Praise for *The Magician's Assistant*

"Patchett's third novel is something of a magic trick itself—a '90's love story wrought with the grace and classic charm of a 19th century novel. . . . We read [*The Magician's Assistant*] with the same pleasure and awe of an audience watching a chained Houdini escape from an underwater chamber."
—Veronica Chambers, *Newsweek*

"Patchett's lush and suspenseful story is also a portrait of America, which—with its big dreams, vast spaces, and disparate realities lying side by side—proves to be the perfect place for miraculous transformations, including Sabine's own."
—*The New Yorker*

"Magicians—and their assistants—may be masters of misdirections and sleight of hand, but novelist Ann Patchett is the real thing. Patchett does have a trick or two up her sleeve in *The Magician's Assistant*—her controlled, evocative prose for one; the uncanny way she makes the most surprising twists seem absolutely inevitable; not to mention the wisdom and tenderness with which she portrays the illusions that keep lovers and families together and those that render them apart. But the magic she creates in this enchanting novel is of the alchemical kind—it transmutes baser elements into gold and changes things irrevocably."
—*San Francisco Chronicle*

"Captivating . . . Patchett's novel entrances . . . [She] artfully transforms the apparently innocuous setting of Nebraska in the middle of winter into a charged domestic arena that inspires sizzling encounters worthy of Tennessee Williams."

—*Chicago Tribune*

"Breathtaking complex and neatly executed . . . Patchett is a strikingly original writer."   —*The Boston Globe*

"Patchett is an elegant and lyrical writer. . . . Like Alice Hoffman, she writes about stripping away reality's illusions to discover the underlying magic."   —*USA Today*

"Reading *The Magician's Assistant* is like watching a master illusionist at work. Ann Patchett fills her reader with wonder, delight, and a new sense of possibility. And with this work, Patchett's career dazzles in much the same way: anything is possible for her."   —Robert Olen Butler, author of
A Good Scent from a Strange Mountain

The
Magician's
Assistant

Ann Patchett

The Magician's Assistant

A Harvest Book • Harcourt, Inc.

Orlando   Austin   New York   San Diego   London

Requests for permission to make copies of any part
of the work should be submitted online at
www.harcourt.com/contact or mailed to the following address:
Permissions Department, Harcourt, Inc.,
6277 Sea Harbor Drive, Orlando, Florida 32887-6777.

www.HarcourtBooks.com

Library of Congress Cataloging-in-Publication Data
Patchett, Ann.
The magician's assistant/Ann Patchett.
p.   cm.
ISBN 978-0-15-100263-4
ISBN 978-0-15-600621-7 (pbk.)
I. Title.
PS3566.A7756M34   1997
813′.54—dc21   97-2139

Text set in Bulmer.
Designed by Geri Davis, the Davis Group, Inc.
Printed in the United States of America
First Harvest edition 1998
BB DD FF HH JJ KK II GG EE CC

to
Lucy Grealy
and
Elizabeth McCracken

At the Intersection of
George Burns and Gracie Allen

PARSIFAL IS DEAD. That is the end of the story.

The technician and the nurse rushed in from their glass booth. Where there had been a perfect silence a minute before there was now tremendous activity, the straining sounds of two men unexpectedly thrown into hard work. The technician stepped between Parsifal and Sabine, and she had no choice but to let go of Parsifal's hand. When they counted to three and then lifted Parsifal's body from the metal tongue of the MRI machine and onto the gurney, his head fell back, his mouth snapping open with no reflexes to protect it. Sabine saw all of his beautiful teeth, the two gold crowns on the back molars shining brightly in the overhead fluorescent light. The heavy green sheet that they had given him for warmth got stuck in the guardrail lock. The nurse struggled with it for a second and then threw up his hands, as if to say they didn't have time for this, when in fact they had all the time in the world. Parsifal was dead and would be dead whether help was found in half a minute or in an hour or a day. They rushed him around the corner and down the hall without a word to Sabine. The only sound was the quick squeak of rubber wheels and rubber soles against the linoleum.

Sabine stood there, her back against the massive MRI machine, her arms wrapped around her chest, waiting. It was, in a way, the end of Sabine.

After a while the neuroradiologist came into the room and told her, in a manner that was respectful and direct, the one thing she already knew: Her husband was dead. He did not pluck at his lab coat or stare at the floor the way so many doctors had done when they had spoken to Parsifal and Sabine about Phan. He told her it had been an aneurism, a thinning in a blood vessel of his brain. He told her it had probably been there Parsifal's whole life and was not in any way related to his AIDS. Like a patient with advanced lymphoma who is driven off the freeway by a careless teenager changing lanes, the thing that had been scheduled to kill Parsifal had been denied, and Sabine lost the years she was promised he still had. The doctor did not say it was a blessing, but Sabine could almost see the word on his lips. Compared to the illness Parsifal had, this death had been so quick it was nearly kind. "Your husband," the doctor explained, "never suffered."

Sabine squeezed the silver dollar Parsifal had given her until she felt the metal edge cut painfully into her palm. Wasn't suffering exactly the thing she had been afraid of? That he would go like Phan, lingering in so many different kinds of pain, his body failing him in unimaginable ways—hadn't she hoped for something better for Parsifal? If he couldn't have held on to his life, then couldn't he at least have had some ease in his death? That was what had happened. Parsifal's death had been easy. Having come to find there was no comfort in getting what she wanted, what she wanted now was something else entirely. She wanted him back. Sick or well. She wanted him back.

"The headache this morning," the doctor told her, "would have been brought on by a leak." His beard was not well trimmed and his glasses were smudged, as if set in place by greasy fingers. He had the paleness of so many neuroradiologists.

Sabine said she'd like to see the film.

The doctor nodded and returned a minute later holding a large paper envelope stamped DO NOT BEND. She followed him into what looked to be a closet and he put eight large sheets of gray film on the lightboard. Each had fifteen separate pictures, Parsifal's brain sliced in every conceivable direction. In the dark, narrow room Sabine studied the information, her face painted in a bluish white light. She stared at the shape of Parsifal's head, at the deep, curving trenches of his brain. In some pictures things were recognizable, the strong line of his jaw, the sockets of his eyes. But most of the pictures were patterns, aerial views of an explosion taken at night. Again and again she saw the shadow, the dark, connected mass the size of a pinto bean. Even she could see where this was going.

The doctor tapped the obvious with the tip of his pencil. "There," he said. He faced the light when he spoke, and the pictures of Parsifal's brain reflected in his glasses. "In some people they stay that way forever. In others they just give out."

Sabine asked for a moment alone and the doctor nodded and backed out of the room. When these pictures were taken, just slightly over an hour before, Parsifal had been alive. She raised her hand to the film and traced her finger around the top line of his skull. The beautiful head she had held. The night Phan died, Sabine had thought the tragedy was knowing that Parsifal would die, too, that there was only a limited amount of time. But now Sabine knew the tragedy was living, that there would be years and years to be alone. She pulled down the films and put them back in the envelope, tucked the envelope under her arm, and tried to remember where the elevators were.

The empire that was Cedars Sinai hospital lapped up the last blocks of Los Angeles before it became Beverly Hills. Buildings were connected by overhead tunnels called skyways. Waiting rooms were categorized by the seriousness of the wait. The halls were lined with art that was too good for a hospital. Sometimes it seemed that every wealthy person in Los Angeles had died at Cedars Sinai, or their loved ones had died there, and what they had been left with was not bitterness or fear but a desire to have their name on a plaque over some door. The abundance of money took away as many outward signs of hospital life as possible. There were no sickly green walls, no peeling floors or disinfectant smells. There had been nights when Sabine had walked those halls so short on sleep that the place became a giant hotel, the Sahara or Desert Sands in Las Vegas, where she and Parsifal used to perform their magic act years before. But tonight, as Sabine went to the nurses' station to call the funeral home, it wasn't even late; the sky still had the smallest smear of orange over Beverly Hills. All the people who would one day come to Cedars to die were only beginning to think about going to sleep.

Sabine knew what had to be done. She had practice. Phan had been dead fourteen months and fourteen months was long enough to forget exactly nothing. But with Phan it had been different. He had worked towards his death so steadily that they knew its schedule. After the doctor came to the house for the last time and told them a day, maybe two, Phan had died the next morning. With Parsifal, it was only a headache.

"I had a dream about Phan," Parsifal had said that morning.

Sabine brought him coffee and sat down on the edge of his bed. It had been Phan's bed, Phan's house. Parsifal and Phan had lived together for five years. Since Phan's death, Parsifal had had a handful of dreams about Phan which he recounted faithfully to Sabine, like letters written by a lover in another country.

"How's Phan?"

Parsifal woke up quickly, clearheaded. He took the cup. "He was sitting by a pool. He was wearing one of my suits, my pearl gray suit and a white shirt. He had taken off his tie." He closed his eyes, searching for details. Phan was in the details. "He was holding this big pink drink, a mai-tai or something. It had fruit all over the glass. He looked so rested, absolutely beautiful."

"Was it our pool?"

"Oh no. This was a capital-*P* Pool—dolphin fountains, gold tiles."

Sabine nodded. She pictured it herself: blue skies, palm fronds. "Did he say anything?"

"He said, 'The water's just perfect. I'm thinking about going for a swim.' " Parsifal could mimic Phan's voice, perfect English sandwiched between layers of Vietnamese and French. The sound of Phan's voice made Sabine shiver.

Phan didn't swim. His house had a pool, but pools dominated the backyards of Southern California. Having one was not the same as wanting one. Sometimes Phan would roll up his pants and sit at the shallow end with his feet in the water.

"What do you think it all means?" Parsifal asked.

Sabine ran her hand over the top of his head, bald now from who knew what combination of things. She put no stock in dreams. To her they were just a television left on in another room. "I think it means he's happy."

"Yes," he said, and smiled at her. "That's what I think."

There was a time not so long ago that Parsifal never would have told his dreams to Sabine, unless it was a ridiculous dream, like the time he told her he dreamed about going into the living room and finding Rabbit in the wingback chair, two hundred pounds and six feet tall, reading the newspaper through half-glasses. And maybe he hadn't had that dream, maybe he only said it to be funny. But Phan's death had made him sentimental, hopeful. He wanted to believe in a dream that told him death had been good to Phan, that he was not lost but in a place where Parsifal could find him later. A place with a pool and a bar.

"What about you?" Parsifal said, covering her hand with his hand. "Any dreams?"

But Sabine never remembered her dreams, or maybe she didn't have them. She shook her head and asked how he was feeling. He said fine, but there was a little bit of a headache coming on. That had been eight o'clock in the morning. That had been on this same day.

After basic arrangements had been made, Sabine took the elevator to the main lobby and the electric glass doors opened up to turn her out into the night. It was January and seventy-two degrees. A light breeze had blown the smog far out over the Pacific Ocean but had left nothing behind it. She wished she could still smell the blossoms from the distant industrial orange groves, the scent of flowers and citrus that as recently as May had settled on her clothes and in her hair like a fine dust. She kept expecting someone from the hospital to come after her. "Where are you going?" they would say, and wrap her in their arms. "You're in no condition to be out here alone." The nurse had asked her if there were someone she could call, but Sabine said no. There were a hundred people to call, and none of them the person she wanted. Parsifal had no family at all, except for Sabine, who was always moved to see her name on the line of the medical records that said "Next of Kin." She would wait until she was home to call her own parents, because if she called them now they would insist on picking her up from the hospital and bringing her home with them. Sabine wanted to be in her own home tonight. Phan's home and then Parsifal's home and now her home.

It felt a little bit like being drunk, the way her knees grew soft from the shock, the very edges of the grief that was coming for her. She had to concentrate to keep from stepping into the bank of rubbery green ice plant along the sidewalk. She couldn't remember where she'd left the car. She walked down Gracie Allen Drive and when it intersected with George Burns Road, she stopped. Outside a hospital where every building was named for someone, and every floor of the building and every room on the floor, Gracie Allen had a street, something that couldn't be bought. The street did not call to mind Gracie Allen's life, but her death, running, the way it did, between two sides of the hospital, the Broidy Family Patient Wing and the Theodore E. Cummings Family Patient Wing, stopping there at the Max Factor Family Tower. Every time Sabine walked down that street she thought that Gracie Allen must have suffered at the end of her life, and that it was her suffering that led the city to give her a street. And maybe her husband had walked down that street some evenings. Maybe when he missed her most he would drive to Cedars Sinai and walk past the ficus trees and the agapanthus bushes and all of the needle-point ivy, the full length of the street that bore his wife's name.

Then one day when he felt himself getting older and the walks more difficult to make, he had gone to his friends and asked if possibly he could have a street for himself. It was not vanity. It was a marker to say he was in love with her. Sabine wished that streets could be bought, like patient wings, so that she could buy one for Parsifal. She would buy it as far away from Cedars Sinai as she could get it. She would give him that, knowing full well that the street that would intersect it would not bear her name.

It was almost nine o'clock at night when Sabine found her car parked at the emergency entrance. She thought on the drive home that she could use the guest list from their wedding to contact people for the funeral. "Not just for tax reasons," Parsifal had said in front of the rabbi. "I do love you." Parsifal said he wanted Sabine to be his widow. And Sabine deserved to be married. She had been in love with Parsifal since she was nineteen, since that first night at the Magic Hat when he had done the passing-rabbit trick, pulling rabbits out of his sleeves, his collar, his cummerbund, the way Channing Pollack pulled out doves. She had been a waitress at the Hat, but on that night she became his assistant, putting down her tray of drinks when he held out his hand, coming up on the stage even when the owner had clearly told her that to volunteer was the God-given right of the drink-buying audience and did not belong to staff. She had fallen in love with him then, when he was twenty-four years old and stood in the pink stage light wearing a tuxedo. She had stayed in love with him for twenty-two years—let him saw her in half, helped him make her disappear—even when she found out that he was in love with men. "You don't always get everything you want," Sabine told her parents.

At the turn of the key in the lock Rabbit hopped slowly down the hall, making a thumping sound like loose slippers against carpet. He raised up on his hind legs and stretched his front legs up towards her, his nose pulsing in lapin joy after such a long, dull day alone. Sabine picked him up and buried her face in the soft white fur and for the first time thought of the white rabbit muff her parents had bought for her as a child. There had been many rabbits, but none as smart, or large, as this one. "It's more impressive to make a tall woman disappear," Parsifal had told Sabine. "And it's better to pull a really big rabbit out of a hat." Sabine was five-foot-ten and Rabbit, a Flemish giant, weighed in at just under twenty pounds. Like Sabine, Rabbit had once had responsibilities. He practiced with Parsifal and learned the tricks. The third of the white working rabbits Parsifal owned, he was by far the smartest and best behaved. Rabbit wanted to work. But since he'd been retired he'd grown fat. He hopped aimlessly from room to room, chewing electrical cords, waiting.

Sabine carried Rabbit down the hall towards Parsifal's bedroom. Her own bedroom was upstairs. She had lived there since before Phan died, when they needed so much help there was never time to go home anyway. And besides, the house was huge. She had slept in four different bedrooms before choosing the one she liked. She had taken another room as a studio. She set up her drafting table. She brought over her architectural models. At night, after everyone was cared for, after everyone was asleep, she sat on the floor and made tiny ash trees that would one day line the front walkway of an office complex.

Sabine did not turn on a light. She ran her hand along the wall to find her way.

"My funeral...," Parsifal had begun. He'd said it at the breakfast table, eating a five-minute egg the morning after they were married.

Sabine put up her hand. "I'm sure this is a very healthy

thing, that you're able to talk about it, but not now. That's a long time off."

"I'd like to do it the Jewish way, buried by the next sundown. Your people are so much more efficient than mine. Catholics will lay you out in the front parlor for a week, let all the neighbors come by."

"Stop it."

"Just don't do the part where everyone has to shovel in the dirt," he said. "I find that very morbid."

"No dirt," Sabine said.

"I don't suppose cremation is terribly Jewish."

"You're not Jewish. I wouldn't worry about it."

"I just don't want to offend your parents." Parsifal closed his eyes and stretched. "Do you think Johnny Carson would come to my funeral? That would really be spectacular. I wonder if he remembers me at all."

"I imagine he does."

"Really?" Parsifal brightened. "I had such a terrible crush on Johnny Carson."

"You had a crush on Johnny Carson?"

"I was too embarrassed to tell you back then," he confided. "See, Sabine, I tell you everything now that we're married."

Sabine put the rabbit down on the floor and switched on the lights. The bed wasn't made. Parsifal had stayed in bed that morning until he couldn't stand the headache anymore. When they left, they left together, in a hurry. He wore dark glasses and held her arm.

What she needed now was clothes. Fourteen months and still Phan's underwear was in the dresser drawers. Phan's and Parsifal's clothes filled two walk-in closets: suits and jackets, wire racks of ties. (Did they have any sense of ownership where ties were concerned? Did a tie belong to one and not the other?) The white shirts were first and then the pale blues and then the darker blues. She knelt beside them, ran her hands down the sleeves. The shoe trees held the shape of their shoes. Sweaters were arranged by material and folded into Lucite boxes. Parsifal needed something to wear, something to be cremated in. Parsifal and Phan had talked together about what Phan would wear. When they decided, Parsifal took the suit to his tailor and had it cut down to fit. All of the clothes grew in the night, Phan used to say.

"It doesn't matter," Parsifal told Sabine later, his voice thin and tight. "It's all going to be burned up anyway."

Sabine left the closet and called her parents.

"Shel," her mother said when Sabine told her the news. "It's Parsifal."

Sabine heard her father hurrying towards the bedroom. She thought she heard her mother say, "My poor girl," but she couldn't be sure because her mother turned her face away from the receiver.

There was a click on the line, her father picking up the phone. "Oh, Parsifal," he said. "He wasn't so sick yet."

"It was an aneurism," Sabine said. "It was something else."

"Are you at the hospital? We'll come right there." Her father was crying already, something Sabine herself had not begun to do.

"I came home." Sabine sat down on the bed and pulled the rabbit into her lap.

"Then we'll come there," her mother said.

Sabine told them it was late, she was tired, tomorrow there would be endless things to do. The rabbit pulled away from her, burrowed into a tunnel of sheets.

"We loved him," Sabine's father said. "You know that. He was a good boy."

"Nothing will be the same without Parsifal," her mother said.

Sabine told them good-night and hung up the phone.

Phan and Parsifal's bedroom was at the far end of the house, big enough to be a living room. After Phan died, Parsifal and Sabine had spent all their time there. This was where they watched television and ate Chinese food from white paper cartons. Sometimes they would practice tricks in front of a sliding mirror, even though they were no longer performing by then. On the bedside table there were framed pictures—Parsifal with his arm draped possessively around Phan's neck, the two of them smiling at Sabine on the other side of the camera; Parsifal and Sabine with Rabbit in a publicity shot for the act; Parsifal and Sabine on their wedding day, standing with Sabine's parents. There was a picture of Phan's family— his French father and Vietnamese mother, Phan in short pants, three tiny girls with round black eyes, one of them still in her mother's arms. The portrait was formal, arranged. On each face there was only the slightest indication of a smile. Sabine took the picture from the table and brought it into bed with her. She lay on her back and studied their faces one at a time. The children looked only like their mother. The father, too tall and fair for the gathering, looked hopeful, as if he had just been introduced. Sabine had never talked to Phan much about his family. She didn't know the names of these people and she didn't think they were written down anywhere. Parsifal would have known. She had to assume that every person in the picture was dead. She wasn't even sure about that. She curled herself around the rabbit. She put her hand on his back and held it still to feel the manic beating of his small heart.

After the funeral Sabine moved downstairs into Phan and Parsifal's room. She slept in their bed. She pushed her head beneath their feather pillows. She slept like Parsifal used to sleep, endlessly. She stayed in bed when she wasn't asleep. She used their shampoo and dark green soap. The room smelled like men. Their towels were as big as tablecloths. Hairbrushes, toothbrushes, shoe polish, every item took on the significance of memory. Suddenly Sabine could see just how full the house was, how much they had owned. She was now responsible for Parsifal's two rug stores, for every sweater in the closet, for Phan's toy mouse, the only thing he had left from his childhood in Vietnam, who watched her from the dresser with painted-on eyes. She had the IRAs, CDs, money markets, insurance premiums, quarterly tax reports, warranties. She had the love letters that were not written to her, the paperback mysteries, the address books. She was the last stop for all of the accumulations and memorabilia, all the achievements and sentimentality of two lives, and one of those lives should not have come to her in the first place. What would she do with Phan's postcard collection? With his boxes of patterns for bridal gowns? With the five filing cabinets that were stuffed full of notes about computer projects and software programs, all written in Vietnamese? Closing her eyes, she imagined her parents' deaths. She imagined her loneliness taking the shape of boxes and boxes of other people's possessions, a terminal moraine that would keep all she had lost in front of her. She was nailed to this spot, to the exact hour of Parsifal's death. And then what about when she died? Who was going to look at the picture of Phan's family and wonder about them then? Who would possibly wonder about Sabine?

The phone rang constantly. It was mostly Sabine's parents, checking on her. It was friends, people who had read the obituary. It was the polite managers from the rug stores who had a few questions. It was strangers asking to speak to

Parsifal. For a while it was the hospital and the funeral home; the director at Forest Lawn, where Sabine had Parsifal's ashes buried next to Phan's. When the phone rang at ten o'clock on the fourth morning of his death and found Sabine still in bed but not asleep, it was the lawyer. He asked her to come in for lunch.

"I know there's a lot to do," Sabine said, pulling the comforter up over her shoulders, "but not today, Roger. Really, I promise I'll come in."

"Today," he said.

"I'm not going anywhere."

"There are some things I need to tell you, and I need to tell you in person, and I need to tell you now. If you can't come to lunch, I'll come to the house."

Sabine put her hand over the receiver and yawned. Roger had been a friend of Parsifal's, but Sabine thought he was pushy. "You can't come to the house. I'm not cleaning it."

"That means you'll come to lunch."

Sabine closed her eyes and agreed, only to get him off the phone. She did not have an especially curious nature. She did not care what the lawyer had to say. The worst thing he could tell her was that it was all a joke and Parsifal had left her nothing; and that, frankly, sounded like the best news possible.

If it had been Parsifal, she would have told him he needed to get out. After Phan died she'd had to beg him to even open the front door and pick up the newspaper. She would sit on the edge of his bed, this bed, holding his bathrobe in her lap. She would tell him how much better he would feel if he just got up and took a shower and got dressed, tell him that Phan would never have wanted things to be this way. The difference being, of course, that there was no one sitting on the edge of the bed now. Even Rabbit had gone off somewhere. Sabine got up and found the bathrobe but then dropped it on the floor, took up her old spot in the nest of the comforter, and went back to sleep.

Phan is in the swimming pool.

"You don't swim," Sabine says, but clearly, he does.

He is swimming with his eyes open, his mouth open. He shines like a seal in the light. He rolls into a backstroke and comes straight towards her. "I learned," he calls. "I love it."

Parsifal's gray suit jacket is draped neatly over the back of a white wrought-iron chair. Outside it is warm but pleasant. When Phan reaches the edge of the pool, Sabine holds out her hands to him and he lifts himself up and into her arms, the cool water from his body soaking her blouse as he holds her. The gold has come back to his skin and he smells of some faint flower, jasmine or lily, that makes her want never to let him go. Phan is clearly much happier since his death. Even in his best days with Parsifal, she has never seen him so relaxed. In life he was shy and too eager to please, in a way that reminded her of a dog that had been beaten. In the fullness of life Sabine had been jealous of Phan, jealous that Parsifal had found someone else to love so much. Jealous because she had wanted that for herself and so understood. What was Sabine, then, but an extra woman, one who was inevitably dressed in a satin body stocking embroidered with spangles? A woman holding a rabbit and a hat. But Phan was always gentle with her. There was nothing about exclusion that he didn't understand.

Sabine smiles and sits down with Phan beside the pool, letting her legs dangle in the water. The dolphins' necks are strung with flowers. The water is the blue of the little mountain bluebird she once saw outside of Tahoe. "What do you do now?"

He takes one of her hands between his. The eczema that

plagued his palms for years is gone. "Most of the time I'm with you. I stay with you." He stops for a minute. Phan was never one to talk about himself. "Now and then I go back to Vietnam."

"Really?" Sabine is surprised. Phan would hardly speak of Vietnam.

"It's a very beautiful country," he says. "There are so many things I remember from when I was a boy, things I haven't thought of for thirty years—grasses in the fields and the rice, when it first comes up in the spring. It's difficult for me to explain. It's a comfort, like listening to so many people speak Vietnamese. Sometimes I stand in the market and cry. You'll know what I mean someday when you go home."

"I am home."

"Israel," Phan says.

"It isn't the same," she says. "I was so young when we left there, I don't even remember it."

Phan shakes his head. "This isn't our country," he says.

Los Angeles is Sabine's country, the only one she loves. "Where do you think Parsifal goes?" she asks.

Phan looks at her with enormous tenderness. The wind blows her hair, which is nearly as black and straight as Phan's. Somewhere beyond the pool a mockingbird is singing. "Most of the time he's with me," Phan says. "We stay with you together. We go to Vietnam."

Immediately Sabine sits up straight; she looks behind her, down a long allée that leads to a gazebo. "He's here now?"

"He didn't want to come."

"No?" She whispers it.

"He's just embarrassed. And he should be, really, he left you with too much."

Sabine looks around, hoping that he's close by, that he will see her there and come to her. She can hardly breathe for missing him. "It's not like there was something he could do about it. He tried to make things easy for me, he married me."

Phan pushes his wet hair back with his hands. He is anxious to get to his point. "You're not the only one who was in the dark about this whole thing. I didn't know, either. I want to tell you that. Parsifal kept this to himself. It was a decision he made a long time ago, and once he made up his mind he never went back. Not ever. So it was nothing against you or against me. It wasn't that he didn't love us enough." Phan ran his foot lightly over the surface of the water, sending out a long series of tiny waves. Clearly he was thinking about going back in. "This is going to make things more difficult for you. He says he was going to tell you; he just thought there was going to be more time. The aneurism caught him off-guard. I guess that was my fault."

Sabine has no idea what Phan is talking about, not any of it. "Your fault?"

"The aneurism," Phan says, and snaps his wet fingers. "Quick."

The memory is extremely far away and yet she knows this has something to do with her. She uses her hand to shade her eyes from the sun and squints at him. "You killed him?" she asks, sure that the answer is no.

Suddenly it is the old Phan next to her. His head bends down, doglike. He seems naked without a shirt. "Please don't say that," he says softly.

"Then explain it to me." She feels something crawling in her throat.

"You had asked—"

"I had asked?"

"Not to suffer."

It takes her a minute and then she remembers—how she would hope there would not be too much pain for Parsifal, how she would say it to herself as they drove home from doctors' appointments. But to hope, to think something, that was nothing like asking.

Sabine's legs swing out of the pool. She stands up. Her head is clear. "Jesus," she says. "Jesus, I didn't mean for you to kill him. I meant for you to comfort him. Comfort. If you didn't understand you should have asked me."

"The difference in time was very small."

"Small?" Sabine said. "What's small? What do you think is small?"

Phan looks at his feet. He presses his toes hard against the cement wall inside the pool. "Two years." He shrugs, helpless. "A little more than two years."

Sabine is dizzy and lifts her hands to her head. For the first time in her life she feels like her head is going to simply break free of her body, sail over the wall that is covered in heavy purple grapes. "How can you say two years is a small amount of time?"

"It is small," Phan says. "You may not understand that now, but once you're dead you'll see. It means nothing."

"I'm not dead." Her voice is high. "I wanted that time." She is crying now, inconsolable. Parsifal could still be sleeping in his own bed. This is all because of something she said, something she did. This is loneliness she has brought on herself.

The breeze over the pool is pleasant and dry, coming in from the ocean. It is a bright afternoon in Southern California. Phan is crying as well. Though his face is damp from the swimming, she can see it. His shoulders are shaking. "I had meant to make things easier for you," he says. He slips off the edge of the pool and sinks into the water. It is not the water that is blue, nor is the blue a reflection of the sky. The pool itself is painted blue on the inside. Sabine watches him. She is trying to stop her own crying.

"Come up," she says. Phan is swimming along the bottom. He is swimming in circles. His body is distorted by the depth into something long and dreamy. Phan does not come up because he does not need to come up. He only needs to keep swimming. She knows that he will stay down there all day.

"I'm sorry," Sabine whispers. "Come back." She twists her hands around themselves. She is so tired. It's so long since there has been any rest in sleep. She waits and waits, but she might as well be waiting for a fish. Finally there is nothing left to do but go, and so she walks towards the gate. She is almost out of the garden before she remembers something and comes back to the water's edge. "Phan?" she says. "What about the rest of it? What were you supposed to tell me?"

Phan is swimming, swimming. She doesn't think he can hear her; or at least she knows that if she were the one underwater, she wouldn't be able to hear.

When the telephone rang, Sabine screamed.

"You're a half hour late," Roger said. "Does this mean you're standing me up?"

"What?"

"Sabine? Are you awake?"

She swallowed. Her heart was beating fast as Rabbit's. "I forgot," she whispered.

"Don't clean the house," he said. "I'm coming over."

There was no way to make sense of the half sentences of information flooding her head. She felt that she was still trying to dig up from some terrible thickness. She put on Parsifal's robe and washed her face several times with cold water. She was just finishing her teeth when the doorbell rang.

It is the responsibility of any good magician's assistant to misdirect the attention of the audience, and Sabine had taken her responsibility to heart. She had worn lipstick to the breakfast table in the morning. She owned cuff bracelets and strappy high-heeled shoes. She had known how to put herself together. That was then, this is now, she thought as she made her way to the front door.

"I meant to come," she said.

Roger kissed her on the cheek and looped a piece of her hair back behind her ear. "The place has a dress code," he said. "They wouldn't have let you in."

"I'm having coffee." Sabine walked to the kitchen and Roger followed. The house was swimming in light, but these days Sabine could sleep through any amount of brightness.

He stopped at the brain scan she had masking-taped to the refrigerator. "What the hell is this?"

"Parsifal," she said, looking for filters.

Roger sat down at the breakfast table and lit a cigarette. He was one of the few people Sabine knew in Los Angeles who still smoked, and the only person she knew who would smoke in your house without asking, something she might have minded at another time in her life. "What do you know about Parsifal's family?" he asked her.

Sabine shrugged, switching the coffeemaker on. "I know they lived in Connecticut. I know they're dead. I know he changed his name from Petrie. If you've come to break the news to me that he has some long-lost cousins who are looking for money, don't worry; I promise to take it well." The pieces of the dream were slipping away from her. Phan. Pool. She wished she could excuse herself for a minute and just sit down to think.

"I always thought of Parsifal as someone I knew fairly well," Roger said, tapping an ash into a dark purple African violet on the table. "But there were a lot of things I didn't know. The same things, I guess, that you didn't know."

I didn't know about it either, Phan said. *I wanted to tell you that.* There. That much she remembered. Sabine stayed between the two worlds, waiting for her coffee. She wanted to be neither awake nor asleep.

"So," Roger said, tenting his fingertips together like a corporate executive. "Here's the thing." He waited for a minute, thinking she would at least turn and look at him, but she didn't and didn't seem like she might, and so he went ahead. "Parsifal's name wasn't Petrie. It was Guy Fetters. Guy Fetters has a mother and two sisters in Nebraska. As far as I can tell the father is out of the picture—either dead or gone, I'm not sure which."

She got down two yellow cups and poured the coffee. To the best of her knowledge, there was no milk or sugar in the house. "That isn't possible," she said.

"I'm afraid it is."

"We were together for twenty-two years." Sabine sat down at the table. She took a cigarette out of Roger's pack and lit it. It seemed like a good time to smoke. "So I guess I knew him better than you. That's the kind of thing that comes out after twenty-two years."

"Well," Roger said, thinking it over. "In this case, it didn't."

The cigarette tasted bad, but she liked it. Sabine blew the smoke in a straight line to the ceiling. There had been a swimming pool. Phan was there. He had said he didn't know about it either. About? Sabine looked at Roger.

"There was a letter in his will. He wanted me to tell his family about his death. He's set up a trust for them, the mother and the sisters. You're not going to miss the money. The bulk of the estate is yours."

"I'm not going to miss the money," Sabine said. It wasn't just Parsifal's money she had, it was Phan's: the rights to countless computer programs, the rights to Knick-Knack. Everything had come to her.

Roger ground his cigarette into the soft black dirt around the plant. "I want you to know I'm sorry about this. It's a hell of a thing, him not telling you. Everybody has their reasons, but I hardly think you need this now."

"No," Sabine said.

"What I need to know is if you want to call them. Certainly I plan to do it, but I didn't know how you'd feel about being in touch with them yourself." He waited for her to say something. Sabine wasn't going to be able to keep her eyes open much longer. "You can think it over," Roger said. He looked at his cigarettes, trying to decide if he would be there long enough to make lighting another one worthwhile. He decided not. "Call me tomorrow."

Sabine nodded. He took a file out of his briefcase and laid it on the table. "Here are the names, addresses, phone numbers; a copy of Parsifal's request." He stood up. "You'll call me."

"I'll call you." She did not get up to see him out, or offer to, or notice his awkwardness in waiting. He was almost to the front door when she called to him.

"Yes?"

"Leave me a cigarette, will you?"

Roger shook two out of the pack, enough for him to make it back to the office, and left her the rest on the table in the entryway.

Sabine smoked a cigarette before opening the file.

Mrs. Albert Fetters (Dorothy). Alliance, Nebraska.

Miss Albertine Fetters. Alliance, Nebraska.

Mrs. Howard Plate (Kitty). Alliance, Nebraska.

There were addresses, phone numbers, Social Security numbers. Miss Albertine Fetters lived with Mrs. Albert Fetters. Mrs. Howard Plate did not. Sabine read the letter from

Parsifal, but all it told her was how he wanted the trust structured. She wondered if there were a way the letter could have been forged. Which scenario seemed more unlikely? Three women in some place called Alliance, Nebraska, made up a connection to a total stranger in order to get what was, Sabine noted, not such an enormous amount of money; or the man she had loved and worked with for her entire adult life was someone she didn't actually know? Sabine ran a finger over the names as if they were in braille. Albert. Albertine. She shook her arms out of her bathrobe and let it fall backwards over the chair.

His story had been absolutely clear. They had been working together for two weeks. Sabine had asked before where he was from and Parsifal had told her Westport; but it was when they took a break from rehearsal one day so that they could get some lunch that she had asked him about his family. Parsifal, who had a great deal of youthful melodrama at the time, put down his sandwich, looked at her, and said, "I don't have any family."

For Sabine, life without family, without parents, was inconceivable, a hole of sorrow that made her love him even more. The details of the story came slowly over the next year. The questions had to be asked delicately, at the right time. There could not be too many at once, there could not be follow-up questions. What worked best was soliciting the occasional fact: *What was your sister's name?* "Helen." To press the subject too hard made Parsifal despondent. She discovered that when he said he did not wish to speak about it, he wasn't secretly hoping she would try to coax him into conversation. *There must be other family, uncles, cousins?* "A few, but we were never close. They didn't try to help me after my parents' death. I'm not interested in them."

Slowly the small stream of information dried up. The story

25

had been told. It was over, leaving Sabine with only the vaguest details of sorrows best forgotten. Once, many years later, when they were playing in New York, she had suggested that they take the train out to Westport. She wanted to see where Parsifal grew up, maybe they could even go to the cemetery and put some flowers on the graves.

Parsifal looked at her as if she had suggested they take the train to Westport and dig his parents out of the ground. "You can't mean that," he said.

She did mean it, but she did not mention it again. There was a certain perverse benefit to the situation anyway: Sabine was his family. Hers was the framed picture at his bedside. She was always his past, his oldest friend, mother, sister, and finally wife. History began in a time after they had met. She did not complain.

Sabine closed the file and tapped it on the table. She needed Parsifal. If he were here, there would be a sensible explanation to this. She ran through the facts until her head hurt. Then she called her parents.

Of course they wanted to see her, to listen to her problem. They told her to meet them at Canter's. For Sabine, they would do anything, do it gladly.

Sabine and her parents had had lunch at Canter's every Sunday that they lived together, and most Sundays after Sabine left home. They knew the menu like they knew each other, two sandwiches named for Danny Thomas and one for Eddie Cantor, the introduction of quesadillas and pasta in the middle eighties. Sometimes they went there for dinner during the week, if Sabine's mother had a math student who needed tutoring after school and there was no time to make dinner. But Sabine could not remember ever going there at three o'clock on a Tuesday. Once she was inside the restaurant, the smell of lox and lean corned beef overwhelmed her. She couldn't remember the last time she had eaten, and she put her hand on the overflowing pastry case and leaned towards the glass, suddenly mesmerized by kugel.

"Wait until after lunch," her mother said, getting up from the booth where her parents were sitting. Sabine kissed her mother and allowed herself to be led back to the table.

"Sabine," the waitress said, and took her hand. "I've heard about your sadness."

Sabine nodded.

"I'll get you something nice," she said. "Something special. Would you like that?"

She said that she would. She would like nothing more than not to have to make a decision at that exact moment.

As soon as the waitress was gone, Sabine told her parents there was news she needed to discuss with them and took the folder out of her purse. Her parents sat on the opposite side of the orange booth, watching, barely breathing.

"Not your health," her mother said. She rested one finger on the edge of the file.

"God, no," Sabine said. "Nothing like that." Although she desperately needed some advice, she hated to tell them. It had taken so long for them to come to accept Parsifal, to love him, that even after his death she felt cautious. She put the story out truthfully: Roger, the lawyer; Guy Fetters; Alliance, Nebraska; a mother and two sisters. Her father looked inside the file. He studied the information so hard she wondered if there were something she had missed.

Her mother shook her head. "Poor Parsifal," she said. Her father sighed and put the folder down.

"Why poor Parsifal?" Sabine asked, certain now that she had missed something.

The restaurant was bigger than an ice-skating rink, but

at three o'clock it was nearly empty, just a few old men in pairs who were drinking coffee, and they were all far away. They bent forward over their cups, their bald heads lacy with freckles. Still, Sabine's mother lowered her voice. "Don't you think something must have..." She paused and opened up her hands. They were empty. "Happened to him?"

"What?"

"Well, I wouldn't know," her mother said. "But he was a loving boy, always hungry for family. One would imagine that these people, these Fetter people, wanted nothing to do with him. They probably sent him away for being a homosexual. There isn't likely to be as much tolerance in Alliance, Nebraska."

It had not occurred to Sabine. She sat back while the waitress brought her a bowl of mushroom barley soup and two knishes that looked very promising, flaky and golden in the soft light of the fake stained-glass ceiling. Sabine thanked her but was no longer interested in food.

"Of course he wanted to forget the past," Sabine's mother said. "He made things up, okay, he shouldn't have done that, but I imagine these people did not do right by him, otherwise he never would have denied them. If you ask me, it's remarkable that he left them all that money, money that should rightfully be yours."

"Stop that," Sabine said, and waved her hand. "There's more money than anyone could possibly spend."

Sabine's father inhaled slowly, sadly. They waited. "Another possibility," he said. He had spent his life in America just down the street, working as a tape editor for CBS news. He was used to changing things around to alter their outcome. "Someone could have hurt him."

"Hurt him how?" Sabine asked.

"It's possible," her father said reluctantly, "when he was a boy." He rubbed the back of his neck.

28

How Parsifal would howl at this, Sabine told herself. *You and your parents sitting in Canter's talking about whether or not anybody put his hand in my pants when I was a kid.* Sabine looked again at the pages she had memorized. Mrs. Albert and Albertine, but no Albert.

"A terrible thought," her mother said.

Sabine was ashamed of herself for not rushing to Parsifal's defense. Her parents had assumed that there was a perfectly good, if perfectly horrible, reason for his lie, but she had not. She believed their answer was somewhere in the neighborhood of correct, if not the exact facts, then the general tenor. Someone in Nebraska had wronged Parsifal enough to leave him unable to speak of what had happened.

"So do you think I should call them?" Sabine asked.

"That's what you pay the lawyer for," her mother said. "You don't need to waste your time talking to people like that. Parsifal clearly didn't want you to know them, so respect his wishes. Don't know them."

Sabine's father nodded in agreement and picked up a potato knish that was growing cold on his daughter's plate.

Sabine was grateful to her parents. Time after time she had asked them to understand things she didn't have much of a hold on herself. They had wanted her to be an architect, but instead she built miniature versions of suburban developments for architectural firms. They thought that with her beauty she would have married well, but she had devoted her life to a man who loved men. The years they had fought and wept and not spoken and made up were so far behind them now that the things that had been said were both forgiven and forgotten. Parsifal had come to their house for many Shabbat dinners and for every Passover and Thanksgiving. He had his own place at the table and there were always plenty of macaroons because he had once said how much he liked them. Parsifal had helped Sabine's mother wallpaper the kitchen. He had taught Sabine's father a particularly difficult card trick that mystified her father's friends. At the wedding her parents stood with them beneath the chupah and cried, if not from happiness exactly, then from love. They had disliked the circumstances, her mother would say, but they had always loved the man.

"We can't leave here until you eat something," her mother said to Sabine. "If you keep going like this you're going to vanish."

The waitresses skated by with coffeepots. They kept the old men happy. The manager brought Sabine a slice of chocolate cake she hadn't asked for and made it clear that she was welcome to stay in that booth for the rest of her life.

On the phone that evening, Roger said of course, no problem. He thought it was just as well that he contact the family. "But if they want to get in touch with you?"

"They're not going to want to talk to me," Sabine said. "No one likes to open up old wounds."

"But I need to know, if they ask me."

Sabine was drawing a picture of a small black top hat on the back of the phone book. After a moment's hesitation, she put Rabbit inside. "If they ask, then"—she bit the end of her pen—"then you tell them yes. They won't ask."

"If you're sure," Roger said.

Sabine said she was sure.

When Sabine was nineteen and had bothered to think about these things at all, she'd pictured Parsifal's mother as being extremely beautiful. That was when his mother was still the tragic heroine of the story. Her hair was thick and dark and she wore it pulled back carelessly in a barrette. She had long legs and tasteful gold jewelry and a good strong laugh. Her eyes tilted up at the corners like her son's. They were his eyes, pale blue like a husky dog's and rimmed in spiky black lashes. She kept one leg tucked beneath her on the front seat of the car as the family drove up to Dartmouth to see their son. They worked the crossword puzzle together aloud. *A five-letter word for African horse.*

Had Parsifal gone to Dartmouth?

The father was behind the wheel, getting the answers to all the difficult questions *(five letters, Gulf of Riga tributary)*. Sabine was never told what he did for a living, and so she imagined him a scientist, spending his days in a white lab coat, checking on beakers and Bunsen burners. He was handsome, quiet, hopelessly in love with Parsifal's mother.

In the backseat was Helen, who tilted her head out the window because she liked to feel the full force of the wind coming down on her. She was still in high school, all legs and arms. She read magazines in the car. She answered all puzzle questions concerning movie stars.

Sabine made them out of bits of Parsifal's personality, characteristics of his face. She made their skin from the pale color of his skin. She put them together in her spare time, and when she had them all exactly right, she arranged them in the car and sent them speeding towards their death.

Dorothy, Albertine, and Kitty, quite alive in Nebraska, eluded her entirely. In fact, the entire state of Nebraska defied imagination. Who actually lived there? Every day that Parsifal lived in Los Angeles, he denied them, scraped them from the landscape again and again until they were hardly outlines. What had they done? Who had cut off whom? Parsifal at four, ten, fifteen—what could a boy have done that was so wrong? Sabine got the Rand McNally road atlas out of the trunk of her car and thumbed through to Nebraska, a page kept perfectly clean and uncreased from lack of use. Other pages showed green for hills, darker green for mountains, blue for rivers and the deep thumbprints of lakes, but Nebraska was white, a page as still as fallen snow. It was not crosshatched with roads, overrun with the hard lines of interstate systems. It was a state on which you could make lists, jot down phone numbers, draw pictures. And there, in the beating heart of nowhere, Sabine found Alliance. Alliance, Nebraska. How could he not have mentioned that? It didn't look like something you would simply forget.

Sabine took the atlas back to Parsifal's study, a small room with a corner fireplace that looked out over the swimming pool. A favorite black-and-white picture of Phan holding Mouse on the flat of his palm was on the desk. Parsifal had conducted much of his rug business from home in the last two years. In drawer after drawer she found invoices, a sheaf of receipts, notes about particular Kashan and Kerman rugs he was looking for, names of buyers in Azerbaijan, a folded-up sheet of notepaper that said, in his own writing, "Poor wool was cheaper than good wool, and various processes of chemical washing temporarily concealed the deficiencies and imparted an enticing sheen to the carpet, which the unsophisticated thought charming." There were meticulous records of purchase dates and rates of exchange, employee 1040s that she thought she probably should send to someone. In other drawers she found notes on magic, mostly descriptions of other magicians, tricks he'd liked and wanted to figure out later: "From his mouth he expelled eleven yellow finches, one at a time, his arms straight out to either side." One note mentioned her: "His assistant balanced everything he needed on top of her head. Rather doubt I could talk Sabine into this." She put her face down in the notebook and smelled the pages.

In a folder marked "Phan—1993" was a copy of every lab report, every T cell count, every pill swallowed, with no editorializing other than the occasional "Color is bad today," or "No sleep—night sweats." Behind it, a considerably thinner folder that just said "Parsifal," in which he had tried to keep a similar record for himself and then quickly given up. He should have told her he wanted to keep track, or she should have known.

There were some letters in a box in the closet. There were letters she had written to him when she was much younger. She knew what they said and didn't open them. He had saved some birthday cards she had given him, a postcard she had sent from Carmel, though she couldn't remember going to Carmel by herself. There were some letters from Phan. Sabine sat on the floor and held them in her lap. The envelopes had been opened carefully, so as not to rip the paper. She slipped her fingers inside one and took the letter out. *Most Beloved,* it began, and for some reason this was the thing that started Sabine crying, so that she folded it up right away and put it back. There were a few letters from other men that she didn't bother with, and then, at the very back, a postcard from Nebraska addressed to Guy Fetters / NBRF / Lowell, Nebraska.

Dear Guy,
Just to say you have a beautiful baby sister waiting for you at home, very healthy, as am I. Kitty says come home soon.
Sent with Love from your Mother.

Sabine turned the card over and over again. The picture on the other side was of a grassy field with some snow-tipped mountains in the background that said "Beautiful Wyoming." This made it all true, truer than anything Roger could have told her. All she could read of the postmark was "MAR 1966," which meant that this new sister, who must be Albertine, was fifteen years younger than her brother. What was Parsifal doing away from home in February? And what was NBRF? Sabine flipped through the box again. One lousy postcard from an entire life? This was all that was sent? Sabine wanted to know where the pictures were, report cards, wedding announcements and obituaries clipped from the paper. Where, exactly, was the proof?

Those were long and quiet days for Sabine, every one sunnier and more relentlessly beautiful than the last. A week passed and then another one started right behind it. In the backyard, limes and avocados fell to the ground, rolled under the low palms and rotted. Hot pink azalea blossoms clotted the pool skimmer. She went back to work on the strip mall in her studio. She made shrubbery for hours at a time while Rabbit slept on her feet. When it was finished she went back and covered the bushes in bright red inedible berries. The work was good because she knew what to do, how to mix the glue into a thin wash, how to cut the steel. She studied the floor plans. She made a rare interior, a boardroom for an office building with deep blue chairs that swiveled beneath her fingertip, a cherrywood conference table whose tiny planks she sanded and stained. She did not decide what to do about the rug stores, although they told her there needed to be a buying trip. She did not look over the papers that Roger sent, and she did not call the Fetters of Alliance, Nebraska, to ask them what the hell had gone on during childhood. What stopped her was her mother's voice in Canter's saying that, clearly, Parsifal had not wanted her to know. If she had found a way to respect his wishes at nineteen, surely she could do it at forty-one; but she kept the postcard on her desk, the words face-out.

Parsifal did not believe in magic. Everything was a trick and some tricks were better than others. He was openly hostile to any magician who claimed to have powers above and beyond good acting and good carpentry. He couldn't even speak of Uri Geller's spoons. But Sabine was a little more sentimental. She knew that there was no such thing as a true Indian rope trick, but she thought that maybe death was not always so final, that sometimes it was possible for someone to come back.

"Dead is dead," Parsifal had told her. "Period."

She said she believed in telepathy, in a few rare cases. She believed that she had it with Parsifal.

"No such animal," he said.

But then how did she always know what he needed? How did she always know it would be him when she picked up the phone? How was it she so often knew what card was on the top of the deck when he held it out to her?

So on the ninth day alone in the house, when the phone rang in the middle of the afternoon Sabine was so sure it was Parsifal that she tripped over the rabbit while lunging for the phone. On the second ring she remembered he was dead. On the third ring she knew it was his mother. On the fifth ring she got up off the floor and answered the phone.

"Mrs. Fetters?" the voice asked, not stating a name, but requesting one.

"No," Sabine said, as confused as the voice.

"I'm calling for Mrs. Guy Fetters. Mrs.— The lawyer said there was another name."

"You're Mrs. Fetters," Sabine said.

"Yes," the voice said, friendly, Midwestern, relieved. "Yes, that's right. Is it—Mrs. Parsifal? That's the name I have here. He was Parsifal the Magician."

"I'm Mrs. Parsifal," Sabine said, and it was true, she had taken his name when they married. She had answered to that name to the doctors, to the coroner, to the undertaker. She said it with authority now.

"Oh, well, I'm glad I got you. I'm glad." But then she was

quiet. Sabine knew she should assume some responsibility for the conversation, but she had absolutely no idea what to say. "This is very awkward for me," Mrs. Fetters said finally. "Guy was my son. I guess you know that. I want to tell you how sorry I am about his dying. I mean, sorry for you and me both. There's nothing in the world that compares to losing a child."

Sabine wondered if she meant losing him now or all those years before.

"Do you have children, Mrs. Fetters?"

"Mrs. Parsifal," Sabine said. "No, I don't."

"Parsifal," she repeated. "That'll take some getting used to. You get used to thinking of your children by one name. You don't expect that to change. 'Course, I shouldn't say that. It changes for your daughters. How long ago did he change his name?"

"Twenty-five years ago," Sabine said, realizing that she was not entirely sure.

"Fetters is not such a pretty name. I can say that, I've lived with it long enough."

Sabine would admit to curiosity, but she wasn't comfortable making idle conversation with a mother who could manage no better than one three-line postcard to her son over the course of a lifetime. She felt the weight of all of Parsifal's loss and loneliness married to her own. "Mrs. Fetters," said Sabine, "you've received the information from the lawyer. I'm assuming that's why you're calling me."

"Yes," she said.

"Then tell me how I can help you."

"Well," she said. Sabine thought she heard a catch in the voice. "Let's see. I'm sure you don't think so much of me, Mrs. Parsifal."

"I don't know you," Sabine said. She pulled the sleeping

rabbit off his pillow and into her lap. He was as warm as a toaster.

"Then I guess that's what I'm calling about. I hadn't seen my son in a long time, and I missed him every day, and now I know that I didn't do anything about it so I'm going to be missing him, well, from now on. My daughter Bertie and I were talking and we decided to come to Los Angeles and look around, see what his life was like, see where he lived, at least. Kitty can't come, she can't leave her family, Kitty, she's my oldest girl. We weren't asked to Guy's funeral. I'd like to at least see where he's buried."

"I didn't ask you to the funeral because I had no idea where you were. All of that information was in the will. It wasn't opened until later." Sabine couldn't quite bring herself to say that she had thought Parsifal's parents were dead.

"Where to find me?" Mrs. Fetters laughed. "Well, I've always been in the same place."

"I didn't know that."

"I'm sure he didn't tell you. There'd be no sense in that. All I want is to come down and see where my son is and to meet his wife—that is, if you'll meet us."

Sabine's studio was large and mostly empty. She was far away from the light over the drafting table. She would meet them. She might not have called them, but she would certainly meet them. "Of course."

"I went ahead and made reservations. We'll be in on Saturday. I figured I'm coming if you'll see me or not, but it makes it a lot better this way. I've got your address, the lawyer gave it to me. We'll rent a car at the airport and come by your house, if that's all right with you."

"Have you been to Los Angeles before?"

"I haven't been farther than Yellowstone," Mrs. Fetters said. "There hasn't been much reason to travel until now."

"Give me the flight number," Sabine said, leaning over for a pencil. "I'll pick you up."

Sabine would not go to bed until she was so tired that she was making mistakes, putting windowpanes in backwards, spilling glue. She drank coffee and played Parsifal's Edith Piaf records loud to stay awake. She liked the music, the pure liquid sadness in a language she could only partially understand. With proper diversion, there were nights that things didn't start going wrong until after four A.M. Only then would she put down her angle and X-acto knife and stretch her legs. She would take Rabbit, who was already asleep on an old pillow left in the studio for that purpose, under her arm and head down the long dark hallway to Parsifal's room. The rabbit's back legs hung down and gently tapped her side while she walked. Those nights she would lie in the big bed and say Guy Fetters's name aloud. Was that Guy Fetters in the photograph, his cheek pressed close to Phan's cheek, or was Guy Fetters someone else entirely? Did Guy Fetters live in Nebraska and work at a Shell station? Was his name embroidered over his heart in a cursive red script? Did he wear fingerless gloves in the winter as he stood at the window of your car, counting out change? She could not make out his face beneath the white cloud of his warm breath. It was one thing to have spent your life in love with a man who could not return the favor, but it was another thing entirely to love a man you didn't even know.

Some nights she was kind. What if you were born in Alliance, Nebraska, only to find that you looked your best in a white dinner jacket? What if you found that the thing you knew the most about wasn't cattle but the ancient medallion patterns in Sarouk rugs? What place would there have been for magic? Could he have sawed apart waitresses in all-night diners along the interstate, could he have made sheep disappear without someone reporting him? "Guy," his mother would say. "Leave your sister alone. If you pull one more thing out of that girl's ear, so help me God." At school he would beg for art history and they would tell him, *Next year, next year,* but it always got canceled at the last minute, replaced by a section of advanced shop; this semester: The Construction of the Diesel Engine. And then there were the girls, the ones he had to dance with at the Harvest Dance and the Spring Dance and after every rodeo to avoid being found out, to avoid being beaten with bottles and fists and flat boards found in a pile behind the gymnasium. He held the girls close and with deadly seriousness. He had to make up one more thing to whisper into their small, shell-like ears and too-delicate necks. He kept his eyes down and free of longing for the ones he longed for, the ones who danced in circles past him without notice, though he suspected some noticed but could not speak. Finally, alone, at home at night in bed, he read movie magazines beneath plaid wool blankets. He looked at the glossy pictures of Hollywood and Vine, tan boys on surfboards, endless summers. Why wouldn't Los Angeles be the promised land? Eight-lane highways and streetlights that stay on all night, stoplights that don't give up and begin to flash yellow at ten P.M. Think of what he loved and had never had before, festivals of Italian films from the fifties, Italian sodas in thirty-four flavors, unstructured Italian linen jackets in colors called wheat and indigo, the ocean and restaurant coffee at two A.M. and the L.A. Contemporary and men. Suddenly to have the privilege of wearing your own skin, the headlong rush of love, the loss of the knifepoint of loneliness. That was the true life, the one you would admit to. Why even mention the past? It was not his past. He was a changeling, separated at birth from his own identity.

Sabine moved the rabbit off her pillow and rolled over. Other nights were different. Other nights he was a liar: Every minute they were together he had thought of what she didn't know. He had held himself apart from her. He did not notice that she had given up everything for him, that she had put her love for him above logic. He thought she was simple because she fell for the story about the dead New Englanders. It was all he could do to keep from laughing when she took the hook into the soft part of her mouth. Her questions made him impatient. When, exactly, was she planning to let this drop? He fed out enough line to keep her going, a name here, a place, and then, as if the thought pained him too greatly, he closed the story down all together. And she believed him. Lies sprung up like leaks. They were too easy, too inviting. He told her he was going to San Diego when he was going to Baja. No reason, except he knew she'd believe him. He told her the club canceled the date when he didn't feel like working, told her he wanted to be alone for an evening when he'd brought home some bartender whose name he didn't remember. He told her the six of clubs was the ace of diamonds. And she believed him. That was her habit, and every time he lied he slipped further away. Sabine woke up twisted in the sheets, the pillow deep inside her mouth. There would have been no reason to lie, not when she loved him the way she did.

She imagined there would be plenty of answers in the Fetters; probably just seeing them walk off the plane would make it clear that these were people you'd want to cover up. Maybe they made his life hell. Maybe it was worse than that, as her father had suggested. Sabine closed her eyes. What kind of mother would never put her head inside the door to see how you were doing? What kind does not call on birthdays? And sisters! Who were these women who called themselves sisters and didn't even know their brother was dying? Sabine would have felt the loss of Parsifal anywhere in the world.

And so she changed her mind, made it up, and changed it back. She made plans to see friends and then canceled. She saw her parents, who thought that no good could come of a woman knocking around alone in such a big house. She would be better off coming home, at least for a while. What would she do if someone broke in?

She asked them, "Do you think Parsifal scared burglars away?"

A breeze came in on Saturday and blew what little smog there was out of the valley. From the beach you could see the islands, dreamy silhouettes of someplace to be alone. Sabine had called the pool girl, the yardman, and a service of off-duty firemen that came in teams of six and cleaned the house in under an hour. She went to the garden and cut some orchids that had thrived through the period of utter neglect, and put them on the table in the entry hall. She had Canter's deliver.

At some point during the week it had occurred to her that there was a very good chance that the Fetters didn't know that Parsifal was gay, that they thought they were coming to Los Angeles to meet his wife, as in his partner, the woman he loved. And why shouldn't they? For an afternoon she would be a daughter-in-law. It came with the territory of being a widow. But it was Phan who should have been the widow. He would have cleaned the house himself, washed the windows with vinegar. He didn't know the meaning of catering. He would have spent the day at the market buying fresh mussels and rosemary. Phan should have lived to see this through. His gentleness put people at ease. He would not have been angry. He would have had these people in his home out of some genuine warmth, a common bond of loss, not a twisted need to prove who had loved Parsifal best. Sabine took off the dress she was wearing. It looked like she was trying too hard. She put on some black linen pants and a heavy blue shirt. She wore the necklace Parsifal had given her for her fortieth birthday, a tiny enameled portrait of the Virgin Mary to whom, in this particular rendering, she bore an unnerving resemblance.

At the airport, limousine drivers with dark mustaches and darker glasses held up pieces of paper with names. Sabine wondered if she should have brought a sign that said FETTERS, but she imagined they would be easy to spot. They would look confused. They would look like Parsifal. Sabine blotted off her lipstick on the side of her hand and rubbed it into her skin. People poured off the plane. Some were embraced warmly, some passionately; some strode towards the main terminal with great purpose; some consulted the overhead monitors for connecting flights. There seemed to be no end to the number of people coming down the ramp.

"My lord," a woman said to her. "You're the assistant."

She was short, maybe five-foot-two, with a corn-fed roundness. Her gray hair had been recently permed and Sabine could see the shape of the rollers on the top of her head.

"Mrs. Fetters?"

The woman took Sabine's arm and squeezed hard. There were tears puddling behind her glasses. "On the plane I said to Bertie, 'How are we going to know it's her?' But of course it's you. I'd know you anywhere. Look, Bertie, it's the assistant."

In Bertie Sabine could see the slightest trace of Parsifal, but it had been very nearly scrubbed out of her. She was almost thirty but did not look twenty-five. Her face was pretty but blank. Her hair had also been recently permed and was a tangle of brown curls highlighted in yellow that came halfway down her back. "Nice to meet you," Bertie said, and shook Sabine's hand hard.

Mrs. Fetters put her hand up to Sabine's face as if to touch it but then pulled it back again. "Oh, you're so pretty. His life must have turned out okay if he had such a pretty wife." The tears had dammed at the bottom of her glasses but suddenly found free passage out the sides. "I wish I'd known that you were the one he'd married. Did you meet him on Johnny Carson?"

"You know me from Johnny Carson?" Sabine said. People were knocking against them in the race down to baggage claim. A family of Indians walked by and Bertie turned to stare at a woman in a gold-flecked sari.

"Well, sure. I didn't know you were together, though. We thought maybe they gave people assistants at the show. Everybody we knew said you looked like one of those girls who hand out the Academy Awards."

"No," Sabine said, feeling confused. She was trying to take it all in.... Parsifal's mother. She had on a green wool coat with a line of wooden toggles up the front. She held a rectangular overnight bag in one hand, the kind of tiny suitcase Sabine had taken to slumber parties as a girl. "I'm surprised that you saw that show, that you remember me."

"Saw it?" Mrs. Fetters said.

"She watches it almost every night," Bertie said.

"My daughter Kitty got it for me on video. It took forever to track it down, but they found it for her. All you say is one line at the end, you say, 'Thank you, Mr. Carson.' "

"Do I? I don't remember."

"Don't you watch it?" Mrs. Fetters asked. Sabine tried to guide them out of the path of an electric cart coming down the concourse.

"No, we don't have a copy," she said, taking the overnight bag from her mother-in-law's hand. Of all the urgent things there were to talk about, *The Tonight Show* didn't even make the list. "We should go downstairs."

"Were you on television all the time?" Bertie asked.

Sabine shook her head and took a few steps towards baggage claim in hopes of getting them to move. "Just that once."

"Well, I'll make a copy for you," Mrs. Fetters said. "You won't believe how pretty you are."

The airport engaged the Fetters. They could barely make it three steps without stopping to look at something and usually someone. Every race and nation was fairly represented in the domestic terminal. They stopped and whispered to one another, "Do you think they're from—?" "Mother, did you see—?" But when they reached the escalator they were silent. They stretched their arms to grip the moving rails on both sides and would not let go when a man in a black suit and a cellular phone wanted to get past them. It was a long ride down, past the finalists of the junior high school "California in the Future" art contest, tempera paintings of orange trees encased in plastic space bubbles. Sabine did not look back. She was trying to sort through the information. Had Parsifal broken with his family out of boredom? Could this really be his family? She couldn't make a picture in her head. She saw Bertie's hand beside her, a pinpoint diamond on her ring finger. She was engaged. Sabine had worn her own ridiculous engagement ring, a four-carat D, flawless, that Parsifal had bought in Africa ten years ago as an investment when someone had told him that diamonds were the way to go. She kept meaning to put it back in the safety deposit box. It looked like a flashlight on her hand.

"I didn't know they made escalators that long," Mrs. Fetters said to no one in particular when they got to the bottom. Her face was damp. A man dressed as a priest held a can that said BOYS' TOWN on it, and Bertie stopped and fumbled with the clasp on her purse. Sabine slid a hand under her arm and steered her away.

"He's not really a priest," Sabine whispered.

Bertie looked horrified. "What?" She glanced back over her shoulder. In Los Angeles there were no laws against pretending to be something you weren't. Behind them, twenty Japanese men in dark suits compared their luggage claims. Clearly there had been some mistake.

The wait at the luggage carousel seemed endless. Bags flipped down the silver chute as the crowd pressed forward, everyone ready to be the next winner. No one ever knew what to say while they waited for their bags. "How was your flight?" Sabine asked.

"I couldn't believe it, mountains and deserts and mountains. It all looked so dead you'd have thought we were flying over the moon. Then all of a sudden we go over one last set of mountains and everything's green and there are about ten million little houses. Everything's laid out so neat." Mrs. Fetters looked at Sabine as if perhaps she had answered the question incorrectly and so tried again. "My ears got a little stopped up, but the stewardess said that was normal. I wasn't half as scared as I thought I'd be. Do you fly much?"

"Some," Sabine said.

Mrs. Fetters patted her arm. "Then you know how it is."

"Here we go," Bertie said as a red Samsonite hardside made its way towards them. Together they walked out of the terminal and into the rush of traffic and light. Mrs. Fetters made a visor with her hand and looked in one direction and then the other, as if there were someone else she was looking for.

"It's so warm," Bertie said, pulling down the zipper of her coat with her free hand.

"It was awfully nice of you to pick us up," Mrs. Fetters said. "I can tell now it would be pretty confusing coming in by yourself. Have you lived here your whole life?"

Sabine said yes. She didn't see that there was any point in getting into her family history.

She had brought Phan's car to the airport because it was the biggest. It was also a BMW, which made it the nicest. "Mouse," Mrs. Fetters said, looking at the license plate. "Is that a nickname?"

Every question, no matter how unimportant, exhausted Sabine. It felt like a turn onto a potentially never-ending off-ramp. "No, it's a pet. It's the name of a friend's pet."

"A pet mouse?"

"Yes." Sabine slammed the trunk. She needed some basic parameters. She did not have the slightest idea who these people were. She did not know why she had offered to pick them up. When they got in the car she turned to Mrs. Fetters in the front seat. "Just when was the last time you saw Parsifal?" she said.

"Guy?"

Sabine nodded.

"Two days after his birthday, so February tenth." Mrs. Fetters looked straight ahead out of the cement parking garage. "Nineteen sixty-nine."

Sabine did the math in her head. "You haven't seen him since he was seventeen?" For some reason she had thought that maybe Parsifal had sneaked away at some point and gone for a visit, at least one visit.

"Eighteen," Bertie said from the backseat. "It was his eighteenth birthday."

"And I saw him on television," Mrs. Fetters added in a sad voice. They sat quietly with that information, the car idling in reverse. "I'd like to go right to the cemetery. If that's okay with you."

Sabine pulled out. She would take them to the cemetery. She would take them to the hotel. And then she would get these people the hell out of her car.

Los Angeles International Airport was a pilgrimage, a country that was farther away than anyplace you could fly to. They exited and made their way down Sepulveda, past the dried-out patches of grass along the sidewalk and fast-food restaurants that lined the way to the 105 east. With three in the car they could forgo the light and ease out into the diamond lane, where they sped along past a sea of traffic waiting anxiously to get out of the city. Angelenos were loners in their cars. That was the point of living in the city, to have a car and drive alone. They got onto the Harbor Freeway north. They passed the Coliseum ("Look at that," Mrs. Fetters said) and the University of Southern California; went through downtown, where they had to crane their necks backwards to see the housing of the criminal justice system. Sabine stayed left through the bifurcation, moving smoothly towards Pasadena and the series of tunnels where murals marked Latino pride and African-American pride and the pride of a washed up Anglo movie star turned boxer, his fists wrapped in tape and poised beneath his chin. Sooner or later it all gave way to graffiti: some twisting, ancient alphabet legible only to the tribe. The senseless letters arched and turned, their colors changing with mile markers. They took the Harbor to the Pasadena to the Golden State Freeway, north towards Sacramento, though no one ever went that far. The median swelled with deadly poisonous oleander bushes. Sabine went to the Glendale Freeway and then took the first off-ramp on San Fernando Road, which she took to Glendale Avenue, which left them, when all was said and done, at the towering wrought-iron gates of Forest Lawn Memorial Park. UNDERTAKING, CEMETERY, CREMATORY, MAUSOLEUM, FLOWER SHOP. ONE CALL MAKES ALL THE ARRANGEMENTS, the sign said.

"Oh," Bertie whispered.

In the fountain, bronze frogs spit water onto the legs of bronze cranes, which spit water straight into the sky. Real ducks and one adult swan paddled serenely, doing their job. Forest Lawn was Mecca for the famous dead, the wealthy dead, the powerful dead. They were buried beneath the tight grass or in their beautiful sarcophagi. George Burns was now filed away beside his beloved wife in a locked mausoleum drawer. All of the headstones were laid down flat, which the cemetery claimed gave a pleasing vista but in fact just made the hills easy to mow. Tourists ate picnics on the lawn. Lovers kissed. The devout went down on their knees at the Wee Kirk o' the Heather. There was politics in where you were buried, under trees or near water. The cheap seats were beaten by the sun or sat too close to the edge of the drive. Phan and Parsifal had decided on the best, a center courtyard behind an eight-foot brick wall with locked bronze doors that made casual viewing impossible. When they told Sabine, they were practically giddy—twin plots! Who would have thought there would still be two left? They reeled through the living room, arms around each other's waists, laughing.

"Forest Lawn?" she had said.

"It's so beautiful," Phan said. He had spent twenty years in this country and still cynicism eluded him.

"It's so crass," Sabine said.

"This is Glendale Forest Lawn," Parsifal said. "That's the original of the five. It's so-o-o much nicer than Hollywood Hills. The shade is stunning."

"Glendale isn't even close." They were moving too far away. "You don't want to go there."

"It's Los Angeles," Parsifal said. "This is our city. If you truly love Los Angeles, you want to be buried in Forest Lawn." He leaned back into the sofa and put his feet on the coffee table. "We can afford it, we're doing it."

Sabine decided to drop it. Who was she, after all, to say where another person should be buried?

After dinner Phan found her alone by the swimming pool. He sat down beside her. The night sky was a dark plum color and in the distance it glowed from the streetlights. "I bought three," he said.

"Three what?"

"Three plots." His voice was gentle, always asking a question. It grew softer every day he was sick. Phan's hair, so black and beautifully thick, had turned gray in a month and he wore it cut close to his scalp now. "We should all be together. That is the truth, the three of us are family. I don't want you to be alone."

Sabine kept her eyes down. Through the generosity of the offer she saw that she was alone. Even in death she would be the third party, along for the ride.

It got darker every minute they waited. The birds were almost quiet. Phan patted her hand. "It is a very difficult thing to discuss. I imagine that when we are gone your life will only be beginning. You could marry, have a child still. You have so far to go before you'll know how things will end. So this plot is only insurance. It says that Parsifal and I love you always, that we want you with us; and if you don't come, it will always mean the same thing. It will stay for you."

Sabine nodded, her eyes filling with tears. Thoughts of their deaths, her life alone, an amendment to twin plots, overwhelmed her. Though she and Phan had very few moments when they could be close out of a true fondness for one another, instead of their mutual fondness for Parsifal, she dipped her head down to his shoulder.

"I can't imagine this," Mrs. Fetters said, looking out over the rolling hills of the cemetery, dotted with the occasional winged angel, marble obelisk, Doric columns. "I'm looking at it hard as I can and I can't imagine it. California and Nebraska shouldn't even be in the same country. Do you think there's someplace I could buy flowers?" Her voice had an almost pleading sound to it. "I don't want to go without bringing something."

"Of course," Sabine said.

"I appreciate your being so patient with me." She touched her hand to the window. They passed a statue of the Virgin, her bare feet balanced delicately on top of a globe. "Bertie, do you see how beautiful it is?"

"It's like a park," Bertie said. "What would it be like to die here?"

Sabine pulled up in front of the flower shop, information center, and sales office which were all housed together in a rambling imitation English Tudor manor. She should have thought about the flowers. When she came out with Parsifal to visit Phan, they always stopped off in Pasadena and bought their flowers from Jacob Maarse. Cemetery flowers tended to rely heavily on gladiolus and carnations. They were also criminally overpriced. But Sabine was out of practice. She hadn't been out here in two weeks, not since the funeral, and she wasn't buying anything on that trip. She reached into her purse and put on her sunglasses. Her palms were beginning to sweat against the wheel.

The air in the florist shop was so sweet that they all had to stop for a minute at the door, as if they were trying to walk through something heavy. The colors were too bright, too many pinks and yellows clustered together. The walls were too white, the sun on the floor too severe. The place was as cheerful as a candy store. Business was booming: customers pointing at ready-made arrangements in glass coolers or pulling out flowers stem by stem from the buckets on the floor. A Mexican woman in a white uniform held a bundle of dark waxy fern leaves in her hand.

Bertie wandered in a trance, running her fingers along the flat faces of red Gerber daisies.

"I have never," Mrs. Fetters said slowly, "seen so many flowers."

Sabine wished they had gardenias. Parsifal loved gardenias. He put them behind his ear and said they made him feel closer to Billie Holiday. She settled for an Oriental hybrid lily called Mona Lisa. She bought all they had, eighty dollars' worth. Eighty dollars' worth of Mona Lisas would make two nice bouquets. She turned down an offer of baby's breath and buffalo grass. She took her flowers plain, swaddled in thin green tissue. Holding them in the bend of one slim arm, she looked like a pageant winner.

"I can't decide," Mrs. Fetters said, staring into the glass case.

Sabine said that what they had would be plenty, that there was only one water holder at the grave, but Bertie and her mother each bought a single yellow rose for five dollars apiece.

They drove to the caretaker's cottage, signed out for the key, and drove to the Court of David. The statue of David was gone, a sign explained, because it had been damaged in the Northridge earthquake. In the field where David should have been gazing down, a group of people gathered around a John Deere tractor and a hole.

"Listen to this," Parsifal had said. "First you go through the Court of David, into the Garden of the Mystery of Life, and then through the locked doors of the Gardens of Memory." He held the map up for Sabine to see. "Those are the directions! Don't you love it?"

"Why is it locked?" Bertie asked.

"It's a very nice part," Sabine told her. "They want to keep people from just walking through and looking." Sabine fumbled with the key. She could hear the light strains of music that were pumped into the private area through speakers on the top of the walls.

"I wish I was wearing a dress," Mrs. Fetters said. She pulled her sweater down smooth over the top of her pants. "Do you think I ought to have a dress on? Maybe we should wait until later."

"You look fine," Sabine said.

"I didn't get cleaned up at all after the flight. It's disrespectful that I should come over here this way. After all the time that's passed."

"Mama," Bertie said, and touched her mother's neck.

Mrs. Fetters took a deep breath and ran her fingers under her glasses. She was sixty-six, but at that moment she looked considerably older. "All right," she said. "I'll just come back tomorrow, too. Tomorrow I'll come back looking nicer."

They went inside.

Over in the far corner, beneath a Japanese plum tree, the grass had been taken up in a sheet and neatly replaced, but still you could see a difference between Parsifal and Phan. There was a small seam where they had buried Parsifal's ashes, a perforation in the green, whereas everything on Phan's side was settled. Two weeks Parsifal had been down there, way beyond Lazarus. And Lazarus hadn't been cremated. Sabine felt a great, bending wave of grief rise up in her chest and push to the top of her shoulders. There was a reason she hadn't come before.

Bertie hung back at the gate, unsure, but Mrs. Fetters moved like a mother. She crouched down and ran her hand over the flat brass marker as if wiping it off. "Parsifal," she read aloud. "Well, if that's what you want, I'll get used to it. Guy, you were always one to make the change. Surprised us so much it wasn't even surprising anymore." Her tone was light, conversational. She had practice talking to a son who wasn't there. "Oh, it's nice here, and you've got yourself the prettiest wife. You did all right, kiddo, better than anyone could have ever made up. You have yourself a good laugh at your daddy's expense. You stand up and show him how good you turned out." She looked up and spoke to Sabine, who was pushed back against the brick wall as if espaliered there by years of careful pruning. "You wouldn't believe the way we fight the crabgrass out where his father's buried. If I didn't cut it back every two weeks in the summer, I wouldn't know where he was. Kitty says it's him that grows it, just to torture me . . . Kitty," she said, turning back to Parsifal's place in the lawn. "Oh, what Kitty wouldn't give to see this! She would be so proud of you. She misses you something awful, Guy. When she heard you'd died, the doctor had to come and give her something. It broke my heart, the way she cried. You were everything in the world to her. Every single day. But Bertie's here." Mrs. Fetters held out a hand to her youngest. "Bertie, come and say hello to your brother."

Bertie moved tentatively towards her mother's hand, as if she were inching across a narrow ledge, looking down into a gorge.

"Say hello," Mrs. Fetters repeated.

"Hey, Guy," Bertie said in a small voice.

"Look how big she is, a full-grown woman. Last time you saw her, do you even remember? She was a speck, three years old. She says she doesn't remember you."

"Mama," Bertie said, as if her mother were telling on her. There were tears running down Bertie's cheeks, and Mrs. Fetters stood up, leaving one child to comfort another.

"There's nothing wrong with not remembering. You were too young. No shame in that."

Bertie looked younger, her face flushed so pink with crying. Sabine, stranded, knelt on the ground and began to separate the lilies into two equal bunches.

"Look how close those headstones are," Mrs. Fetters said.

"You'd think for the money they'd give you a little elbow room."

"Phan was a friend," Sabine said, and put half of the flowers on her friend's grave.

"Phan Ardeau? What kind of name is that?"

"Vietnamese. Vietnamese and French, really."

"Did Guy go to Vietnam?" Mrs. Fetters said, her voice full of panic, as if that were where he was at that very minute. "I didn't think they'd send him."

"Phan lived in L.A., they met here. Parsifal didn't have to go to Vietnam," Sabine said.

"Because of his ulcers," his mother said. "There was no way they could send that boy, the kind of ulcers he had."

Sabine looked at her. That was one thing they both knew.

"It was awful nice of Guy to buy that poor boy a funeral plot." She took one of the yellow roses off Parsifal's grave and gave it to Phan in charity.

"Phan bought the plots," Sabine said. She knew it would be better to just let it go, let everything go, but she couldn't think of Phan being dismissed. It was mostly his money they would all be living on from now on. "He bought one for me, too. The one you're standing on."

Bertie looked down at her feet and took a quick step to the side, but Mrs. Fetters held her ground, green grass cushioning the bottoms of her sensible shoes. "That was real nice of him," she said. "Guy always could make friends."

They stayed a little longer, none of them talking. They were all worn out from the sadness and the smell of the flowers. The beautiful day had hurt them. Parsifal was wrong, Los Angeles was no place to be buried. It was five o'clock when they left, and the January sun was just making its way down.

"It was an aneurism, right?" Mrs. Fetters said, as if she

were not at all sure that was right. "That's what the lawyer told me."

"An aneurism," Sabine said, glad she had remembered to take the brain scan off the refrigerator. The car hummed at the front gate of Forest Lawn. "I'll take you to your hotel," she said, but she didn't know where they were staying, which way she should go. "Unless you want to see the house, but we could do that some other time."

"The house," Bertie and her mother said together with a fresh burst of energy.

"It's nice of you to ask us," Mrs. Fetters said.

Sabine could only nod. It was nice of her.

Phan had bought the house on Oriole seven years ago, when he first came down from the Silicon Valley. By then the traffic was thick with people trying to move away from Los Angeles, and houses that had been bought and sold for hysterical amounts of money only a few years before now waited on the market like pregnant dogs at the pound. The agent was delighted by his call. She had six properties lined up to show him the first day, with plans to show him six more every day of the month, but Phan bought the first one. He refused to see the rest. The house on Oriole was built in the twenties as a contractor's gift to his wife, in a neighborhood where every street was named for a bird, Wren and Bunting and Thrush. Phan had always wanted a Spanish-style house. To him, they looked like California. The creamy stucco swirled like frosting, the red tile roof, the high archways between the rooms, the fireplace big enough for two people to sit in, the careless way in which the house seemed to amble on forever. It reminded him of one of the administration buildings at Cal Tech. "Six bedrooms, a study, guesthouse, mature fruit trees," the agent said, ticking off the points with her fingers; "a pool." Phan went through the glass doors in the back. The water sparkled, hot blue diamonds. Perhaps he would learn to swim.

"You live here by yourself?" Bertie said, tilting back her head in the driveway to try and take it all in.

"I do now," Sabine said.

Bertie stopped and maybe for the first time she looked at Sabine directly. She wrapped her arms around her waist. "I'm sorry. I don't know what made me say that."

"It's a big house," Sabine said, punching in the code for the alarm. The girl who did the yard had filled the planters with white winter pansies.

In the front hall their voices echoed. The Fetters began by complimenting the things that were closest, the curve of the staircase, the little table in the entry hall, the yellow-throated orchids on the table. "I have not seen anything like this in my life," Mrs. Fetters said. "Nothing close."

They went through the house as though they were half starved. They could barely restrain themselves from opening closets. "Is that a guest bath?" Bertie said, pointing to a closed door, and then, "Mama, would you look at this mirror in the bathroom." They picked up the fancy soaps shaped like seashells and sniffed them. They went through the guest rooms, the study, Sabine's studio. They commented on her interesting work, the perfection of such small trees. They petted the rabbit, who barely woke up, his flop ears stretched in either direction like an airplane. They followed the runner down the hall to her bedroom before Sabine could think about whether or not she wanted them there. But it was in the bedroom that Mrs. Fetters found the thing she had been looking for, the thing she had come to her son's house hoping to find.

"Oh," she said, sitting down on the edge of the bed, holding a picture from Parsifal and Sabine's wedding. "Look at him," she whispered. "Look how good he turned out."

Bertie came and sat beside her mother. "He looks just like Kitty," she said. "It's like Kitty with short hair and a suit."

"They always were just alike when they were children. People who didn't know us used to always ask were they twins." Mrs. Fetters touched her finger to the tiny image of his face. "Look at this one," she said, picking up another frame—Parsifal and Sabine in costume for the show. Sabine felt embarrassed; in the picture she looked naked but covered in diamonds.

"You sure do take a good picture," Mrs. Fetters said to her. "Are these people your parents?" Another frame.

Sabine nodded.

"I could see it. Are they still living?"

"About five miles from here," Sabine said.

"And do you see them?" Mrs. Fetters asked. A real question, as if there were a chance Sabine had left her family as well, only five miles away.

"I see them all the time," Sabine said.

"Oh, that's good," she said, smiling sadly. "That's good. I know you must make them so proud. Who's this?"

Parsifal and Phan at the beach, red cheeked, laughing, arms around necks. "That's Phan."

"The man at the cemetery."

"That's right."

"And this is Phan." A black-and-white picture of Phan working. It was bigger than all the other pictures. It was a beautiful picture. Sabine had taken it, a birthday present for Parsifal in a silver frame. Phan was writing on a tablet, his hair had fallen forward. The tablet was covered in numbers and symbols, hieroglyphics that only he would understand. "And this is Phan's family," Mrs. Fetters said, pointing to the portrait from Vietnam. Sabine confirmed this and waited for the next question, some inevitable question about why a friend's family was on her bedside table. But the Fetters were quiet, too busy feeding on photographs to ask.

"If there are more pictures of Guy, I sure would love to see them sometime." Mrs. Fetters got up from the bed.

"Plenty."

The three of them left the bedroom. The tour was over.

"It's perfect," Mrs. Fetters said. "Every last thing. How long have you lived here?"

"Just over a year," Sabine said, speaking for herself.

"You put a house like this together in a year?"

"Parsifal lived here for five years before me," she said, again, peering over the edge into the mire of complications. "It's his house. He was the one with the taste."

"So how long were you two married?" his mother asked. "I should have asked you that before. I don't even know how long you were married."

"A little less than a year," Sabine said, stretching out her six months. "It was after I moved in."

Mrs. Fetters and her daughter looked at Sabine suspiciously, as if suddenly she was not who they thought she was.

"We worked together, we were together for twenty-two years. We'd just never seen the point in getting married before. I'm afraid I'm not very old-fashioned that way." She did not wish to lie or explain. It was, after all, her life. Her private life. "I haven't even offered you anything to drink. Let me get you something. A soda, a glass of wine?"

"So why did you end up getting married? What changed your mind after all those years?"

Sabine put her hand on the banister. These people didn't know Parsifal. They did not know his name. If there were questions to be asked, she should be the one doing the asking. They were probably wondering why the money was all hers, why she had the house, an interloper married less than a year.

"We were all getting older," she said. She heard her own voice and it sounded clipped, nearly stern.

Mrs. Fetters nodded. "Older," she said. "I for one am getting older." They all at once understood that the family reunion was over. Everyone had seen more than they had planned to see, no one had gotten what they wanted. "Bertie, I think it's time we headed back to the hotel and got rested up."

"You're welcome to stay," Sabine said, following some code of social interaction her mother had drilled into her from birth. She could not help herself.

"I'm tired," Mrs. Fetters said. "It's bad enough that I have to ask you to drive us to the hotel."

Another trip in the car seemed a small price to pay for getting her privacy back. Sabine already had her keys in her hand.

"I told the travel agent I was willing to pay more for something safe," Mrs. Fetters said when Sabine pulled up in front of the downtown Sheraton Grand. "For what this place costs I think I ought to have a guard standing outside my door. Do you think this is safe?"

"You'll be fine here," Sabine said. "I can come in, make sure you're checked in okay."

Mrs. Fetters held up her hands. "I wouldn't think of it. You've done too much as it is. I know it was hard on you, going out to the cemetery. I'm afraid I was just thinking of myself."

"I wanted to go," Sabine said.

For a minute they all just sat there. Finally it was Bertie who opened her door. "Well, good night, then," Bertie said.

"If you need anything..."

"We're fine." Mrs. Fetters looked at her, everyone unsure of how to part. Finally she patted Sabine on the wrist, a gesture of a distant aunt, a favorite teacher. They got out of the car and waved. Sabine waited until they were safely inside before punching the gas. The BMW could exit parking lots at record speed.

Parsifal's family, his mother and sister, and Sabine had not invited them to sleep in one of the guest rooms. She had not offered them the enormous amount of food that was waiting in the refrigerator. Would it have been too much to be a little bit nicer? She gunned the engine and cut deftly into the left lane. Let them catch her. Let them try and take her in. She pushed the button down on the power window and let the wind mat her hair. Nights like this, the freeway was an amusement-park ride, a thrilling test of nerves and skill. Sometimes it was all she could do not to close her eyes. She would have to assume that Parsifal wouldn't disapprove of her leaving his family in a hotel, after all, he had been polite enough to leave them a small inheritance but not warm enough to tell them where he lived. There was a reason he stayed away. Even if it wasn't exactly evident, she trusted his judgment completely now. There was something wrong. Something that did not concern her or include her. It was dark and Sabine took the Coldwater Canyon exit over to Mulholland Drive. This was when she felt the most inside the city, when it was all broken down into patterns of lights.

There would have been something to gain by having them around. There were questions, giant gaping holes she would have loved to fill in, but when had the moment presented itself in which she could have said, and why, Mrs. Fetters, did you not speak to your son for all those years? Why the sudden interest now? Those were confidences, things that had to be earned. It took intimacy and that took time, and while she had seemingly limitless amounts of the latter, she had no stomach for the former. People made her tired. The way they were easy with one another, the way they seemed so natural, only made her sad.

At home she pulled out the trays of food and fixed herself a plate. She made a salad for Rabbit and put it on the floor, tapping her foot until she heard his gentle thump down the hall. What, exactly, was it worth without Parsifal to tell it to? How she wanted to find him at the breakfast table, waiting. She would spin it out, the airport, Johnny Carson. He would never believe his mother had a tape of Johnny Carson. In her mind she told him about the trip to the cemetery, how Bertie had stood back while his mother chatted up the grave marker. She told him about how they went through the house as if he were there but hiding, just out of earshot. For twenty-two years Sabine had told her stories to one person, so that the action and the telling had become inseparable. What was left was half a life, the one where she lived it but had nothing later to give shape to the experience.

"I don't want to wind up some old woman who talks to her rabbit," she said to Rabbit, who was chewing so furiously he didn't even bother to lift his head.

That night, while she sat in her studio carving a hill out of Styrofoam, trying to get the sweep to be gentle, she thought about them. She thought of Bertie's pale hands, the tiny diamond, and wondered who had put it there. Had Bertie thought about this brother she could not remember? Would it have made a difference in her life if he had been there? Mrs. Fetters didn't seem like a bad mother, the way she spoke to him at the grave site. She was direct. She was clearly proud of him, even in his death. And what could they know about Los Angeles? Would they go home tomorrow? Would they go back to Forest Lawn? Would they be wandering around the city, in and out of neighborhoods they shouldn't go to, trying to put together something they couldn't possibly find? Sabine was feeling guilty that she hadn't tried harder, asked more; and it was in the distraction of guilt that she slid the knife she used to cut the Styrofoam through the thin skin at the top of her wrist and into the base of her palm. It took a tug to pull it free. She started to say something, to call out, but then didn't. She closed her other hand around it and sat for a minute, watching while the blood pulsed out between her locked fingers. Then she went into the bathroom.

It was deep, no doubt about it, and it stung like the knife was still in there and very hot when she held her hand under the water, but all her fingers moved properly. The sink turned red. It looked like the kind of cut that would need stitches, but she would rather have bled to death sitting on the side of the tub than take herself to Cedars Sinai. Using her teeth, she tore open five packages of gauze pads and piled them onto her wrist and the bottom of her hand, then she taped them in place. Phan and Parsifal stocked a spectacular selection of first-aid paraphernalia. She could see the blood seeping around the edges and she raised her hand above her head. That's when she heard the phone ring.

It was nearly eleven o'clock. It would be Mrs. Fetters, though Sabine hadn't expected her to call. She sat on the floor, hand raised as if she had some urgent question.

"Sabine?" There was noise in the background, music and talking, a party. *Sabine.* "It's Dot Fetters."

Dot. She hadn't thought of that variation. "Are you all right?"

"Oh, I'm fine. I'm sorry to be calling so late. I'm waking you up."

"Not at all."

"Well, Bertie's asleep and I just couldn't, you know, so I came down to the bar. They have a nice bar here."

Sabine was glad she had called. She felt the blood running in a thin stream from her upturned palm down her arm.

"So I was wondering," she said, "and this is stupid because it's the middle of the night and everything and I know you don't exactly live next door, but I was wondering if you'd be interested in coming over for a drink."

Sabine thought that Dot Fetters had already had a drink or two, but who wouldn't? How would such a call be possible otherwise? "A drink."

"It was just a thought—too late really, I know, but I felt bad about the way things went today. I was hoping to have the chance to talk to you, and—I don't know. You have to bear with me, this is all hard."

"I know," Sabine said, her voice small in the room. It was very hard. And though she could not imagine going out to drink with Dot Fetters she could imagine even less being alone.

"All right," she said.

"Really? You could come?"

"Sure. It will take me a minute, but I'll be there."

Sabine changed her shirt, which now had a bloodstain under the arm, and wrapped her hand up tightly with an Ace bandage until it looked like some sort of club with long, cold fingers wiggling out of the end. She didn't know why she was going back, when only a few hours before she'd been so glad to be away, but this was new territory. There was no reason she should be expected to understand. She didn't even think about the drive. She was from Los Angeles; driving was simply part of it.

The bar at the downtown Sheraton Grand was alive and well, late on a Saturday night. The lights were turned low and the televisions played without volume. A man in the corner picked at a piano but did not sing. Cocktail waitresses in blue suits and white blouses threaded through the tables, most of them were Sabine's age or older, their heels mercifully low. When Dot Fetters saw her, she waved from a bar stool, and then, as if that had been insufficient, got up, went to Sabine, and hugged her. They had met, had parted, and had come together again, which by some code meant there could be physical contact.

"I want to buy you a drink," she said, raising her voice a bit over the din of clinking glasses. "You tell me what you want."

"Scotch," Sabine said, naming Parsifal's drink instead of her own.

Mrs. Fetters leaned over and spoke to the bartender, who laughed at whatever it was that Sabine couldn't hear and nodded his head.

"This is all so much to take in," Mrs. Fetters said. "Bertie was whipped, went right to sleep. You can do that when you're young, but I knew I was going to be up all night."

A man with dark eyes and expensively capped teeth brushed against Sabine, smiled, and asked for forgiveness. She ignored him and took up her drink.

"I didn't even ask you how long you were planning to stay," Sabine said.

"Day after tomorrow. Bertie has to get back to work. I work in the cafeteria where Kitty's boys go to school, but they're real flexible. Kitty thinks I ought to retire now that we've got this money, but I like seeing the boys. They're good kids, and they're already so big, I mean, practically grown-up. I want to be around them while I can. Her older son is Howard Junior, for his dad, but her younger boy's named Guy. Kitty named him for her brother. Now, there's something I bet you didn't know." Something caught her eye in the dim light. She was looking in Sabine's lap. "What did you do to your hand?"

Sabine looked down at it herself. She had been trying not to think about it, but it was throbbing as if she were holding a small heart in her fist. Perhaps she'd wrapped it too tight. "I cut myself," she said.

Mrs. Fetters reached down into Sabine's lap and brought her hand up to the bar. "Either you don't know anything about bandaging something up or this isn't just a cut." Then she took the hand as if it were something not connected to Sabine, a wallet or a comb, and held it closer to the light over the bar. "Jesus," she said. "This thing is soaking through." She reached into her purse and tossed some money on the bar. "Come on in the bathroom and let me have a look at it."

"It's fine," Sabine said.

But Mrs. Fetters wasn't listening, she was off the bar stool, pulling Sabine along like a woman with vast experience in flesh wounds. In the bright light of the bathroom, things didn't look very good. She had the Ace bandage halfway off before they were down to a solid red wetness whose color matched the flowers in the wallpaper. Sabine felt suddenly dizzy, and she didn't know if it was from the loss of blood or the sight of it.

"Do you want me to take all of this off and tell you you have to go to the hospital or do you want to save the time and just go now?"

"I'd really rather not," Sabine said, but in her own voice she heard doubt. She was moved by the sight of so much blood. Part of the cut, she knew, was in her wrist, that delicate network of things not meant to be severed. "I hate that hospital."

"Well, it's a big town, there has to be more than one." Mrs. Fetters looped the bandage back around carelessly. "Come on," she said, leading again. "I guess it's a good thing I called you. You probably would have bled to death in your own bed."

Sabine stopped her at the door. "If I have to go, that doesn't mean you have to go. I'll be fine."

Mrs. Fetters looked at her, puzzled. "You don't think I'd have you going to the hospital in the middle of the night by yourself, do you? What do you think your mother would say if she ever found out?"

My mother, Sabine thought, would be too busy asking you questions about how you raised your own children.

Good Samaritan was less than a mile from the hotel. There was no need to drive all the way to Cedars Sinai. Could a person really bleed to death from sticking themselves with an X-acto knife? Probably not, but she liked the thought of it, committing suicide while she slept with no intention of doing so.

The lights of the emergency room blazed. The electric doors flung themselves open at the slightest touch. They wanted you here. They pulled you in.

Children lay flushed and dozing in their parents' laps, a woman with her arm slung in a piece of floral sheeting stared straight ahead, a man with no shirt and a large piece of cotton padding on his chest lay on a gurney in the hall, a woman with blood-matted hair and bruises only on one side of her face sat away from the rest with a police officer. People cried, sweated, and slept. Some people sat next to suitcases and watched through the window as if they were waiting for a bus. Two old men who looked like they should be at Canter's talked and laughed aloud at each other's stories. Sabine went to the front. She filled out her forms, had her insurance card copied, and was not reassured that her turn would be soon. She went and sat beside Mrs. Fetters in the waiting area.

"Do you think there's something particularly bad going on tonight?" Mrs. Fetters asked in low voice.

Sabine shook her head. "I'd guess this was pretty calm."

"I don't think I'd ever get used to living in a city."

"This isn't a very glamorous way to spend your first night in Los Angeles."

Mrs. Fetters laughed. "Well, what was I going to do? I'll tell you one thing, spending the night in a bar never did anybody any good. I'm better off here." She looked at Sabine's hand and lightly touched the tips of her fingers. "Those nails of yours are getting kind of blue. I think we should loosen this thing up a little bit. They won't let you bleed to death right here." She took her hand and carefully wound back the Ace bandage, then put it on again, letting the weight of the soggy cloth hold it in place.

"Thank you," Sabine said. Dot Fetters got a tissue out of her purse to wipe the blood off her fingers. Several drops of blood fell on the white floor. No carpet around here. "This is where they brought Bobby Kennedy, the night he was shot."

"Really?" Mrs. Fetters said, looking around the room with new respect. "What a tragedy that was. What a sweet boy."

They sat quietly, both of them trying not to look at anyone in particular. "Do you remember that scar Guy had—it was right here?" Mrs. Fetters put her finger beside Sabine's left eye and traced a line down the side of her face, back along her hairline, in front of her ear, and down to the very top of her jaw, following the exact course of a scar Sabine had looked at for twenty-two years. The touch was so light that it chilled her.

Sabine nodded.

"Where did he get that scar?"

"Playing hockey at Dartmouth. Someone got him with the stick."

"I got him," his mother said, crossing her arms around her chest. "Seven years old. I was working in the yard and Kitty and Guy were playing. I was trying to cut back a bush but my shears were too small and I told Guy to go to the garage and get the big shears. But Guy was all busy with Kitty, they were making something and I had to holler at him again, told him he better run 'cause I wasn't going to ask him a third time. Well, then he drops everything. He went off in a flash and not two seconds later he's coming back and he's got the clippers and they're open, like this"—she put her palms together and turned back her hands. "Well, I saw those things coming, they caught the sun. It's like he's running with a couple of butcher knives, and I say to him, 'Don't run,' though not a minute before I'd told him *to* run, and he gets confused, looks at me, and down he goes over the hose line, just like that." She snapped her fingers. The nurse looked up, puzzled, and then looked away. "Damned if he didn't slice his beautiful face halfway off, right in front of me. I'll tell you, if you have kids you spend your whole life thinking how you'll never forgive yourself. You always think you should have been watching them better, but half the things happen when you're looking right at them."

Sabine saw him, his back narrow in a blue T-shirt, his hair cropped short. The blood on the blades of the shears, on the grass. "What happened?"

"Everything happened," Dot said, holding herself tightly, "at exactly the same minute. I'm crying, he's crying, Kitty is absolutely beside herself. I turn him over and I have to push the skin back over the bone with my fingers." She held up her hand to show Sabine the fingers she had used. "I was covered in dirt, of course. You've never seen the likes of it. I tell Kitty to get my car keys and just like that we're off to the hospital, not that you'd even call it a hospital after being in a place like this. Everybody comes out to see what's going on. I've got Guy in my arms, Kitty's holding on to his feet, she's got blood on her, I'm all bloody. The three of us look like we just walked away from some sort of wild burning car crash. I tell them what's happened, so the doctor says he's going to take him in the back and sew up his head and that I am to wait in the other room until it's over. At this piece of news

Guy grabs onto my shirt, right at the neck, for everything he's got and he starts to really scream. So I say, 'cause I'm feeling so bad about telling him to run, 'No, I'm going in there.' 'No, no, Dot,' they say. 'You won't like this. You trust us, you stay out here.' " Dot Fetters took a breath and looked at the double doors going back to wherever it was they sewed up children's heads.

"I see how scared he is, and I know I'm going back with him. I've already made my point and there's no getting out of it. Besides, nothing bleeds like a cut on the head, so we're all pretty much standing in a pool now. Well, a nurse comes and she tells Kitty that they're going to go get cleaned up, get a little present maybe. 'Course, Kitty is not one to be left out, and the next thing I know this woman is hauling my girl bodily away, and Kitty is howling like a dog. She's got Guy's shoe in her hand where they tugged her loose. Now it's me and Guy and the doctor. We go back in a little stitch-up room and another nurse and I put him out on the table and tell him to hold real still, that they're going to sew him right back to- gether. 'Just like mending a shirt,' I say, 'absolutely good as new.' But when he sees that needle coming he starts to thrash. They damn near put that needle in his eye. I'm holding him down on one side and the nurse has got him on the other and for a kid who must have about a half cup of blood left in him he's fighting like a grown man. He's screaming, and I can still hear Kitty screaming down the hall. Well, nobody's got the time for this, and nothing I say is making any sort of impres- sion on him, so they bring out a sack—it was like a little laundry bag—and they stuff him inside and they cinch it up at the neck. There's my baby in a bag, just his little head sticking out, and I really thought I was going to fall over. Then they strapped the bag to the table, strapped it down tight, so he's held just so, and the nurse takes his head and the doctor gives the shot and starts to stitch. I never saw anything like it. Once Guy knew he was whipped he settled down, but his eyes were wide open and he stared at me while I stood there and cried like an idiot. That doctor took pretty little stitches, better work than I ever did."

Sabine thought about the straitjackets, water boxes, chain acts, MRIs. Do not be tied down, locked up, no matter what. "He had claustrophobia," she said. "I know that. He hated to be confined. He told me it was because he got locked in a refrigerator once."

"Oh," Mrs. Fetters said, looking tired. "That, too."

Sabine was about to ask, but they called her name. "Sabine Parsifal," the nurse said. Mrs. Fetters stood up with her.

"I'll be right back," Sabine said.

"Oh, I've come this far, I might as well go along."

"You can't come back there with me," Sabine said.

"May I come back?" Mrs. Fetters asked the nurse. "I'm her mother-in-law. It's just stitches."

"Sure," the woman said. It was the emergency room. Everyone there could come back for all she cared.

When they were seated in the little white cubicle, Sabine looked at her, Dot Fetters with her tight gray curls and plastic-frame glasses. Everyone's mother. Sabine didn't even know her. "There's no reason for you to do this," she said. "I'm going to be fine."

A young Chinese woman came in wearing a white lab coat, her straight black hair caught in a ponytail that hung halfway down her back. "So, Mrs. Parsifal, you cut yourself," she said, taking off the layers of wrapping. She did not look judgmental, she just ran water in a basin. "When did you do this?"

Sabine told her it had been an hour ago, maybe two.

The doctor touched the cut gently and a sharp wire of pain came up Sabine's arm. She liked the way it felt, the simple clarity of pain. Cut your hand and get it stitched up, wait and the hand will mend, the stitches come out. The idea that she would have the opportunity to get over something thrilled her. The doctor rested Sabine's hand in the warm water of the basin and cleaned the wound. Sabine watched the doctor's two hands working over the pale fish of her one. The water turned pink. Her hand was removed, patted dry.

"I'm going to give you a shot," the doctor said, filling up a needle for proof, "and when everything is good and numb we'll sew it up, all right?" Everyone was so wide-awake, even Sabine. They did not feel the time.

Mrs. Fetters stood up then and took hold of Sabine's other hand, the good hand. "This is the part that hurts," she said. "Squeeze hard."

It was all a business, part of a larger service industry. The doctor was good, though she had only been a doctor for six months. She somehow managed to give the illusion of time, but from her arrival to the positioning of the last bandage, only ten minutes passed. Papers were exchanged, signed, duplicates received. Sabine and Mrs. Fetters touched their feet to the black rubber mat of the exit door at the same moment, and it swung open and set them free.

"I appreciate your coming along," Sabine said in the car. It was after one in the morning and yet there were people everywhere. Slender palm trees cut outlines against the night sky.

"You always want to feel like you've come along at the right time, and besides, I wanted to see you again."

Sabine nodded but didn't say anything. Phan's car was an automatic. Her left hand sat in her lap, face up, useless.

"I just hated getting stitches. I don't know how many times I went in or took in one of the kids. Something always had to be sewn up." Dot thought about it for a minute, maybe ran over the entire catalog of life's pains in her mind. The burst appendix, the broken wrist, the endless litany of tears in the skin. "That story I told you, about Guy falling on the shears?" She asked as if she thought Sabine might have forgotten it in the last hour.

Sabine took her eyes off the road for a minute and looked at her, nodded. The traffic was light.

"It was awful, start to finish, and I was eaten up by guilt, thinking I had done it to him, that he'd have such a scar on his face, but not for one second during the whole thing did I think he was going to die. It never even occurred to me."

It was the thing that happened when you ventured outside, people started talking. Everywhere she looked the citizens of Los Angeles were awake, talking. Their heads bent towards one another in the front seats of the cars that flashed by. On the sidewalks they stood close and whispered, or they stood apart and screamed. Those who had no answers had sense enough to stay home in bed. "I don't know why he's dead, Mrs. Fetters, if you're asking me."

Sabine pulled into the circular loop in front of the Sheraton reserved for registering guests, which they weren't. They sat there together in silence.

"So," Sabine said, because it was late and the not-asking had, at that exact moment, become as difficult as the asking, "why did you and your son not see each other for twenty-seven years?"

"What did he tell you?"

"He told me you were dead."

Mrs. Fetters sat quietly, as if, of all the possibilities she had been privately mulling over, this was not one of them. "Oh," she said finally, sadly. "When did he tell you the truth?"

"He didn't. The lawyer told me when he went over the papers. He didn't know, either."

"Dear God," Mrs. Fetters said, her hands pressed hard against her thighs, bracing herself. "You mean all this time—" She stopped for a minute, trying to piece together so much information. "Come inside and have a drink. I need a drink."

"It's too late," Sabine said.

"Park the car," she said. "Or leave it here, either one. What about his sisters? Did he say his sisters were dead? He wouldn't say Kitty was dead."

"Helen," Sabine said. "There was one sister named Helen. Everyone died together in a car accident in Connecticut."

"Connecticut," Mrs. Fetters repeated to herself; a state she had never seen, had barely imagined. "Well, you must be wondering what I did!" She looked like she was ready to walk to Forest Lawn and dig Parsifal up with her hands. "What can a mother do to make her son say that she's dead, the whole family dead?" It was as if he had killed them.

"He wanted to separate from his past," Sabine said. "That's what I know. Nobody's saying that it's because of anything you did." But of course, Sabine thought, that is exactly what I'm saying.

The bar stayed open until two A.M. Who would have thought it? It was quieter now, no piano player, one waitress. The bartender waved them back into the fold like lost friends, brought them the same drinks without being asked. It seemed like a miracle, a bartender who remembered.

"We'll drink to your husband and my son," Mrs. Fetters said, and they touched their glasses.

"Guy," Mrs. Fetters said.

"Parsifal."

They drank. It was that wonderful, fleeting moment when

the scotch was still warm on top of the ice cubes, so very nearly sweet that Sabine had to force herself to pull the glass away from her mouth. There was so much to say it was impossible to know where to start. But the place Mrs. Fetters picked to begin was a surprise.

"Tell me about that fellow in the cemetery."

"Phan?"

Mrs. Fetters nodded, her hair holding fast. "Him."

"He was a friend, a friend of Parsifal's, a friend of mine."

"But more a friend of Guy's."

Sabine ran the thin red straw around the rim of her glass. "Parsifal met him first."

"And what did he do?"

"He worked in computers, designed software programs. He was very successful. He developed Knick-Knack."

"Knick-Knack?"

"It's a game," Sabine said.

It meant nothing to her. Ask anyone else in the bar and they would have gone on and on about how they'd thrown half of their life away playing Knick-Knack. Sabine watched while Mrs. Fetters sorted things out in her head. At the table beside them a man was telling a woman a story in a low whisper while the woman bowed her head and wept.

"Listen," Sabine heard him say to her. "Listen to me."

"I know nothing about Parsifal," Mrs. Fetters said. "I've been out of the picture for a long time. But I know one true thing about my son, Guy, one thing that is making all of this difficult to figure." She looked as if she were trying to remember how to say something, as if the words she needed to complete the story were Swedish and her Swedish was no longer very good. "Guy was a homosexual."

Sabine took a sip of her drink. It was something like relief. What she did not have in life she would not have in death. It was only fair. "Yes," she said, "so was Parsifal."

Mrs. Fetters nodded like a satisfied detective. "So now where does this leave you, exactly? You're too pretty to just be faking it for somebody."

"We were very close," Sabine said. Her voice was quiet. The bar seemed to press forward; the bartender pushed his upper body across the polished wood, pretending to reach for a bowl of salted nuts. There was no answer, not unless you were willing to sit down and look at all the footage, sift through the ephemera. "We worked together, we were friends. After Phan died, I think we both had a sense that it was just going to be the two of us, and so we got married."

"But why didn't you marry somebody else?"

There was a votive candle in a pale orange cup burning between them on the table. A whole host of somebody-elses stretched out in front of her, all the men who were in love with her, who begged her to be reasonable. Architects, magicians, rug dealers, the boy who bagged her groceries at the supermarket—none of them were right, none of them came close. "I was in love with him," Sabine said. Everyone knew that.

"Everyone was in love with that boy," Mrs. Fetters said, making Sabine's confession common as ice. "But weren't the two of you ever"—she tilted her head to one side, as if straining to hear the word—"together?"

"No."

"And that was okay with you."

"Oh, Christ, I don't know," Sabine said. "No, not at first." It embarrassed her even now, and Parsifal was dead. "When I was young I guess I thought he'd come around, that it was all about having patience. I'd get angry at him and then he'd get angry at me. Finally we broke up the act. I was maybe twenty-five then. We were only apart for a week, but—" She stopped and looked at Parsifal's mother. Maybe she could see him there, just a little bit around the mouth. "When we were apart something changed for me. I missed him so much I just decided it was better to take what I had. To accept things. I really believe he loved me, but there are a lot of different ways to love someone."

"It seems to me that you got a bad deal," Mrs. Fetters said.

"I had a very good deal," Sabine said, and picked up her drink.

Mrs. Fetters nodded respectfully. "Maybe you did. There are a lot of things in this world I'm never going to understand."

"Do you understand why Parsifal told me you were dead?"

Mrs. Fetters polished off her drink in a clean swallow and caught the bartender's eye, which was easily caught. "I do."

"Good," Sabine said. "Tell me about that. I'm tired of confessing."

Mrs. Fetters nodded, looking as if the late hour of the night was finally catching up with her. "I was born in Alliance. I lived there all my life. When I was growing up, if you had told me there was such a thing as a man who loved another man—" She stopped, trying to think of something equally impossible, cats loving dogs, but it all fell short. "Well, there was no such thing. There were two men I remember worked for the railroad who lived together just outside of town. There were lots of fellows worked for the railroad that lived together, but there was something about these two made everybody nervous and after a while they were run off, and even then I don't think folks could put their finger on what it was, exactly. We were a backwards lot, and I was way out there in front, the most determined to keep myself backwards. I was a grown married woman before someone told me what it was to be gay and it was a while after that before I believed it. And yet all the time I knew something was different with Guy, and he was only three or four before I knew that was what it was. I never exactly said it to myself, and I sure never said it to anyone else, but I knew."

The bartender arrived with two fresh drinks. "Coming up on last call," he said helpfully, picking up the used glasses and damp napkins.

"We'll think about it," Mrs. Fetters said. She drank while Sabine waited. "I'm taking too long to get to my point. That's because I'm not so interested in getting there. By the time Guy was fourteen there was a little trouble, him messing with friends, playing games that I didn't think were games. I sent him to Bible camp, I got him saved, but all over him I saw his nature. I thought it was something that could be changed, a sickness, and so I sent him away when I was pregnant with Bertie. I sent him to the Nebraska Boys Reformatory Facility up in Lowell to get cured. I sent him into the worst kind of hell so that what was wrong could get beaten out of him. The day he turned eighteen he came home, packed up his things, and left. That was that. He didn't want anything to do with us after that, and once some time had gone by I couldn't say I blamed him. I never knew what happened to him, not until fifteen years later, when I saw the two of you on the Johnny Carson show. You can't imagine what that's like, thinking your child is probably having some miserable life somewhere because of what you've done to him and then seeing him on television, a big famous magician. I liked to fell out. I wrote to the people at the show and asked them to forward a letter on to Guy—Parsifal the Magician. Oh, I was sorry and I told him how sorry I was and how we all wanted him to come home. I just about held my breath every day going out to the mailbox. Then, sure enough, I get a letter with no return address and a postmark from Los Angeles. It was very polite.

He said all was forgiven and forgotten and the past was in the past, but the past needed to stay right where it was. He said he just didn't want to think about it, not ever again, and would I please respect that. He sent us some money. Every now and then more money would come. In the last few years it was a whole lot more money, but he didn't write to me again and he didn't write to Kitty, which I think was wrong of him no matter how mad he was." Mrs. Fetters looked right at Sabine and Sabine did not look away. "So that's what I did."

Sabine tried some of her drink, but now it tasted spoiled in the glass. "Well," she said.

"I'm not looking for your forgiveness," Mrs. Fetters said. "I haven't even come close to forgiving myself. I'm just telling you what I know. He should have told you. You're a nice girl. You deserve to know what's going on."

"I appreciate that," Sabine said. Parsifal in prison. Parsifal in hell.

Then, for the last time that night, Mrs. Fetters surprised Sabine. She reached across the table and picked up Sabine's good hand and held it tight inside her own. "I'll tell you straight, Sabine, I'll tell you what I want from you. Give me and Bertie one more day. Take us around to the places he went to. Show us what he liked. I want to see how it was for him, give myself something good to think about for a change. Even if it's not good, it will be good, because it will be the truth. I'll be thinking about him, how he really was, not just some idea I had. I want that to take back to Nebraska with me." She smiled at Sabine like a mother. "It's a long winter out there, you know, lots of time to think."

Sabine looked down at the table where her hand was swallowed up. Suddenly she was tired enough to cry, tired enough to sleep. She knew it would come sooner or later. "I need—," she said, but could not finish.

"You need to think about it," Mrs. Fetters said. She squeezed the hand and let it go. "Of course you do. You know where you can find me."

Sabine nodded. "I can tell you in the morning. It would be wrong for me not to give this some thought."

"Sure, honey," Mrs. Fetters said.

Sabine pushed back from the table and stood up. "Good night," she said. She waited but it looked like Mrs. Fetters planned to stay for a while, contemplating last call.

"I'm glad you came over," Mrs. Fetters said.

Sabine nodded and got to the door before she stopped. There was no one left in the bar. Just the bartender. The music was off. It was like speaking across a dining room. She did not raise her voice. "Thank you for going with me," she said, and held up her hand.

"That?" Mrs. Fetters said. "That's nothing."

In the car Sabine turned the music up loud. Parsifal kept the glove compartment stuffed with cassettes, mostly operas, scratchy recordings from the twenties. He liked Caruso. He liked Wagner, the story of Parsifal he had named himself for years before he had listened to the opera all the way through. The name sounded so much more like a magician than the more traditional Percival. The brave underdog knight. The one who finds the grail. The only one, in the end, who is left standing. She did not think of Lowell, Nebraska, then, sailing over the empty freeways home. She did not think of it driving on Sunset Boulevard, which was always awake, the billboard advertisements for new films bright as movie screens, the twenty-foot faces of famous people staring vacantly in her direction. She did not think of it as she drove into the hills of bird-named streets, or locked her car inside her own garage, or walked down the dark hallways of her own house. She did not think of it at all until she was in bed and it was quiet. Nebraska Boys Reformatory Facility. Facility. Boys who habitually stole from grocery stores. Boys who loved fire and burned up dry grass fields in summers, hay barns in the winter. Boys who would not stop fighting, broke the noses and jaws of smaller boys. Mean, stupid boys who could not be taught the difference between right and wrong, never having seen it themselves. Boys who took girl cousins down to the creekbed at family reunion picnics and raped them. Boys who held those same girl cousins under the water later on to keep them from talking. Boys who knew what to do with a lead pipe, knew how to make a knife from a comb. The authorities locked them together in Lowell, Nebraska, let them discipline each other. And then they disciplined them. Parsifal, in his white tuxedo shirt of Egyptian sea-combed cotton. Parsifal, who walked out of the theater when the space alien split through the lining of the astronaut's stomach. He gave money to Greenpeace. Where, exactly, was Greenpeace when the seven boys in the shower went to put their shoes on before kicking you in the stomach, in the back? But he never let on, not for a minute. He picked up checks, wasted time, slept late. In Los Angeles he was never afraid. So maybe that was why he didn't tell her. Maybe it was better to keep it that far away, to never have to look at someone who was remembering when you have made such a concerted effort to forget.

But Sabine would never know for sure. This was one more legacy. Something else to keep watch over.

The field is so flat that she cannot judge its size. It goes on forever and in every direction it is flat. There is no point on which to fix her eyes, just green, a green so tender and delicate it makes her want to bite into it. Sabine is standing in warm water, the new green shoots surrounding her ankles, her feet sinking into a soft mud she cannot see. There has never been so much flatness, so much green.

"Sabine!" Phan says, and waves. In his hands he is carrying a bouquet of Mona Lisa lilies. Their slender leaves reflect the brilliant sun. He walks towards her like a man who knows how to walk through rice. He moves without losing his balance or damaging the plants. His pants are neatly rolled to his knees. They are dry and clean.

Sabine loves him. She cannot remember ever being so happy to see anyone in her life. "I am not alone," she says. She doesn't mean to say it aloud, but it makes Phan smile hugely. The air is humid and sweet. Like the water, it seems to be alive.

"I behaved so badly," he says. He leans over and floats the heavy bouquet beside them in the water and then takes her hands, but she pulls her hands away so that she can hold him in her arms, put her arms around his neck. She can almost smell the sun on his skin as she presses her lips to his ear.

"I'm so sorry," she says. "To think that I could have blamed you for anything. I know you were doing what you thought was best."

"I should have explained—"

"Sh," she says. "Don't think of it." It is such a strong feeling, the joy of being with Phan, who understands, the joy of not being alone, that for a minute she thinks she is in love with him. In love with the dead gay lover of the dead gay man she was in love with. She laughs.

"What?" Phan asks.

"Just happy." Sabine steps back to see him. He looks even better now. He is perfect in this field, breaking the line between the green shoots and blue skies. "Where are we?"

"Vietnam," Phan says proudly. "I was going to come back but I thought, Sabine should really see this."

"Vietnam," Sabine says. Who would have thought it could be such a beautiful place? All the times that Sabine had heard about Vietnam, thought about it, no one had mentioned it as beautiful. "I can't believe it."

"My father came here from France in 1946. Did I ever tell you that?" Phan takes her arm and walks her down the long wet path through the limitless fields. "He was a contractor. He was supposed to come here for two years and build roads but he stayed and stayed. He married my mother, they had a family. In his soul, my father is Vietnamese. He loves it here."

"Your father still lives here?" Sabine says, her toes tracing through the soft muck.

Phan laughs. "Good Lord, Father has been dead forever."

Sabine nods. Clearly condolences are not in order. "When did you leave?"

"My parents sent me to study in Paris in 1965. It was a difficult year. 65. I never came back until now." He stops and looks out at the landscape. "I had a little white dog," he says. "The dog had a red leather collar." When he turns to her there are tears in his eyes and he touches her hair with the very tips of his fingers. "Isn't it funny, the things we miss the most, the things that really can break our hearts?"

"What was the dog's name?" she asks.

"Con Chuot. Mouse. My father said I couldn't take the dog and so he gave me the mouse, a tin mouse to remember my Mouse at home. Do you still have it?"

"Of course," she says.

"I was very loyal to that mouse," he tells her. "I took it everywhere with me. All the time I wanted my dog." He sighs and then smiles. "I'm happy in Vietnam, Sabine. I find it relaxing. We keep saying once things settle down we're going to spend more time here."

Sabine looks behind her. Nothing could hide in this field. "Is Parsifal here?"

Phan reaches up, rubs her neck in the exact place it has been bothering her. "Not this time. He's back in L.A. He stays very close to you. It's just that he's so—well, so embarrassed about all of this."

"But he shouldn't be. My God, with all that happened to him."

"Ah," Phan says, "things happened to you, to me. He shouldn't have kept this to himself. I understand, but still, he should have thought it through."

"You may be underestimating things," Sabine says, but her voice is kind. It is very important not to frighten Phan off, never to hurt him. For one thing, she has no idea how she would get home from Vietnam.

Phan smiles at her. "Death gives a person a lot of perspective."

"Well then, Parsifal should know that he can talk to me, that he should come to see me."

"He will," Phan says, "he's getting there."

Sabine reaches down and brushes the top of the rice with the flat of her palm. The bottom of her nightgown is soaked and it clings to her legs. "But now you want to talk to me about his mother."

"It comes back to perspective," Phan says, "the larger picture. There is a woman with a good heart. A woman who maybe didn't make all the right choices, a woman who's told a few lies, but really, when did any of us get everything right?"

"But if Parsifal didn't want to have anything to do with her, why should I? I like her fine, I do, but when I think about all of it . . ." She can hardly make herself think about it. Parsifal not in heaven, not in Vietnam, but in hell.

"In his life Parsifal, like his mother, probably did the best he could. But in his death he wants better. He looks back and sees where there could have been reconciliation, forgiveness. These are the things you think about. But what can he do?"

Phan looks away, as if he is looking for Parsifal to walk up out of the field, and Sabine looks, too. "What he can do, Sabine, is ask you to do that for him, and even though he wants it, he can't ask because he knows it's too much. So what does he do? He asks me to ask. That is the way we are joined, you and me: We don't know how to turn Parsifal down. His heart is perfect. It isn't that he wants to take advantage of either of us, but what he wants to do he can't, because he's dead." Phan stops and looks at her closely to make sure she's following everything he's saying. "That leaves you."

"It's all right," Sabine says. "So I take them out. So I forgive her. She says she doesn't need my forgiveness, but I know she does. If that's what Parsifal wants, forgiveness and a day's tour of Los Angeles, I can do that. Tell him I can do that."

Phan puts two fingers to his lips, and then, as if he remembers he no longer has a need to bite his nails, drops his hand. "That's good," he says. "And if—if something else was needed, something you felt you could do, you'd do that, too, wouldn't you?"

"You're not giving me much information here."

"I don't know the future. I have my suspicions, but who can really say for sure? All I care about now is that we understand each other. You know what Parsifal wants—forgiveness, support. And if it took a little more time to achieve this . . ."

Sabine waits, but he never finishes his sentence. "Of course," she says.

Phan hugs her again. "He does believe there will be a benefit in all of this to you, and so do I." She can hear the relief in his voice. "We worry about you. You spend too much time alone. Too much time on grief."

"It's only been two weeks," she says.

"Still," Phan says. He looks at the bandage on her hand,

touches the white tape around the stitches. "I was sorry about this. I saw that knife go straight into your hand. Did it hurt much?"

Sabine thinks about it, but it all seems so far away. "I can't remember," she says. "I don't think so."

"Good," Phan says, and he kisses the bandage over her hand. "That's what we like to hear."

Sabine slept late. Despite the sun in the room and the rabbit nudging at her, wanting food, she did not wake up until after nine. When she did wake up, she felt better about everything. What else was she going to do today, anyway? Work on a shopping mall? Go through the dresser drawers again? Sleep? Why not call Dot and Bertie? All she knew for sure was that the story was complicated, it happened a long time ago, and she was only getting part of it. Parsifal had taken care of them in the will, he had been helping them for years. Wasn't that a sign, a kind of forgiveness? Besides, whatever it was, it was one day. Tomorrow they would be going back to Nebraska.

The phone hadn't made it through one whole ring when Bertie answered. "Hello," she whispered, her voice low and suspicious.

Sabine had almost forgotten about Bertie, who had slept peacefully through all the revelations of the night. "Bertie, it's Sabine."

"Sabine?" she said. "How are you?"

"I'm fine. Your mother and I talked last night about going out today. I could drive you around, show you some places that Parsifal liked."

"Mom's not up yet," she whispered. "It isn't like her, but the room is so dark, and the time change and all. Maybe it just threw her off."

It was an hour later in Nebraska. "We were up pretty late,"

85

Sabine said. She found that she was whispering back and stopped it. "After you went to bed, we got together and talked. Have you been out yet? You're not just sitting there in the dark, are you?"

"I don't want to wake her," Bertie said.

Sabine thought about how often she had sat in a dark hotel room, waiting for Parsifal to wake up. All the endless places she had sat, waiting. It must be a family trait. Half of them sleep, half of them wait. "Put your mother on the phone."

"She's sleeping."

"Well, she told me to call her in the morning and wake her up so we could go. I'm just doing what I said I'd do." Enough of waiting for Fetters to wake up.

"Um," said Bertie. The line was quiet for a minute, as if she were really thinking it through. "Okay," she said finally, "hold on." She put the phone down softly. Sabine could hear her cross the short distance between the two hotel beds. "Mom?" she said, her voice still a whisper. "Mama, wake up. It's Sabine. She says we're going out today." There was a pause, most likely for a touch to the shoulder and then a gentle shake.

Sabine wondered how much longer Mrs. Fetters had stayed on in the bar. Last call had only been minutes away, but clearly that bartender liked her. Maybe she should have let her sleep.

"Mama?"

"Hum?"

"Sabine's on the phone."

"Sabine?"

"She's taking us someplace, she says. She wants to talk to you."

There was rustling, the click of the light switch. Sabine could almost feel Dot's bones shift as she stretched. "Hello,"

Mrs. Fetters said. It was the voice of a late sleeper, someone who would not be awake for at least an hour after they were up and dressed.

"It's Sabine. I'm sorry to wake you."

"You didn't wake me," Mrs. Fetters said.

Just like Parsifal, who slept more than anyone in the world and always lied about being asleep. "I just wanted to tell you, yes, I'd be happy to take you and Bertie around today if you're still interested." It was easier now. They had found something out about each other. They knew, to some small extent, what they were dealing with.

"How's your hand feel?"

Sabine looked down at her hand and was half surprised to see it taped up. She had forgotten about it until the question was asked. "It's fine," she said. She lifted it, turned it side to side. "It feels much better."

Even under these difficult circumstances, Sabine was glad to show off her city. Los Angeles, she felt, was maligned because it was misunderstood. It was the beautiful girl you resented, the one who was born with straight teeth and good skin. The one with the natural social graces and family money who surprised you by dancing the Argentine tango at a wedding. While Iowa struggled through the bitter knife of winter and New York folded in crime and the South remained backwards and divided, Los Angeles pushed her slender feet into the sand along the Pacific and took in the sun. The rest of the country put out the trash on Wednesday nights and made small, regular payments against a washing machine and waited through the long night for the Land of Milk and Honey to get hers. And, oh, how America loved it when it happened. They called in sick to work and kept their children home from school so they could watch it together on television as a family, the fate of a city too blessed. The fires shot through the canyons, the floods washed the supports out from beneath the houses that lined the hills over the Pacific Coast Highway in Malibu. There were earthquakes. There were riots. America leaned over: "Dangerous," they whispered to their children. "I always told you that." It was true, in the orderly city the boys packed together and murdered one another and then themselves in brutal festivals. There were places you could no longer go at night and then places you could not go during the day. The city kept its head down. Everyone would say, *It is not the same.*

But Sabine never thought in terms of having allegiance to her country. She loved Los Angeles. Sabine would always choose to stay. She had lived through every tragedy and shame and they only served to draw her and her city closer together. What would she be without the palm trees, without the Hollywood Hills? She had been born in Israel, but she was shaped by tight squares of regularly watered lawns, by layers of deep purple bougainvillea blooming on top of garages. She heard languages she could not identify and they were music. She smelled the ocean. She loved to drive. After she and Parsifal finished a show, they would almost always drive the long way home, up and over Mulholland, to watch the lights in the canyon. "Try getting that in North Dakota," he would say to her. They lived in the magnificence of a well-watered desert where things that could not possibly exist, thrived. They lived on the edge of a country that would not have cared for them anyway, and they were loved. They were home. Do not speak badly of Los Angeles to Parsifal and Sabine.

Dot and Bertie Fetters, rested, washed, fed, and dressed, were back in Phan's car. They were ready. They gave no hint that they had thought all along that Sabine would come through. They never said she owed them a ride in Los

Angeles. On the contrary, they were overwhelmed. They trembled with gratitude that she should give them such a gift.

"Really," Bertie said from the backseat. "This is so nice of you." The top section of her hair, whose curls today appeared more gold than brown, was pulled away from her face in a mock-tortoise barrette. It was a pretty face, though it took some getting used to. The spikes of her eyelashes had left tiny black dots of mascara beneath her eyebrows. Of all the different styles represented in Los Angeles, the Midwestern look was rarely seen.

Mrs. Fetters, either not fully awake or just slightly hungover, kept touching Sabine's arm as a way of expressing her thanks.

Sabine had not forgotten what had been said the night before. She kept the Nebraska Boys Reformatory Facility close to her heart. But this morning she felt unable to pin it on the small woman who sat beside her in the car. All that had stayed with her from the conversation was the sadness. The blame, somehow, had gone. "So is there anything in particular you want to see? Any place we should go first? We can go to the studios, the tar pits, the ocean."

"Where did Guy work?" Bertie asked, leaning over the seat. "Is there one main place magicians work or do they go from place to place all the time?"

"He was only a part-time magician," Sabine said. "We never made our living at it." She thought she saw a look of disappointment cross Dot Fetters' face, as if her son were a failed magician. "Nobody makes a living at it, maybe a few dozen people in the country. It's a terrible life, really, you have to travel all the time. Parsifal had two rug stores. That was his job."

"A rug salesman?" Dot Fetters asked.

"He worked in an antique store when I first met him, then

he got into fine rugs. The stores are very successful. He had a wonderful eye."

"I thought you had awfully nice rugs in your house," Bertie said, happy to have put something together.

"Then we'll go to the rug store first," Mrs. Fetters said. "And if there's someplace he did magic, then we'd like to go there, too. And back to the cemetery. But we don't have to go every place. I don't want to be taking advantage of you here."

Sabine told them no one was taking advantage.

Sabine hadn't been to the stores in a long time. When Phan was sick and after he died, she went often, ferrying papers that needed signatures and couldn't be faxed. Parsifal would ask her to go and look at the color and the weave on something that had just come in. Again and again she said she knew nothing about rugs. "You have eyes," he would say. "You have good taste. I want you to tell me if you like them. I want to know if they're pretty."

They were pretty, always pretty, because Parsifal knew his business even when he couldn't go to the store. And in truth, over time, Sabine had picked up some things through constant exposure. She never had Parsifal's talent, but she had been with him on how many buying trips? She had been to Turkey. She had sifted through piles of prayer rugs in Ghiordes and Kula, stood in the sun until her sweat had made mud out of the dust on her legs. Maybe she had missed some subtle values, some rugs that were fine although possibly drab, but the great rugs she could always spot. She could read the patterns, knew at a glance a Melas from a Konya, a Ladik from a Sivas. She loved the Ladik. Parsifal said Sabine was invaluable because she had classic American tastes. Whatever she loved would be the first rug to sell when they got home.

It wasn't just her taste that was helpful. She was strong,

though you might not know it to look at her. Sabine could hold up in the heat longer than Parsifal ("Yours are a desert people," he would tell her as he went to sit in the shade) and she could lift the rugs, peel them back, separate the piles. Back in the old days, when there was only one store and the host of healthy young men Parsifal was given to hire had not yet been found, Sabine would climb the ladder and attach the rugs to overhead displays.

Sabine had no plans to keep the stores and run them herself, but she hadn't yet thought of letting them go, either. She drove the way Parsifal liked to go, down Santa Monica Boulevard, past Doheny, and through the abundance of boys. They roamed the street like beautiful moths in tight black jeans and draping trousers, their white T shirts absorbing light. Blond curls dipped naturally; straight black hair, recently trimmed, swept into eyes. So many white teeth, so many square jaws. Black-brown skin pulled taut over biceps, heavy lashes fell softly on pink cheeks. They walked arm around thin waist, chin nuzzling neck. Bertie put both hands on the windowsill of the car. She started to say something, but then didn't.

" 'Parsifal's on Melrose. Fine Rugs,' " Mrs. Fetters said, reading the neat gold letters of his name on the front window. How happy he had been the day the painters came. Sabine had taken his picture that day, standing next to his name. Where was that picture? "Will you look at that."

The fan of bells that Parsifal bought in China bumped against the glass and sang out when they opened the door. Salvio nearly cried when he saw Sabine. He put down his coffee and walked all the way across the store with his arms stretched out towards her, and she stepped into those arms like a woman stepping into a coat held out to her by a man.

"My angel," Salvio said. He kissed her neck beneath the straight line of her hair. "We've all been hoping you would come down when you were ready. We miss you, everybody misses you so much."

Sabine nodded and touched his head. She knew who he was missing. Siddhi and Bhimsen, the two men from Nepal whose job it was to unfold the rugs for customers, came and shook her hand warmly, offering sympathy in sketchy English. Mrs. Fetters and Bertie stayed by the door beneath a towering arrangement of tightly wrapped calla lilies, watching.

Sabine squeezed her eyes shut for a second and then pulled back. "You're never going to guess who I've got with me," she said. She held out her hand and they came to her in shy obedience. "Salvio Madrigal, this is Dot and Bertie Fetters. Parsifal's mother and Parsifal's sister."

Salvio was a champion. He would not engage in price haggling but always let the rugs go out on trial. He was helpful but never made anyone feel crowded. Whatever was said, Salvio took it as something expected, something completely natural, so he did what any person would do when meeting family, even though he knew Parsifal's family was dead. He held out his hand. "Mrs. Fetters, it is such an honor to meet you. Your son was a dear friend of mine, one of the best men I ever knew. I am very sorry for your loss."

Mrs. Fetters held his hands and looked at him with such tenderness a passerby would have thought this woman had finally found her son.

"Salvio runs the store," Sabine said. "He does everything."

"Did Guy ever run the store?" Mrs. Fetters asked Salvio. "Did he work in here?"

Where did he stand? Which chair did he sit in? May I hold the phone that he held? Show me the way he held it. Did he stand here and look out this window? Was there something in particular he watched for? Tell me, and I'll look for it, too.

"Guy was Parsifal," Sabine told Salvio.

"Parsifal," Mrs. Fetters said, repeating a difficult word she was trying to memorize. "It's right there on the window."

Salvio didn't throw one questioning look to Sabine. He picked up the dance step, followed the lead. "He used to be here all the time, seven days a week. But then there was another store, other things going on. It was good for him to take some time away. Everybody knew he worked too hard."

"Once Phan got sick," Sabine said, because Salvio couldn't, wasn't sure, "Parsifal turned it all over to Salvio."

"Did you know Phan?" Bertie asked. Mrs. Fetters had clearly brought her daughter up to speed this morning: The History of Your Brother as I Know It, over breakfast. And Bertie, in all her sweet Midwestern dullness, had taken it in, made the information part of her so that now, a few hours later, she was asking about the dead lover of the dead brother she did not know.

Salvio dressed like an aging tough boy—black jeans, black T-shirt, his black hair, just now gray at the edges, slicked back. "I knew Phan well. I was here in the store on the day that they met. He was a very sweet man, thoughtful, generous. Very quiet."

"They met here?" Mrs. Fetters said.

"Phan came in to buy a rug. I think it was"—he looked at Sabine—"was it a Vietnamese rug?"

Sabine nodded.

"They never did find that rug," Salvio said.

Los Angeles gleamed. January and sixty-eight degrees. A light breeze hustled the smog out towards the valley and left the air over Melrose as fresh as a trade wind in Hawaii. The streets were so wide it felt like luxury. It was not Manhattan, nothing pressed close together, nothing strained,

Instead it stretched, relaxed, moved slowly. It was not Alliance, Nebraska. Everything beckoned. Every store was a store you wanted to step inside of. Every girl was a girl you wanted to kiss.

"I thought we'd go to the Magic Castle for lunch," Sabine said.

"Castle?" Bertie said. She was looking over her shoulder, watching the rug store recede behind them. She had been happy there. She had wanted to stay.

"It's a club where Parsifal and I used to perform, a magicians' club." Sabine was glad it was Friday and they could go to lunch and not dinner. There would be fewer people she knew there for lunch, but there would still be too many people she knew no matter when they went. Magicians were notorious for hanging out. Each one had his own very specific seat at the bar, a drink that everyone was supposed to remember. They wanted to perform, they wanted people to see them, they wanted to steal each other's tricks. The thought of the Castle depressed her.

But people loved it, the massive old house on the top of the hill, all the cupolas and leaded windows, the secret rooms and sliding walls. They made the place feel haunted by leaving it dusty and dim. Even at a quarter to twelve on a bright afternoon it felt like the middle of the night in there, dark wood and heavy blood-colored carpets, chandeliers turned low.

They squinted as they stepped inside. The woman at the desk was on her feet and coming at them before their eyes had fully adjusted to the dark. "Sabine!" She hugged Sabine hard around the neck. "Monty!" she called over her shoulder. "Sabine's here." She touched Sabine's face, touched her arm. "Look at you. Look how skinny you are. We've all been wondering when you were going to come down."

"I haven't been getting out much," Sabine said.

"Well, it's early yet. It hasn't been any time at all."

Sabine introduced the Fetters to the woman, whose name was Sally. Sally had worked the door at the Castle for the twenty years Sabine had been coming, and in that time her hair had become blonder and her eyeliner darker, but the woman was still essentially the same. She didn't know that Parsifal didn't have a family, so meeting them was no surprise. Monty came down from the office, kissed Sabine, shook everyone's hands.

"People ask about the act all the time," Monty said. "Everybody wants to know when Parsifal and Sabine are coming back."

"We won't be coming back," Sabine said. Wouldn't that be a trick.

"I know, I know that," he said, and draped an arm over her shoulder. Monty had taken off his tie because lunch wasn't so formal. "All I'm saying is that people remember. Everybody loved you guys. Really, Sabine, you should think about coming back on your own, when you've had a little more time. We've got lots of women magicians now. It's not like the old days."

But everything in the Castle was the old days. It was forever a Hollywood set, a soundstage for some Dean Martin film. Parsifal was always telling Sabine he wanted her to take over the act, start performing on her own.

"There's no reason that you couldn't do this," Parsifal had told her. "You know all the tricks. All the props will be yours, you know everybody at the clubs."

"We haven't done a show in two years."

"Those people haven't all died, Sabine. You could go back to them. You could get someone to help you. You could even get an assistant of your own."

"Why are you saying this?"

"Because I did all the work. I made those tricks." He

spoke so loudly he frightened the rabbit, who flattened himself down to scoot underneath the sofa. "There are things I do that no one else but you knows how to do. I don't want all that work to be lost. It was a good show. There's no reason you couldn't do it."

"Except for the fact that I'm not a magician. I'm the assistant. It isn't the same thing."

"You're the one that does the tricks," he said bitterly. "You just refuse to see it. You do the tricks hanging upside-down in a box."

Sabine shook her head. "I couldn't even think of it," she said to Monty. "That's not what I do."

"Well, you should think of it." He winked at Mrs. Fetters, who looked flattered. "She should think of it. Sabine's great."

"You go on in," Sally said. "Get lunch over with so you can come down for a show. Sam Spender is doing close-up. You know Sam."

"Sure," Sabine said.

Sally nudged Bertie and pointed at the stuffed owl perched inside the bookcase. "Go up to the owl and say 'Open Sesame.' That's how you get in."

Bertie looked shy. She didn't want to speak to the dead owl. Sabine herself simply refused to do it. She would always wait and slip in behind someone else. "Go on," Sally said. "It's the only way."

But Bertie just stood there. "I'd really rather not," she said. "Mama, you do it."

So Dot Fetters, without giving it a thought, walked up to the bird and did what needed to be done. If you had to say "Open Sesame" to get through the door, then that's what she would do. The bookcase slid open.

"They really want to give you a job," Dot Fetters said, taking Sabine's arm. "You should be flattered."

All through lunch there was a steady stream of people at the table paying respects, giving condolences, heaping Parsifal's memory with lavish compliments to honor the Fetters. One by one, magicians left their scotch-and-sodas at the bar and came to sit with them for a moment, tell a few stories, as if these women were some leftover Mafia wives. The Fetters were overwhelmed by the attention. They let their hands be kissed by showmen. And Sabine was glad to do it, glad to show them how greatly Parsifal was loved, but for herself she felt like the secret panels in the walls were closing in.

"So now I've taken the guy's watch," the magician at the table next to them told the magician he was eating with. "I do a few little tricks for the other people and I'm waiting and waiting for this fellow to notice his watch is missing, until finally I got to move on so I say to him, 'Can you tell me the time?' And the guy looks at his wrist and he says, 'I'm sorry, I'm not wearing a watch.'"

"He doesn't know?" the other magician said.

"No idea. So I say, 'Did you have one on earlier?' I mean, hint, hint, and the guy touches his wrist, like maybe he's double-checking, and his wife pipes up and says, 'He can never remember anything. He'd leave his arms at home if they weren't attached.'"

"Now there's the kind of broad you want to have around. What kind of watch?" the other magician asked.

"It's a Sea Master. It's no Rolex, but still we're talking a grand."

The other magician whistled.

"Well, you know this trick. I got the watch sealed up in an envelope inside a zipper wallet in my pocket. Perfectly done. A sweet trick, if someone misses their watch."

"But in this case . . ."

"Exactly. I can't just give it to the guy, say, 'Oh, in fact you did put your watch on this morning, you idiot.' "

"So?"

"So I turned it in to the lost-and-found, thinking sooner or later he'd wise up. Stayed there for a month and then they gave it to me." The magician pushed up his shirtsleeve to show the watch. "Omega," he said. "Keeps time like a Swiss train."

Sabine sighed and accepted a refill on her coffee. A magician's assistant was flatly nothing without a magician. There would never be a night when the assistant took the stage alone. "Look how well she holds the hat," they would say as she stood there, hat in hand, her face one bright smile. No one wanted to watch her put herself in a box and take herself out again. No one cared how gracefully she moved, how good the costume was. She held the rabbit tenderly. She caged up the doves. Who cared? They didn't know how often she was the one working like a plow horse while Parsifal fluttered his hands through the spotlight and smiled. Back in the old days, before Parsifal decided the three-part box was an exercise in misogyny, she was sliding around inside a platform on her back, sticking up a leg, popping her seemingly disconnected head into the top box, waving her hand through a trapdoor. And when Parsifal finally reconstructed her, she could not appear sweaty or out of breath. She had to look surprised, grateful. By professional standards, Sabine was much too tall to be an assistant. The little women, like Bess Houdini, could squeeze themselves into anything, while Sabine had to be vigilant to keep herself thin and limber. Still, Parsifal said, better to have an assistant who looked like a stretched-out Audrey Hepburn, and there were plenty of tricks she didn't figure into at all. Magicians all across the world managed quite well without assistants, but without magicians, the assistants were lost. Even if Sabine had never loved magic the way she loved

Parsifal, she realized that it was one more thing that was over for her. She had been a brightly painted label, a well-made box, a bottle cap. She was never the reason.

After lunch she took them to the Houdini séance room, the Dante room, the Palace of Mystery. They went backstage, where Mrs. Fetters tapped her foot suspiciously on the floor. What a night it had been when Parsifal first took Sabine to the Castle, how impossible it was to think that someday they would perform there. Inconceivable that one day they would get tired of performing there.

"Look at this," Bertie said, and touched the figure of Houdini wrapped in chains. His eyes looked as if he suffered from lack of oxygen, or possibly a thyroid condition.

Everything was a prop. Once it had thrilled Sabine, too, now it made her feel abandoned. "Come on," she said. "We need to get to the show if we want a seat."

The meal was the price you had to pay to see some magic. That was the trick of the Castle. You had to make it past the food and drinks, give them a chance to make their money before you got to see the show.

"How often did the two of you perform here?" Mrs. Fetters asked Sabine.

"A week a year, usually, sometimes more if there was a cancellation. It was a lot of work for not a lot of money."

"But it must have been so much fun," Bertie said. "I can't even imagine it, getting to come here every night."

Sabine nodded and turned away, pretending to study the framed caricatures that lined the walls. She focused her eyes on the blank space in between Harry Blackstone, Senior, and Harry Blackstone, Junior. Bertie was right. It had been fun. It was a completely different lifetime, one without sickness, without knowledge of past or future. It was just Parsifal, Sabine, and Rabbit. Fun.

For the lunch crowd there was only close-up magic, mostly card tricks, hoops, and coins, maybe a little mentalism. No one got sawed in half at lunch, no one vanished. Like Parsifal, it was this smaller magic that Sabine had come to prefer, not as showy and, therefore, more difficult. It was always harder when the audience was pressed up against you, the closest row practically pushing on your knees.

"I can't believe you did this," Mrs. Fetters whispered as Monty came out to introduce Sam Spender. "It's so exciting."

Spender was a thin, dark-haired man in his middle thirties. He and Parsifal had only overlapped by a year or two, Parsifal winding down from the business just as Sam was coming up. All that Sabine knew about him was that he was two people, one on the stage and one at the bar after the show. His true self, she believed, was onstage, where he was graceful and nearly handsome. He had what Parsifal used to call bravado. But at the bar after the show he was nobody, a man who could vanish in a crowd without any tricks.

He began the patter, the Ladies-and-gentlemen-I-want-to-welcome-you-to. Dot and Bertie Fetters sat forward in their seats, so thrilled to be entertained that for the moment they forgot that the purpose of their trip was to mourn. But then that was the point of magic, to take people in, make them forget what was real and possible. They were so utterly game that when Sam Spender asked if there was anyone in the audience from out of town, they raised their hands, not knowing that everyone in Los Angeles was from out of town.

Sabine turned her eyes away. She could not imagine how she'd thought that going to the Castle would be a good idea. She felt the pressure of sadness rising up in the back of her throat. She stared at the bandage on her hand, at that damn engagement ring she had forgotten to take off. Think about none of it. She tried to concentrate on the strip mall she was building. She would need to buy some small-grain veneer, some corrugated plastic. She would make a list of what she needed to buy. But even as she concentrated, she could hear it. From someplace far away, the farthest left-hand corner of hell, she heard her name. Dot Fetters touched her wrist.

"It's you," she whispered.

"Sabine," Sam Spender said, and held out his hand to her.

She shook her head.

"Ladies and gentlemen, Sabine Parsifal, one of the truly great magicians' assistants."

One of the truly great hood ornaments. One of the world's best bottle caps. There was applause.

"Now, when you take someone you don't know from the audience, everyone suspects they're a plant, that person must be in on the trick," Sam Spender's voice chimed and sang. "But when you pull a professional out of the audience, then everybody knows something must be up. Sabine, come on down here."

She held the armrests of her chair. She would bury herself in that seat. They would never find her.

"Sabine," Bertie said, and shook her as if asleep. "Go on up, he wants you."

People never seem to take into account that they can say no. In Sabine's life she had seen people who truly, desperately did not want to be called onto stage, who begged to be passed over, but when they were pressed, they always went, resigned, as if to their deaths. When the magician asked, no one ever thought to tell him to go to hell.

She was lifted up, Bertie and Dot Fetters lifted her from her seat. She was not walking. She was being passed hand over hand through the air, above the audience, until she was delivered to the stage. Once their hands were free of her they clapped wildly. Sabine smoothed down the sleeves of her blouse. Sam Spender kissed her cheek, said something about having her back and how it was good. The lights were in her eyes.

No one had ever been alone this way before.

"So, are you going to be able to help me out with a couple of things, Sabine?"

She looked at him, begged him in the secret language of assistants and magicians. There was still time to get out of this, even if it didn't seem that way. She knew the location of every trap in the floor. There were lines in the light scaffolding over-head; if she could only reach them, she could pull herself up. It is a fact about human nature: People look down, not up.

"What I'm going to ask you to do is just hold on to this hoop, just a plain silver circle."

He put the hoop in her hand. It was cold, thin, light. It trembled with her hand.

"You got that there? Now I want you to pull on it. Go on and really give it a good pull, feel it all over and tell me if it's solid."

It was solid. It would be solid to anyone but Sabine, who knew the trick, knew the hoop like her name. She moved it around and around through her fingers. Parsifal hadn't done a hoop trick in fifteen years. It was a good warm-up, it looked good from the audience, but it had become too easy for him and so he stopped. When things were too easy, they didn't interest him anymore. Some of the things he did that were the hardest didn't even look so complicated, but those were the ones he stayed with and loved. He was that sort of magician. She was that sort of assistant.

"How does that look to you?"

The hoop fed itself endlessly through her fingers. She could not see Sam Spender, but she could remember him. A decent magician, a dull man. She and Parsifal were years past hoop tricks, lifetimes past. There was no need to check the hoop. It was rigged, there was a hair catch. Nothing you could see, you just had to know it was there. You knew because someone had told you. But there was nothing to do but check it over and over again. No place to go. Sabine stood there, hearing Sam Spender's questions without being able to answer. She couldn't answer. She couldn't walk off the stage. All she could do was check the hoop, and so, over and over again, she did.

"Come on, Sabine." She felt something, a tug and then emptiness. The hoop was out of her hands. "Here you go," Mrs. Fetters said, and gave the magician his hoop. "Come on, let's go home." Mrs. Fetters put her arm around Sabine's waist and led her off the stage, down the three short steps. Sabine was crying in a way that kept her from seeing. She would never stop crying. Bertie ran her hand in circles across the small of Sabine's back. They left the magic parlor, the three of them together.

When people approached them, Mrs. Fetters waved them away. "She's fine," she told Sally. A lie so obvious that it said, none of your business, leave us alone. The valet brought the car up without questions and Bertie got into the driver's seat. Mrs. Fetters got into the back with Sabine. She held her there, stroked her hair.

"Which is worse," Mrs. Fetters said, "that man asking you to come up on stage or me telling you to go?"

Bertie drove out of the parking lot and safely to another street before parking in the slim shade of a palm tree. "I'm so sorry," she said. "We never should have asked you to take us there."

"We've been thinking about ourselves," Mrs. Fetters said. "We should be thinking about you. Poor baby, all you've been through."

Sabine was embarrassed in so many different ways she

couldn't begin to list them. What had she done up there? What was she doing now? She tried to tell the Fetters it was all right, that she would be fine in just one minute, but she couldn't make the words. Parsifal would never be in the house when she came home. She would never open the door and find him there again. Not even once.

"I've got some Kleenex," Bertie said, and began rifling through her purse.

Sabine thanked her, took a deep breath, and tried to sit up straight. "I'm fine, really. I'm sorry." She wiped a straight line beneath each of her eyes. There were dark, wet stains on the front of her blouse.

"Nothing for you to be sorry about," Mrs. Fetters said.

Sabine looked at her hands and laughed.

"So why don't we take you home?" Mrs. Fetters said.

Sabine shook her head. "We'll go out to the cemetery." It seemed fine, better even, to go to someplace Parsifal was rather than someplace he was not. Sabine opened up the car door and got out. "Come on," she said to Bertie. "I can drive."

"You don't want to go to the cemetery," Bertie said.

"Sure I do." Sabine could breathe again. She stretched up on her toes. "Nobody minds a crying woman in a cemetery."

Bertie scooted awkwardly over the gearshift and let Sabine have the driver's seat.

"When my husband died, I used to cry like that," Mrs. Fetters said, leaning forward, her safety belt undone. "I cried like that, and I hated the man. I cried just because everything was different. So I can't imagine what it would be like, crying over a husband that you loved as much as you loved Guy."

Sabine was touched by Mrs. Fetters calling Parsifal her husband. "When did Mr. Fetters die?"

Bertie looked down at her hands. She adjusted her engagement ring so that the tiny diamond stood straight up.

"Albert died when I was pregnant with Bertie. That's why I named her Albertine." Mrs. Fetters reached up and patted her daughter on the shoulder. "The only thing this girl got from her father was his name. That's why she's so sweet."

"How did he die?" Sabine wouldn't normally have asked, but obviously no one was going to be breaking down over this particular loss.

"He was in an accident," Mrs. Fetters said. "It was a real shock. One minute he's there, the next minute—" She swiped her open hand through the air and then made a fist. "Gone."

The lilies had opened up. Their white waxy petals made twin bridal bouquets on the grass of the twin graves. Sabine sat with her back against the brick wall that protected them from seeing Lincoln Heights. She watched the flowers and listened to the light music that was pumped in for the wealthy dead while Mrs. Fetters chatted with the marker, retelling the day's events, the rug store, the Magic Castle, what she took to be her fault in all of it. Sabine considered getting up and correcting her, explaining to Parsifal that it, in fact, was not his mother's fault at all. She smiled to know that she wasn't so far gone that she couldn't see what a stupid idea that was.

Mrs. Fetters licked her finger and rubbed at a tiny spot on Phan's marker. "Everything is so clean around here, there's nothing to do. The people running this place don't understand psychology. People need things to do at cemeteries to make themselves feel useful. It's like fluffing up pillows for the sick. It doesn't make the sick person feel better, it makes you feel better."

"You want to fluff pillows?" Sabine said.

"I want to weed something. There aren't any weeds. This is the nicest damn grass I've ever seen in my life."

Sabine looked down at the grass and saw it was lush and

soft and the color of emeralds and so she lay down on it and closed her eyes against the sun. "I like it here," she said, thinking about the empty spot beside Parsifal that was her real estate.

"How did you meet Guy, anyway?"

"I was a waitress at a club called the Magic Hat. Parsifal was a magician."

"Is it still there?" Bertie asked.

Sabine shook her head. "It's Italian now." She didn't go on. She thought that was the end of the story.

"You were a waitress at a club called the Magic Hat," Dot Fetters said.

Sabine rolled over on her side. It was like being in the locked garden of a resort. The tiles in the grass were stepping-stones. "This is twenty years ago, more than twenty years. I was going to school during the day to be an architect and waiting tables at night. One night I was serving a drink, and I remember this, I don't know why, a Manhattan with double cherries, and I look up and I see the most beautiful man onstage."

Mrs. Fetters, unable to stop herself, jumped in. "Guy."

"Yes."

"I wish I could have seen him," Bertie said.

"No one ever looked better in a tuxedo." Sabine was happy to tell them. It was a story in which Parsifal was beautiful and young. It was the moment when neither of them knew what would happen. The beginning of everything. "I put down my tray on the table where I had served the Manhattan, and I just stood there and stared. He was doing something he called the Rabbit Pass, where he'd put a rabbit down his collar and take it out of his sleeve. Put it in his hat and take it out of his pants leg. It was all very graceful, very funny. Parsifal had such beautiful hands."

"Even as a little boy," his mother said.

"And then he said, 'For my next illusion I will need an assistant,' and he held out his hand to me. I was all the way in the back of the room but I knew it was to me. So I went up on stage."

"Did he saw you in half?" Bertie said.

"I don't think I did anything particularly interesting that night. I think I held the rabbit and drew a card from a deck. I barely remember that part. I was so nervous, I'd never been up onstage before. I wasn't used to the lights."

"And after that?" Bertie said. She sat down on the grass.

"After that he gave me a job. He made me promise that I wouldn't drop out of school. I had this idea that I was going to make a fortune as a magician's assistant."

"And you waited all those years before you got married," Bertie said, her voice saddened at the thought of having to wait any longer herself.

"When are you getting married, Bertie?"

Bertie turned over her hand to look at the ring as if it were a watch that would tell her exactly when. "Next month."

"Bertie's marrying the nicest fellow in Alliance," Mrs. Fetters said. "Finally, someone in this family has good taste in men."

Sabine shrugged. "Parsifal had good taste in men."

"Really?" his mother said.

"Nice guys, almost always, and Phan." She pointed to the grave, as if they might have forgotten. "There was no one better than Phan. That was true love."

The Fetters looked over at Phan's marker, hoping to be able to tell for themselves. "I love Haas," Bertie said.

"Haas?"

"Eugene Haas. But nobody calls him Eugene." She ran the flat of her hands back and forth over the grass. "Maybe you'll come to the wedding, Sabine. I know it's a big trip, but you'd like Haas. And you could meet Kitty. Kitty would love you."

Sabine smiled at the thought of Bertie in a wedding dress, how the dress would be shining white with mutton leg sleeves and a sweetheart neckline. How she knew that Bertie would be the type to cry at her own wedding. "I've never been to Nebraska."

"Well, then, you have to come," Mrs. Fetters said. "You're the rest of the family now. It would be like Guy coming to the wedding. Can you imagine that?"

"What was your wedding like?" Bertie asked.

Parsifal had wanted to get everything in Sabine's name so that she could avoid being crushed by inheritance tax. "We were married at the house in the late afternoon," she said. "It was a beautiful day. Parsifal had figured out that the light hit the pool in just the right way at four-thirty. Parsifal was always worried about lighting. All the magicians were there, and the rug and antique people, and all the architects. It was a good party."

"I love you," Parsifal had said. "I want you to be my widow."

"Did you serve dinner?" Bertie asked. "Was there dancing?"

Sabine nodded. She could smell the lilies from the graves. "We ate dinner outside and put a dance floor down on the lawn. There was a lot of dancing." The people who loved them drank too much and cried.

"If you want to get married," Sabine had told him, "it doesn't mean we have to have a wedding."

"I want to have a really great party," Parsifal said.

When the last napkin was collected from the lawn, the host of handsome waiters took the rented dishes away, leaving the house, remarkably, as they had found it. Sabine and Parsifal recounted who was making passes at whom and who looked the best and who seemed not to be doing so well. He took her in his arms and they danced a few steps in the kitchen while Sabine hummed. "My wife," he said. "My beautiful wife." And then he kissed her, one, two, three times, and they both laughed and said good-night and went down the hallway in different directions as they had at the end of any number of parties they had given over the years.

"Good night, Parsifal," Sabine said.

"Good night, Mrs. Parsifal," Parsifal said.

The light was good now in the cemetery. Parsifal would be pleased. He had been right about the wedding. It had helped Sabine. It was a strange piece of comfort he had given her.

"Did you have a minister?" Dot Fetters asked.

"A rabbi."

The Fetters looked puzzled. They both had the same tilt of the head, which made them look like mother and daughter. "Why a rabbi?"

Sabine laughed because the question struck her as so strange. "Because I'm Jewish."

There was a light wind coming down from the direction of the Wee Kirk o' the Heather, but the grass was too closely cut to be stirred. "Oh," Dot Fetters said finally.

"Is that all right?" Sabine asked.

Her mother-in-law smiled. "Of course it's all right," she said. "I just don't think I've ever met anybody who's Jewish before."

On the way home Sabine stopped by the downtown Sheraton Grand and the Fetters packed their bags and came home with her. She thought they might protest, but they smiled and nodded, said yes and thank you. They wanted to stay in the house, to be close to Sabine. Dot and Bertie Fetters wanted her attention. They wanted her love. It was not in their nature to shy away from what they wanted. She fed them dinner from Canter's. She laid out their towels and folded extra blankets at the feet of their beds. She asked them what they needed, what they wanted. They all kissed one another good-night and while she was walking down the hall they called to her again, "Good night." She left her door open so that she could hear the faint sounds of their voices. She thought she could hear water running through the pipes. The house was not empty. Rabbit came down the hall at a better than usual clip and stood up on his hind legs until Sabine reached down and brought him up into bed. Outside, the thick green magnolia leaves lost hold of their branches and floated like flat-bottomed canoes around the edges of the pool. A helicopter made a soft chop overhead. Everything was in its place.

A wedding, Bertie's wedding, might be reason enough to go to Nebraska. She closed her eyes and tried to picture the state. She told herself there were cows, it was cold, they grew corn. But no matter how hard she tried, she couldn't make the words into landscapes. It was a country she couldn't imagine. What could be more foreign than Nebraska? It was farther away than Israel. It was farther than Vietnam. Finally she stopped trying in favor of sleep, and the sleep was long and deep and dreamless.

In the morning they sorted through pictures while eating bagels and eggs. There were a few albums, well organized and clearly marked with dates that Phan had put together; but pictures from the time before Phan and the ones taken after his death were dumped unceremoniously into a Bloomingdale's box large enough to hold the fox-fur jacket Sabine had bought for her mother's birthday in a year of largesse. Her mother had let her keep the box.

In the early years together, Sabine had asked to see pictures of Parsifal's family, but he said there were none. She held her position that that wasn't possible; if your family is killed in a car crash you don't deal with it by throwing all their pictures away.

"I didn't keep anything from that time," he had said. "I told you that."

"Nothing? Not even a sock? You stripped yourself naked and started over again?"

He looked at her, that special look reserved for conversations about his past that said, Drop it. No more. "There are no pictures," he repeated.

Maybe Sabine could have believed this, but Parsifal was a fool for documentation. Look at the evidence on the kitchen table, the pictures sliding onto the floor in every direction. Eight rolls of film, thirty-six exposures each, from one trip to India. Sabine in the marketplace wearing a wide straw hat. Parsifal coming down a ghat to the Ganges, shirtless, laughing. There were pictures of the rug stores. Pictures of nameless magicians. Picture after picture of white rabbits doing cute things, sleeping on their backs, looking out the window, eating Cheerios from a bowl.

"Is this Rabbit?" Bertie asked.

Sabine looked at the picture, held it towards the light. "That was the rabbit before this one. Not such a good rabbit. Kind of stupid, God rest."

Parsifal had kept the bad pictures, half a face out of focus, the blur of a tree taken from a speeding car, unflattering photos of friends with flame red eyes, their mouths open. "I have to throw these away," Sabine said.

"Maybe later," Mrs. Fetters said, taking the stack out of

her hands. "There's no sense in doing it now. Where was this?"

Parsifal in his camel overcoat, unshaven, looking serious. To his left there was a mass of dark wire that Sabine knew to be the Eiffel Tower. "Paris."

"Really," Mrs. Fetters said. "You two went everywhere."

Sabine didn't remember it that way, there were plenty of days spent at home, vacuuming, doing taxes, but confronted with so much proof she could only think that in the last twenty-two years she had seen a great deal of the world. She never thought about the trips, the dinners or days spent in museums. She only remembered his company now. Why had he always taken her? There were plenty of men, men at home and men whom he met while he and Sabine were gone; their pictures were on the table now, on the floor and in her lap, nameless, with such beautiful faces. But none of them had stayed on the way Sabine did, the way Phan would have.

"I like the ones of the two of you onstage the best," Bertie said, and handed Sabine a picture taken at the Sands in Las Vegas.

"We're both wearing too much makeup," she said, and flipped it aside.

Mrs. Fetters grabbed the picture back. She studied their faces. "You're beautiful," she said, her voice nearly angry. "Both of you."

Sabine thought the bright lights made them look sickly and she didn't like to see herself in costume. But no one ever looked better than Parsifal on a stage. Tuxedos always made her think of the night they met.

"I'd like to have this one," Mrs. Fetters said. "If you don't like it."

"Of course," Sabine said, "take whatever you want. Clearly I have too many of them. And the negatives are all in here, too." She shook the box for effect, though she could hardly imagine finding the negative for one particular photograph. The picture of Parsifal in front of the rug store slid by and then was reabsorbed. She had enough to remember Parsifal by, more than enough. The Fetters could take what they wanted. "If there's anything else," she said, looking up suddenly. "I don't know what you'd like, clothes or books, furniture. Just tell me." They deserved things. She would pack up boxes of memorabilia. She would ship things to them later. Anything.

Mrs. Fetters was going to say something, but a picture, just that moment revealed in the shift of paper, caught Bertie's eye "Well, hey. Look at this." She reached into the box and plucked it up. The winning ticket. After looking at it herself for a minute, she gave it to her mother.

Of all the photos, this one seemed to please Dot Fetters the most. Sabine leaned in. It was a black-and-white picture of a dark-haired girl about eight or nine years old. She was wearing jeans and a cowboy shirt. She was standing in front of a car, smiling, doing nothing but waiting to have her picture taken. The face was familiar, but maybe just because Sabine had sorted through those pictures so many times before. It was largely a box of strangers. It seemed perfectly reasonable that there would be a child in there that she didn't know.

"That's not me," Sabine said.

"Of course it's not," Mrs. Fetters said, so happy to have the picture.

Bertie was the one who told her it was Kitty.

Sabine looked again. She had not seen a picture of Parsifal as a child and yet this was Parsifal as a child. Parsifal with long hair and a girl's tip of the head. Parsifal's other sister.

Mrs. Fetters fanned the picture slowly back and forth, holding it by the corner as if it were damp. "I knew it. I knew he wouldn't have written us off altogether. Or at least he wouldn't write off Kitty. He loved her too much. Those two were a pair, right and left. When he left he took a picture of Kitty. That's proof. He leaves everything behind, but he takes a picture of his sister."

The little girl had the sun in her face, but the sun, either early-morning or late-afternoon or hidden halfway behind a cloud, didn't seem too strong for her, and she looked straight into it. Sabine wasn't sure what it proved, one picture in a fur-coat box with a couple of thousand others. It wasn't as if he'd kept it on his desk, or put her in a frame in the bedside table with the people considered family. But who could say? Maybe having it meant something, maybe it meant everything. She was certainly comfortable letting Dot Fetters think that it did.

"Do you want that?" Sabine asked.

Mrs. Fetters looked surprised. "No, no. This one's yours. I have plenty of pictures of Kitty. This is the only one you've got." She handed it to Sabine, who took it carefully and put it in the breast pocket of her blouse, not because she wanted it, but because she understood the gesture to be important.

Dot and Bertie Fetters made modest piles of pictures they wanted to keep for themselves. Mrs. Fetters liked the pictures in foreign places best, while Bertie preferred the ones from magic shows. Bertie took one of the ocean with no one in it at all. They both took as many pictures of Sabine as they took of Parsifal. Mrs. Fetters took one of Phan.

"I'm going to take one of you now," Bertie said, pulling an Instamatic from her purse. "One of the two of you together." She bit her lip thoughtfully. "We'll go out back, by the pool."

Mrs. Fetters touched her hair. The curls sprang around her fingers. "Just take one of Sabine," she said.

"Both of you," Bertie said. She looked around on the floor, then reached down and scooped up the rabbit with her other hand. She handed him to Sabine. "Him, too."

They went out through the French doors in the dining room. Rabbit blinked and twitched in the sun. "Over by the purple flowers," Bertie said, the camera making her suddenly confident. "Come forward just a little, I want to see the pool, too. That's good."

Mrs. Fetters put her arm around Sabine's waist and pulled her close; with her other hand she petted the rabbit's head. Sabine felt Mrs. Fetters' soft midsection against her hip. Dot Fetters smelled like vanilla.

"Smile," Bertie said.

Places were exchanged. There was a picture of Bertie and Sabine and then one that Sabine took of Bertie and her mother, Bertie holding the rabbit. There they were, in Parsifal's yard, in Phan's yard. Maybe Parsifal had done the best that he could, going on with his life without them, maybe the Nebraska Boys Reformatory Facility was something that no one could be forgiven for, but Sabine couldn't help but think he would have liked these people. It was a shame that he had spent his life without this love that was available to him. "You'll send me copies," Sabine said.

"You bet," Mrs. Fetters said.

Rabbit was tired of being held and he squirmed and kicked in hopes of being set down in the sweet dichondra. Sabine was always afraid he would find his way under the fence or fall into the pool and drown. It was only on the rarest of occasions, only when she was right there all the time, watching, that he was allowed in the yard.

After the dishes were put away and bags were packed, it really was time to go to the airport, although no one seemed to be in a hurry to leave. Mrs. Fetters saw that there was a bit more coffee left in the pot and decided to go ahead and drink it.

"It hardly makes any sense to come all the way here and not see anything," Sabine said, her voice sounding wistful in a way that she could not entirely account for. "If you wanted to stay a couple of extra days, you could stay here. I'd pay to have your tickets changed."

Bertie smiled, her blue eyes bright and clear like her brother's. The more Sabine looked at her, the more beautiful she became. "You're sweet," she said. "It would be heaven to stay, but I've got to get back to work, and besides, I've got to see Haas."

Sabine thought for a minute, scanned back over conversations. "God, Bertie, I don't even know what you do."

"I teach first grade. They got a sub for Friday, but Monday I have to be back."

Swarms of children, pots of thick white paste and snub-nosed scissors, construction-paper leaves in red and yellow taped to the windows. "First grade," Sabine said.

"Oh, Bertie's the best," Mrs. Fetters said. "She got the teaching award for the whole school last year."

Bertie shrugged. "It's a good job."

"Anyway," Mrs. Fetters said, "Kitty counts on me to help her with the boys, and we've got this wedding to plan for. But it won't be that long till we see you. You'll come to the wedding?"

The last wedding Sabine had been to was her own, and she couldn't tell the Fetters her best memories from that day. Parsifal danced with the rabbi, who was a remarkably good dancer, while the band played "Girl From Ipanema." Architects lined up to kiss the bride and one by one brushed their lips to her ear, begging her to meet them later in the evening. There was talk in the crowd of putting Parsifal and Sabine into chairs and lifting the chairs above their heads and dancing out onto the street, but people were drunk by then, their train of thought was easily lost. "Maybe I'll come to the wedding," Sabine said.

What they accomplished by their dallying was the elimination of time for long good-byes. All the way to the airport they looked at their watches, wondering if they would make the plane. They were silent in the car. There was too much left to say and not enough time. There was no one place to start. Sabine wanted to ask what subjects Parsifal had liked in school as a boy. Had he done well, was he interested in magic? And what about his father? Did Parsifal ever say what had happened at the boys' reformatory? Had they ever gone to visit him there? Sabine wanted to say that even if Mrs. Fetters wasn't in the market for forgiveness, Sabine forgave her anyway, because as they took the San Diego Freeway towards the airport, she knew with sudden, utter clarity that his mother had not understood what she was doing, and, if she had, she never, never would have done it. But Sabine said none of this. She parked the car, checked their bag, and led them through the snaking concourse without a word. The Fetters no longer seemed interested in LAX.

At the gateway, in clear view of so many strangers, Mrs. Fetters began to cry.

"Don't," Sabine said. "You have to go."

"You were so sweet to us."

"You'll come back," Sabine said. "You'll come back and stay for as long as you want."

"You shouldn't be by yourself." Mrs. Fetters slid her fingers beneath her glasses. "I've got my girls and the kids. I don't want you to have to be alone."

"I'll be fine," Sabine said.

The crowds moved around them, pressing them closer together. From overhead came an endless stream of information: *If stand-by passengers would please... Rows twenty-nine through seventeen... announcing the arrival... final boarding ... Ladies and gentlemen, there's been a delay...*

"That's us," Bertie said, but Sabine didn't know which part she was referring to.

Mrs. Fetters stepped back, stepped directly onto a five-year-old girl with lank yellow hair, who shot out from under her foot and ran away for all she was worth. Mrs. Fetters did not notice. "You'll come with us," she said, her voice filled with wonder at her own good idea. The plan that would solve everything. Sabine would come with them.

"Now?"

"Get on the plane. You have the money. We can get some clothes, whatever you need. Come home with us."

Bertie looked at them, interested.

"I can't come with you. I have to go home." She held Dot Fetters in her arms for a moment and then let her go. "Who would feed Rabbit?"

"Mama, we're boarding," Bertie said.

"It's not a bad idea," Mrs. Fetters said. "Even if it's not right now."

A tall black flight attendant in a tight blue suit stared at them from her podium and then gestured with her head towards the door. All the other tickets had been collected. Everyone was onboard, ready to go.

"Good-bye, Sabine," Bertie said, and kissed her quickly. "I hope you come. I really do." She took her mother's arm and guided her towards the door, making Dot Fetters appear older than she was. When they handed in their tickets Dot blew a kiss and waved. Sabine felt sure they would come back, one more idea, something else to tell, but they turned around and then they were gone, down into the tunnel that would take them to the plane that would take them to Nebraska.

Sabine stayed to watch the plane take off, and even after it left she stayed. All around her people were crying in the wake of arrivals and departures. They clung to one another as if a plane had nearly crashed or was about to crash. They held their children, kissed their lovers. She heard their voices all around her—*It's so good to see you... What will I do when you're gone... I thought you would never get here... Good-bye.* The good-byes wore her out. She'd had enough of them.

In the days after the Fetters left, Sabine slipped back into bed, back into the deep nest of dark sheets and king-sized pillows. A late Santa Ana wind howled around the house and loosened the ivy from the gate. Low waves crested and broke in the swimming pool. The half-constructed mall sat in her studio, no walkways, no roof, the windowpanes sealed in polyurethane bags. Salvio called from the rug store and even before he asked his question, Sabine told him he would have to decide himself. She told him to decide everything. Most of the calls she didn't return, including a nervous message from Sam Spender, the magician. On television the local news focused on murder, suspicion, prosecution. What would that be like, to have someone to blame death on, to stand across the courtroom from that person and point them out, say, *You, you took everything I had.* Little did they know that everything they had would be taken anyway. The thought of accusation exhausted Sabine. There wasn't any order. There wasn't any sense in trying to find it. On the day she was due to go back to the hospital to have the stitches taken out of her hand, she sat on the bath mat and cut them with cuticle scissors and then pulled the stiff thread out with tweezers. They lay scattered on the white floor like the spiky legs of a disembodied insect. The scar was pretty, dark red and thin. It didn't hurt.

Eight days after they left there was a letter from Dot Fetters. Four pictures fell out when Sabine unfolded the paper. Three had been taken in her own backyard, but it was the fourth one that interested her. It was of a boy, thin chested and bright faced, maybe eight or nine years old, but Sabine was a bad judge of children. He wore a band around his forehead with a lone feather jutting up from the back, his eyes damp with pleasure. A sweet-faced, dark-haired boy who was her own boy. She would know him anywhere, in an instant. His jeans were faded and loose, his T-shirt striped. Sabine could barely make out the freckles that had left him long before they met. She studied his neck, his delicate shoulders. She memorized the gate behind him and the scalloped white border of the photograph. On the back, written in ink, were the most basic facts: "Guy, 1959." 1959. Sabine wished she had known him then, when she was a girl in Los Angeles. What had been wasted when she was only a well-loved daughter, her mother walking her to school in Fairfax every morning, lunch in a brown-paper sack, her father taking her to CBS, telling her she was sitting in Walter Cronkite's chair, even though Cronkite delivered the news from New York. What had happened to this little boy while she was sitting in Canter's after Hebrew school on Sunday, drinking cream soda and reading the funny papers while her parents divided up the *Los Angeles Times*? What had she lost that she could never account for? She reached over and pulled open the drawer on the bedside table where the picture of Kitty sat, faceup. Sabine lay on her back and held the two side by side. It was the same sun, the same scalloped edges; on the back there was the same handwriting, which said, "Kitty, 1959." Maybe the pictures were taken on the same day, or at least during the same summer. It was true, what Mrs. Fetters said: They were nearly twins; except, of course, for the wonderful feather. That was Parsifal's alone.

She looked at the pictures, one and then the other, for nearly an hour. She would buy a twin frame and put them with the family pictures on the table. She was just beginning to see the edges of a hunger she didn't know she had. When Parsifal died she lost the rest of his life, but now she had stumbled on eighteen years. Eighteen untouched years that she could have; early, forgotten volumes of her favorite work. A childhood that could be mined month by month. Parsifal would not get older, but what about younger?

So much time passed that she forgot completely that there was a letter. She didn't find it, half covered in the tumble of sheets, until she was ready to go to sleep.

Dear Sabine,

Many thank-you's for our very good time in Los Angeles. Bertie and I have not stopped telling stories about all our fun. I am sending you copies of the pictures we took. I look awful, but the one of you and Bertie is very nice, I think. Do you ever take a bad picture? I am also sending one of Guy, which I have always thought was sweet. I thought that you might like to have it.

I am still thinking that you should come to Alliance. There's no need to wait until Bertie's wedding. Come now and stay, we have plenty of room. I think that you are maybe sadder than you think and that being alone right now may not be the best thing. Maybe I'm not the person to be giving advice, but I feel like you are one of my own girls, and I know that this is what I would say to Kitty and Bertie and it would be right.

So now you know that you are welcome. In the meantime,

thanks again for your time and generosity and for the pictures,
which Kitty was so glad to see.

Love from Bertie and from me,
Dot

The handwriting was schoolgirlish, all the heights and curves evenly matched. It was the handwriting on Parsifal's postcard at the reformatory, it was the handwriting on the backs of the pictures. Had they had a minute of fun in Los Angeles? Sabine could not remember it.

"They only made things worse for you," Sabine's mother said at Canter's on Sunday. They were sitting near the counter. Sabine stared at the fruit in the display case, fruit salad in parfait glasses next to halved grapefruits. The cavities of the cantaloupes were clean and hollow, everything sealed in Saran wrap. The waitress came by and Sabine's mother mouthed the word "Horseradish" to her. She nodded in complicity and went on. "You're more depressed now than you were before."

"I'm not more depressed," Sabine said. "I am depressed, same as before."

"They had no business coming."

Sabine's father sat in silent agreement, stirring his black coffee to cool it down.

"I should have brought them over to meet you. I wish I had. You would have liked them. No one was more surprised than me, but I'm telling you, they are very decent people."

"Decent mothers don't send their sons to some children's prison for being homosexual." Before Parsifal's death, Sabine's mother had always dropped her voice on the word homosexual, but now that she saw it as the source of his persecution, she spoke it clearly; even, Sabine thought, loudly. "I will admit it, I think it is easier to have a child who is not a homosexual, but if I did I would have loved that child, not tortured him. What happened to poor Parsifal was sheer barbarism. A loving mother does not send her son off to be tortured."

Sabine sighed. It was not her intention to argue in favor of the Nebraska Boys Reformatory Facility. "It's awful, I know that. I just think it was a different time. I know that doesn't excuse it, but I don't think she understood what she was doing, what it meant."

"Nineteen sixty-six was not the Dark Ages. We were all alive in 1966. We are all held accountable for our actions."

They sat together in a family silence, listening to the sounds they understood, heavy china cups against white saucers, forks against plates, ice ringing against the sides of glasses, and everywhere, everywhere, voices. No one could make out a whole sentence; but words, every one a free agent, fell against the sound of the cutlery and made a kind of music. A hand swept over the table, depositing a silver cup of horse-radish beside Sabine's mother's plate.

"I was thinking," Sabine said, her eyes cast down, "of maybe going to visit." She had not been thinking of it exactly, but the minute she said it, it was true.

Sabine's father put down his knife, which had been raised in the act of putting jam on his bread. "Nebraska?"

"There's a lot I want to know. Things about Parsifal. There's so much I don't know." Sabine was speaking quickly, quietly, and her parents leaned forward from the other side of the orange booth. "You think you know someone, one person better than anyone else, and then there's all this." She spread her hands as if to indicate that what she didn't know was the food on the table. "What if you found out that Daddy wasn't who you thought he was? What if he'd been married before, had children you knew nothing about. Wouldn't you be curious?"

Her father looked startled and then confused. When he opened his lips, her mother spoke. "I know everything about your father. You shouldn't even think such a thing."

"I want to know what happened," Sabine said.

"He didn't want you to know," her mother said.

"But I do now. I know part of it."

"You never should have seen them."

Sabine closed her eyes and leaned her head back. "I did see them, there's no use in going over that." Even in her frustration, Sabine felt sorry for what she was doing to her parents.

Her mother pushed her plate away so as to put both hands flat out on the table. "Listen to me, Sabine. You had a long and very unusual relationship with a good man, but that's over now. Parsifal's death was a tragedy and we will all miss him, but you're no girl anymore. There are no more years to waste. Don't pursue dead men." She slapped the table gently, as if to say, enough. "Don't pursue dead men. I don't think I have any advice clearer than that."

Sabine didn't think of the boy who Parsifal had been as dead. That boy was in Nebraska, waiting for her. He was there with his mother.

The house got bigger. Every day the staircase grew by ten steps. In another week it would be impossible to climb. Sabine didn't go into most of the rooms anymore. When the firemen came on Tuesdays they ran the vacuum over old vacuum marks, picking up only the most subtle layer of dust and rabbit fur generated by life. What had possessed Phan to buy such a big house? Coming to Los Angeles alone, not knowing a soul, hadn't he rattled around in there? Didn't he find that loneliness was exacerbated by space?

Sabine tried to think about Parsifal's life, but all she

seemed able to remember was the nagging infection in his hep-lock. In her mind, he was always thin. He was already deep inside his spiral of aging. She wanted to think about him in Paris or in the backyard in summer or up onstage in the flattering light, but the thoughts were always crowded out by that last headache.

In the place where they did the MRI testing, Parsifal had barely opened his eyes. The machine was big enough to be a room itself, solid enough to have its own center of gravity. They must have built the hospital around it. Even broken into pieces, it could never have come through doors, down stairwells. Tiny beads of sweat began to surface on Parsifal's ears. He stayed on his back, on his gurney, next to the sliding tray they would move him onto.

"It looks like a clothes dryer," Parsifal said to her, and shuddered. "They're going to put me in the dryer." Parsifal was a magician, but magic wasn't escape. Parsifal could make Sabine disappear down to the heel taps of her shoes, but he had no interest in restraining himself. He would not get into the disappearing closet, nor would he lie down in the saw box, even to see what Sabine had to do to make the blades miss her stomach. He was never once padlocked and chained. It was all he could do to see a film of Houdini hanging upside-down over Fifth Avenue in a straitjacket. Magic for Parsifal did not include being stuffed into a milk can filled with water or being buried in a coffin six feet underground. He could not speak of such illusions. Sabine never minded a tight squeeze. Despite her height she could tuck herself into whatever small corner Parsifal requested.

"I got locked in a refrigerator when I was a kid," he told her once, when they were looking at some equipment that a retired magician was selling. The attic was hot and the ceiling low. Sabine had slipped in between two panels in a magic box that were so close she had to turn her face to the side. "I was playing and the door slammed shut." He sat down for a minute on a stool. When Sabine asked him if he wanted a glass of water, he shook his head.

At the end of his life, Parsifal was trussed like a mental patient, stuffed, terrified, into a narrow tube so that the doctors might find the source of his crushing headache.

"You're not wearing a watch. Do you have any metal on your body?" the black nurse said, his voice low but clear, nearly musical. "Do you have a pacemaker?"

"I really don't want to go in there," Parsifal said. His closed eyelids fluttered from the headache.

"Nobody wants to go in there," the technician said. He was a Filipino who wore a gold cross on the outside of his blue cotton scrub suit. "Some people don't mind and some people hate it, but nobody wants to go."

"It doesn't hurt," the nurse said.

"Doesn't hurt at all," the technician said. "We're going to lift you up, get you over onto the table. The pretty lady here is going to hold your head." He looked at Sabine.

Sabine put one cool hand on either side of Parsifal's head, and Parsifal cringed. No matter how gentle she was, she was causing him pain and it was something she did not think she could possibly stand. She concentrated on the shape of his ears inside her palms. Beautiful ears. At the count of three they lifted, brought him only a few inches into the air, moved him barely more than a foot. It was gentle, everything was easy, but there were tears pooling up in the corners of his eyes and they spilled into her cupped palms.

"Not so bad," the technician said. "Raise up your legs now." He slipped a pillow under Parsifal's knees. "Is that comfortable? Do you feel all right?"

"I'm sorry," Parsifal whispered. Now the tears were running into his ears. "I just can't go in there."

"He's claustrophobic," Sabine said, stroking his arm. She was worried that she was going to faint.

The nurse and the technician looked at one another. They were a comedy team, each responsible for half a sentence. "The claustrophobia we've seen in here—," the technician said.

"—one woman put out her arms and stopped the tray at the last minute—," the nurse said, spreading his arms.

"—another one just scooted out the bottom and left," the technician said. "Not a word to us."

For a moment they were all quiet. They were all waiting for different things.

"This is a problem," Sabine said finally.

The nurse looked through Parsifal's file. He was clearly mulling things over. "I can give you a little Xanax, under the tongue. It's bitter but it makes you feel better right away. That's going to help you." He stepped out of the room for no more than half a second and came back holding a tiny white cup, as if the pills were kept in a bucket just outside the door. At some point he had put on gloves, or maybe he had been wearing them all along. Then the nurse did something that surprised Sabine: He put his full open hand on the side of Parsifal's face, a touch that seemed almost loving, and for a minute Sabine wondered if they knew one another. Parsifal opened his eyes as if kissed awake. "Open up," the nurse said.

Parsifal parted his lips and the thin, covered fingers of the nurse dipped beneath his tongue. The technician turned without another word and went back into his booth where he sat behind a glass window. He busied himself at a control panel, not watching.

"I don't like these machines," the nurse said. "I've been in there myself lots of times. They test things out on us. But it isn't bad." He kept his hand on Parsifal's face. He ran a thumb across Parsifal's forehead in a way that did not seem to hurt him. "You just have to go. Just for a little while and then he'll let you out. The pretty lady, is she your wife?"

"Yes," Parsifal said.

"Your wife is going to stand right here at the bottom and she's going to hold on to your foot." He turned to Sabine. "Go hold his foot," he said softly. And Sabine let go of Parsifal's hand and walked to the end of the table and held both of his bare, sheet-covered feet. "All this is is magnets. There's nothing in there that can hurt you."

"I just don't like being closed in," Parsifal said.

"Nobody does," the nurse said. "Nobody does. Is that pill gone?"

Parsifal nodded.

"Then you're feeling a little better. I'm going to put some earplugs in because it gets noisy in there." He slipped two small foam corks into Parsifal's ears and then began putting padding around his head. "This is to hold you in place," he said, his voice suddenly much louder. "You have to promise to stay still for this so you don't have to do it again later on." He put a strap under Parsifal's chin and snapped the end above his head. "Now, this is the part that I don't like. I'm going to put a trap over your head, just to keep everything in place. Close your eyes." Even raised, his voice was sweet, hypnotic. Sabine knew he would have made a fine magician and she knew that even in his pain Parsifal was thinking the same thing. The nurse reached up and pulled a white steel cage over Parsifal's head. Then Parsifal was Houdini, but he hadn't practiced. "Now, I want you to stay real still, but if you need something, you say it, we can hear you, and you can hear us, and your wife, she's right here holding your feet and if anything goes wrong she'll just pull you out. Is that okay?"

Parsifal didn't answer. He waved his hand.

"Okay," the man said, and went behind the door.

The voice of the technician came over an unseen speaker.

It filled the room. "I'm going to move the table now. This is going to be very slow." When the tray moved into the tube, Sabine followed it. Parsifal wiggled his toes and she squeezed them back, and in this way they communicated.

"He's doing all right in there?" the voice asked.

"He's all right," Sabine said. Squeeze.

There is a certain feeling when the spotlight is directly in your eyes. You know the house is full, the manager has told you, but everything in front of you is wrapped in a black sea, so you stop trying. To try and see is to strain your eyes against the light. It will give you a headache. When you look out, you are blind. The only person who knows this is the one standing next to you on the stage. He is all you can see. Together you speak and smile into the blackness. He is blind and he leads you. From this close you think he is wearing too much mascara.

"You're doing just fine," the technician's voice said. "You are holding perfectly still. Just keep holding still."

There was a drumming in the room, an industrial rhythm of hammers and gears, low thuds that at times seemed so frantic that it felt like something had gone wrong. The test took half an hour. Sabine watched the clock over the tube click along like an oven timer. She wanted to tell Parsifal something, to keep him occupied, but there was nothing to say. It was all she could do to speak. "Are you doing okay?" she called, and he bent his foot by way of acknowledgment.

"You're halfway there," the voice said. "You are so still. You're perfect." The sound of bedlam, jackhammers and lead pipes on lead walls. And then later, "Three more minutes. One more set of pictures and then you're out of there." That was when Sabine felt Parsifal's toes flex and pull with happiness in her hands.

The nurse came into the room, his blue scrubs dazzling against his black skin. He pushed a switch to set Parsifal free.

"Over, over, over," the nurse said. "Never have to go in there again." He slid the head cage up and flicked the chin strap loose. It came apart so much quicker than it went together. The padding was gone, the earplugs. Parsifal was free. "You're feeling okay now. Aren't you fine?"

"My head hurts so much," Parsifal said, his eyes still watering. There were wet stains beside his head.

"They'll know something soon. Come on and I'll get you back to your room so you can rest."

"Can I stay here, just for a minute? I don't want to move yet." Parsifal tried to smile at the man for his kindness. "I just need a minute to rest."

"You want to stay on the machine? Wouldn't you like it better if I moved you onto your gurney?"

"Not yet," Parsifal said. "If that's all right. Not just yet."

"Sure," the nurse said, patting his shoulder so lightly that they almost didn't touch. "We'll be right behind the window. We have a few minutes. You take your time."

Sabine thanked him and the man left. All those people she met on the most important day of her life and never saw again. Sabine took Parsifal's hand.

"I wish we were home," he said.

"We will be. We'll go home today. No matter what they tell us, we'll leave."

"Lean over," he said. "Come close to me."

Sabine bent forward. Her hair slipped from behind her ears and fell onto his forehead. His eyes were blue like the sky over Los Angeles in winter.

"Open your mouth," he said.

And as soon as he said it she felt the cold weight on her tongue and tasted metal in her saliva. She opened her mouth and he reached up to her and took the silver dollar off her tongue.

"Look at that," he said, and put it in her hand and squeezed her hand tight around the coin. "Rich girl," he said.

Sabine waited three more days before calling Dot Fetters.

"Just checking to see how the wedding plans are coming," Sabine said, but she could not make her voice sound like her voice. It shuddered and broke.

"Sabine?" Dot said.

Sabine put her forehead against the heel of her hand and nodded.

"Are you all right?"

"I'm good."

"You're coming out, aren't you? That's what you're calling to tell me."

"I was thinking . . . ," Sabine said, but didn't finish.

"Bertie," Dot Fetters called, "it's Sabine, pick it up in the bedroom."

In the distance, Sabine could hear a scramble. Dot Fetters was no fool; two would be more persuasive than one. In the moments it took Bertie to reach the phone, Sabine saw the rooms of the house on the other end of the line. She saw the living room where Dot Fetters sat in a reclining chair unreclined, pale tan walls and practical carpet with a braided rug over that. The kind of rug that Parsifal referred to as a big doormat. The light was dim and gold and the house was as small as Sabine's was huge. The halls were hung with family photographs from generations back. The double bed that Bertie was now sitting on was covered in a white chenille spread. She didn't stop to turn on the light on the bedside table before picking up the receiver.

There was a click and then a breathless excitement on the line. "Sabine! Are you coming?" she said in the dark.

"She's thinking about it," Dot Fetters told her daughter.

"You have to come now," Bertie said. "We could use help with the wedding. You've got such good taste and I don't know what I'm doing. I need help fixing up Haas's house, too. There's so much around here that needs to be done."

"Don't make her think we want her to come just to put her to work," Mrs. Fetters said.

"She doesn't think that, do you, Sabine?" Before Sabine could answer, Bertie went on. Sabine thought of her pink hand clutching the phone, the engagement ring making a brave light. "I'm just making excuses. I'm just trying to make you think that we need you so you'll come. We just miss you, is all. You don't have to do anything once you get here."

"You fly to Denver," Dot Fetters said. "Then you take the shuttle to Scottsbluff. We'll pick you up there. Unless you're afraid of those little planes. If you're afraid, I've got no problem driving to Denver to get you."

"They plow all the roads to Denver," Bertie said.

"No problem getting to Denver," Dot Fetters said.

"Do you have warm clothes?" Bertie asked.

"She's got warm clothes. There were pictures of her and Guy in the snow."

"I wasn't sure. It was so warm in Los Angeles. Well, don't worry about it. There are plenty of clothes here. Everything's going to be too big on you but between me and Mama and Kitty there's a ton of stuff. Don't go and buy anything."

"Do you mind the cold?" Dot Fetters asked.

At first Sabine thought she was asking Bertie, but when there was silence on the line she knew it was her turn to answer. "No," Sabine said.

"It's cold here," Mrs. Fetters said. "I don't want to mislead you about that."

"I understand."

"So when are you coming?"

Sabine leaned forward in bed and looked down the hall. It went on forever. It went on so long that it simply got dark and faded into nothing. "Tomorrow."

"Tomorrow?" Dot Fetters said. "Honey, do you have a ticket?"

From the extension in the bedroom, Bertie made a squealing sound of perfect joy.

"Those tickets are an absolute fortune if you don't buy them in advance," Dot Fetters said, her voice bewildered.

"Mama, be quiet," Bertie said. "Don't scare her off. Don't make her think we don't want her to come."

Nebraska

"IT'S USUALLY NOT as bad as this," the woman said to Sabine once the plane had righted itself again. "I make this flight sometimes once a month, and most of the time it's fine."

Sabine's seat was shaking. She could hear the strain in the hardware that bolted it to the floor. She tried to keep her body relaxed, not to take every jolt in her spine. The plane dropped a hundred feet, as if it had been suddenly seized with the realization that it was deadweight, then just as abruptly it was caught by some invisible upsurge in the air. Sabine's head hit against the window next to her. She touched her temple lightly with her fingertips. She took a deep breath and tried to focus her eyes on the bright white light on the tip of the wing.

"Oh," said the woman across the aisle.

Sabine looked at her and smiled sympathetically, but she did not speak. Even opening her mouth felt dangerous. The woman smiled back. She was, in fact, not much older than

Sabine, but she had lived a different kind of life. With her gray hair and wide lap she appeared to be well past fifty. In this particular circumstance of fear, they were very much united. Sabine had never been afraid of flying, but this felt more like a preparation for crashing. From time to time the stewardess made a low moaning sound from the back of the plane.

Sabine was thinking about her parents, the rabbit tucked between them on the sofa in the living room, getting the news. Hadn't they told her not to go? Didn't they cry, both of them, not much, but still a few tears, when she left off the food and the pillow Rabbit used for a bed? Her father had held him in his arms; running his thumb back and forth in the soft dent between his ears. "Sabine is going to a place where they eat nice bunnies like you," he whispered.

They had asked her very pointedly to forget about Nebraska. They had tried their best to be understanding and kind when she decided to go just the same. That would be the story they would always tell. How they begged her not to go, their only child, and how she left.

"Ladies," said a buttery voice over the intercom, dropping the "gentlemen" because it was only Sabine, the one other woman passenger, and the stewardess on board the little plane, "this is your captain speaking. It's a little rocky out there tonight, so we're going to ask the flight attendant to postpone the beverage service. We're hoping you can just bear with us and we'll see if we can't find a better altitude. In the meantime I'm going to leave the seat belt sign illuminated and ask that you please remain in your seats."

"I was really thinking about stretching my legs," the other woman said.

Sabine smiled again in polite acknowledgment. The woman sighed and shook her head. The stewardess was in the center of the very back of the plane, strapped into a jump seat with a crossing shoulder harness. She was flipping through the pages of a magazine, but when the plane pitched sharply to the left for no apparent reason, the magazine flew from her hands. Sabine turned around again and closed her eyes.

Everything would go to her parents. Salvio was staying at the house and she hoped he would have the good sense to take the gay porn videos out of the drawer under the VCR. If she ever got back to Los Angeles, she would make a point of giving them to him. The truth was her parents would deal with the burden of all those possessions much better than she had. They would wait a decent amount of time and then they would go into the house and methodically break it down, save a dozen pictures out of the fox-fur box, and then throw the rest away. They would sell things of value. They would give wisely and generously to charity. They would choose a handful of memorabilia: Sabine's scrapbook of the magic act, one of the model houses she had built from her own designs that proved what a fine architect she could have been, the real pearl necklace they could not afford when they had given it to her for her sixteenth birthday. They would take a few things they simply liked, the extravagant Savonnerie rug from her dining room, which would fit perfectly in their living room; the pair of brass stags whose antlers held candles at different heights; the small Paul Klee painting that Phan had bought for Parsifal on their one-year anniversary. The rest of it would go. The house would go, even though they liked it, even though they had greatly admired the yard and had always wanted their own lemon trees; they would not move. What Sabine realized as the commuter plane from Denver to Scottsbluff tossed and dived, the wings shearing through dirty clouds, was that her parents would get on with their lives in a way she had been unable to. In spite of whatever immeasurable grief this would cause them, they were the sort of people who picked up and went on. In a wave of nausea, Sabine felt inestimable love. What greater comfort was there than to know that they wouldn't fold under this potential loss?

When her parents had told her not to leave Los Angeles, she had known they were right. Sabine's best interest was always what they had in mind. It was for Sabine's sake that her parents had left Israel. They looked at the baby in the crib and thought of all that uncertainty. A place that was only for Jews was too new, the world would never permit it. All around them countries were full of anger; and much of it, or so it seemed with this child, was directed towards them. Sabine's father had cousins in Montreal and Sabine's mother spoke French, and so they thought they had found their place. In August, when they arrived and moved into the little apartment over the cousin's garage, they felt sure they had done the right thing, but by December they were not so sure. The winter paralyzed them. There were too many unhappy memories in cold weather. As soon as there was enough saved to make a second trip, just barely enough, with nothing left over, they moved to Los Angeles, a place like Israel, so warm that the citrus fruit stayed on the trees year-round. They went to the Fairfax neighborhood, where the public schools closed down for High Holy Days and the menus came standard in Yiddish. They stayed there even after the neighborhood declined, even after there was money enough for a better house in the Valley, because, as Sabine's mother said, they were through with change. Four countries were more than anyone should suffer in a lifetime. How could one street be so different from the next? If they didn't feel the need to wander, why should she?

For one full second the plane seemed to stop. It hung in the air, motionless, and for that second Sabine could see the snow falling straight down. Then the plane caught on something and sputtered forward. Sabine had a single memory of Canada, and that was of snow. Standing in the snow and seeing white in every direction she looked, up and down, behind her, to the side. She turned and turned and swung her head around until she knew that this was an envelope from which she would never escape. Sabine's mother tells the story of hearing a scream that was the sound only a dying person would make. She thought that a wolf or a bear, animals that had never before come into the city of Montreal, was at that moment in her yard, eating her daughter alive. But when Sabine ran to her, it was only the snow she was screaming at, and her mother said she understood. She had felt like screaming herself. All of Sabine's other memories were of Fairfax, a place where a person could live in America without going to all the trouble of figuring out the country.

"When I was in high school I wanted to be a flight attendant because I thought it was the only way I was ever going to get out of town," the stewardess said blankly from the back of the plane. Sabine and the other woman turned around. The stewardess had bright blond hair and wore her eye makeup like Natalie Wood. "I thought, How else am I ever going to get to go to Europe? Meet a wealthy businessman, get married? Nobody told me that I'd be flying to the same little fucking towns I came from."

"Are you okay back there?" the other woman said.

"These are the planes that go down, girls." The stewardess narrowed her eyes. "It's hardly ever the superjets. Look at the numbers. It doesn't get the big press because it's just a handful of us who get killed. These things are death traps with wings."

The plane could potentially hold eighteen passengers in its moist and tinny walls. Tiny pearls of water shot across the plastic windows, which were etched with delicate patterns of frost. The blue carpet was frayed at the edges and the brighter blue chairs were made shabby by the pieces of white paper Velcroed over every headrest to protect the fabric from the stains of oily hair. The plane pitched so completely to the left that Sabine had to grab onto the armrests while her purse shot across the aisle and lodged itself beneath another seat. The stewardess screamed.

"Hello?" said the other woman to the curtain up ahead of them. "Could somebody up there do something about her?"

There was a pause and then a man leaned back through the soft folds of fabric. "Bad weather," he said, either the pilot or the copilot. Sabine hoped it was the copilot. She did not recognize the voice. "We're perfectly safe."

"Her," the other woman said, pointing to the back of the plane. The stewardess hung limply forward in her shoulder harness, big, inky tears smearing her face.

The pilot or copilot watched for a minute. "Becky," he said, trying to make his voice loud enough to reach the back of the plane, but she didn't seem to hear him. The engines roared against the wind. He looked first to the other woman and then to Sabine, and when neither of them presented an idea he disappeared back behind the curtain. "Becky," his voice came over the intercom. The girl sniffed and raised her stained face to the ceiling. "Pull it together now, we've got passengers."

Exhausted, she nodded at no one. She brushed her hands back and forth across her cheeks and blew her nose on a cocktail napkin. She was quiet.

And in that quiet, Sabine felt very clearly that she would not mind dying on this night, with these people, in this plane. The memory of Los Angeles seemed to pull away from her, thousands of tiny houses on neat curves, their roofs glistening like dimes in the bright sun as she looked out the window after takeoff. It looked like a world she would build herself, the order and neatness of miniature. She thought that maybe she would be lucky if her life ended quickly, like Parsifal's, and once she felt that peace in her heart, she knew just as certainly that the plane would land and they would all be safe and it would be a good thing not to die.

The plane was clearly losing altitude, although this time it seemed to be doing so with a sense of purpose. Sometime later Sabine felt the landing gear move down and lock. The fields below were blowing white, a whiteness interrupted only by the occasional shadow thrown from a drift of snow.

"Ladies," said the pilot, "we are making our final descent into Scottsbluff."

The woman on the other side of the aisle held out her hand, and Sabine took it and squeezed hard. There was a roaring like a tornado when the plane touched down, a roaring and a shaking that threatened to pull their hands apart, but they held on. The warmth in those fingers felt as much like love as anything Sabine had ever known. They were in Nebraska now.

Even when the plane was parked, Sabine still felt the ground moving. A man in blue zip-up coveralls held her hand as she walked down the movable metal staircase into the snow. Immediately snow blew down the neck of her sweater and dampened the bare skin of her wrists between the ends of her coat sleeves and the tops of her gloves. Snow filled her pockets and pressed into her mouth. She had to stop and lean against the jumpsuited man.

"Not much farther," he yelled over the wind, and put his hand beneath her arm in a professional manner. As they walked across the tarmac, sheets of snow pooled and vanished beneath her feet. It was like walking on something boiling. In every direction the snow was banked into high hills. Plows worked on either side, nervously rearranging what could not be made right. The flat, smooth place they were walking across now had been carved out like a swimming pool. The man worked hard to open the heavy metal door, and the wind made a sucking and then howling sound when it, with Sabine, was let into the warm building.

Dot and Bertie Fetters were waiting.

They looked different in Nebraska. Even at the first sight of them in the hallway, Sabine could tell they looked better here. Instead of seeming merely bulky, the heavy coats with toggles made them look confident, prepared. Sabine wondered if she too could buy high boots with rubber covering the feet. When they saw her, they called her name with a kind of joyful wonder that she had never heard in the word Sabine before. They threw themselves together onto her neck. What was lost is now found.

"I half thought you wouldn't be on the plane," Dot said. "I tried and tried to tell myself that you were really coming but I couldn't make myself believe it." She hugged her again, hugged her hard enough to empty out Sabine's lungs. "Have you gotten thinner? It couldn't be possible that you've gotten thinner?"

"Sabine," Bertie said, stepping back to see her fully, "it's so wonderful that you're here. Was the flight okay?"

"Good," Sabine said.

Bertie leaned towards her, her mouth up close to Sabine's ear. "You've got to meet Haas." She held out her hand to a man standing away from everyone, his back pressed against the wall. When she motioned he came to her, the nylon of his blue down coat making a soft shushing noise as his arms moved against his sides.

"Haas," she said quietly, "this is my sister-in-law, Sabine Parsifal." Bertie's face was so hopeful, so eager to please, that Sabine had to look away from her. She shook Haas's hand. "This is my fiancé," Bertie said, "Eugene Haas."

"Nice to—," he said, but was unable to finish the sentence, assuming, perhaps, that what was nice was implied. Haas was older than Bertie. He looked a little overwhelmed, frightened even. Like Sabine, he seemed unsure as to why he was in this airport. He pushed his hand back into his pocket and stepped away.

"Haas drove us over," Bertie said. Sabine looked at the delicate bones of his face, the way his stocking cap was pulled to the top of his glasses, and thought, He worries about you in this weather. He's afraid you'll get stuck in an embankment and freeze to death on the road. He's afraid of someone skidding on a patch of ice and coming into your lane.

"Come on and let's get you home and settled in." Dot took Sabine's arm and steered her with authority to where the bags were being set out by the man in the blue coveralls.

The airport had two gates and Sabine had arrived at the second. In the lobby, orange plastic bucket chairs stood empty and waiting, bolted into two straight lines. There was a vending machine full of brands of candy she had never heard of before. Chuckles. Haas went on ahead to drive the car to the front door from where it was parked, fifty feet away. The woman who had sat beside Sabine on the plane smiled at her shyly now and without speaking, picked up her suitcase and left.

Sabine looked at the woman at the ticket counter, the man and woman who waited patiently at security, the two girls talking at the car rental booth. She looked at the handful of people who milled around through the airport, and she looked at the Fetters. There was something she couldn't put her finger on exactly, a way they resembled each other and yet resembled no group Sabine had seen before. And they had not seen her before, either, because she felt them looking, the way people had looked at her in the marketplace in Tripoli the first time she went and did not know to cover her head. There was a

Lucite display box in the baggage claim area that held three five-gallon cans of house paint. VISIT SHERWOOD HARDWARE, the sign said.

"Kitty was going to come, but Haas had to drive," Dot said, "so there wasn't enough room in the car."

"He wanted to come and meet Sabine," Bertie said.

"I've never seen a man so interested in taking care of a woman as Haas is. 'Let me get you coffee.' 'Are you sure you don't want to take a scarf?' I swear, if he wasn't so nice he'd drive me crazy."

"You'd get used to it," Bertie said.

"How long have you been going out?" Sabine asked.

"Six years." Bertie seemed more self-assured in Nebraska. She was older here. You could see it in the way she held her head. "It was seven years ago he came to teach at the school, and we started going out a year later."

"As long as you're not rushing into things." Sabine had meant it as a joke, but Bertie just nodded her head as if to say that was how she thought of it, too.

"No one will ever accuse Bertie of not being cautious," Dot said.

The man in the jumpsuit brought Sabine her luggage, never for a moment doubting it was hers. She was suddenly embarrassed by having two bags. She had packed carelessly. She had brought Phan's gloves and was wearing his coat. She had brought the sable hat that Parsifal had bought for Phan in Russia. She had brought Parsifal's sweaters. She had thrown anything that caught her eye into the suitcase. In LAX, where skycaps pushed flatbed carts burdened with hat boxes and shoe trunks, Sabine had never even thought about her luggage. Bertie took the heavier bag and led the way out to the car.

Maybe, if anything, it was like Death Valley. None of the beautiful parts, not Furnace Creek or the range of Funeral

Mountains. No place where the rocks were red. Not in the spring, when the ground cactus bloomed with vicious color out of the sand. But maybe this was Death Valley in its endless stretches of flatness. Death Valley in July at noon in the places where people with flat tires managed to walk three miles or four before giving out, their sense of direction destroyed by the 360-degree sweep of nothingness. Add to that the snow, which pelted the car the way the sand could bury you when a windstorm came out of nowhere. Over and over again Sabine tried to fix her eyes on a single flake hurtling towards them, lost it, and found another. It made her head ache but she couldn't make herself stop. Add to the snow the bone-crushing cold, which was a combination of the cold of the atmosphere and the cold of the wind. It was not so unlike the heat in that it permeated every square inch of your skin and deep beneath it. Cold, like heat, quickly became the only thing possible to think about: how to get out of it, how it was going to kill you. There were no towns in the thirty-five miles between Scottsbluff and Alliance. Sometimes there were billboards, but there was little to advertise, places to eat and sleep that were so far away there was no point in even thinking about them now. Most of what there was to look at was flat land and snow.

"I bet you never thought you'd see Nebraska," Dot said. She was beaming. Nebraska made Dot Fetters whole. They were coming into the town now, driving down streets lined in rows of tiny, identical ranch houses.

"I never did," Sabine said. Was it the snow that made every house exactly the same? Was there something else under that white blanket?

"It's hard to tell it now, but in the summer this place is beautiful. In the summer you'd never want to be anyplace else."

"This winter has been worse than most of them," Bertie

said from the front seat, where she sat next to Haas. "Don't think it's always going to be this bad."

Always? Did they think she was staying? Did they think she'd be around to see the summer or the winter after this? Was that what Parsifal thought as a boy when he looked out into the fields: *Do you really expect me to stay through to the summer?*

"It's a shame you didn't bring Rabbit," Bertie said. "Haas, you should see Sabine's rabbit."

Haas pulled into one of the many driveways there were to choose from. The house was lit up, waiting. They tightened their coats and stepped into the soft, deep snow. They hurried up the front steps and through the unlocked door.

"This is it," Dot said, stretching out her hands. "This is home. I should feel embarrassed. I've seen your house."

Over the sofa there was a copy of a painting, an old covered bridge, a horse and wagon approaching. "When I'm king," Parsifal had liked to say as they wandered through antique stores, "my first edict will be to outlaw all covered-bridge paintings and their reproductions."

Sabine told her she was happy to be there, and it was true.

Dot smiled at the room, the nappy brown sofa with maple arms, the console television set, the two recliners. The bulb on the ceiling was covered with a piece of frosted glass that resembled a handkerchief pinned at each of its four corners. "I've been here a long time. We moved here when Guy was barely walking and I was still carrying Kitty around. Now I think about this being Guy's house and I don't think I'll ever move. It's one of the only links I've got to him. I started feeling that way a long time before he died."

Sabine's parents had told her that the house on Oriole was too much for her, that she should give it up and buy someplace that would be easier to manage, but she wasn't moving, either.

Bertie and Haas, who had been lingering out in the car, came through the door, red faced from the cold or from the pleasure of finding a minute alone. Bertie stamped on the mat to dislodge the snow from the deep treads in her boots. "Kitty!" she called out, her voice loud enough to call Kitty from next door. "Isn't Kitty here?" she asked her mother.

"Sure she's here." Dot went into the kitchen and then looked down the hallway. "Kitty?"

"She was supposed to make dinner," Bertie said to Sabine. Haas unzipped his jacket but couldn't quite bring himself to take it off. He stood on the mat by the door, waiting.

"I'll call her," Dot said.

"Then you might as well do it in the other room." Bertie sat down heavily in a chair and started to unlace her boots, Haas watching her, longingly.

"Don't be silly." Dot picked up the phone. "Sit, sit," she said to Sabine. "This will take one minute. I bet she just had to run someplace with the boys. She's probably on her way."

They were all watching her, waiting quietly while the phone rang for what must have been a long time. Far past the point at which Sabine would have hung up, Dot spoke. "Howard," she said, her voice gone flat. "It's me. Let me talk to Kitty." They waited, all of them. Dot curled the plastic phone cord around her finger. Sabine could barely make out some framed pictures hanging in the hall and wanted to go to them. Now she understood how much Dot had wanted to see the pictures at her house. "Well, she has to be there because she's not here. She was going to come over for supper. Guy's wife is in town from California. You know that." Dot looked at Sabine, to be sure. "Just put her on the phone." After a minute she put the earpiece of the phone on her forehead and tapped the receiver there a few times, then she hung up. "So," she said, her voice steady and reasonable. "Other plans for dinner."

"I'm going to pick something up," Haas said, and slid the zipper of his jacket back into place.

"I shouldn't have asked her to make dinner," Dot said. "I should have done it myself."

"This isn't your fault, no matter how you look at it," Bertie told her mother. Then she put her hands on Sabine's sleeves and she squeezed. Sabine knew that Bertie was telling her something, but she was too tired and confused to figure out what it was. Maybe she meant to say sorry, or, just bear with this and don't ask. Sabine nodded in general compliance. "We've got really good pizza in town," Bertie said. "Tomorrow night we'll cook." She pushed her feet back down in her boots.

"Be careful," Dot said. "It's getting worse out there every minute."

Bertie slipped her hand in the pocket of Haas's coat as if she were looking for something important, and then she left it there. They did not care about the weather.

Sabine moved her hands inside her own pockets. Snow.

"Look at you, standing there in your coat," Dot said to Sabine when they were alone. "I don't get enough practice being a hostess."

Sabine took her coat off and held it in her arms. She would prefer to wear it. The weight of the coat made her feel pinned down. "So, do you want to tell me about this?"

Dot tilted her head to the lacy piece of crocheting that hung over the back of the chair. She closed her eyes. "Not really," she said. "Not if you're giving me a choice. Everything comes out awfully quick, anyway. Don't you think?"

Sabine saw her parents standing just inside the kitchen door. Her father did not look judgmental, only sad. He held the rabbit tenderly in his arms. "You're thirty-five miles from the airport," her mother said. "There is a blizzard outside, and you do not know these people. You've come to Nebraska for what, Sabine? What were you thinking about?" They looked cold, standing there in winter clothes meant for Southern California. Her mother shivered and pushed close to her father, close to the rabbit.

"Let me see Parsifal's room," Sabine said.

Dot smiled, her eyes still closed. "Good," she said. "Now's the time, when we have the house to ourselves. I still never get this house to myself. Everyone always asks me, 'What will you do with Bertie gone?' Bertie was about ready to ask Haas to move in over here after they got married, she was so worried about me, and you've got to know he'd do it. But I told her, there have been people in my house every day of my life. I moved from my folks to Al's, then I had the kids. It would be nice, you know, to wake up one morning and have a place all to yourself."

"I just got that little bit of time when I lived with Phan and Parsifal, and then the year after Phan died."

"I'm not saying I hated it. I'm just saying after a while enough's enough." Dot stood up and stretched. "Come on," she said. "I'll show you."

There was a hallway with four doors off the living room. Two bedrooms on one side and a bedroom and bathroom on the other. "This is me, this is Bertie," Dot said, and when they got to the last door she opened it and said, "This is you."

Of course what struck Sabine right away was the rug, which was a red plaid tartan of the kind used to make kilts for Catholic schoolgirls and dog beds in New England, only this plaid was bigger, more inescapable. How he must have lain in bed at night dreaming of carpets, of nimble, delicate fingers securing a thousand knots per square inch. The rug was the only thing that was unexpected. The twin beds were carved from the same light maple as the furniture in the living room. Between them there was a nightstand with a lamp. There was a desk underneath the window, with a straight-back chair. There was a dresser with eight drawers. There was a bookcase full of Hardy Boys mysteries and volumes A through K of an off-brand encyclopedia, the type that comes from filling up stamp books. There were four plastic horses with removable saddles, the tallest one standing twelve inches at the head. There were three small silver trophies and five blue ribbons commemorating moments of honor in baseball. There was a baseball. Sabine wanted time in that room. She wanted to pull up the rug and look beneath it, check inside the coils of the box springs, see if there wasn't something taped behind a picture. Of course there could not be a message for her, and yet she thought there would be something, a clue that only she would understand. There was a framed photograph of four people—Parsifal and Kitty, younger than they had been in the photographs Sabine had already seen, and Dot and a man who was tall and square jawed with dark eyes and dark hair. A man who should have been handsome but, for some reason that had to do with the spacing of his eyes or the shortness of his neck, was not. It was a studio portrait taken before anyone had even the dimmest notion of Bertie coming along. They looked regular, friendly, close.

"Look how pretty you are," Sabine said, and it was true. Dot Fetters was fine boned, her waist as tiny as a doll's. Her face in the photograph was energetic and bright, hopeful.

"I was pretty then," Dot said, peering into the small face that was her own face. "But it was wasted on me. I couldn't see it to save my life, thought I was the homeliest thing going. Then one day I woke up and I was old and fat and I knew. You don't miss the water till the well runs dry." She stopped to study Sabine for a minute. "I sure hope Guy had the good sense to tell you how beautiful you are. Even if he did go for the boys, a homosexual's got eyes just like the rest of us. I hope he did that for you."

He had said Audrey Hepburn's neck, Cyd Charisse's legs. He said she should stand in a room by herself in the Louvre. "I wish you could see yourself in this light," he would tell her, in the bright sun of Malibu or in the kitchen in the morning or beneath the stage lights gelled pink and forgiving. "You are so beautiful in this light."

"He did that," she said.

"Good," Dot said, nodding. "I would have been disappointed in him otherwise."

Sabine pointed to the frame again. "And that's Albert?"

Dot looked to make sure and then she nodded. "When Guy went away," she said, as if the question had reminded her of something else, "Kitty moved into his room. I was pregnant with Bertie then and not feeling so well, and Kitty made her whole room over for the baby and slept in here. She never changed a thing in Guy's room, never put up any of her stuff. She just made a little place in the closet for her clothes and that was it. Now her boys sleep here when they stay over with me and she won't let them touch anything. She'll let them read the books but only in the room, only if they put them right back, and that's it." She picked up one of the horses and held it to her chest without looking at it. Its beady plastic eyes stared up at her without affection. "I tell her, I don't think it's so healthy. It wasn't so healthy when she was doing it as a girl but then when her boys came along I thought, Hell, these are boy's things, let them have them. Not Kitty. Everything concerning her brother has to be just so. That's why it's such a shame she didn't get to come to Los Angeles. If anyone should have been there it was Kitty, maybe even more than me." Dot looked at Sabine. "There's something I think I should tell you. I kind of told a lie. Not a big one."

"To me?"

She shook her head. "To Kitty. When I got back from California I told her that her picture was on his nightstand. I couldn't tell her it was just in a box, jumbled in with everybody else. You and I know it was something that he had it at all, but it meant so much to her, thinking she was right next to him, that he was looking at her and thinking about her." For a moment Dot stopped, her words choked down with worry. "I love my children," she said. "No one will tell you otherwise, but just between the two of us I have to say I admire you for not having any. The ways they break your heart, Jesus, and it never stops. I mean it, it simply does not stop."

Sabine felt sure that her parents were sitting in Fairfax right this minute saying the same thing about her. She took the horse from Dot's arms and put it back on the shelf. "What do you say you fix me a drink?"

"Oh," Dot said, lifting her head from the reverie of sadness. "You are talking now."

Dot produced a bottle of Jack Daniel's from deep in the pantry and the two of them sat quietly at a small table in the kitchen with their glasses, thinking of what had been lost. The drink reminded Sabine of the confession in the Sheraton bar, the Nebraska Boys Reformatory, and she might have asked about it then had the back door not swung open. Snow skittered across the linoleum so fast that in a matter of minutes the apple green floor would have been white. Bertie and Haas, back with pizza.

In all the confusion over napkins and plates, Haas stayed by the door, his ice-encrusted hat still on his head. In this, her second encounter with him, Sabine knew that the door was his spot, that in any fire, he would be the most likely to survive.

"I'm heading home," Haas said. "Papers to grade."

"Don't you want something to eat?" Dot asked.

"I got a little something while we were waiting. I'm set."

Sabine thanked him for the ride and Haas assured her it was nothing. Bertie gave him a polite kiss and then he was gone.

"It looks bad out there." Dot stood up to serve their plates.

"The radio said ten to twelve inches is all." Bertie seemed a little put out, maybe that Haas had left or maybe because she had not gone home with him. She was nearly thirty, surely she must go home with him. "Did Kitty call while we were gone?"

Dot shook her head. "Your sister gets busy."

"The hell she gets busy." Bertie didn't so much slam down her fork as place it down decisively. "Howard gets busy."

"Whatever it is, I don't think it's call to raise your voice when Sabine is here. Let's at least put on a good front for one night, show her what a happy family we are."

Bertie picked her fork up again and absently began pricking holes in the cheese. "I don't see why we're not allowed to talk about Kitty."

"We talk plenty and it does no one any good. You can't make somebody else's decisions for them," Dot said wearily. "I've spent my whole life trying."

Suddenly Bertie turned to Sabine. "Do you have brothers and sisters?" she asked, hoping to guide the conversation into more polite terrain. Her curls were wet from where the snow had melted on them and they glistened as if recently varnished.

"Just me," Sabine said. "My parents seemed to think that that would be enough."

Dot and Bertie looked at her in silence, waiting for more, when there was no more coming. They had hoped the question would take them away from their own worries and when it didn't they had no idea what else there was to say. Sabine would have been glad to know the story of Kitty, but if Bertie was interested in telling it, Dot was certainly not interested in hearing it. Besides, Kitty's story was not the one Sabine had come for. She'd just as soon be in Parsifal's bedroom now, staring up at the ceiling he had stared at all those years. "You know, I'm awfully tired, to tell you the truth," she said, and gave a halfhearted stretch.

"The flight will take it out of you," Dot said, relieved. "And it's not like your life has been so normal lately. You don't need to eat this. Have you had enough?"

Sabine said she'd never really been hungry at all.

"Sure, baby. This has been a long day. You go on to bed. If you need anything, sing out. I'll be up for a while still."

Bertie looked up from her dinner. "I'm sorry about all this," she said. "Mama's right. I could keep it to myself."

"You have," Sabine said. "I have no idea what's going on."

They all said their good-nights and Sabine headed down the dim hallway, past pictures of people she did not know and some who looked familiar. The voices of her parents stayed in her ears. What, exactly, could she have been thinking of?

But in the room that was his room, Sabine felt different. She felt a rush of that privacy that comes not from being alone but from being with the one person you are completely comfortable with. The door was made of hollow plywood, so light that one good slam would take it off the hinges. It had no lock and there was a full inch gap beneath it where the light from the hall came in. But closed, this door was freedom itself. How he must have hidden in that room, begged to be sent there for punishment. There was not a single corner of it that he hadn't memorized, no pale water stain on the ceiling or separation of baseboard and wall that he didn't know. She ran her hands flat over the top of the dresser and felt his hands, small then, reaching for socks inside the drawers. Sabine sat down on the red bedspread. Every night he had slept in one of these beds. On some fortunate weekends, a boy from school had slept in the other, and they would lie awake in the dark and talk about what life would be like once they grew up and left. Parsifal would wake up in the middle of the night and watch that boy sleeping, the warm expansions of his narrow chest, the legs a careless tangle in the sheets; and he wanted to crawl into that bed without knowing exactly why. With his head on that boy's pillow, he knew sleep would come quickly.

It was a long way from the bedroom she had imagined in Connecticut, the one with the yellow Labrador and the big windows and bunk beds.

Sabine put on a pair of pajamas she'd bought for Phan to wear in the hospital and slid into the small bed. The sheets smelled pleasantly of laundry detergent, though what had she been expecting? When she turned off the light, she listened to the wind circle the house like a pack of howling dogs. The wind made Sabine nervous. She thought of all that emptiness, Nebraska stretching out flat in every direction like a Spanish map of the world. In her mind she tried to conjure the sounds of helicopters and police cars to sing herself to sleep, the reassuring hum of civilization.

During the night she finds herself in the middle of a snow-field. She is not in Vietnam, but she is not afraid because her feet are bare and the snow is deep and the pajamas she bought for Phan that he never got around to wearing are thin as the wind presses them hard against her chest, and still she is not cold. This is how she knows it is a dream. The sky is clear and the moon is so bright against the snow that Sabine could read a letter. As long as it is light and she is not cold, there is nothing to be afraid of. She waits less than a minute before seeing Phan, a small black outline moving towards her. His legs are working hard against the drifts. He is wearing the sable hat that Parsifal bought for him in Russia, the hat that is now lying beside her suitcase, which is on the twin bed she is not sleeping in. "Hey," she calls out, and waves as she starts towards him. It is like walking through a field of deep, loose flour that forms itself to the impression of her foot after every step.

"I can't believe you got here first."

"I was already here," she says, knowing good and well that even in her sleep she is still in Nebraska. The closer she gets to him through the labor of snow, the lighter she feels. Sabine never had a real lover. There were men she had dinner with, men she slept with, some for long periods of time. But there was never a man she wanted to run to when she saw him, a man in whose neck she longed to bury her face and recount every detail of her day. There was never a man she felt could make every difference simply by holding her to his chest and saying her name. Except for Parsifal, and he was not a lover. Except, now, for Phan, who takes her into his arms and lifts her up above his head, towards the clear night and the stars.

"I have absolutely no reason to be here," he says. "I just wanted to see for myself how you were doing. Nebraska," he says, gesturing out to the field. "Can you believe it?"

"No," she says honestly.

"Growing up, I was Saigon, Paris, L.A. Nothing like this. When Parsifal first brought me here—"

"Do you come here much?"

"Parsifal likes it," he says. "He's very interested in his family, very interested in reviewing his life. It's a phase. At first I was in Vietnam all the time, now I only go because I enjoy the country."

"Have you been to his house?"

"Oh, sure," he says. "He wants to see his sisters, his mother. One night when we were there we lay down on the beds, those little twin beds."

Sabine closes her eyes, sees them there in the darkness, fully dressed, their hands clasped formally over their chests as if dead. They were not there with her. They were there together, with each other. "I don't know why I'm here," she says.

"There's a reason. When you can get some distance, you start to see patterns. Everything falls into place." He lifts his hand to the darkness. From the moonlight on the snow, Sabine can see his face so clearly. Phan is happy, death has given him that. "It's all so orderly, really, it's shocking."

"But I don't have distance," she says, her voice failing her for a second. "I'm here by myself. I'm in the middle of it. I can't make sense out of anything."

He cups his hand around her neck, skims a thumb across her smooth cheek. She does not mean to be comforted, and yet she is. It is what she wants, to be touched and held, to be promised things regardless of the truth. "Everything will be fine," he says.

He opens up his coat for her, though it isn't cold, and she steps inside it and leans against the soft sweater on his chest. When he folds his arm over her back she thinks, Keep me here, exactly like this. Let me stand here forever. "All right," she says.

"All right," he says, and rests his cheek against her hair, and if they do not stand there together forever, they stand for a very long time, and Sabine has no memory of it ending.

There was nothing like waking in an unfamiliar darkness. Sabine blinked, her fingers tried to understand the blankets. Is it home, is it my bed? No. The hospital, then, Phan's room?

Parsifal's? No. Am I somehow back in my old apartment, my parents' house, did none of this happen? No. Far away she heard the faintest sound, a second of scraping, a chair against the floor, and she used the sound to navigate her way back to Parsifal's room in Nebraska. She thought she smelled a cigarette and then didn't, but it stayed in her mind. The electric clock said 1:30. Sabine closed her eyes and waited but nothing came. She turned and pushed her head under the pillows and then turned again. Sleep felt like it was over for good.

There was nothing to do but get up. Barefoot and dazed, Sabine went down the hall. Dot or Bertie, one of them, was smoking a cigarette in the kitchen. Sabine had gone to sleep too early. She should have known she would wake up. If she had been smart, she would just now be going to bed.

The woman in the kitchen had her back to the door. Her dark, shoulder-length hair was pulled into a ponytail so that her pale neck was exposed. With her head bent forward, Sabine could see the shadows cast from the top vertebra of her spine. She was smoking with too much concentration to know that anyone else was in the room. There were already two cigarettes crushed out in the saucer beside her. A light haze of smoke ringed the overhead light. Even from the back, even without knowing her, Sabine recognized the girl in the picture.

"Kitty?"

The woman looked up at her and smiled from her brother's face, the pale blue dog eyes tilting up ever so slightly, the shadow smudged beneath the lower lip. Sabine felt confused, suddenly remembering that she had been dreaming and thinking that this was part of the dream: She goes to Nebraska to find Parsifal but he is a woman. The woman was wearing a sweatshirt and slim jeans, socks but no shoes. She was Parsifal's mother, the one Sabine had made up, the one who worked crossword puzzles in the car in Connecticut, the woman Sabine made from his rib while he slept.

"Sabine," the woman said. She dropped her cigarette in the saucer and rose from her chair. She came right to Sabine and took her in her arms. Sabine had been held minutes ago and it was like this and not like this. The woman smelled like smoke and salt, and beneath that she smelled like soap and powder. Sabine brought up her arms, lightly touched the woman's back. Kitty held Sabine just a second longer than she should have and when she stepped back she was smiling and just beginning to cry.

"What a good first impression I make," she said. She wiped her face with the back of her hand and laughed. Parsifal always laughed when he cried. He laughed when he was embarrassed about anything.

"I cry all the time these days."

"I'm so sorry about dinner. I thought I'd get over here fine and I didn't get here until the middle of the night."

Did she know how much she looked like Parsifal? Could she see it in the photographs? "I wasn't even hungry."

"I probably woke you up. Did I wake you up?"

"I don't think so," Sabine said. Had she been awake? She had the distinct impression of having been outside and she wondered if she would ever walk in her sleep. The thought made her shiver and she peered out the window. In the light of a street lamp she saw two aluminum poles with no clothesline strung between them.

"It's still going like a son-of-a-bitch out there."

"I'm not entirely awake," Sabine said.

Kitty looked worried. Parsifal's face, so completely his face that Sabine could look at it all night. She had watched that face for twenty-two years. She had seen that face in stage makeup, she had seen it with fevers and asleep. She would know it anywhere. "Go back to bed," Kitty said. "You must be exhausted. I know I woke you."

Sabine yawned, shook her head, sat down at the table. "May I have one of these?" she said, picking up the pack.

"You smoke? I didn't think anybody in California smoked."

"I don't, but I'm not in California."

Sabine tried three times to work the lighter and then Kitty reached over and took it from her. When she pushed the button down, a flame shot out of the blue plastic. "Childproof," she said. The two women sat and smoked, each trying not to stare at the other.

"I appreciate your being so nice to my mother," Kitty said. "Looking after her when she was in Los Angeles and then coming out here to visit. It's really helped her."

"Your mother's great."

Kitty gave a small nod of halfhearted agreement. "She is, but still a lot of people wouldn't have done it. They wouldn't want to be bothered. We're all way back there in the past."

There was a time when Sabine believed in keeping what was private to herself, but now everything that mattered to her felt spilled. It had all gotten away from her somehow. "I haven't been doing so well with all of this," she said. "Your mother and Bertie were good to me, too."

Kitty seemed to understand; maybe she wasn't doing so well herself. "I'm sorry about not coming to Guy's funeral. If there had been any way, I would have been there."

"You didn't know," Sabine said. "I didn't know."

"I still feel bad about it." She covered her eyes with her hand and shook her head. "I can't believe I'm sitting here talking to Guy's wife."

Why did there seem to be such a difference between being Guy's wife and being Parsifal's wife? Sabine didn't know Guy.

She felt like she was lying, setting herself up for another evening of revelation like the one she'd had with Dot at the Sheraton. She was Parsifal's wife. "Listen," she said. "I just need to be clear about something."

"Guy was gay."

Sabine sighed. "Did your mother tell you?"

"He was always gay," Kitty said, blowing smoke towards the ceiling, her neck stretched back. "I think I may have been the one who told my mother. I can't remember."

"Okay."

"I don't care how you worked out being married. What I care about is that you knew him, you were there with him. You were with him all those years when I wasn't. You were with him when he died." Kitty stopped and considered this. "Were you?" she said. "Right there with him?"

Sabine nodded. She went back to that room again, saw him there in the blank white light of the Cedars Sinai basement, laid out on the tongue of the MRI machine. She pushed the thought away.

Kitty waited for something else. When nothing came she asked, "And it was . . . ?" Kitty looked at her so hard. Sabine's hand holding the cigarette stayed perfectly still, halfway between the table and her lips.

"Very quick. He had a headache, the aneurism burst. That was it."

Kitty's eyes filled up again, and she turned them away. Sabine would have said Kitty looked older than her brother, were it not for the fact that he had aged so much at the end. For years he was younger, for a while they had been the same age, and then, at the end of his life, he was older again.

Kitty dabbed her nose on the cuff of her sweatshirt. "Did my mother tell you I have a son named Guy? My younger boy. My oldest is Howard, for his father, but my other boy is

Guy. I wonder if I should change his name now. I think it's harder to get a good spot on the football team if your name is Parsifal."

"Might as well leave it alone, then."

Kitty smiled so slightly, so quickly, that when it was over Sabine wasn't sure she had seen it at all. "Parsifal is a good name for a magician. It's a lot better than anything he had picked out when we were kids. He had a whole school note-book full of names. There were three categories." She held up three fingers to make the point. "There was general alias, that was going to be his everyday name, then there would be a stage name, and then he would pick out a third name that would be his backup, so that if anyone ever found out he changed his name he would give his third name as his real name. The third name was the real genius of the plan. The third name was always deceptively dull. He practiced writing them all the time. He said he wanted his signatures to be convincing."

No one knew more about practice than Parsifal. Work a routine until it was inside you, until you could feel all fifty-two cards in the deck as separate pieces in your hand. Work it until it no longer looked like work. "You can't always trust what you think, what you know," he would tell Sabine. "But you can always trust your nature. You have to make the tricks your nature."

"Ted Petrie," Sabine said. "That was the third name. There was no alias."

Kitty nodded. "That one was on the list. Ted for Ted Williams and Petrie for Rob Petrie on the Dick Van Dyke show. Rob Williams was on the list, too."

"He must have really wanted out of here," Sabine said.

"Like you wouldn't believe."

Sabine's feet were getting cold and she pulled them up on

the chair. In Los Angeles it had been hard not to take things personally: What reason did he have to lie to her? But in Nebraska, in this kitchen, it didn't seem so much like lying. He had remade his life, and when he was finished it was the only life he knew. In Nebraska this seemed reasonable, smart, a wool coat with toggles. "What about you?" Sabine said. "Did you have a book of names?"

Kitty shrugged. The gesture made her seem oddly girlish. "There were a few. I never had Guy's imagination. He had real vision when it came to these things. Sometimes he made up names for me. Assistant names. Ophelia, Candy—we had a big range."

"Magician's assistant?"

"I was going to have your job, but that was only on the days he was going to be a magician. He was still thinking of a lot of things back then. If he'd decided to go with being a professional baseball player, there wouldn't have been much of a spot for me. Batgirl, maybe."

When Guy was twelve years old, there was no Sabine. Sabine was a child in the Fairfax neighborhood of Los Angeles, drinking orange juice her mother squeezed in their juicer, checking out books from the library on the great castles of the world. No one in Alliance could have imagined Sabine. There was no need for her because her part would be played by Kitty, patient in instruction, diligent in practice. What was needed was a girl who could hold a hat and appear amazed every time a rabbit was extracted. A girl who knew how to smile and wave. Kitty was that girl. Spine straight, shoulders back. Kitty had thought, in the way that children think of such things, that this would be what she would do forever. In truth it was not such a great job, but all these years later Sabine felt she had somehow stolen it from this woman on the other side of the kitchen table. The life that Parsifal had left had come down hard on Kitty—marriage, two children, all that work and endless winters. Every day of it showed on her. But had she left with him at sixteen or seventeen, Sabine could see how she would have been the beautiful girl. Put her in lilac silk, wrap netting and beads around her bare shoulders. She would have done fine. She would have done well.

It was past being late. Even the snow had given up. In every direction there was sleep and stillness and dark. There was no time like this in Los Angeles. It was never this late.

"I'll admit it," Kitty said. "That night we first saw you on Carson, I thought, That was supposed to be me."

"But it could have been," Sabine said, and the thought troubled her. "Just as easily you as me."

"My brother and I were very close when we were growing up," Kitty said. Her voice was tired, as if she'd had enough of going over this. "The plan, our plan, was that we were going to wait out childhood as best we could and then go away together, maybe go to New York, change our names. I know there are kids all over the world who go to bed at night saying that they're going to move to New York and change their names, but you get older and you forget about it, except Guy. He did that, exactly. He did everything he said he was going to do except"—she stopped and smiled to show that she had made peace with everything—"take me with him, and I understand that, you know, I really do. It's like a prison break. There's just a lot better chance of being successful if you go it alone." She put out her cigarette with one clean twist and then lit another one. Her hands were perfectly steady. "That was all a long time ago. I don't think about it now. I have two wonderful boys. I'm very close to my family." She shook her head. "I'm talking too much," she said. "I don't think I'm making sense."

"No," Sabine said, "I understand." Children wanted to change their names and move to New York? She, who had been read to every night, whose hand was held at the crossing of every street, did not understand. Sabine in Los Angeles, where everything in the world was available to her, peaches in January, a symphony orchestra, the Pacific Ocean. It was not the city children dreamed of leaving. It was the one they dreamed of coming to.

"There's a real high price for getting out of a place like this." Kitty smiled. "Alliance, Nebraska, doesn't like to let go once it's got its hooks in you. There aren't any new people coming in to take your place. But Guy did it."

"How?"

"He suffered," Kitty said, making "suffered" sound like a bright word, a fine plan.

"You mean reform school?"

"I mean reform school, I mean killing my father. That's creating a circumstance where you just can't come back."

Sabine sat up in her chair. Her fingers fluttered in front of her face as if something cold and wet had touched her there, and the cigarette, smoked almost down to the filter but still glowing orange, dropped to the floor and rolled beneath the table. "What?"

Kitty looked so startled one would think she had received the news, not given it. "My father," she said.

The words were somewhere in the catalog of words Sabine's mind had memorized. "Your father."

"They told you this," Kitty said, her voice neither a question nor an answer. Her voice was wishful.

"Who?"

"Guy told you, Mother told you, Bertie told you. Fuck." Kitty reached under the table and retrieved the cigarette, which had burned a small black reminder into the green floor. "That mark on the floor," people would say, "that was the moment that Sabine knew."

"No one told me anything."

167

Kitty stubbed out what was left of nothing and went to the sink to wash her hands. When she was through she dried them and washed them again. "Why would no one tell you that?"

"Do you think I know?"

Kitty wrapped her hands in the dish towel hanging from the refrigerator door. Her face was pleading, guilty, and for an instant Sabine thought if there had been a killing, Kitty was the one who'd done it. "I'm sorry," she said. "I didn't mean to tell you. I never thought you didn't know—I mean, that's the story. That's everything. If you know about this family at all, then that's what you know."

"You're saying Guy killed his father." Because it was Guy.

"He did," Kitty said, her voice quiet.

"And this is true. This is a known fact. Did someone see it?" She would not misunderstand this. She would not let him be accused of something impossible.

Kitty raised her head, repeated the list of all in attendance. "I saw it. My mother saw it. Guy saw it. My father saw it." She braced herself against the counter, as if Sabine might come at her.

Was it still snowing? Did the wind still circle around the house? Shouldn't the others be up by now? Shouldn't they wake them?

Sabine asked when.

"New Year's Eve, nineteen sixty-six. Guy was fifteen. Almost sixteen."

She asked how.

"Hit him."

"With his fists?"

Kitty shook her head. She had been the one to tell. It wasn't a secret. Every paper for five hundred miles had printed the story, printed it again when Guy got out of Lowell. "A bat," she said. "His baseball bat. One hit. He didn't mean to kill him, he meant to stop him. He pulled him and slapped him but it was like he was just a fly, like Dad didn't even feel it. And the bat was right there, right by the door, where he always left it. There wasn't one second to think. He was just going to stop him but there was something about the way ..." She stopped and waited and then tried again. "My father was moving very quickly. There was no time. Guy couldn't get a good fix on where, and the bat came down on his neck. He broke his neck. In two minutes, in a minute, he was dead."

"Stop him from what?"

"Kicking Mother on the floor," she said, and then she repeated it because it was the part of the story that so many people would leave out later on. "She was pregnant with Bertie then."

On the night that Phan died, they knew it was over before it happened. Phan couldn't speak anymore but there were sounds that he made, crying, infant sounds. Sounds from the back of his throat in a pitch unlike anything they had heard before. You could hear them no matter where you were in the house, even though they were soft, and they froze you to that spot and broke you there. Phan was blind by then; he could not sit up. All he knew for sure was pain and fear. And he knew that Parsifal was there. Parsifal was not beside the bed, but in the bed. He took off his shirt so that he could hold Phan against his skin. He held him all day that last day, through the stink and the sounds and the terrible fear of what he knew was coming for him, too. He held the man that he loved, rocked him and kissed his hair as he had rocked him and kissed his hair on the first night they were together. Parsifal was afraid of death but he was never afraid of Phan. He loved him. Every minute he loved him.

"Why didn't your mother tell me?"

Kitty bit down on her lip harder than was thoughtful. She

was trying to understand and trying to explain simultaneously. "I'm only guessing, but I imagine at first she didn't want to scare the hell out of you. She wanted you to like her, to like us. She wanted you to come here. My mother does what she has to. She's got experience in that. Then later, she let it slip her mind. Why think about it, you know? This isn't something we talk about. Even then we didn't really talk about it." Kitty closed her eyes, shook her head. "Would you have come if you'd known?"

There, in that second, the exhaustion came, broke down like a wave the way it did on the nights Sabine worked so late. "Christ, I don't know. I would rather have known about it when I was home. I wish I could go and get into my own bed now. I would rather have known about all of this a long time ago, mostly so I wouldn't be hearing it now."

"Guy was the best man I ever knew, even when he was a boy. It was an accident, how he killed him. He didn't mean to."

"I'm sure he didn't mean to," Sabine said. Sure of what? Of nothing. She ran her hands up and down the sleeves of Phan's white cotton pajamas, pajamas she'd picked out herself for him to wear in a hospital in Los Angeles.

"When it happened, when he fell, I thought, God, let him be dead, because if he's not dead he'll get off that floor and kill us all. Mama and Guy, they were half out of their minds, but I went over to him, knelt down on the floor and touched his neck and I felt his pulse kicking away. His eyes were open, not that he was looking at anything. My mother propped up on her hand and she said, 'Is he okay?' And I said, 'He's dead.' I believe those were the last words my father heard, me pronouncing him dead. I said it because I wanted that much for it to be true, so he wouldn't kill Guy for hitting him. Then it was true. Just like that."

"Where," Sabine said, but she couldn't quite make it into a question.

"Where what?"

"Did this happen."

Kitty looked around the room as if trying to remember exactly, and Sabine felt something like a small hand, a child's hand, creeping up the back of her throat. It laid a tiny finger against her tonsils. Kitty pointed, the nondescript corner of green linoleum near the back door. A broom stood in that corner, a pair of snow boots, one turned on its side. "There."

It must have made an excruciating sound, a hollow crack of contact that would have precluded anyone crying out. There would have been the sound that any man would make falling to the floor.... There was Dot, on the floor herself. And where was Guy then, the boy who Parsifal was? Standing above them? Was the bat still locked in both hands, raised above his head while he waited to see what would try to lift itself up, or did the bat swing limply at his side? Did he lean on it, drop it? Did he back away? Cry out? "Why did you stay?"

"Stay where?" Kitty pulled the elastic out of her hair and nervously reshaped her ponytail.

Sabine redirected Kitty's attention by turning her head to that side of the room. "You didn't move."

"Houses in small towns where boys kill their fathers are tough to sell. Kids weren't allowed to walk down our street for months, and when they were allowed, they didn't anyway. And there wasn't any money and there wasn't anyplace to go and when there was, if there was, years and years after that, hell, we didn't even care anymore." Kitty put out her cigarette, though she'd barely smoked this one at all. "Forgive me, but I think I need to stop this now. We can start it again later, but right now I think I'm at my limit."

"It's so late," Sabine said, not having any idea what time

it was but knowing instinctively it was no time to be up. "You must need to get home."

Kitty stood up. She was tall but not as tall as Sabine. "I'm home for tonight."

"You're sleeping here?"

"For tonight," Kitty said. That was another story, a story that neither of them had the energy for. She picked up the saucer and dumped the ashes in a trashcan under the sink. Then she washed the saucer with hot water and soap and put it in the rack to dry. "You go on to bed."

"I'm sleeping in your room."

"No, you're not. I'm on the couch. It's only a few hours. I have to be at work in the morning. It's a good couch."

Sabine had slept on so many couches. In dressing rooms and Parsifal's old apartment and the hospital waiting rooms. She was too tired to even consider hunting up blankets, a spare pillow. Too tired to think of someone else having to do it. "Come on and sleep in your room. There's another bed."

"I'm fine," Kitty said, and raised up her hand.

"I won't talk anymore," Sabine said. "Sleep in your room. I'm going to sleep. It doesn't matter to me."

Kitty meant to decline, but, like her mother and her sister, she was unable to refuse what she wanted. "Maybe then we won't have all those dreams," she said.

They walked down the hall together, dragging their long tails of information. They did not turn on the light and Sabine got into the bed that was unmade and as cold now as the snow on the windowsill. She pulled up her knees, shivered. Kitty took off her jeans and got into the other bed wearing a sweatshirt and anything else she had on. She was lying on her back, and Sabine could see her profile clearly in the light that came in under the door. She recognized it.

"I'm sorry about this," Kitty said.

"I would have found out sooner or later." Sabine turned on her side to face her.

"Who knows, maybe not. You made it this far."

There were so many other things to say, but sleep was pushing Sabine down under the water with both hands. Questions struggled to shape themselves into half sentences, but she didn't have enough energy left to form her mouth around them. Already Kitty's breathing had become regular and deep. Sabine thought that there would be someone waiting for her on the other side. She thought there would be information, but when she went to the snowy field, she waited and waited and she was alone.

Before her eyes opened, Sabine's hand skimmed the crumpled bedspread, looking for the warm bundle of rabbit fur that usually slept near her stomach. When her fingers found nothing there, she remembered and opened her eyes. This was a boy's room, brightly lit because the rolled shades had not been pulled down the night before. There was sun covering the beds and the desk. Sun coming off the hot tin of the baseball trophies and washing over the red plaid rug. She was alone in the room and there was no indication that she hadn't slept there alone all night, never waking, barely turning over. The other twin bed was neatly made, so exactly as it had been when she arrived yesterday that for a minute it seemed that nothing had happened. It wasn't snowing now. Outside the window was divided into two planes, blinding blue and blinding white. The snow was snapped down over the field like an ironed bedsheet. It was a clean, orderly world.

Sabine would have had to stoop to get all the way under the shower but instead she stood there, eyes closed, and let the water beat against her face, her nose almost touching the flat silver disc of the showerhead. Everything in the story had

173

been reversed. Los Angeles was the place to kill someone, Nebraska was where you went later to forget. The openness would hide you. No one would look in Nebraska. Probably every third house on the street sheltered a member of the Witness Protection Program. Yet somehow Parsifal's plan had worked. He moved through the city of patricides without detection. Sabine was waiting to feel devastated by what she knew, but the longer she waited, the more she was sure it wasn't coming. She had taken all her blows with proper heartbreak: Phan's death and then Parsifal's, the surprise of his family, and then all the other surprises. Yet somehow the news that Parsifal had killed his father, killed him, albeit accidentally, with a baseball bat, called up very little this morning. The steam in the bathroom released decades of soap and shampoo smells from the wallpaper. Sabine turned her naked body in a coastal fog of herbal-floral steam and let the water, which was slightly hotter than she could stand, pound on her neck. She wouldn't have told, either. That was where the comfort was, the thing that made sense. Now she understood why he had lied to her, and how it was less a lie than the complete burial of an unmentionable truth. Where we are born is the worst kind of crapshoot. Sabine was not entitled to her birth in Israel, to the loving nest of Fairfax. This could have been her house. She could have picked up the bat, felt the coolness of the wood in her hands. And if she had, she would have cut off the past as well, clipped it like an article from the newspaper so that people might see that something was missing but no one would know what it was. And even as she wished he had told her, so that she might have comforted him, forgiven him, she knew that had it been her life she would not have told him, either; because there never would have been a morning, sitting in the kitchen over coffee, that she could have pushed the plates aside and taken his hands and said, "Listen,

listen to me, there's something I have to tell you." Parsifal, her friend, her husband, had made himself a happy life like someone else would make a seaworthy boat, following step by careful step. The past was no longer his past and it slid away from him like an anchor, unattached, to the mossy darkness of the ocean floor. She had watched him sleep for years, seen his face the first moment he opened his eyes, and she knew he was not troubled by dreams. This was Sabine's comfort, her joy: Parsifal had gotten away. He was in the boat that saved his life, the boat that was Los Angeles. He had let the blue water run over his open hand. It was Sabine who had come back. Sabine who was now at the bottom of that ocean, holding the anchor to her chest.

The water went quickly from hot to lukewarm to cold and forced her out of the shower. In the mirror she saw nothing but thick steam. When she was dried and dressed, she went to the kitchen, where Dot Fetters sat with her coffee, staring into the unbearable brightness of snow.

"I slept so late," Sabine said.

"You were up late," Dot said dully. She did not look up.

Sabine got her coffee in a SEE MOUNT RUSHMORE mug, the rocky faces of three important presidents and one minor one floating in a pale blue oval. "Bertie's gone to school?"

Dot nodded.

"And Kitty?"

"Gone first thing to work. I saw her, though."

"So she told you we met. I liked her. Bertie was right. She looks so much like Parsifal."

"She told me." Dot nodded, agreeing with herself that it was right to acknowledge this. "Told me she told you everything. She was none too pleased about it, either, thought surely I wouldn't have brought you all the way out here without coming clean first. I guess we need to get our stories straight, have a big family conference. Forgive me, but we don't get a lot of new people around here. We've got Haas, but I know for sure Bertie has told him every single thing starting with Moses. He always looks so nervous when he's here." Dot looked up at Sabine for the first time. "Did Kitty tell you anything about Kitty?"

"No."

"Well, I was just checking. Got to see who knows what. Kitty thinks you're going to want to leave today, that I ought to plan on driving you to Scottsbluff."

Sabine thought about the plane, the screaming stewardess, her raccoon eyes melting down her cheeks. "I don't have any plans to go."

Dot chose to drive her point home, just to make sure there was absolutely no misunderstanding it. "Guy killed Albert, right there in that corner." She picked up her cup. The coffee had cooled to a point where she could drink it quickly. "My son, your husband. Baseball bat. Al was dead right away. Ambulance came, and then the police."

"That's what she told me," Sabine said, thinking it pointless to add, more or less. She felt a great well of sympathy for Dot. She was seeing the part where Dot was kicked, not the part where Parsifal stopped it. It wasn't this Dot, but the one in the picture. Small, pretty, hopeful. Sabine got up and went to the refrigerator to find some milk for her coffee. She saw the eggs waiting in their blue depressions on the door and felt that they must be a good omen. She slipped one into the pocket of her sweater. Then she pulled her chair around so that she faced Dot, so that their knees touched. She considered saying that it would be fine if Dot wanted to stop there, but she was afraid Dot would think she wasn't willing to listen, that she was repulsed by what was, in fact, a repulsive story.

"I don't know how much of this you can understand," Dot said. "I know you're plenty smart, but you weren't here and it's hard to get the whole picture sometimes. It's hard for me to understand it all, and I was there."

"I can't imagine how you must have felt." Sabine wanted her coffee but did not pick it up.

"I can tell you," Dot said, pushing her glasses up the bridge of her nose. "I felt bad. I felt bad that my husband was dead, even though I had prayed that he would leave or die for nearly as long as I'd been married to him, and then I felt bad for all those years of prayers. I felt bad my son had been sent off for doing it, for trying to take care of me, because that's when I realized that Guy had always been my favorite, and then I felt bad for having favorites. I felt so bad that when Bertie was born two months after all of this I named her for Albert, which was maybe the worst thing I ever did because it sent a real clear message to Guy about which one of them I was missing most. I handled it poorly, start to finish, but I've got to say life doesn't prepare you for this one. There are no examples to follow, no other families you can look to. It's all running blind. Kitty was so angry at me for not being able to keep Guy at home she said it was all on my account that he was in Lowell, which was true. But what she never understood was how lucky I was to get him in at Lowell. He was close enough to sixteen that there was talk of trying him as an adult, and that's prison, something else altogether. No one seemed to give two cents that he was a good boy trying to stop a grown man. No one cared about what Al had put Guy through all those years. Things then weren't like things now. Your husband beats you, your father beats you, you take it like it's your duty. And if you lift a finger back, well, the law is going to be so deep down your throat you'll feel it in your stomach. So Guy's gone, and I've got Kitty and then this little baby, no money." She shook her head. "Forget it. I'm feeling sorry for myself. I don't like to think like this."

Dot was right about one thing: There were no examples

to follow. No card that read, *I'm so sorry your son killed your husband.* "It seems fair," Sabine said helplessly. "I'm feeling sorry for myself all the time these days."

The snow in the sun had a certain ground-down, glittery brilliance. In the white bed there were flecks of color, bright pinpricks of green and yellow and red, the colors you saw when you pressed in on your eyes as a child. Parsifal may have taken the hardest hit, but he had gotten away, safe, in his boat. Dot and Kitty had stayed, circling that same spot on the kitchen floor. Dot was crying now, and Sabine knew from too much experience that crying in the morning practically guaranteed a headache for the rest of the day. She leaned over and stroked Dot's hair, felt the stiffness of the curls beneath her fingers. Then she did something that she had seen a million times but had only done herself years before on the rarest of occasions. She extracted a hen's egg from Dot's ear.

White and cold, it came out smoothly. She had applied just the right amount of pressure so as to give the feeling of the egg being birthed through the tympanic membrane—not too much pressure, of course. More than once she had seen an amateur crush an egg against the side of some unsuspecting head, a mixture of yolk and white slipping beneath the shirt collar. Sabine, who had been nervous about pulling this off, felt so enormously pleased with herself she considered palming it again and trying the other ear. Dot Fetters touched her ear nervously and then took the egg from Sabine's hand as if it were something more miraculous than her breakfast.

"Oh," she said. "Sabine." She traced her finger across chalky white shell. "This is so sweet of you."

"Plenty more where that came from." Parsifal's line.

"I should have told you."

"You should have."

"In California, it was all so overwhelming. You and that house and the palm trees."

"So what was the story in the Sheraton? What was all that about his being gay?"

Dot tilted her head towards her right shoulder, her ear coming close to the wool of her sweater. "Well, it's true that I knew he was gay and it used to worry me when there was free time to worry. Guy's being gay and his going to Lowell got tied up together in my mind somehow. I think that really sealed things for him. Maybe if he'd been brought up in a better home, stayed in Nebraska, it would have gone different."

"Not a chance," Sabine said.

"You think?"

"He liked men. No one knows that better than me. That's just who he was." Who he was in the bone marrow. He loved the comfort, the sameness of himself. He loved the narrow hips and the rough brush of the cheek.

"So you aren't mad at me? You aren't leaving?"

"I'll leave eventually." Her mind was still on the egg. "But I just got here."

There were too many other things to know. It doesn't just happen that one day the father knocks down the mother and the son knocks down the father and then everybody goes their own way. And besides, even in this short time Sabine had gotten the thing she'd most hoped for: She felt closer to Parsifal here. It should have been in Los Angeles, in the house where they lived, in the clubs where they played, on Mulholland late at night; but all the places she knew him to be only showed up the fact that he was gone. In Nebraska, where she had never imagined him, she could see him everywhere.

"Guy could do the silver dollar really good towards the end." Dot made the movement of taking something out of her own ear. "Smooth as silk. All the kids in the neighborhood waited around for him. They were crazy for it, even if he wouldn't let them keep the dollar. But he never could do the egg. He tried it on me, but I always saw it coming. Not that

I ever told him, of course. But he knew." She patted Sabine's knee, happy and proud, like a parent. "You, on the other hand, wow. I felt that thing coming right out of the center of my head. I don't mean to compare, but you're a lot better at this magic stuff than he ever was."

"Oh, God, no," Sabine said, strangely shaken that such a thing could even be said. "He taught this to me. I don't know a thing about magic that I didn't learn from him. Taking an egg out of somebody's ear, that's nothing. It's a kid's trick. The things he could do ... Well," she said, struck by the loss of all those things, "you wouldn't have believed them."

Dot nodded appreciatively. "I'm not saying he wasn't good. He was wonderful. Good at everything he tried his hand at, baseball and math and cooking, even. All I'm saying is that with this magic business you've got something ..." She pursed her lips together. A mother looking to be completely fair to all parties involved. "Extra. You've got a good move. I think it's because you don't ever draw attention to yourself. Beautiful as you are and elegant, you don't do anything to make people look at you. You don't show off. When you pulled that egg out of my ear, you looked just as surprised about it as me."

"That's because I didn't think I could do it." The praise irritated Sabine. Dot didn't understand. She had missed those crucial twenty-five years in the middle of the story.

"Well, I'll drop it. I just don't want you to sell yourself short, is all." Dot stood up energetically, relieved to have the weight of that conversation thrown off her. She kissed the shiny crown of Sabine's head and held the egg out to her. "I'll make you breakfast. Any way you want it. How about that?"

At ten-thirty Dot left the house to go work in the cafeteria of the high school, where Kitty's boys were in the ninth and eleventh grades. She stood on the side of the hot-food line opposite the students and dished mashed potatoes and creamed corn into indented plates. Sabine believed Dot would be fast and give out fair and equal portions. "It's good work," she told Sabine. "I like seeing the kids. Not just Kitty's boys, but all of them. Kitty says I shouldn't work now that we've got this money, but I'd miss it. What's there to do at home all day? There'll be plenty of time for that." Up until four years ago, Dot did forty hours a week at the Woolrich plant and overtime when she could get it. But then the money that Parsifal sent once in a while became regular and generous, and though she could never ask him if she could count on it, after a while, she did. That was when she quit the plant and went to the high school.

"I hate to leave you here like this," she said when she was bundled inside her coat. "You're sure you don't want to drive me over, keep the car?"

"I'm going to be fine," Sabine said.

"Not that there's much to drive to, really. It's not like leaving someone alone in Los Angeles for the day."

"Go to work."

Dot nodded but didn't go. She stalled at the door, fussing with her gloves. It had been the same way at the airport when she didn't want to get on the plane. She was afraid that if she left Sabine alone she would lose her. Alone, Sabine would start to think. Losing Sabine would be too much like losing Parsifal again. The very idea froze Dot to the floor. "Do you have my number?"

Sabine opened the door. The air was so cold she stepped back as if slapped. Dot, not wanting to chill the whole house, hurried outside.

Sabine waited, craned her neck to see the car turn around the corner. Its exhaust threw a huge plume in the frigid air.

Then she went to the phone and dialed her parents' number. She was glad when it was her father who answered.

"Angel," he said. "You'll never guess who's here, who is sitting right on my lap helping me read the newspaper."

"You'll spoil him."

"No such thing as a spoiled bunny. This is an animal who possesses a limitless capacity for affection."

In Alliance, Sabine curled inside the soft arm of the recliner and held the phone with both hands. She closed her eyes and studied her parents' living room. In the gold morning light of Los Angeles her father, her mother, her rabbit were together, safe, waiting. "How are you, Dad? How's Mother?"

"We, Angel, are always the same. We are fine except for missing you. Tell me how is this Nebraska? Are there many cows?"

Sabine told him. She told him about the snow and the house and Bertie and the snow and Dot and Parsifal's room and meeting Kitty in the middle of the night and the snow and the snow and the snow. She did not tell him about Parsifal's father, although she knew she would when she got home. There could be no association for her parents now between where she was and a violent death, no matter how long ago it had happened. They depended on Sabine to be safe, as she depended on them to be.

"Your mother has gone to the store. I almost went and then I didn't. Maybe it is because I knew you would call."

"Possible," Sabine said.

"That would make your father a mind reader, a sort of magician. Maybe we could get a little act together."

"I'd like that."

"Well, then, come home and we'll get started. Have you seen enough of it now? I wouldn't think you'd need too much time to figure out Nebraska. Are you coming home?"

"I just got here last night."

Her father laughed as if she'd said something terribly funny. She wanted him to laugh. She wanted him to talk to her all day until Dot came home. She wanted to hear the sound of his voice, safe and happy. Her father, who had set his alarm for two A.M. so that he could get up and drive to the Magic Hat to pick her up because it was too late for taking buses home from work.

"I am only wishful thinking. Nebraska is too far away to go for the night, I know that. Should I have seen Nebraska, Sabine-Love? What do you think? Your mother and I talk about vacations. You couldn't list all the places we didn't go."

Sabine lifted her head, opened her eyes. Outside was snow and sky, a house across the street that was a mirror image of the one she was in. "There are better vacation spots."

"Do you think you will know Parsifal better now?" His tone was confidential. Either way it would be their secret.

Sabine's eyes were still open. Parsifal had shoveled the walk that led to that street. He had cut his face open with hedge shears in that yard. He had killed his father in one accidental second and changed the world. She told her father yes.

"Good, then. Good. You are in the right place."

Sabine tried to go back to sleep but could not. No matter how far she pulled the shades down the room wasn't dark. She wandered through the house, studying the pictures on the walls, looking in drawers and finding nothing that mattered. She lay across Parsifal's bed and read an entire Hardy Boys mystery. The plot involved a cave and the kidnaping of the boys' father. She shook the other books to see if anything had been left behind and found the wrapper from a stick of Doublemint gum, but that was probably from one of Kitty's sons.

She poked through the room, lonely and restless. She looked beneath the baseball trophies, behind the pictures on the wall. When half the afternoon was gone she found something that interested her high up in the closet, a Mysto magic kit, the corners of the box held together with strips of masking tape that were themselves so old that they were nothing but dried-out pieces of paper formed to the box. On the cover was a photograph of a somewhat sinister-looking man in a top hat and cape leaning over two children. The children were looking at a small white rabbit and a couple of rubber balls. Their oblivion to the magician seemed dangerous. The live rabbit seemed misleading. This had been the kit that Parsifal talked about, "impressing your friends." Inside there was a set of interlocking rings that reminded her unpleasantly of Sam Spender and her breakdown at the Magic Castle. There was the set of rubber balls pictured on the box, a series of cups for hiding the balls, a black wand with a white tip. It had been so long since Sabine had seen anybody use a wand that it took her a minute to figure out what it was for. There was a deck of cards that didn't belong with the set. From the diagram on the lid it was clear that a few items were missing: the magic twine, the five enchanted coins, and the bouquet of silk flowers. Silk flower bouquets turned ratty the third time you used them. Over thirty years they were bound to have disintegrated.

Sabine skimmed over the instructions, which were nearly impossible to follow. To do the cups and balls the way they described it would take eight arms, dim lighting, and an audience recently injected with Versed. What torture this must have been for a child who had never before seen magic performed. Sabine dropped the papers back in the box. She picked up the rings, hit them together and locked them, snapped them hard and set them free. It wasn't a bad set of rings. Thirty years ago there was more integrity in a cheap box of tricks than there was now. She held all three rings together in one hand and then threw one up in the air, hit it, and locked it on. She threw up the second one, hit it, and then all three were connected. That was a little bit of a trick, to throw them up, to lock them where anyone could see without anyone being able to tell. That had taken them some practice. Sabine used to throw them to Parsifal and he would lock them on in the catch. It took forever to figure out exactly how hard to throw them and at what angle. It took forever again until they could do it in their sleep. Sabine liked the sound they made, the short clang and rattle of the metal running into itself. How long had it taken little Guy Fetters to figure this one out? Was he eight then? Ten? Twelve? She turned the lid of the box over and dropped the balls inside. She covered them with their cups and sent them spinning cup to cup. She hid two extra balls in the stacked cups. It was never just three balls. Sabine had fast hands. She knew how to make her hands go in one direction and the cups skid off in another. She could have made a fortune running three-card monte at Venice Beach. A good assistant had to be that smooth; faster than the magician, even. So fast as to be completely still.

There was no such thing as being a magician's assistant without knowing the trick. People are misguided by the assistant's surprise, the way her mouth opens in childlike delight as her glove is turned into a dove. But if you didn't know how it would all turn out, you wouldn't know where to stand, how to turn yourself to shield the magician's hand or temporarily block the light. And if, in some impossible, unimaginable circumstance, the trick was not explained to the assistant, she would get it sooner or later out of sheer repetition: The egg comes out of your ear, the rabbit is between your breasts, your head is sawed off, it happens over and over and over again. Sooner or later you are bound to know it like your name.

But knowing a trick doesn't mean being able to pull it off. That's what Parsifal didn't understand, or maybe it was just the sickness and sadness at the end of his life that made him forget. Sabine was an encyclopedia of magic, a walking catalog of props, stage directions, cues, but she wasn't a magician. Most people can't be magicians for the same reason they can't be criminals. They have guilty souls. Deception doesn't come naturally. They want to be caught.

There were sounds, rustling and then the stamping of boots coming from the kitchen. Sabine quickly put everything back in the box and slid it under the bed. It was a toy, a game. Forty-one years old, what was she doing on the floor, playing with balls, feeling guilty?

"Sabine?" Dot called from down the hall. "Are you here?"

"I'm here," she said, scrambling up, her left leg sound asleep. She limped down the hall, hitting her thigh with her fist.

"I've got a real treat," Dot said.

When Sabine rounded into the kitchen, there was Dot and, on either side of her, a boy. Each was tall. Each was beautiful, so red faced from the cold that he appeared to be just that instant awake. They were swaddled in clothing, plaid wool scarves wrapped half around necks, wool sweaters over plaid shirts, down vests over wool sweaters, and coats that looked to be borrowed from Admiral Byrd. Their hands were bare and chapped. The taller of the two wore a blue knit hat. They resembled their uncle at that time in his life when Sabine had first met him, when she first saw him take a rabbit from his shirt cuff. Beautiful.

"This is How," Dot said, putting her arm recklessly around the taller, darker of the two. "And this is Guy." Guy, slightly fairer, was smaller only from being two years younger. His body's clear intention was to outreach his brother's. When his grandmother embraced him he stiffened slightly. "Boys, this is your Aunt Sabine."

"Aunt Sabine?" she said.

"Well, you're their uncle's wife. That's how it works. Do you think 'Mrs. Parsifal' would be better? I should have asked you first."

Sabine puzzled over it. Certainly not "Mrs. Parsifal." But "Aunt Sabine"? "Aunt Sabine, or Sabine, either one," she said, and stepped forward to shake their hands, both of them cold and impossibly large. Both of them with nails bitten nervously down to the quick.

" 'Lo," How said. (Howard? Sabine thought. Doesn't anybody around here go by their name?) He shook her hand gently, awkwardly, as if the occasion to shake a woman's hand had not come up in his life until now.

"Hello," said Guy. His shake was more defined. He looked at her clearly for a minute before dropping his eyes back to the floor.

"They've been so excited about coming over to meet you," Dot said, completely oblivious to their lack of excitement. Or maybe that was just the way boys were at that age. Sabine couldn't remember. She hadn't been around teenagers since she was one herself, and even then she hadn't had much of an understanding of them as a group. She felt as if she were trying to speak to someone without knowing a word of their language. She fought an impulse to raise her voice.

"Parsifal, your uncle, he would have loved to have met you." He would have. These handsome boys, Kitty's boys, would have thrilled him.

"Parsifal," Guy said. "Mom told us he changed his name."

"He was a magician. That was the name he used for the act, and then it turned into the name he used all the time." Was she pitching this too low? How much information did these boys have, anyway? *Uncle Guy killed Grandpa years and years before you were born, not two feet from where you're standing.*

"I was named for him," Guy said, making the connection just in case she'd missed it.

"Then you're lucky," Sabine said.

"I made cookies," Dot said. "Could I interest you boys in some cookies and milk?"

To Sabine this seemed ridiculous, a parody of some television idea of what goes on between grandmothers and grandsons, but the boys brightened considerably at the mention of food. They made agreeable sounds that were not exactly words, took off their coats, and sat down at the table while Dot poured tall glasses of milk as white as their young teeth.

"So what did you do all afternoon?" Dot said, laying cookies out on a plate.

"Looked around at Parsifal's things. I read a book." Sabine hoped she wouldn't be asked what book she'd read, although she wondered if the Hardy Boys would be a topic for conversation.

"Aunt Bertie says you've got a great place out in L.A.," Guy said.

Sabine looked back at him, the salmon flush of his cheeks, the brilliance of such thick, straight hair. "It's a nice house."

"I'd like to go to L.A.," he said. "Maybe get a band together. Could I visit sometime?"

"Sure," Sabine said, although she couldn't imagine what you did with a teenager if he wasn't your teenager. The chance that a boy from Nebraska would meet with a significantly tragic outcome in Los Angeles seemed nearly certain. And then she remembered Parsifal.

"What about you, How?" Dot said. "Any interest in Los Angeles?"

"He'd never go," his brother said for him.

"I'd go," How said. His cheeks were so red he looked as if he'd been slapped. His mouth was red. His darker hair waved like his uncle's. Uncle—she could not get used to the word. He never knew he was an uncle, but couldn't he have guessed as much?

"I've got plenty of room," Sabine said. "You could both come."

"I'm not baby-sitting him," Guy said.

"Guy." Dot made his name long and low, getting the most out of the three letters.

"Nobody asked you to," How said, quiet.

"He's never going anywhere," Guy said to Sabine. He was like a dog. He was on the scent now and could not let go. "He's a mama's boy."

The absurdity of the insult caught Sabine so off-guard that she smiled hugely before realizing that a smile was not appropriate. This was the cut? The terrible accusation? What could be better, she thought, than a mama's boy? How was out of his chair as quick as Sabine's smile, his body moving over the table towards his brother like it was a thing over which he had absolutely no control. Guy, possibly tougher, was still smaller, and he leaned backwards, away from what was coming.

When Sabine spoke the room froze. She possessed an intrinsic understanding of men. It was from a lifetime of being beautiful, even to children. "Your mother? I met your mother last night. Did you know that?" The sound of her voice soothed them, made them nearly sleepy. The boys dropped back in their chairs. "The middle of the night, I woke up and she was in the kitchen. She reminded me so much of your uncle. They look so much alike. You look like him when he was young," she said, giving that prize to How. "I had never met your mother before, but she was so much like her brother that I felt like I knew her."

They did not hear her words as much as absorb them.

Magic was less about surprise than it was about control. You lead them in one direction and then come up behind their backs. They watch you, at every turn they will be suspicious, but you give them decoys. People long to be amazed, even as they fight it. Once you amaze them, you own them. What was nearly a fistfight on top of the kitchen table was now completely forgotten. Like the flash floods in Twenty-Nine Palms, it surprised them both coming and going.

"How long will you be here?" How said, grateful now.

"I'm not sure. We'll see how it goes."

It was the wrong thing to say. Dot and the boys all lowered their heads, as if his or her own bad behavior might be the thing that would send Sabine packing.

"Why don't you boys clear out for a while, and Sabine will help me get started on supper. Do you think you can watch a little television without killing each other?"

"Sure thing," Guy said. He stood up, stretched, and took a cookie from his brother's plate. His brother, feeling so recently vindicated, decided to let it pass. They walked out of the room together without ever picking up their feet.

Dot watched them go, shaking her head. "I love Guy, but that boy is turning into his father," she whispered to Sabine. "I'd like to give him a good smack sometimes."

"Do you want to give his father a good smack, too?"

Dot raised her hands in innocence. "Don't even get me started on that one."

"They seem like nice boys."

"They are. Good boys. How is like Guy—your Guy. Doesn't have his personality, but he's got the sweetness to him. In a kid that age it seems like a miracle. I wouldn't want to have kids now. There's too much going on in the world. It would all be too hard for them." As if harder things had been invented since her children were growing up.

Dot squatted down and shoved her ᵇ
cabinet beneath the sink. She said someth
was no telling what.

"What?"

She leaned back slightly but kept he
"Did Guy ever talk about having childre
still turned away. "I mean—I know, we
want kids?"

Not only did he not want them, he hated them. He had
rolled his eyes in restaurants, on planes. He had taken Sabine's
arm tightly when he saw one on the street, whispered to her
dramatically, "Well, at least we were spared that." The mocking was so bitter and constant that in the years that Sabine
thought she wanted a child she never once spoke of it. She
bit down and waited until it passed. But so many years later,
when it was Phan who wanted a child, there were no more
jokes. "You feel differently when it's your own," Parsifal told
Sabine, explaining his sudden change of heart. They talked
about adopting, about surrogate mothers. They even talked
about Sabine, and while she knew it would be disastrous for
her, she would have leapt at the chance. It wasn't too long
after that that Phan had a blood test and none of them mentioned children again.

"No," Sabine said. "He didn't want children."

Dot raised herself out of the cabinet, white rose potatoes
filling both of her hands. "I think that's my fault. He was afraid
he was going to turn out like his parents. He would have been
a good father. You could tell by the way he was with his sister.
He had it in him. It's too bad." She looked at Sabine, suddenly
aware. "That's why you never got to have children. You were
waiting around on him."

"No." Sabine took the potatoes from her. "I never wanted
them, either."

191

't believe you."

"ow much do the boys know about Parsifal?" Sabine
d in the Fetters family spirit of keeping the story straight.

Dot was peeling now. Her hands were as round and white
as the potatoes. "They know about what happened with
Albert. That's absolute legend around here. Nobody lives in
Alliance without hearing about that. And even if by some miracle the boys missed it at school, their father isn't above
screaming it out in a fight, reminding Kitty she comes from a
murdering lot." Dot tried to throw the sentence off cavalierly,
but the sound of it saddened her and she set the peeler down
on the sink. "Kitty's always done a lot to counteract all that.
She told the boys what happened, how it wasn't Guy's fault
but that he had to go to Lowell anyway. Lowell's got real
power when you're a boy. That's the big threat, the worst
thing that can happen to you. And of course it makes perfect
sense to them that somebody would want to leave this place
and never come back, especially if the whole town was talking
about you. That one gave them no problems at all."

"And the rest of it?"

Dot took a quick look around the door to make sure the
boys were stationed in front of the television set, volume up
high. "We never told them Guy was gay. That's real important
to Kitty. If Howard hounds her about having a murderer for
a brother, she'd never hear the end of it if he found out he
was a queer, too. God help us all. At least Howard can
semirespect the notion of killing somebody. I don't think he
was any too crazy about his old man, either."

Sabine looked at her. She put her own potato down.

"Oh, come on," Dot said. "I know what you're thinking.
You've got to be honest about who you are—Guy was always
honest and all. But I'm telling you, there's more than that.
You've got to think about who you're living with."

"Parsifal lived with it."

"Sabine, some things you just don't tell."

In Southern California there was very little that went unsaid. People lived their lives, heads up, in the bright sun. Take it or leave it. "It's your own business," Sabine said. "I'm not going to volunteer information."

Dot smiled, relieved. "That's all I'm asking."

Everything happened early in those short winter months. Dot and the boys were home at three o'clock, Bertie was in by four. At five o'clock the moon was visible in the trees and dinner did not seem out of the question. The darkness pushed them together. The boys grew quiet, abandoning television for homework when the news came on. Dot, Bertie, and Sabine stayed at the sink, chopping vegetables, their heads nearly touching. Sabine was glad to have a moment when the three of them were together. To her it seemed just like Los Angeles, although it was nothing like Los Angeles.

As soon as they finished eating, Kitty arrived, her face luminous in the dark window. She waved to them from the cold before opening the door. What would it have been like to see her standing next to Parsifal? Were they really so much alike, or did Sabine's loneliness just make them that way? Kitty looked better than she had last night. The cold flushed her cheeks. How stood up to help his mother off with her coat.

"School okay?" she said.

"All right." How held her small coat close to his chest, as if he were suddenly cold.

Kitty picked up a circle of carrot from the top of the salad bowl. "This is what I meant to do last night."

"Enough about last night," Dot said, and smiled. "You've come just in time. We're going to watch the video."

"A movie?" Sabine asked. Phan loved old American

movies, Cary Grant and Joseph Cotten. Watching videos at home was one of the things that Parsifal did with Phan. It was something he did not do later, without him.

"A movie, and you're the star," Dot said, stacking the dishes into impossible piles.

"It's your Carson show with Guy," Bertie said. "We thought you'd want to see it."

"You've seen that a million times," Sabine said, feeling breathless because she so clearly remembered being breathless when they were on the show. "I'll watch it tomorrow."

Dot looked at her, her face stricken, her hands holding tightly to the plates. "I thought..."

The boys twisted their napkins in their laps.

"This is religion." Kitty pushed back from the table and stretched. "We watch it together. It's five minutes. We won't watch the whole show. The whole show we do maybe once a year. Around Christmas, usually. We just saw it not too long ago. Joan Rivers doesn't hold up to repeated viewing. You do."

"It's cool," Guy said, pushing back his hair with both hands. "He looks like us."

First there had been the invitation to audition. A scout had seen them doing a weekend show in Las Vegas. They were opening for Liberace after his regular magician was swiped on the cheek by his own tiger during rehearsals. "If you're going to work with animals, remember," Parsifal had told her on the plane going out there. "People, rabbits, and birds. Little birds." After the show, a bald man with a suntan and a sports coat met them backstage. "Next Thursday." He handed Parsifal a business card. "I think the boss will like you. You come, too, sweetie," he said to Sabine, tapping a careless hand on her hip. "Did you get her here or is she yours?" People thought that magicians' assistants were coat-check girls, Tropicana dancers off for the night.

"Mine," Parsifal said absently, looking at the card.

"Yours?" Sabine said.

The man laughed, clamped a firm hand down on Parsifal's shoulder. In Las Vegas everything was for sale. People were used to touching. "She's yours, all right. I'll see you next week."

Sabine turned to Parsifal and the tiny gold beads that dangled from her torso turned with her. He held up the card to stop her. As quickly as she saw the word, there were tears in her eyes.

Carson.

Trial lawyers wait for their first murder case, painters for a show at the L.A. Contemporary. Actresses wait for feature films, weekly sitcoms, cat food commercials, or a well-attended party. Magicians waited for Carson. There was very little justice. If Carson went down to the Magic Castle after *The Tonight Show*, had a couple of drinks, there was no telling what assistant-sawing half-rate would be invited back to national television. Still, who could complain? If it weren't for Carson, the only magician America would have access to would have been Doug Henning, his big-toothed grin floating through the occasional special.

The producers told them to come in costume. Sabine picked her favorite, lilac with blue satin trim. She held it up in front of her, hugged the waist to her waist. "Wear the red," Parsifal had said to her, so distracted that all he could see was a blur of color. She wasn't sure she wanted to have her parents see her on television wearing the red.

When they arrived for the audition, they couldn't find the man who had given them the card, only a restless crowd of hopefuls packed into the greenroom. The comics were nervous, overeager. The singers sat by themselves, mouthing words but making no sounds. There was a magician there they knew who called himself Oliver Twist, but when they went to him, Twist picked up his things and waited in the hall.

"I'm so nervous," Parsifal whispered. "I'm afraid my hands will shake."

"Okay," Bertie said. "It's all cued up. Hit the lights."

Dot was in her chair. Bertie rushed back to take her place at the end of the couch—Bertie, Kitty, and then Sabine. Guy was in the other chair and How stretched out on the floor in front of their feet like a giant dog. Kitty leaned over to Sabine, whispered, "I'm glad you decided not to go. I've felt terrible all day."

"Sh," Dot said. "It's coming."

Kitty, shushed, slipped her hand over Sabine's and squeezed. Sabine was surprised to find she felt the touch travel all the way up her arm.

Parsifal had put down the phone and thrown his arms around Sabine's back, pulling her in to him so quickly her feet left the floor. "We're in," he said. "We're in, we're in."

"Play!" Guy said, and hit the button.

There was applause for someone. Carson was at his desk, smiling his closed-mouth smile that was slightly embarrassed and completely knowing. His pencil balanced delicately between his fingers. Sabine remembered suddenly his handsome face, how he had that particular glow of celebrity that everyone recognized but no one could quite identify. He was wearing a tan suit. His gray hair was cut close.

Of course Parsifal was in love with him.

"When we come back, we have a big treat. For the first time on the show, Parsifal the Magician." Carson flipped over his pencil and deftly hit the eraser two times on the desk as if to drive the point home. "So don't go away." Doc

Severinsen's band struck up some music that Sabine remembered as completely deafening when she was in the room with it, but on television it seemed quite reasonable. Then the screen was covered by a drawing of a television being chased by a floor lamp. Both of their plugs were undone and whipped up in the air behind them, small, two-pronged tails. The television screen said, THE TONIGHT SHOW, STARRING JOHNNY CARSON. As if they didn't know.

For an instant there was a color field with a bull's-eye on it. Three, two, one. "That's where they put the commercial," Guy told Sabine. "We didn't get the commercial."

Behind a multicolored curtain, a man with a headset and a clipboard had stood beside them. They had been prepped, drilled, rehearsed, but still he went over it all one more time. When the curtain opened they were to go, no questions asked. When the curtain opened again they would come back. Joan Rivers and Olivia Newton-John were sitting on the sofa next to Johnny Carson. They were lucky that Carson was hosting the show himself that night. It could well have been Joan Rivers, host, instead of Joan Rivers, guest. When there was a substitute host the numbers went down precipitously.

Parsifal and Sabine held hands tightly and leaned into each other. "Three, two . . . ," the man with the headset told them, but instead of saying *one* he pointed viciously at the opening of the curtain. Get out, was the general gist of it. Get out there.

"There you are," Kitty said.

Dot's eyes spilled over the second she saw them. She pressed her fingers to her mouth.

"She always cries," Kitty whispered, her breath a layer of wintergreen mint over a layer of tobacco. "Even if she watches it ten times a day, and some days she does."

Young. That was the only word. They were young. Slim

and tall, handsome and beautiful. Young. Parsifal shone with health. It came like light from his skin. He was an advertisement for milk. For fresh air and sunshine. For life in beautiful Southern California. Sabine had forgotten that such health had ever existed, in him or in the world. It hurt her. She had lost everything without understanding. The life she wanted was on television now. His youth, his life. This was the way she had felt when she was a teenager and saw a man walk on the moon. It was so spectacular that you knew it had to be faked. She could not look away from the perfect structure of Parsifal's bones to see the girl beside him. She saw only her outline, a shadow in red.

"Man," Bertie said, "are you good-looking or what? Not a lot of women who could pull that outfit off."

"I wouldn't have looked good in that when I was fifteen years old," Kitty said.

"Hush," Dot said. "This is the part."

"Good evening," Parsifal said, his voice spilling over the room. "Thank you."

As they walked forward a black velvet curtain crept down unnoticed over the bright silk stripes. The audience had been applauding thunderously, screeching their appreciation for two unknown performers who had done nothing to earn it. Sabine hadn't understood at the time. She was afraid they were mocking. But now she could see it was their youth that was being cheered, their beauty. That was why they got the job. It was her legs, the sweep of his hair off his high forehead. It was something they projected together but not apart. They were in love, or at least that was how it looked on television.

"My name is Parsifal, and this is my assistant, Sabine." The camera panned to her face and then stayed there for an impossibly long time. Her mouth was wide and painted the red of her costume. Her eyes were as dark as her hair.

"Look at you," Kitty said. As she said it the face on the television broke into a blinding smile, riches of perfect white teeth.

Sabine looked hard at the face. She could identify it as beautiful because it knew nothing. That face believed the man beside her on the stage would always be beside her, believed she would always be that young. No one had explained anything at that point.

The camera pulled away abruptly, a man caught staring.

Parsifal put a board between two chairs, a blanket over the board. He took Sabine's hand and helped her lie down. She followed obediently, did everything he wanted. There was something about the sight of her body stretched out, so relaxed, eyes closed, that embarrassed her. So much leg. Parsifal crossed her arms over her chest. She did not help him, so limp and doll-like she didn't know enough to fold her own arms. He bent over to kiss her forehead, at which point her heavy eyelids dropped closed and she was assumed to be in a trance; and maybe for a moment she was, because she could not remember the feel of that kiss.

Levitation was invented by John Nevil Maskelyne in 1867. He manually placed his wife in the air. The trick then went to Harry Kellar, who sold it, along with the rest of his act, to Howard Thurston upon retirement. After Thurston, it went to Harry Blackstone. Sabine soothed herself with facts, gave her mind over to trivia. Too many people had the trick now. It wasn't enough to just do it straight anymore. They had all seen a girl in the air.

Parsifal wrapped her in a blanket and tied it down. He ran a hand through the air across the top of her and beneath her, and then he took the board away so that her head stayed on one chair and her feet on the other and her poker-straight body rested in between. It was a good effect, but the audience hardly found it miraculous. In fact, this was the hardest part of the trick, because Sabine was rigid; she was balanced between two chairs weighted down to hold her steady. Parsifal and Sabine looked careless, but every inch was plotted, retraced, mastered. On the television in Nebraska, Sabine watched the way her feet slipped into the blanket. There would have been no way to catch them. No way to tell the truth of their movement. The black velvet curtain made everything a mystery. Parsifal's hands swept over her, beneath her. Then he pulled away the bottom chair and held her feet in his hands. Look at the tenderness on his face, the tenderness for her! He lifted her feet to his chest, testing her at first, and then trusting, going higher and higher. He lifted her feet over his head, walked his hands down the backs of her legs and slowly to her back. His hands moved down and her feet lifted higher, and then impossibly high, until Sabine was balanced, tightly wrapped like a papoose, on the very crown of her head on the back of one chair. Oh, the audience loved this. On her head, Sabine heard the applause. The crowd in the living room loved it, too; the women clapped politely, both of the boys made appreciative sounds. Parsifal, silent, kept just the tips of his fingers on her back to give the appearance of steadying her, when in truth Sabine steadied herself. His face was the very picture of caution. So tentatively, so delicately, he pulled his hand away and then put it quickly back; then, with more confidence, took it away again and again, and then altogether. Sabine, eyes closed, hair fanning over the top of the chair, was Venus inverted. All the work of this trick was hers, staying perfectly still, asleep. Her face was easy, peaceful. She kept herself from swaying, took shallow breaths through her nose while every muscle ripped apart from its neighbor. From the studio audience in Burbank, more hearty applause. Parsifal stepped away from her. For a minute she was forgotten while he bowed. Sabine remembered feeling like the top of her head was going to crack open. Then he saw her again. He studied her, studied the chair. He bent from the waist and, with great effort, lifted the chair with the balanced Sabine up into the air with both hands; but the higher up she went, the lighter she became. Only the chair was heavy. Parsifal the actor. Sabine the gymnast. At waist level Parsifal took a hand away, and then he lifted the chair above his head. The camera pulled back and back. He was tall, and then there was the chair, and then tall Sabine, her toes pointing into the hot stage lights. The audience was not used to looking so far up, and it thrilled them. They were applauding wildly now. Parsifal bowed again, still balancing. Then he ran the entire trick in reverse. The chair grew heavier as it came down. He brought back the second chair and the board. He tipped her down, suddenly careful with this woman he had been waving like a flag. Flat on her back, all her weight returned, he unwrapped her, flicking off the blanket, uncrossing her arms. Gently, sweetly, he kissed her forehead again, at which point the magnificent eyes fluttered and opened. The generous smile spread across her face. With his help, she sat up and stood, waved and bowed. It was a beautiful trick, but it took the whole five minutes they were allotted. They were good, Parsifal and Sabine, their abilities to amaze were limitless. There were hundreds more tricks they weren't given time for.

Then Johnny Carson was with them, applauding as he walked across the stage. This was a clear sign of approval. Usually he thanked people from the distance of his desk. They were not stars. They would not be invited to sit on the couch with Joan Rivers and Olivia Newton-John.

"Great," he said, shaking Parsifal's hand. "Just great. That's one trick you wouldn't want to blow."

"I haven't dropped her yet," Parsifal said. An unrehearsed line. He sounded witty, at ease.

Then Johnny Carson turned to Sabine. "And I certainly hope you'll come back to see us."

(In fact, two days later Mr. Carson's secretary called Sabine at home and said that her employer would like the pleasure of Sabine's company at dinner. She declined.)

And then came her line. "Thank you, Mr. Carson." Again the camera held her.

Johnny Carson clapped his hands together, pointed out to the cameras, said blithely, "Right back." Doc's band struck up the theme song. More applause. The color field returned, the series of numbers.

How rolled towards the VCR and shut it off. They sat for a while in the darkness, a reverential silence that no one wanted to break. Kitty was right: religion.

"Proudest moment of my life," Dot said finally, blowing her nose.

"You just happened to be watching Johnny Carson that night?" Sabine asked. What were the chances?

"Mama watched Carson every night," Bertie said. "When he had his last show, we all sat here and cried our eyes out."

Sabine had watched the last show with Parsifal and Phan. Parsifal cried. Maybe it was hereditary.

"Johnny Carson grew up in Nebraska," Dot said.

"So," Guy said, clicking on the light next to his chair so that he could get a good look at Sabine. "How'd you do it?"

"We auditioned," she said, knowing what he meant. "We had to go back twice."

"The trick. How did you balance there for so long? How did he lift you over his head? I've been watching this since I was a little kid and I never have been able to figure it out."

The room pressed towards her. They were all wanting to know. Guy was just the one who had asked. Maybe this was the reason they'd come looking for her in the first place. Year after year of watching the same magic trick and not being able to figure it out would make any family restless. "I can't tell you that," Sabine said.

"Why not?" How propped up on one elbow. His face was full of the painful earnestness of a good person receiving bad news.

"That's the whole point, that's why it's a good trick, because you can't figure it out."

"You can tell us," Guy said.

"I can't. I won't," Sabine said. Was this what Parsifal had felt? All of the attention was on her. Everyone wanting the answer that only she had. No one had ever asked her how the tricks were done before, because what would the point be, asking the assistant when the magician was right there? No one asked her because no one even considered that she might know.

"You're not going to do it anymore," Guy said, his voice taking on just the slightest edge of a whine. "We're never going to tell."

"I was the only person your uncle ever explained the tricks to and he wouldn't have told me if he didn't absolutely have to. Magicians take this very seriously. It's like a code of honor for them." Listen to her, wouldn't Parsifal be laughing now. You never told because people wanted so desperately to know. They wanted what you had and therefore what you had was all the power. Who would give that up? What possible benefit could there ever be in telling? A minute of gratitude and then the dull falling away, the boredom that always followed knowledge. For fifteen years the Fetters had wanted to know how Parsifal balanced Sabine on the top of a chair. Waiting for the answer hadn't done them any harm.

"I bet he told plenty of people," Kitty said. "I bet they were just people he liked better than us."

A flicker of hurt went over Dot's face, a remnant of a very old fight.

"I promise you," Sabine said. "He never told anyone. He didn't even tell Phan how it worked."

The women tensed. Kitty pressed her hands between her knees.

"Who's Phan?" How said.

So she had made a mistake. Did they think this was hard? Did they think she didn't know how to get out? "He was my best friend. He came to all our shows. I wanted to tell him how we did some things, just a couple of tricks, but your uncle said no."

"What kind of name is Phan?" Guy said. The word came out of his mouth like something that tasted bad.

"Vietnamese."

"Don't make fun," Dot said, relieved. "You can bet there are a group of Vietnamese sitting around right now wondering about a family in Nebraska who've got people named Guy and Dot."

"And How," said How.

"Bertie and Kitty," Bertie said.

Hearing her own name, Kitty started and looked at her watch. "I've got to get you boys home. It's late."

How rolled over on his stomach and laid his head down on crossed arms. Guy leaned back in his chair, as if meaning to dig himself deeper into the upholstery. Kitty stood and clapped her hands together as if she were rounding up cattle. "Come on, let's go."

Guy stretched, pushing his long arms out in front of him, and then both boys closed their eyes. "For God's sake," Dot said, standing up and kicking How lightly on the leg. "Listen to your mother. Get up and go home."

"I'm not going until she tells us how they got her on her

head," Guy said. Eyes closed, Guy looked like a huge child, a three-year-old whose pink cheeks and round lips were large beyond reason.

"You can sit there all night if you want to," Sabine said. "It's fine with me if you stay."

And they might have. It was impossible to gauge their seriousness. But before there was time to try to talk them into getting up, someone was knocking on the front door, and long before there was time to answer the door, they had barely turned their heads in the direction of the sound, the man who was outside simply walked in, as if the knock had been less a request for entry than an announcement of it. He kept his head down and shook dramatically from the cold, slapping his bare, open hands against his arms, trying to coax the circulation up again. He was wearing a denim jacket over a sweatshirt. It was not enough. "Damn," he said. "Some night to be out in the cold looking for your family."

Now the boys' eyes were open. How sat up. They looked like deer, ears pricked and alert, their noses sniffing the air.

"I said we'd be home by eight." Kitty lifted her wrist towards the man, showing her watch as proof. "We'll be home by eight."

"Well, you said you had company. I thought it would be nice if I came over and met your company." If he had come to see Sabine, he had not yet noticed her. His attention was fixed on his boots, which were miraculously free of snow.

"Then you're not out looking for your family in the cold," Kitty corrected. She held her shoulders back and leaned slightly in towards the man. "Now shut the door."

Mrs. Howard Plate (*Kitty*), that's what the lawyer's papers had said. Which would make this Mr. Howard Plate. Mr. Howard Plate was big like his sons, with hair that might have been red when he was their age and now was that colorless sandy brown that red hair can become. But it was his face that drew attention, the way it was fine on one side and collapsed on the other, as if he had been hit very hard and the shape of the fist in question was still lodged beneath his left eye. It had the quality of something distinctly broken and poorly repaired. The bad light cast by the living room lamps threw a shadow into the cave of his cheek, where a random interlacing of scars ended and began. He slipped one hand behind his neck and pulled down hard, as if he were trying to make himself smaller. "Do you want me to go?"

"Sabine," Dot said, "before this gets any worse, let me introduce you to my son-in-law. This is Howard Plate. Howard, you've heard all about Sabine, Guy's wife."

"I hear you've got a big house in Los Angeles," Howard Plate said, looking at her. Seen straight on, it was not such a bad face. It was the kind of face that in Los Angeles could make him seem exotic but in Nebraska only made him look poor.

"It's a good-sized house," Sabine said. She held out her hand and he shook it. It was a big hand, rough on the palm and cold as the iron railing around the front porch. Did people have something against gloves?

"Don't bother her about the size of her house," Kitty said. If she had left five minutes before then her car wouldn't have been in the driveway and Howard would have slowed down but not stopped. He would have driven on home when he didn't see her there.

"Well, since Dot and Bertie came back from California that's all I hear about, what a big house she's got. There's no crime in having a nice house, is there?" He looked at Sabine, turning slightly to show her the better-looking part of himself. "I never met Kitty's brother. We all thought he was dead forever—I mean, a long time before he was dead. So it's been a real surprise finding out that he's been alive all this time and doing so well. Most people come and visit their families when they do well. They're proud of what they've got."

Sabine realized that all of this was meant to insult her, that the great wave of awkwardness that came up from every corner of the room, save Howard Plate's, was the embarrassment generated on her behalf. But Sabine herself, still standing after the handshake, didn't feel insulted or embarrassed. She only felt a vaguely tired sort of depression because it wasn't summer, because she wasn't sitting next to the pool underneath the shade of the big red umbrella with Phan while Parsifal brought out three tall Beefeater tonics. How he loved to bring them out with a knife and walk to the lime tree and snap one off, slice through the thin green skin right there on the glass-topped table. "You're really living when you're living off the land," he'd say. He stirred the drink again with the knifepoint, the fuzzy effervescence of very fresh tonic looking celebratory although at the time they'd thought there was nothing in particular to celebrate. What she wanted to say to Howard Plate, what she could not say and he could not possibly understand, was this: If you've had good gin on a hot day in Southern California with the people you love, you forget Nebraska. The two things cannot coexist. The stronger, better of the two wins out.

"Well, that's it for me," Bertie said, getting up heavily from the couch. "I'm going over to see Haas. You have a good evening." In her voice there was a tremble of barely contained rage. Every muscle in her body strained to keep her from taking on Howard Plate.

"Bertie, don't go," her sister said. She reached up for her wrist, but Bertie deftly moved her hand aside so that even when Kitty stretched, she fell short.

"Take Haas some cookies," Dot said. "There's a bag of them on the kitchen counter."

"I'll be back by twelve." They all watched her go. In the

lamplight Bertie's hair seemed like almost too much luxury, all those brown-and-yellow tangled curls. Haas would separate each one, comb it out gently.

"She just can't wait to get married," Howard Plate said to Sabine, as if he were saying something dirty.

"I know," Sabine said. "I remember that feeling exactly."

Howard sat down on the couch in the warm spot that Bertie had left, and Sabine took her place on the other side of Kitty, but the swap of Bertie for Howard Plate had stripped everyone in the room of their language skills. Even Dot seemed at a loss as to how to rally the conversation. "Did you eat?" she asked Howard finally.

"I did."

The room fit them snugly now, three women, two such large boys, a man that none of them wanted to talk to. With all the windows locked tight, storm windows down, window seals caulked, curtains drawn, Sabine became aware of how much oxygen they were all taking in.

"Did you watch the video?" Howard Plate asked his wife.

Kitty nodded without bothering to look over, as if the question had been a particularly boring one.

"Sabine had never seen it," Dot said. "Can you imagine that?"

"You were on television and you never saw it?"

Sabine twisted her wedding ring around and around on her thin finger. "The show wasn't live. They taped in the afternoon, so we were home to watch it that night. I saw it the night it was on." But the night it was on they'd had a party. Not magicians, whose feelings were too easily hurt. They would have said that Carson was trash magic and they had no interest in lowering themselves to it. This was years before Phan. Parsifal lived in that bright apartment in West Hollywood, which on that night was full of rug dealers, architects, neighbors, old boyfriends of Parsifal's, and one or two of Sabine's, people who whistled at the television set and pounded on the floor when their faces filled the screen. That was what Sabine remembered, not how they looked. When she saw the tape tonight there had been no part of it that struck her as familiar.

"How'd you do that trick, anyway?" Howard Plate said.

All this time the boys had stayed quiet, not crossing their legs or shifting their weight. Even their breathing had seemed shallow, like they were balanced on a high and precarious branch of a tree. But at their father's question How laughed, and then Guy laughed with him.

"What?"

"I think we should get these boys home," Kitty said. She looked at her mama's boy, her favorite. "You about ready?"

"Sure," How said, the color up in his face.

"Somebody going to tell me what's funny?"

Kitty reached over and patted her husband on the knee, giving him that small acknowledgment. "We'll tell you on the way home."

"I've barely met your company," Howard Plate said. He had not been in the house long enough to get completely warm, and already it was time to go.

Sabine shrugged and smiled, as if the meeting had been a pleasure, as if she would try and hide her disappointment at this early departure. "I'm not going anywhere for a while."

Howard Plate said he was glad to hear that. The boys drew themselves up to their full standing heights. How was taller than his father, just slightly wider through the shoulders, as he was thinner in the waist. Guy, who seemed to be busy growing while the rest of the group wasted the evening in talk, was fast gaining on them both.

While the Plates were replacing all their clothes in the

proper order, Guy said he couldn't find his scarf and a search was launched. That's when How touched Sabine's arm and motioned for her to follow him into the hall. She did, followed him all the way to the end, past all the bedroom doors. They left the lights off. How stood very close to Sabine and whispered in her ear. "I have to ask you."

"What?" Sabine whispered back.

"Maybe—it wasn't just a trick?" His voice was soft and uncertain, desperate that neither a father nor a brother could overhear.

"What do you mean?" She could smell him, warm and not entirely clean. Smelling sweet somehow and like a boy.

"I've watched that for so long and I've always kind of wondered if maybe. Well. Maybe there's nothing to figure out. I mean, maybe he just did it."

"Like magic?" Sabine said, feeling ridiculously soft for this boy suddenly, wanting to pull him close to her and whisper in his ear, "It's all in the chairs."

"Yeah." He nodded. He was glad to be understood, glad he didn't have to speak any more than this.

"No," Sabine whispered. "It's a trick. A really difficult, complicated trick that's supposed to make you think that magic happened, but it didn't."

"Oh." He stayed quiet for a while but didn't move. "Okay. That's what I thought. I just wanted to be sure."

"Sure," she said. In the dark she thought she could make out disappointment, a Santa Claus kind of loss, but she couldn't bring herself to lie to the boy. They walked together back into the kitchen. Guy had decided that he hadn't been wearing a scarf after all.

The Plates bundled into their separate cars and backed away from the house. From the kitchen window Sabine watched the red taillights down the driveway, first one set and then the next. She was sorry to see them go, to see Kitty go, because there was such comfort in her face, which had disappeared into darkness as soon as the car door was shut. Kitty wasn't Parsifal, but she was the only thing Sabine had found that came close.

As soon as the crowd was safely gone Dot turned on her heel to ferret out the bottle of Jack Daniel's from the back of the pantry. When she had assembled their drinks, snapping the ice cubes from their blue plastic trays with an authoritative twist, she held both glasses still in her hands. Once those ice cubes had settled down in the whiskey she said to Sabine, "Listen. Have you ever heard such a quiet?"

Sabine listened, for at just that moment the refrigerator had stopped its electric rumbling, and there was a great Midwestern silence filling up the kitchen. She was not accustomed to this kind of quiet, the kind that grew and flourished on the spread out outskirts of an already too-small town in the deadest part of a dead state, buried in the insulation of snow.

"I love them." Dot handed Sabine her glass and they both took a long drink with no formalities. "I don't love Howard, but I love the rest of them. But when they're all gone, my God. I think sometimes I might cry, I feel so relieved." She slipped down into a kitchen chair and turned her face up towards the covered light fixture on the ceiling as if she were taking in vitamin D from the sun.

"Maybe I should go do a couple laps around the block, clear the place out for a while." When she said this Sabine realized she had not set foot outside the house since she'd come in from the airport yesterday, and that it was only yesterday when she had been in her own house. "Have you seen enough of it now?" her father had asked her.

Dot swung out a chair. "Sit, sit. I'll keep you here. You're a treat, so much like Guy, my Guy. I look at you and I know exactly the kind of man he grew up to be. The two of you together, though, all those smarts and good looks in one room, it must have been something else." She tilted back her glass and drained it. When she set it back on the table, she studied the bare ice cubes with relief. One more task accomplished.

"I'm nothing like him," Sabine said regretfully. The list of ways they were different scrolled through her mind, over-whelming, endless. "He was a real crowd-pleaser. He could talk people up, charm them, make deals." At the rug auctions, the way he bid so forcefully, so completely without hesitation that other people dropped out thinking that there was no point, this man would bid until the end. Then he'd take that same rug back to Pasadena and double the price, make some old lady from Glendale think he was all but giving it to her for Christmas, it was such a sweet deal. And in magic he invented misdirection, could have had the entire audience studying his kneecaps while his hands took oranges from his pockets.

Having left the bottle of Jack Daniel's on the counter by the empty blue tray, Dot was forced to stand up when she hadn't intended to. "I have two daughters," she said. "I know all about daughters. You remind me of my son." She gestured the bottle towards Sabine before filling her own glass, but Sabine shook her head. "Half an inch," Dot said, putting a splash in anyway. "Otherwise it makes me look bad. Kitty and Bertie, they can't hold anything back. They can't get what they want out of people, except maybe for me, because they're too busy turning themselves inside out trying to be helpful. You think they could have stood up to a room full of people and not told them how to balance on top of a chair?"

Sabine shrugged. "If they wanted to."

Dot tapped her finger hard in front of Sabine's glass, nail-ing her point in place. "Not in a lifetime. They'd spill before the question had been all the way asked. But Guy, hell, you felt lucky if he told you what time it was. He was like you. He kept things in because we all wanted to know them. He was always entertaining us, juggling baseballs, doing impressions of people from his school or famous people or us. Guy never was a bully, but he stood up to people, he got his way. Howard could have barked at Guy all night and Guy would have never lost his head, just like you. That's what made his father so crazy." Dot closed her eyes and watched it all spread out before her in bright colors. "No matter how much Al screamed, how much he kicked Guy around, it always wound up looking like Guy was the one in charge. Plain and simple, Guy was smarter than Al, and god, did it make Al mad. There was no amount of punishment Al could dole out to stop him. Guy just wasn't afraid. And I'll tell you what, he should have been. I told him all the time. 'Be smart,' I'd say, 'be afraid of your father.' That's all he really wanted from all of us, a little fear."

"But he was afraid," Sabine said. "He did lose his head. Everything that happened proves that." Sabine looked down at the floor and saw the little black smudge where she had dropped her cigarette. Look to the other side and she would have seen the place where Dot and then her husband fell. It was like touring the beaches of Iwo Jima.

"No." Dot had the authority of an eyewitness on a clear day. "What he did was the only thing there was to do. He hadn't meant to kill his father, but he meant to stop him. That's what mattered most to Guy, stopping him. He didn't lose his head, he was thinking. He couldn't get Al off of me and he saw there was no time to call anybody for help. Guy had to be the help himself. He saw that, understood that, and he did something. That's not called losing your head." Dot took a slower sip of her drink and it calmed her some. "I wish he had told you this himself, because he could have explained it so much better than me."

"I wish he had, too."

"I know that he didn't have regrets about what he did. Maybe he felt sorry that Al died, and maybe he felt guilty about having done it, but he told me himself on the day he came home from Lowell that he'd done the right thing. What a grown-up boy he was, saying something like that. There he was, eighteen, and he'd already figured out all sorts of things I wouldn't come to for years and years. I used to wish so bad I could talk to him, tell him once I'd finally put it all together, but nobody can be expected to wait around. By the time I understood what had happened he was already a famous magician. He had you. By the time I'd figured it out he had forgotten about me altogether."

"He didn't forget you." But that was just something to say. Actually Sabine had no idea. Maybe he had forgotten. She never saw a trace of past in him. Maybe he had put every scrap of it to bed, including the woman sitting in front of her now. "When I think of my mother, I think of her playing the piano," Parsifal would say to Sabine in their early days when she still bothered to ask. There was no piano in this house.

"Don't try and make me feel better."

"I'd love to make you feel better," Sabine said, taking her drink down to bare ice. "I'd like to make us both feel better."

The refrigerator made a low rumble and then resumed its deep electric grind. Dot blinked, as if suddenly awake. "You know, I gave myself a lot of comfort these last ten years or so, thinking he'd come back. Once I saw him on television and then when he started sending me money, I just knew, one of these days I was going to open up the door and there he'd be. The girls and I would talk about it all the time. Sometimes I'd be driving home from the grocery store and my palms would start to sweat on the steering wheel and I was sure, I was just absolutely sure."

"I know," Sabine said. If he had lived another twenty years, another forty, he would not have come back to this place. He had forgotten it. Even as he put the money into the envelope every month, it did not exist.

"And what I think is that this belief I had was what ruined everything. That's the thing that kept me from going out and finding him, this idea that when he was ready he was going to come and find me. That's the thing I've lost, that excitement, the nervousness I had from waiting. So just when I stopped waiting, that's when you came."

"When I came?"

"You take up that place. That's what Kitty said, that all the years we've been saving a place for him and with you here, that place is full again. It is better."

Dot smiled at her, not unlike the way Sabine's mother used to smile when Sabine did well in ballet as a child. "I hate to bring this up," Sabine said, and moved the ice in her glass in circles with her finger, "but you know I'm not going to stay here. Sooner or later I have to go back to L.A."

"We'd talked about putting you in the basement, but with all the tricks you know you'd probably figure out how to escape."

"It's true."

Dot patted her hand. "Go to bed, Sabine. It's late. Nobody's going to ask you to live in Nebraska. You have to be born in Nebraska to want to stay here, I know that. Half the time that doesn't even do the trick. You're my daughter-in-law, my family. You can live anywhere you want and that's still going to be true."

Sabine gave Dot a kiss and headed down the hallway to her room. The cold weather made her sleepy, even when she stayed inside. She would go home. She thought about walking down the long hall to her bedroom on Oriole Street. She thought about the smell of the lemon trees mixing with the smell of the chlorine from the pool as she ran her hand along the paneling of the house that Parsifal had lived in as a boy. In a couple of days, in a little while, she would go home.

In Los Angeles, every day came with a series of tasks: Pick up the Bactrim, deliver the condominium complex, lunch at Canter's, take the rabbit to the vet. There were things she had to maintain, like the magic. Parsifal had told her in the very beginning, for magic to work it had to be a habit. Magic was food, it was sleep. Neglect made her awkward. She spun three balls in one hand while she brushed her teeth with the other. Add to that her job, the panes of glass that needed to be cut, sheets of grass to be painted. On the walls of her studio were the tacked-up drawings of buildings she would not get to for months, two dimensions she was to pull into three. Sabine made lists, things to buy, things to make, things to practice. All day long the list propelled her forward. When she went to bed at night her mind would reel through all she had forgotten, all the things there hadn't been time for. It had been like this even when she was a child, going from Hebrew school to painting class to ballet, working her math problems in the evenings, and then setting the table for dinner.

It wasn't like that in Nebraska.

She slept. She memorized the black lines of the branches that brushed against the storm windows of Parsifal's bedroom. She waited for Dot and Bertie to come home. She waited for Kitty and the boys. They were regular, punctual. She shaped herself around their coming and going. The house was clean, but when she was alone she cleaned it again. She read half of *The Joy of Cooking* and then made a cake from scratch, a daffodil cake. She chose the recipe because it was tedious and complicated and because she could find all the ingredients. She used every egg. In the garage, leaning alone in a corner, she found a snow shovel with a red handle and a flat tin bed. She put on her boots and hat and gloves and went outside to shovel the front walk. Then she shoveled the driveway. Sabine had never shoveled snow before. Every load surprised her with its weight, all those tiny flakes. She remembered reading somewhere that men were much more likely to have heart attacks and that it was better for women to shovel snow. What a way to die, pitching over into the soft bank, freezing there until your family came outside to find you. Her back hurt, a pain in a previously unknown muscle. She could feel the blisters rubbing beneath her soft lambskin gloves. Sabine shoveled the sidewalks well into the neighbors' property on either side. When she was finished, she went in and worked herself out of her clothes, which were stiff with ice. She sat in a hot bath and shook from the cold. Her toes were wrinkled, white and numb. Outside, it was starting to snow again.

In Dot Fetters' tiny ranch house, which in this blanket of heavy snow, and probably without it as well, appeared to be exactly like every other tiny ranch house in every direction, Sabine was finding a part of the husband she had lost. Guy the alter ego, the younger self. She imagined him flying down the street in the bracing cold, stomach to sled. She saw him at the kitchen table spooning through a bowl of cereal before school, his eyes fixed to the back of the box. Guy, who would someday be Parsifal, lying on the floor in the living room, reading library books on magic, frustrating books that never gave the information you really needed to have. She imagined him popular, tight with the neighborhood boys, good to his sister. At night she saw him asleep in the bed next to her bed, not the man he would be later on, the one that was gone, but this slighter, very present version of himself. She saw him in Kitty and Bertie, sometimes in Dot and How and Guy. She saw him at six years old and nine and twelve, because she needed to, every minute. Missing him was the dark and endless space she had stumbled into.

"I don't want to put you to work," Bertie said. "I think you should be relaxing, on vacation, but Mama thinks if we don't give you things to do you're going to kill yourself." She set a stationery box on the kitchen table. "Maybe you could address some wedding invitations—only if you feel like it. I know your handwriting is better than mine."

Sabine touched her fingers to the edge of the lid. She felt hungry.

"Go to bed," Parsifal had said to her. "You're going to go blind."

"Few more," Sabine said, not looking up. Why hadn't she looked up? She needed two hundred ash trees, two and a half inches high. She kept a trunk pinched between tweezers.

He walked behind her, pushed his hands deep into her neck. Sabine's neck was always aching. She spent her time hunched over. "Did you hear the one about the girl with too much work ethic?"

"No such thing." She threaded on a branch.

He bent towards her. "I'm going to take you to the beach," he whispered. "Make you lie on a towel all day and read trashy novels." He touched his lips to her ear and she shivered. "You'll go insane."

Sabine, who had been driving the freeways of Southern California since she turned sixteen, would not drive in the snow, no matter how many times Dot offered her car. It would be like pitching an ice cube across a linoleum floor and then commanding it to stop. On Friday, Sabine's fifth day in Alliance, when everyone was in school, Kitty came by to take her to Wal-Mart. Sabine had taken all the light fixtures off the ceilings that morning and washed them in ammonia and hot water. It had been her plan for the whole day, something to do that no one would notice that she had done. But by ten-thirty every glass cover was screwed back on the ceiling, free of dirt and dried-out flying insects, and there was nothing left. She was staring up at her work when Kitty let herself in the back. Sabine had not heard the car crunching into the recently shoveled snow. When she saw Kitty under those brighter lights she wanted for a moment to cry. It was the joy of having un-expected company, the joy of seeing Parsifal's face, and the joy of seeing Kitty. They kissed each other in the kitchen, quickly on the cheek, as if they were old and wealthy friends meeting for lunch at the Bel Air Hotel.

"I thought you might want to get out," Kitty said. "Mom said you wanted some pens to do Bertie's invitations."

Sabine did want to get out. She did want pens. Yes. "Don't you have to work?"

Kitty shrugged and unlooped her scarf. Her hair was down, straight and shiny in the wonderful overhead light of the kitchen. "I'm working less now, now that we're getting this money from Guy. I'm going three days a week regular, plus filling in for people when they're sick. I figured if I didn't cut back, Howard would. I beat him to it."

Sabine pulled on her coat. "It is your money."

"That's the way I see it. I mean, most of it will go to college for the boys, assuming I can talk them into going. Neither one of them seems to think that spending their lives in Alliance working at the Woolrich plant like their parents would be such a bad way to go. How's got good grades and Guy is smart enough, if I can just sit on him and make him work. They could go to college."

"I don't see why not."

Parsifal had always been so proud of having gone to Dartmouth. He followed their mediocre football team with interest. He would sing the Dartmouth fight song in the shower.

Come stand up, men, and shout for Dartmouth.
Cheer when the team in GREEN appears;
For naught avails the strength of Harvard—
When they hear our mighty cheers:
Wah-who-wah-who-wah!

Now Sabine had no idea whether or not he had gone to college at all.

"Maybe you could mention it to the boys," Kitty said, her face turned away. "Tell them it's important. They'll listen to you."

"Why would they listen to me? They hardly know me." Sabine pushed her feet and their two layers of socks into a pair of warmer boots she'd borrowed from Bertie.

"They're crazy about you. They think you're famous."

"Famous?"

"You were married to their famous uncle. You won't tell them how you got on your head, and besides, as far as they're concerned, you've been on television with Johnny Carson every night for the last fifteen years." She looked at Sabine. "Hat."

Sabine touched her bare head.

If someone were to have pressed a sheet of glass down over the top of Alliance, Nebraska, in winter, it would have resembled an ant farm. Everything was a tunnel eaten neatly, carefully into the snow. The tunnel of the streets branching into the narrower tunnels of driveways and carved-out sidewalks. The snow banked over cars, lawn furniture, porches, like frozen animal carcasses stored for future need. It gave the world the feeling of organization and purpose. Get on one of these paths and it would take you directly to where you need to go, the ice slipping you quickly forward.

In the car Sabine fished her sunglasses out of her purse. "Do you get used to it?"

"To what?" Kitty said, one mittened hand guiding the steering wheel.

"The winter, all this snow. I think I'd feel a little panicked after a while. Trapped."

"I can't blame my panic on the weather," Kitty said. "It's bigger than that."

Sabine smiled because it was what Parsifal would have said, smiled because even if Kitty were serious, she herself had meant it as a joke. Maybe Kitty and Parsifal's similarities were all genetic, the tilt of the eyes, the length of the leg; or maybe they had formed themselves carefully into one person those first fifteen years and it lasted them each a lifetime. Sabine looked out the window. A puff of a child, sexless in a yellow snowsuit, was pulled by a woman with a sled. It felt good to be out. The heater blew warm air on Sabine's feet almost to the point of discomfort. The houses were painted blue, then green, then yellow, and the colors looked so good against the snow, like the green of those tough evergreens and boxwoods.

"I live down there." Kitty pointed down one of the identical chutes.

"It's nice that you're so close." Just as quickly as it had been there, Kitty's street was gone. Sabine wanted to look over her shoulder. She hadn't seen the name.

"Sometimes. My mother and I used to fight a lot. Now everybody's older, it's not so much of an issue anymore. She worries about me too much, though. I don't like that. I have to worry about the boys and worry about myself, and then I have to worry about the fact that I make my mother worry. Wears me out." Kitty pulled off one mitten with her teeth and punched down the cigarette lighter in the station wagon. She took a cigarette out of the pack on the dashboard while she waited for the lighter to pop back out again.

"So why is your mother worrying about you?"

"Why do you think?"

"No one seems to like your husband very much, including you, if you don't mind my saying."

Pop. Kitty held the hot orange coil up to light her cigarette. "We're a fairly transparent bunch."

"How long have you been married?"

Kitty cracked the window and exhaled. It was a long, exhausted sound that was meant to account for all of those years. The sharp, cold air outside blended with the cigarette smoke and then shot it back into the car. "I'm forty-four, so it would be twenty-four years."

"Young." But Sabine would have married at twenty if Parsifal would have married her then.

"So young. There should be laws about getting married so young." Far, far ahead the traffic light switched from green to yellow to red, and Kitty began to pump her brakes slowly in anticipation of the stop. "I would have done it even if there had been a law. It made my mother so mad. I couldn't resist. We got married in the Box Butte hospital. Howard and I were dating and he fell off a train. He was working at the trainyard then. There was some ice on the runner and off he went, right on his head, smashed the whole side of his face in."

"That must have been awful." Sabine remembered the light from the living room lamp throwing a dark shadow into the hole of Howard's cheek, the nest of scars like knotted fishhooks.

"Oh, you should have seen me at the hospital. I sat by his

bed crying and crying, the doctor saying he was probably going to die. I grew very attached to Howard when he was un-
conscious. I'd lost my father and I'd lost Guy, and there I was
about to lose this boy I was dating that I didn't even especially
like, but at the time it all felt very connected. He was such a
sweetheart in that bed, sleeping, all bandaged up. Nobody
thought he'd pull through, and then when he did the first thing
he said was that he wanted to marry me. I got up from my
plastic chair, went down the hall, and got the chaplain. There's
something about a boy with a smashed-in head that's very hard
to resist when you're twenty."

"But that's not why Dot didn't want you to marry him."

"Oh, God, no, nothing like that. Howard was a hoodlum
when he was young. My mother was convinced somebody
threw him off that train for gambling debts or stealing cars or
some such thing. I'm sure he was just drunk or stoned. I never
did ask him. The truth is, he turned out better than anybody
thought he would. He's kept a job, he's stayed with us. But
pretty much as soon as the pain medication wore off, we both
knew we'd made a real mistake." Kitty eased the car into a
plowed lot. "Wal-Mart."

"Is there any sort of art-supply store?"

"The general wisdom around here is if you can't get it at
Wal-Mart, you don't need it."

Sabine looked up at the brown building, which was itself
the size of another parking lot. "I've never actually been in
one of these."

"Go on," Kitty said.

Sabine shook her head. "I've just never had any reason to."

Kitty stubbed out her cigarette and replaced her mitten.
"Well, you are in for a treat."

As they walked together towards the store she told Sabine,

"I bring the boys here in the dead of winter when the weather is awful and they're bored, and I come here when I want to be alone. My mother and I come here when we want to talk privately, and Bertie and I come here when we feel like seeing people. I come here when the air conditioner goes out in the summer and I buy popcorn and just walk around. Most of the times I can remember that Howard and I were actually getting along he'd ask me if I wanted to go to Wal-Mart with him, and we'd look at stuff we wanted to buy and talk about it— wouldn't it be nice to have a Cuisinart, wouldn't it be nice to have a sixty-four-piece sprocket set. It's a very romantic place, really."

On the curb was a soda machine, all drinks a quarter. Kitty leaned in towards Sabine as they pushed open the glass-and-metal doors. The warm air smelled like popcorn and Coke. It smelled like a carnival wearing new clothes. An older woman in a blue tunic who seemed to be patterned on Dot, the same plastic glasses and gray curls, the same roundness, pushed out a shopping cart for them to take. She greeted Kitty by name.

"I buy books here," Kitty said. "I buy my shampoo and underwear and cassette tapes and potato chips, sheets and towels and motor oil." There was something in her tone, so low and conspiratorial, that Sabine put her gloved hand over her mouth to keep from laughing out loud.

"Why?" Sabine said. "Why?"

Kitty raised a hand over her head, gestured magnificently towards the fluorescent lights, the banners hanging from the ceiling that pointed you to specific departments and special values. "There is no place else in town. No place to go. This is it, Sabine."

The place was an airport. Not an airport, but a hangar where planes were kept. Sabine thought of the marketplace in Bangkok, everything you wanted available to you. Somewhere, if they turned the right corner, there would be a row of live rabbits and chickens to buy for their supper. There would be gauzy sarongs and bright green songbirds and huge red fruits for which there was no name. Somewhere there would be an aisle of prostitutes, women and girls and boys in different sizes that could be purchased on an hourly basis. Sabine curled her fingers around the blue push-bar on the cart, even though Kitty had been steering.

"Can you think of anything you need?" Kitty asked. "Anything at all?"

"Just the pens."

There was not one thing that was true about all the people in the store, but so many things repeated themselves, women with perms, men in dark blue jeans and cowboy boots, the dearth of color in their skin and eyes and hair. The people began to run together. And then she realized, they were all white people. Where had she ever been in Los Angeles where all the people were white? The white people looked at Sabine. Some doubled back down the same aisle twice to see her again. In the Alliance Wal-Mart, Sabine appeared famous. Maybe, without being able to remember the exact incident, they sensed that she had been on television. Maybe they could smell all the other places she had been to in her life. They didn't know why it was exactly, but they knew she was different.

Kitty stopped the cart and put in two three-packs of paper towels. "Sale."

Sabine nodded. Was $2.49 a good price? To know if paper towels were a deal this time, you'd have to remember what they cost last time. Sabine could never remember. They passed through the paper products, past the baby oils, lotions, diapers, shampoos. They went through Electronics. The bank of televisions played three different channels. They were all set to soap operas because it was that time of day. Women wearing jewelry and elaborate outfits mouthed their love to handsome men with slicked-back hair. They looked like they meant it, their eyes were bright with tears. The volume was off. Sabine started watching and fell behind. Kitty was making her way towards School Supplies, and Sabine hurried to catch up with her.

"Guy needs posterboard," Kitty said and ran her fingers over the ten available colors. "He's doing a project on food chains."

Ahead of them, a man bent over a stack of spiral notebooks. Sabine recognized his coat, the curve of his shoulders, but couldn't place him until he straightened up. Her mistake had been in trying to remember him as someone she knew in Los Angeles. "Haas," she said.

Haas looked up through his glasses and smiled. "Hey, there." He took a step forward but didn't quite reach them.

"Hooky?" Kitty said.

"Lunch. I needed some things." Haas looked more comfortable in the Wal-Mart than he did in the Fetters kitchen. He smiled easily.

"We came to get some pens. Sabine is going to do your wedding invitations."

"That's what Bertie told me," he said. "It's very nice of you. I think Bertie has good handwriting but she feels self-conscious about it. She wants everything to be perfect."

"She was just trying to give me a task," Sabine said. "I know she could do them."

Haas shook his head. "She's grateful for your help. Bertie's so glad you're here. We both are. It means a lot to have all the family together for the wedding."

"Won't be long now," Kitty said.

Haas picked up a package of gold tinfoil stars and ran his fingers over the edges thoughtfully. "We've waited a long time.

If it was up to me we'd go ahead and get married tomorrow, but Bertie wants a nice wedding and she should have one." Haas waited through an awkward moment of silence and then tossed the stars in his basket. "I should go. The lines looked pretty long when I came in, and I've got to be back in class by one."

"Sure," Kitty said.

"It was good to see you again." He hesitated and then held out his hand to Sabine, who shook it and said good-bye.

"He thinks you're famous, too," Kitty whispered as Haas was walking away. "They make him watch the video every night."

Sabine turned to watch him recede towards Checkout. His legs were thin and long beneath his coat. "Do you think Bertie's doing the right thing? He seems so solemn."

"Did you look in his basket? Almond Roca. Bertie loves that stuff and it's not cheap. He'll buy a couple of notebooks as a cover but he was over here to get her a present, you can bet your life on it. He loves her and she loves him. If you ask me, Bertie made him wait way too long. Even if the women in my family don't have such a good track record with men, she's never had anything to worry about with Haas. He's always going to be good to her."

That's what Parsifal had been, good to her. It was the thing that Sabine believed in, more than passion, more than tradition. Find a man you love who is good to you. She looked at the pens: razor point, fine point, ballpoint, Rollerball, indelible. There was one felt-tipped calligraphy pen, but it wasn't what she'd hoped for. She liked the old-fashioned kind, a set with changeable nibs and a bottle of ink. "It seems like they're waiting kind of late to get these invitations done."

"I don't know why they're bothering to send them at all."

Kitty added a box of envelopes to the cart. "Everybody knows they're getting married two weeks from Saturday. They know when it is and where it is and whether or not they're coming. It's all a formality, sending out the cards."

"Sentimental words from a woman who got married in a hospital room."

"It was a ward," Kitty corrected. "No private room for Howard."

Sabine dropped the pen in the basket and was ready to push on when she was sidetracked by the glue sticks. They looked so much like ChapSticks. Next to them were the X-acto knives. The posterboard was flimsy and cheap, but there was some illustration board that was almost as good as Bristol board. She picked up a metal ruler for a straight edge. Making models of buildings was how Sabine was used to filling up her time. In Los Angeles she was in demand. There was always a greater need than she could possibly meet. "I think I'm going to buy a couple more things, just to give myself something to do."

"Sure," Kitty said. "We're in no hurry."

What she needed she already owned. She had it in triplicate at home. But she wasn't home, and suddenly the idea of building something appealed to her. Maybe she could make something Dot would like. She filled the basket with wire and tempera paint. She found things she never knew she wanted in the hardware section, a lovely jeweler's file and a three-ounce hammer. She doubled back to Beauty and bought Q-tips and rolled cotton. She bought straight pins in the sewing section and pushpins in School Supplies.

Kitty looked in the basket. "We always buy things we didn't mean to. That's the whole point of the place. It's cold outside, there's nowhere else to go, so you might as well stay in here and shop."

Before they left, Sabine bought herself a pair of men's jeans in dark blue denim.

Kitty and Sabine were home long before anyone else. The day, which had been so bright when they left the house, had clouded over while they had been shopping, and by the time they were home again they had to turn on the light in the kitchen in order to see properly. Kitty made tuna-fish sandwiches while Sabine sorted through her purchases.

"My mother told me you took an egg out of her ear," Kitty said.

"I did."

Kitty nodded, mixing a spoonful of mayonnaise into the bowl. "She said you did a great job. I'd like it if you could take one out of my ear sometime, not to show me how to do it, I know you wouldn't do that, but I'd like to see the trick."

"I can't do it if you ask me to. It only works if you catch someone off-guard. I'll take an egg out of your ear sometime when you're not expecting it."

"Guy had a hell of a time with that one. He never could get it right."

Sabine shook her head. "I just can't imagine that. It was the easiest thing in the world for him." When there were omelettes for breakfast he took all the eggs out of Phan's ear. Something about the cold shell on the soft skin of his ears made Phan crazy. He would fall on the floor, giggling and squirming, while Parsifal pulled out another and another. Sabine knew how to palm an egg so well because she had seen it done right there on her kitchen floor a hundred times. Parsifal never did the trick again after Phan died. He wouldn't even eat eggs. "Do you have a deck of cards?" Sabine asked. Think of something else.

Kitty looked in a couple of drawers in the kitchen and then

disappeared into the living room. She came back with a blue Bicycle pack that she handed to Sabine.

"No eggs." Sabine took the cards out of the box, leaving the jokers inside. "So we'll do a different trick." She was wonderful at shuffling. That was one of the great responsibilities of an assistant. After every show they did in Vegas the house would offer her a job. She could have had the best blackjack table on the floor. "A pretty girl like you," they'd say. "You'd make ten times more dealing than whatever Mr. Magic is paying you."

"Can you imagine anything worse than dealing in Vegas?" she'd say to Parsifal. Winners slipping red plastic chips down the front of your blouse as a sign of appreciation.

Maybe it was because she had such long, slim fingers. Hands that were delicate but strong enough to open lids that were sealed onto jars. "With those hands," her mother would say, "you could have been a surgeon, a pianist. But my girl shuffles cards for a magician." In later years, her mother said it proudly instead of sarcastically.

Sabine made the cards fly on the Fetters' kitchen table. She showed off shamelessly for Kitty, who lowered herself slowly into the next chair. The cards shot up, twisted, and arched. She swept them to the left and then right, rocked them back and forth like notes held long on an accordion. She showed their faces, hid them, changed them. Each of the fifty-two was a separate object, a singular soul. That was how you had to think about them. Not one deck but fifty-two cards.

When she wanted them, they came back to her, a cozy stack. She pushed them with the tips of her fingers across the table to Kitty. "Cut?"

"I can't believe the boys weren't here to see this. You have to show them this."

"You bet."

Kitty declined to cut the deck and Sabine took it up again and fanned it out. "Pick a card, any card. Memorize it and put it back in the deck. Don't forget it, don't change your mind, don't lie about what it was later on when I need you to tell me the truth." Card banter. She knew it like a song. She sang it.

Kitty did not reach out at first. The cards still seemed to be spinning. There was not as much air in the room as there had been before. Sabine did not question the wait. She knew it. She had made it herself.

"Okay," Kitty said, blinking. "Okay." She slid one from the pack, looked at it, slipped it back.

"You've done your part, now relax. Don't relax so much that you forget your card." They were not her words, but they came out fine. Whoever really said anything for the first time, anyway? Sabine shuffled again, just a moderate riff this time. The shuffle show was already in place and now what mattered was not disturbing the order of the cards. "There are how many cards in a deck, Mrs. Plate?"

"Fifty-two."

"Fifty-two, correct. And in that deck of cards there are how many suits?" Cut.

"Four."

"And do you know the names of these suits?" Cut. Cut.

"Hearts, diamonds, spades, and clubs."

"Exactly right." Cut. Cut. Cut. Cut. Put the deck down. "So we have fifty-two cards and four suits, which leaves us how many cards in each suit?" Sabine almost didn't ask her this part. So many people got it wrong. The simple math of it froze them and they couldn't tell you to save their lives.

"Thirteen," Kitty said.

Sabine smiled at her. "Beautiful." She dealt out the entire

deck into four piles. She counted to thirteen four times, made neat and even stacks without having to give the edges a straightening brush with her fingernail. Kitty watched her like she was dealing out Tarot cards, the truth of her future. The Sailor, the Drowned Man, the Queen of Wands. "So that's all of them," Sabine said. "Thirteen cards, four piles. My thought then is that this would have to be your card." Sabine turned over the top card of the first pile, a six of clubs.

Kitty looked astonished and then heartbroken. It was better than giving them their card. They believed so completely that you would not fail. Even as they tried to follow you and couldn't, they had seen a lifetime of card tricks. They were sure that the card they selected from the deck would come back to them at the end, even if they couldn't understand how. Which was true, but Sabine was not at the end.

"No."

Sabine looked pensive. She touched two fingers lightly to her lower lip. "I thought I knew how this one worked," she said, not in the magician's voice, but in her own. She tapped the second stack and turned the top card over. Six of diamonds. "This one?"

Kitty smiled. There was the pattern, the superior revelation. "No."

Sabine went on to the third. "It shouldn't be taking this long. Here?" Six of spades.

Kitty, thrilled, shook her head.

"One more chance," Sabine whispered. She flicked the card over. She barely had to touch it, because it moved beneath her hand. Six of hearts.

"Yes." Kitty nodded. "Yes, yes, yes." She fell back in her chair, exhausted from the anticipation. She was smiling like a girl, so huge and open that Sabine could see not only how beautiful she must have been when she was the assistant, but how beautiful she was now. The card trick had made Kitty beautiful. "That was wonderful. Pure genius. You are wasting yourself here with us. You have to be a magician."

Sabine was so pleased to have done well for Kitty. "Just because you can do something doesn't mean you want to."

"Bullshit." Kitty waved her hand. "You just aren't used to thinking of yourself that way. This is brilliant, Sabine. What a waste it would be not to use this."

Sabine smiled, flattered. She swept up the cards in one hand. "There are so many people who can do what I can do. To really make it work you have to have something else. Parsifal had it. He made tricks up. He could convince people of things."

"I have to wonder what would have become of Guy if he'd stayed here. I wonder if he would have been a magician in Nebraska. He could have performed at the schools, I guess. Fairs, parties, maybe."

Sabine tried to see it, the gymnasium hot and crowded, children squirming against the cold metal of folding chairs. The rabbit slips from Parsifal's hands and shoots into the tangle of feet. All of the children go onto the floor, scoot under the chairs. "No," she said. "He was a Californian through and through. He didn't even like to play in Vegas. We traveled all the time but anywhere we went, all he could talk about was going home. I think no matter what happened he would have wound up out there sooner or later."

Kitty's eyes were half closed. Sabine wondered what she dreamed about. "I'm sure you're right. It's just that I remember him here. I know that he hated it, but this is where I see him. I see him in this house. I always have." Kitty picked up the deck of cards from the table. She fanned them out and closed them up again. "Did he do a lot of card tricks?" Her hands were fluid.

"In the end. The last few years, all he wanted to do were cards."

"I didn't picture him sawing people in half."

They had sold the saw box years ago to a married couple who called themselves the Minotaurs. They still had the zigzag box, though. It was such a good one that Parsifal hated to get rid of it, even when he refused to use it. It was made out of teakwood, painted with red and yellow diamonds. The inside was lined in cool blue satin. It was in one of the guest rooms now. It made a pretty little armoire. "He sawed me in half plenty. He folded me down and stuck swords through the box. He made me disappear in a locked trunk and brought me back as a rabbit. That was in a less enlightened time, but we did it all."

Kitty spread out the cards and stacked them up, spread them and stacked them as if she were trying to figure out how they worked. "I'm surprised." She tapped the deck thoughtfully. "He didn't like to be closed in."

"He hated to be closed in. He closed me in, but he never got boxed himself. Parsifal needed a Valium just to get on an elevator, for God's sake." Sabine had looked into the dark barrel of the MRI machine. She had pressed herself into a tenth of that much space. She'd told him it didn't look so bad. "Your mother told me about the time he cut his face with the hedge shears, how they tied him up in a sack."

"I remember that."

"I would think after something like that, small spaces are always going to make you nervous."

Kitty nodded and tapped the deck again absently. "They do." Outside, the dark clouds were making the smallest release, a snow so light it looked like talcum powder. "It wasn't that sack that scared him. I'm sure it didn't help, but that wasn't it."

"The refrigerator, you mean."

Kitty blinked, startled awake. "He told you about that?"

He had told her plenty. He told her about taxes and head-aches and men he was in love with. "He got trapped in an old refrigerator when he was a kid. He was playing and the door shut behind him."

Kitty folded her lips into her mouth to have the pleasure of biting down on both of them at once. The face she made was old, empty. "No."

"Oh, Christ." Sabine put her forehead down on the table. "This is going to be another one of those stories, isn't it? Parsifal's life in hell. Why can't you tell me all of them in one shot? Tell me the worst of it and let me go home."

"You already heard the worst of it. Guy killed Dad with a bat in the kitchen. Guy went to reform school. Guy left Nebraska. That's the very worst of it."

"And the refrigerator? Where does that fit into the picture? How bad on the scale of bad things is this?"

Kitty seemed to mull the question over, to see if there was some sort of rating system. "Our father locked him in the refrigerator. Guy was nine. Eight, nine. He had eaten some-thing, I can't remember what it was now. Something he wasn't supposed to eat. Something my father wanted. He put Guy in the refrigerator."

"Nobody does that. You can't."

"Listen, I'm not making this up to provide colorful stories about the past. This is what happened to Guy. I don't know what I'm supposed to tell you. I don't think about these things. I don't think about them—and now I do. Do you want me to tell you?"

What Sabine wanted was Fairfax. Jews did not lock their children in refrigerators. She wanted her own parents, who were in their yard now, a thousand miles away, watering the azaleas while the rabbit napped at the end of a leash her mother held with two hands. "Your father put him in the refrigerator." The words came out slowly, carefully. She remembered that she wasn't angry at Kitty, though just as quickly she could feel herself forgetting.

"My father had good qualities," Kitty said, "but I can't remember them anymore. I know there were moments that I loved him but I can't remember when they were. With him, you could do something nine times in a row and it was fine, and then the tenth time it wasn't fine. The tenth time he'd kill you for it. He'd kill Guy for it, or my mother. Sometimes me, but not so much at all. I felt bad about that. Who knows what Guy ate, but when my father asked him, just by his voice you knew this was going to be time number ten. There was nothing to say except, 'What? Yeah, I ate it.' "

"So he opened up the door and stuffed him inside? That's a big boy, eight or nine." It was the magician's voice, confident, controlling. Pick a card. Sabine could feel her hands starting to shake and she sat on them.

"He made Guy take everything out first." Kitty picked up the deck and began dealing a single hand; one, two, three, four, five, she counted the cards silently out on the table.

"Made him take out the food?"

"The food, the shelves. There wouldn't have been room for him otherwise. The refrigerator was full and it all went very slow. It took him a long time. He put the food on the counter and on the breakfast table and the floor." Kitty pointed as if to say, that counter there. "Guy was crying a little and my father was harping at him, 'Always stuffing your face, always taking what doesn't belong to you.' At one point he called him a fat boy, which just made no sense. When he took his shirt off you could see his ribs, for Christ's sake."

Parsifal at the beach had taken off his shirt, raised his arms in the Southern California sun, turned in front of Sabine, who was sitting on her towel. "Tell me the truth," he'd said.

"So we were scared, but not so scared. It was crazy stuff. We thought, Guy and I thought, that he was bluffing. If things took too long he just lost interest. We thought once everything was out, he'd turn around and tell Guy to put it all back in and that would be that. That was the sort of thing he'd do, give you plenty of time to think about how you'd never eat something you weren't supposed to again."

"Did you help him take things out?"

"I wasn't allowed." Kitty scooped up the cards and tapped them on the table to straighten them out.

"But you were there."

"I was always there," Kitty said. "When I was there things didn't get so out of hand. Things didn't usually get so out of hand, but this time, I don't know. Finally all the food was out. He left the things in the shelves on the door and he left the things in the freezer. It was just one of those little freezer boxes at the top that pretty much just hold ice. He told Guy to take out the shelves and out they came. By now we're sure it's over. Dad says, 'Get in,' and Guy does. I almost laughed, I was thinking, My father has let this go too far and he's looking stupid now, it hasn't been a good lesson. Guy made a face at me like, Hell, I'm in the fridge. Then just at that minute when it's all supposed to be over, Dad shuts the door. Not even a slam, just a real normal click like he'd just gotten himself a beer. It's one of those big old refrigerators with the bar across the front like a safe and when it's shut it looks absolutely locked and I started screaming my head off. I think the neighbors must have heard me. Guy told me later that once you're in there you can't really hear anything."

Sabine did not turn to look at the refrigerator behind her. She knew it to be a Whirlpool side-by-side, ice through the door, in toasted almond. She didn't know the rest of the story, but she knew how it ended. Parsifal got out.

"My father told me to be quiet. He told me to come in the living room with him, to sit still and be quiet. I'm thinking, How long can a person last? How long until he suffocates? I was a kid, kids don't have any sense about those things. Hell, I don't even think I'd know now, how long it would take. I didn't think he could freeze to death, but it would be cold in there. It was summer when this happened, so he was in there in his T-shirt and shorts. My father picked up the paper and started to read. I look back on this now, I think about it as a parent, and there's no way to understand what happened. He read the paper and I sat there. I sat there and sat there and sat there until suddenly I did this little gulp, like a hiccup, and I realized that I hadn't been breathing, and I bolted up and ran into the kitchen and let Guy out. He was sitting on the bottom and you could see the prints of his sneakers on the inside of the door shelves where he'd tried to push it open. He'd cracked the inside of the door. I don't know, maybe he could have stayed in there another six hours. I have no idea. I remember him being perfectly white, but I don't know if that was from not getting any air or from the cold or just from being so goddamn frightened."

"What did your father do?"

"Not a thing. He didn't even look up. I was supposed to let him out. I really think that was the way he had meant for it to go. I told Guy that I'd put the food back, but he was nervous. He thought it was supposed to be his job, and if he didn't do it he'd wind up back inside. He wiped out the refrigerator, got everything all cleaned up. We threw away anything that looked rotten, and then Guy and I put the shelves back in and then all the food. Everything had gotten sweaty and wet. It was hot in the kitchen. Guy was real shaky but he didn't say anything. He wiped off the milk, he put back the milk. I don't remember where my mother was, but when she came home later she thought we'd cleaned out the refrigerator as a surprise."

"Did you tell her?"

Kitty pressed the heels of her hands into her eye sockets. "Much, much later. Whenever I got mad at my mother, I told her everything. Before my father died, we were all a team, me and my mother and Guy. We were together against him. But after Guy was gone and Bertie was born, I blamed it all on my mother. I thought she could have done something to stop it all from happening. I never thought that at the time, but later, once things were quiet and I could think it all through, I wanted to nail her to the wall."

Terrible things had happened to Phan. Hadn't he been sent off alone as a child? Hadn't his parents, his sisters, been killed in Vietnam? Hadn't he lost everything? Phan had stayed alone in the world until he found Parsifal, and yet his face showed none of that. His face, bright and smooth in the sun as he slept next to the swimming pool, was peaceful. When he came home from work in the evenings there was always something in his pocket for the rabbit, a carrot stick from lunch, a cluster of green grapes. He made elaborate birthday cakes with thin layers of jam in the middle. He ironed Parsifal's handkerchiefs. But what about at night? Did they hold each other tightly? Did Parsifal whisper in his ear, "My Love, my father put me in the refrigerator and left me there to suffocate. It was so dark and so cold and I heard the electricity hum." Did Phan then bury his face against Parsifal's neck and say, "Darling, they killed my mother. They killed the boys who sat next to me in school. They killed even the birds in the trees." Did they rock one another then? Was there comfort? Did they stay up until dawn, recounting things too unbelievable to say with the lights on, and then decide in the morning to keep it all a secret? Was there always a brave face for Sabine?

For Sabine there was always a brave face. Where had her parents met exactly? Not at the beginning of Israel, but before that. Was it on a train? Was it before that? They came from different corners of Poland, but then all of Poland was swept together. They were not from Poznan and Lublin. They were only from Poland. They were not Polish, they were only Jews. What did they say to each other in bed in Fairfax? What did they remember late at night, their voices dropping to a whisper to spare Sabine? "Darling, do you know what became of your sister?" "My Love, I cannot be reminded by the snow." Did they speak in that other language, the one Sabine studied but did not learn. Did they lull themselves to sleep with familiar words?

"I have to lie down," Sabine said, and pushed out of her chair.

"Don't." Kitty took one of Sabine's hands. She pressed it between her own. "Don't be mad at me. I don't know how to tell you these things."

"Not mad," she said. "I'm very tired." Sabine walked down the hallway to Guy's room, Parsifal's room. She appeared to be pulling Kitty with her, but it was because Kitty had fixed herself to Sabine's hand.

"You tell me something," Kitty said, and when Sabine lay down on the bed, Kitty sat down beside her. "That would even it out. You tell me about you and Guy taking a trip or doing a show. Tell me about a time when he was happy." Kitty meant it.

"I can't now. I will later, I promise, but not now."

"I need you to."

Sabine closed her eyes and turned her face away. She hadn't realized that she was crying until she was lying down. "Let me sleep for a little while."

Sabine felt Kitty's feet down near her feet. She felt Kitty's chin brush her shoulder as she stretched out beside her. "Something very small is all I'm asking for. You can tell me about him laughing at a television show. You can tell me he was happy when the pancakes turned out well. He was crazy about pancakes. Tell me about when things were good." Her voice went deep inside Sabine's ear. "It's only fair."

And when Sabine remembered, it was all good. Except for when Phan was dying, except for the loss of Phan, there was something to recount in every single day, twenty-two years of good days. Sabine scanned their life and chose at random. "Okay, this was a long time ago."

"Tell me." Kitty's head settled against the pillow of the single bed.

"He found a Savonnerie rug at the Baldwin Park swap meet, twelve feet, five inches, by seventeen feet, four inches, probably 1840. Absolutely mint. It was in a box under a ratty quilt and a couple of crocheted lap blankets. The guy wanted a hundred and fifty dollars for it." The day was so hot and the smog had clamped down on the San Gabriel Valley like a lid, but Parsifal had insisted they snake their way through every aisle of junk. He said he had a good feeling, there was something out there for him, that nobody went out on such a terrible day and came back empty-handed. "The rug was huge. Parsifal didn't even unfold it. The guy who sold it kept saying he had planned on cutting it up into a bunch of little rugs, the size people could really use. Parsifal paid him in cash and we picked that thing up and lugged it back to the car just as fast as we could go, which wasn't very fast. It was the most beautiful rug I ever saw, before or since. He got more than thirty thousand dollars for it. Every time we went to a meet we looked for that guy. Parsifal wanted to give him more money. He was going to do it, but we never found him again."

"And he was happy."

In the parking lot at noon in August, hundreds of cars flashing in a flat, hot sea of metal and glass, Parsifal throws back his head and screams, the millions and millions of delicate wool knots clutched to his chest. His fingers strain under the weight of so many flowers, the creamy colors, peach and salmon, the filigrees in the design, the well-sewn hem. He screams and laughs and kisses Sabine, who knows enough about rugs to understand what has happened, that this will change everything. "That was the money he used to start his own store. He'd worked for somebody else until then, but when he found that rug he said he could see his name on the glass. We called all our friends that night. We drank margaritas. We went dancing."

"It sounds wonderful."

"It was heaven," Sabine whispered. She told Parsifal he was the luckiest person she had ever met in her life, not just in this, but in everything. Things came to him from nowhere. He got what he needed without ever asking, just like he had gotten her. She didn't say it with any sort of bitterness. She was proud of him. She was thrilled by his limitless good fortune. They were in her car, which had air-conditioning and no radio, as opposed to Parsifal's car, which had AM/FM and a tape deck and was hot as an oven. They passed the gravel pits of Irwindale with the windows rolled up tight. All the way home they sang "Do You Know the Way to San Jose?," the rug lashed to the roof of the car like a grizzly bear, shot dead and ready to be stuffed and mounted. *I'm going back to find SOME PEACE OF MIND in San Jose.* Sabine meant to tell Kitty that part, how they only knew one verse and still they couldn't stop themselves. *L.A. is a great big freeway.* That was the part of the story that she loved, but she had worn herself out, all the telling and listening, and before she could finish her point she fell asleep.

"Even when Paris is horrible, it's fabulous," Phan whispers into the back of her neck. He is behind her on the Pont Alexandre III, the most beautiful bridge in Paris, and when she turns he kisses her, first on both cheeks and then, quickly, on her lips. "Continental and American. Beautiful Sabine, look at you. Maybe prairie living agrees with you after all."

"It's killing me," she says, and wraps her arms around his waist, feels the soft cashmere of his coat with her bare fingers. She is not surprised to see him. She is not surprised that he is there or that she is there. Paris does not surprise her. She knows the heavy statues on either end of Pont Alexandre III, the lights that look like candles at night. It is a city that Parsifal loved. It seemed like every time they left the country they managed to work in Paris. They had their rituals, la Pomme de Pain for bread, Les Pyrénées for café au lait, a Mont Blanc at Angelina's when they were feeling reckless. Sabine knows which evenings the Musée D'Orsay isn't crowded. She knows the hidden sale racks at Au Bon Marché. There is nothing left to surprise Sabine.

"Paris is the perfect antidote for Nebraska. I come here whenever I've been spending too much time in Alliance, even if it's just for a minute. They balance each other out. One probably couldn't exist without the other."

"Paris would survive quite nicely without Nebraska." Together they lean against the railing and stare down into the Seine, which is gray and sluggish in the cold afternoon, and even then it is beautiful. The bare trees and the iron lampposts and the grates that cover the windows, everything that should not be beautiful is that thing exactly.

"I thought about taking you some place where the weather was better."

"The weather is better here," Sabine says. The women

wear their dark hair pulled back. They wear fur coats or fur collars on dark wool coats. Their lips are smooth and red. They have never gone to sleep and dreamed that they were in Nebraska.

"If you really stretch, you can almost see where I used to work." Phan points far down the west bank, past so many gray palaces or annexes to palaces. "I did very good work. They were scandalized, these old French women, giving a sewing job to a boy. A boy touching their bridal gowns. It helped that I was Vietnamese. It made me seem more like a girl to them."

"How did you ever get the job?" The air always smelled of perfume. It smelled of the beautiful women who passed them.

"I said I would work three days for free, all handwork, and then I would go if they wanted me to go. I was so terrified, sitting in the back of that store, all those women watching me. I never spoke to anyone there. They didn't want me, but they couldn't resist either. The French will always take something for free. At the end of the three days, they needed me."

Sabine thinks of Phan coming home from eight-hour meetings at Microsoft and getting down on his knees to pin up the hem of her skirt. He had her stand on a wooden footstool. He did not ask her to turn, but crawled in a circle around her, his mouth full of pins. "Who taught you to sew?"

"My mother, my grandmother, my aunts. We all sewed. They wanted to keep me close, with them, all the time. Children weren't out roaming the streets then in Vietnam. The women sewed to pass the time and then they let me sew. My mother never knew what she was giving me, a means of taking care of myself, paying my way later on when the money ran out. Everyone needs to have something that he knows how to do, something that can support him."

"Did you tell Parsifal?"

"That I could sew? I sewed for him all the time."

The couple who is walking towards them stops and kisses without ever looking out at the water. He cups the back of her head in his hand. For a minute Sabine wonders if she and Phan look like lovers, the way they are pressed together on the bridge, but then she remembers that he is dead and she is asleep in America. She remembers and then she puts it out of her mind. "Did you tell him about living here? I know that he knew, but did you talk about it? Did you tell him how you felt, not hearing from your parents anymore, being alone, having to go to work? Did you talk about the things you were afraid of then?"

Phan runs his thumb back and forth across his lower lip. "It's so hard for me to remember. I'm sure I told him most of it. I know there was nothing I meant to keep from him, but did I tell him about those days in particular? Did I tell him about sewing seed pearls onto the train of a gown for ten days straight, the bride who wanted tiny bumblebees made out of seed pearls all around her hem? My stitches were so even that the woman who owned the shop said she could have worn her dress inside-out and still have had the most elegant gown in France, and I said she couldn't because then all those little bees would have stung her. It was the only time I ever made a joke in the three years I worked there. Maybe I didn't tell him that. It seems like there wasn't ever time to talk about the past. Those were such good days, when we were all together, but everything happened in a rush. When I think back on it now, I want to find a way to slow things down. I have so many memories of leaving the house. It seems like I was always walking away. We went out to dinner, we drank by the pool, we went to work, saw friends. Now I wish we had always stayed inside. We were so in love with each other, we were so relieved that the past was behind us, I don't think we wanted to talk about it."

"I used to think he told me everything," Sabine says, even though it is not her lover she is speaking of. It is her husband, her friend.

"You were his life. There was no one he trusted more than you, but no one tells anyone everything." Phan puts his arm around her and together they watch the river of tourists snaking its way towards the Louvre. "There isn't enough time."

"Kitty tells me," Sabine says. "She's trying to tell me what she remembers. It's hard for her, too. She does it because I ask her."

"I like Kitty. I like her face."

"It's Parsifal's face," Sabine tells him. "At first you can't even see her, she looks so much like him." As she says this Sabine looks up and sees Kitty walking towards them over the bridge. She is wearing a long dark coat and her hair is pulled away from her face. Her hands are buried in a white muff. Sabine stands up straight and shades her eyes with her hand, even though the day is overcast. For a second it is clearly Kitty, and then she folds into the crowd again. Sabine knows Kitty has never been to Paris before, that she may be lost or confused. "Phan." She points as if she has spotted a crime or a rare bird. "Look."

Phan looks and then he smiles. He stands behind Sabine and wraps his arms around her. He puts his face against her hair, whispers in her ear. *"Sabine, regard. Qui est-ce?"*

And she does. It is easier and easier, because with every second there is a step and they are closer and closer together. It isn't Kitty at all. That is not a muff but a rabbit. She breaks from Phan, whose arms bloom open to let her go. She runs and runs through the crowds of beautiful men and women who are walking towards her holding hands. He is beautiful, as beautiful as he was that first night in the Magic Hat, as beautiful as he was on Johnny Carson. Good health has made him young again. Sabine's crying has started and it blurs her vision, but it doesn't matter because he is coming towards her as well. He is with her. He is catching her, holding her, as she cries and cries against his chest. It is overwhelming to feel such relief, the abrupt end of pain. This is everything she has wanted, this instant, the sound of his heart beneath his sweater.

"I'm so sorry," Parsifal says, his voice warm and kind and completely his own, his fingers lacing into her hair. He has put the rabbit down and it waits at his feet. Bosco, a rabbit from so many years ago. It has a brown spot between its ears like a toupee.

She shakes her head no, buries her head against him. She wants to crawl into his chest, to live inside him, to find a hold from which they can never be separated.

"I've put you through so much," he says. "Sabine, Sabine, I should have told you everything. I wanted—"

The bedroom door closed, making a heavy click. At the click, she opened her eyes.

"They're asleep," a voice called down the hall, a voice that should have been quieter since she was sleeping. How's voice?

Sabine closed her eyes and tried to slip back. She had been dreaming, it had left a taste in her mouth. Her pillow was damp from crying. She wanted not to remember but to sleep, to be inside again. Where was she now? Nebraska. Parsifal's room. This should be the dream. The place she had been a minute ago was more familiar. She dug herself into the pillow and took the regular breaths of sleep, but there was no going back. Bit by bit the real world surrounded her. Dot and Bertie were home now, and the boys? She could hear their faint noise down the hall. Dot was laughing. They would wonder what she was doing sleeping in the middle of the day. Sabine felt guilty whenever she was caught napping. Not like Parsifal, who flaunted his naps, stretched out over the sofa in the middle of the day, the ringer on the phone turned off in anticipation of a long voyage. Sabine shifted her weight slightly, rolled forward on her hip, and that was when she noticed the warm breathing on the back of her neck, the weight of an arm across her waist. She was in Parsifal's bed. She had fallen asleep. Kitty had been telling a story, another horrible story. Kitty was in the twin bed, both of them on their sides, Sabine facing the window, Kitty facing Sabine. Of course she could hear her now, the nearly undetectable sounds another person makes when she is at her quietest. She could feel the warmth on her back, warm enough to fall asleep without a blanket. Though she would have been embarrassed if Kitty was awake, for this one minute she was grateful for the luxury of having someone to lie next to. Sabine tried to remember the last time she had slept with another person. She had lain down with Parsifal in the weeks after Phan had died. She had held him when he wanted to be held, but she had never fallen asleep. When she was a child there had been nothing better than sleeping in her parents' bed. They allowed it in cases of thunderstorms, nightmares, and mild earthquakes that did not require them to stand underneath doorways. But when was the last time? In all the nights that came to mind she was alone. It must have been the architect, the one who had the sailboat. She had stayed the night because he always wanted to cook her dinner. He never managed to get anything on the table until ten o'clock, so that by the time they had made love she was too tired to drive herself home. He planned it that way. He wanted her to fall asleep, to spend the whole night—his sheets and blankets, the glass of water he left for her on the windowsill above the bed just in case she should wake up in the middle of the night thirsty. A few times Sabine went along, but there was something wrong about it even as there was something nice. Sleeping together, she believed, was about love, which was what she knew the architect wanted. Which she knew she did not want with him. In the morning he squeezed fresh juice for her breakfast, wanted to brush his teeth while she was in the shower.

Kitty stirred, pressed her forehead against the back of Sabine's neck, moved her knees closer to Sabine's knees. "I fell asleep," Kitty said, her voice thick.

"Kitty," Sabine whispered.

Kitty pulled back and then raised up on her elbow. "Oh, my," she said slowly. "This is a surprise." She sat up and ran her fingers hard through her hair. "I don't usually fall asleep like that. I must have been dead tired. It must have been all the talking. We wore ourselves out."

"They're home. I heard them."

"Who?"

"Dot, Bertie. I think the boys."

Kitty stood up and stretched. Her shirt had slipped out of her jeans and showed a thin strip of white stomach. "I guess I'd better go on out there, see if anybody needs mothering."

Sabine nodded but she did not get up right away. Who would have thought there could be so much room in a single bed? Room enough to fall asleep with someone and forget that they were there.

"We are too skinny," Kitty said, as if she had been thinking the same thing. She slapped her own stomach. "The two of us sleeping in that little bed."

Sabine got up and followed Kitty down the hall without her shoes. She felt stupid, stupid from the sleep and stupid from the dream, which she thought had been good even though she had been crying. Mainly she felt stupid trailing behind Kitty like a silent sheep when she wanted to touch her arm and tell her something, thank you or that they were friends now, absolutely. They had been alone all afternoon. They had gone out and told secrets. They had fallen asleep. Shouldn't there be a moment when they whispered something to each other instead of simply walking single file into the kitchen's throng?

"There are my girls," Dot said. "Sleeping in the middle of the day."

"It did me a world of good," Kitty said, tucking her shirt down. "Is there coffee made?"

"Two minutes." The television was playing in the other room. The theme to *Headline News* was their background music.

"Don't," Kitty said. "Not if there isn't some."

Dot waved her off and picked up the percolator. Who still used a percolator? In Phan's house on Oriole there was a cappuccino machine and an espresso machine, a Melitta, a plunger, and a two-potted Mister Coffee for dinner parties so that they could make regular and decaf at the same time. Parsifal kept the beans in the freezer. "I want a cup."

How and Guy sat at the table. They seemed to be having a peaceful moment, reading two separate pages from the sports section, eating toasted cheese sandwiches. As much as they hated one another, they seemed to be bound at the waist by a three-foot invisible rope. They had finished exactly half of their sandwiches, and the two glasses of milk that sat beside their respective plates were at suspiciously similar levels.

"The Lakers are dead," Guy said in a disgusted voice. "They should have their ball taken away."

"Everything go okay at school?" Kitty asked. She leaned over and pushed back a lank piece of hair that blocked Guy's left eye.

"Um-huh," Guy said.

"There was a food fight at lunch," How said, his face made bright with the memory. "Gram had to break it up. She got right in the middle of it."

"They were only throwing their peas," Dot said modestly.

"Nobody threw anything at her," How said.

"Well, I'm glad to see them showing some respect for the elderly." Kitty's hands were everywhere. She ran them over Dot's shoulders and down How's arm. They settled, comforted.

How looked up at his mother, his eyes full of a dreamy sort of love that made him look sleepy. "You feeling all right?"

"Sure thing," Kitty said.

"I was wondering, since you were lying down."

"What are you," Guy said, without looking up from his reading, "the sleep police?"

How opened his mouth, but it was Kitty who spoke. "Sabine and I bored each other out of our minds. We talked and talked until we got so dull we just passed out. We didn't even mean to. One minute we were talking and the next minute, bang." Kitty looked to Sabine in conspiracy.

"Absolutely," Sabine said.

Bertie came in with her arms full of colored sheets of construction paper. She was wearing a plaid wool jumper over a white sweater. She was wearing tights and flat shoes. Her curls were brushed back hard and caught in a barrette at the nape of her neck. She looked like a larger version of her students, as if she had dressed to reassure them that growing up wouldn't be so different from what they already knew. "I can't work in there. He won't turn the television off."

Kitty looked at her sons, counting them, one, two. "Who won't turn the television off?"

"Howard's here," Dot said. "I told him you were asleep."

"And he didn't wake me up?" Kitty leaned over the percolator and watched the coffee shoot up into the glass dome. The room filled with the tidelike churning of its boil. "I find that hard to believe."

"Gram told him he couldn't go back there because of Aunt Sabine," Guy whispered. "Said we all had to be on good manners."

"Why isn't he at work?"

"He's going to double-shift tonight," Dot said, pulling down cups. She held one up to Sabine. "You going to have some?"

Sabine nodded and rubbed her eyes. The smell of coffee reminded her of something, the first time she and Parsifal went to Paris. They stayed in a pension over a bistro, and the smell of coffee woke them up in the mornings. It got in their clothes, in their hair. When they went walking they could close their eyes and follow the scent of coffee in the breeze. "Not just any coffee," he had said to her. "Our coffee." That was before the rug store, when he was the buyer for French Country Antiques. They spent tireless days at the flea market. Parsifal bought an eight-hundred-pound marble deer that was curled up, asleep. When they finished shopping they showered and changed into their costumes to do a magic show.

"Bonsoir, Mesdames et Messieurs. Je m'appelle Parsifal le Magicien et voici ma merveilleuse assistante."

" 'Ma merveilleuse'?" Sabine had said after the show.

"Haas said he saw you two at Wal-Mart." Bertie poured herself a cup of coffee. "Did you get the pens?"

"Did you get the Almond Roca?" Kitty asked, leaning against her sister.

Sabine thought Bertie would laugh, but instead her cheeks flushed red. She turned away from her sister as if she had been caught.

"Ohh," Guy said, suddenly alert to the potential for humiliation. "Almond *Ro*-ca." He gave the *r* a deep, Latin roll and managed to make the small, nut-crusted candies sound lascivious.

"I found a pen," Sabine said, shifting through the bags she had left by the back door. It would be hard to be Bertie, to be so in love in this house where everyone else was inured to it. She would have been five years old when Kitty got married in the hospital ward, Howard Plate taking his morphine through drip IV while they repeated their vows back to the minister. Sabine held up the pen, which was sealed to a piece of cardboard by form-fitting plastic. *"Voilà."*

"I want to pay you for it."

Sabine smiled. "You're not going to pay me for a pen. You can think of it as a wedding present."

"Well, you're going to have to work fast. Those things should have been in the mail a long time ago." Dot tried to sound like the mother of the bride, but she was paying more attention to making dinner than she was to the conversation. She had been mothering people in one way or another for forty-six years. Her energy for the project had faded.

"We already know who's coming," Bertie said.

"Hey, Dad," How said. The room got quiet and turned collectively towards the living room door, where Howard Plate leaned. His baseball cap, whose neat cursive letters said *Woolrich* across the front, was pulled down low so that he had to tilt his head back to see properly.

"There still coffee?"

Dot brushed her hands against the sides of her slacks. "There should be some. It seems like we all wanted coffee without knowing it."

"That's because some people get so sleepy," he said. If he was looking at anyone in particular it was impossible to tell because of the angle of the cap.

"Some people didn't get a whole hell of a lot of sleep last

night." Kitty picked up the salad radishes her mother had been slicing and continued the job. The knife made a staccato tap against the cutting board.

"Now, whose fault would that be?"

"All right," Bertie said, and pushed up from the table. "If Howard's abandoned the television, then I think it's fair game for me and the boys. What do you say?"

Good, obedient boys, they stood up and began to fold the newspaper, making preparations to follow their aunt into quieter regions of the ranch house. There were too many people in the room once Howard Plate had been added, like the person who makes his way late onto a too-full elevator. Everyone had begun shifting their weight, feeling boxed in.

Kitty put down her knife. "I don't want you to run off. I haven't seen you boys all day. Everything is fine."

"Is that my coffee?" Howard Plate pointed towards the cup Dot had left on the sink. Dot looked at it, surprised, and nodded.

"I want Sabine to show you how she shuffles cards," Kitty said. "She showed me today. I want you boys to see it. Maybe she'll show you a card trick, too, if she feels like it. I was so impressed, I told her I thought she ought to be a magician."

"I told her the same thing," Dot said to her grandsons. "She took an egg out of my ear, you know."

"I didn't think women could be magicians," How said. He thought about it and started again. "I mean, I knew they could be, but they aren't, are they? I can't ever remember . . ."

"In all the many, many magicians you've seen," Guy said.

"On television," How said, his voice taking on an edge like the far-off sound of a storm. "How many women magicians have you seen on television, stupid?"

"I really think I might scream if this goes on for one minute more," Kitty said quietly. She put down the knife and reached into her back pocket, where she had put the deck when she and Sabine had been alone. She handed it to Sabine. Howard Plate, coffee cup wrapped in both hands, was back in his spot at the doorjamb. It was easy to see how he could have been a hoodlum twenty-five years before. There was something in his posture, both hurt and menacing, that might have seemed romantic when he was young and still handsome. When he was young, it might have been enough that he was tough rather than smart, that he drank too much and went around in the winter with no jacket. Boys like that came to bad ends: They went to prison; they slapped their cars into trees late at night and never got out; they left town under the good advice of the local law enforcement agency and were not heard from again. They slipped on the ice late at night in a trainyard and fell beneath the wheels of a train. Rarely, rarely did they survive, stay with the woman they married, the children they fathered, and settle a round stomach on top of their thin legs. Howard Plate had stayed.

Sabine opened the pack. The cards were soft from a hundred games of gin rummy, from all of Dot's late-night solitaire played on a cookie sheet in bed. Once the cellophane was off a deck, and the seal broken, the cards were worth nothing to a magician. Everyone thought you were cheating, and even though you were, every minute, you didn't use marked cards. Parsifal ordered his cards by the case. He threw them away after a few tricks, even if it was only in practice. He had to work with new cards. Once a card was broken in he didn't know how to make it move anymore. But Sabine saved those decks. She practiced with cards until she tore them in half. She glued them together, painted them, and cut them into walls for office complexes. She gave the leftover packs to her mother, who sent them to Hillel House and the Jewish Home and, on one occasion, sent twenty decks to an orphanage in Israel.

She handed them to How. "Ordinary deck of cards?"

How took the deck suspiciously. He knew it. It was the deck he and Guy used to play spit-in-the-ocean on the days they were stuck inside, days it got so cold the wind could burst your eardrums. They played until one of them believed the other to be cheating, at which point they threw the cards down and began to beat each other senseless. Dot always made them count the deck in front of her once they were finished with it. Otherwise cards got lost beneath the couch. How fanned them out and did a cursory inspection, identified all four suits, did not notice an unusual number of aces. The blue-and-white deck had the softness of a well-worn baseball glove. He handed them back to her. "Okay," he said, but with no real commitment.

Sabine started the show. She did it because she felt that Kitty was asking her for help with her family. She did it because a deck of cards always made her feel closer to Parsifal. She started slow, a simple collapsing bridge. She divided the deck into packets of cards and tripped them over in her fingers. These people were card rubes. They had never had the opportunity to be impressed before. She could make them cry out in pleasure just by cutting the deck. "It was your Uncle Parsifal who taught this to me originally."

"God," Bertie said, leaning over the table. "I have to call Haas. He has to see this." She did not straighten up or go to the phone. She stayed fixed to her place by the flash of blue-and-white paper. "Do you think you could come to my class sometime? The kids would love this."

"Wouldn't that be something," Dot whispered.

How's hands stayed on the table, his chapped lips parted so that he could breathe easily through his mouth. Even Guy was quiet. Kitty was standing at the back of Sabine's chair. They were all rocked by the cards, soothed by the rhythmic motion. She could make these people bark if she wanted to. She could make them walk on their hands and knees and bark like dogs if she told them that was the next part of the trick. It wasn't even a trick, it was shuffling. She had paralyzed them by shuffling cards, which said more about Alliance than it did about her talents.

She rolled the deck so fast they would never have caught her doing anything at all. Red cards face-in, black cards face-out, a few more showy cuts where nothing really moved. "One trick," she said, "An easy one, but I'll need a volunteer."

It was a beautiful word, volunteer, the promise of partner ship, inclusion. To volunteer was your chance to step into the light and see the people who were seated down where you used to be. The Fetters and the Plates looked up at her, hopeful, expectant. Each one was sure he or she would be chosen and so did not feel the need to ask.

"You, sir," Sabine said, smiling like a Vegas girl to the man at the door.

The table turned and looked at Howard Plate, who had kept his distance, staying on the far side of the kitchen. "You don't mean me."

"I do." She patted the table, a sign to come.

"Ah, hell," Howard Plate said.

"Be a good sport," Kitty said to her husband.

"I don't know anything about this stuff."

Guy moved over to the empty chair beside him, offering his place to his father. "Come on, Dad."

Howard Plate sighed at the tremendous burden that had been put on him. He walked his coffee cup over to the sink, rinsed it out, set it facedown on the counter, and came back to the table in no hurry at all. "I never liked games," he said, taking his place.

"It's not a game," Sabine said, turning the deck in her hands, making them think the shuffling continued long after it was over. "This is a test."

"I like those even less."

The table was nervous. Maybe Sabine had made a bad pick. Their backs were all preternaturally straight, their breathing shallow, as if they were at an especially convincing séance. "This is for ESP, extrasensory perception. Very easy. It is a proven scientific fact that people can sense things they cannot see—"

"Always tell them it's science," Parsifal had said. "People are suckers for science. If car salesmen wore white coats, they'd make a fortune."

"—so all I'm going to do is test your abilities. If you think a card is red, I'll put it to the left. If you think it's black, I'll put it to the right. That easy. Don't think about it too much, just go on impulse, left and right."

"I don't know what color a card is if I can't see it."

"Maybe you do, maybe you don't." There was no way out. You don't give them one. Ever. "That's what we're going to find out."

Howard Plate lifted his baseball cap high enough for him to comb back his hair with his hand and then set it back in place. He was looking at the spaces on the table in front of him, the right side and then the left. He was thinking it through. "All right."

Sabine held out a card, facedown.

"Left."

They started into the deck, four lefts in a row and then a right; another left, but then he changed his mind and put it to the right. Howard Plate stared hard at the back of every card as if the deck were marked and he had found a way to read the code. He grew quicker, more confident. "Right, left, right, right."

When Sabine had counted to twenty-six she stopped him. "Okay. It's good to switch the piles now. It helps to keep your thinking fresh. So now red is going to the right. Got it?"

"Got it."

Sabine and Howard Plate made their way to the end of the deck. When it was over the table relaxed. Bertie and Kitty both sat down. Dot stretched out her short legs in front of her. Guy slapped his brother lightly on the arm for no reason at all. "I think I did okay," Howard Plate said.

"I have a feeling you did very well," Sabine said. She picked up the stack to the right and began going through the cards like an answer sheet. "Red, red, red, red, red, red, red, red." She flipped them down slowly at first, so that there could be the moment when people were startled not by her, but by the notion that Howard Plate was, in fact, in possession of perfect ESP. In the second it dawned on them that it was all a trick, she started going faster. She picked up the second stack and fanned it out, all black.

"Jesus," Howard Plate said. He reached his hands out to touch the cards on the table. He was careful, as if suspicious of heat. "Would you look at that?"

It was not uncommon. The last person to catch on was the one who stood to benefit, the one who was quickly calculating a life of previously unexplored talents.

How laughed and broke the spell.

Sabine had picked the wrong member of the audience. She knew it the second the last card was turned, but once it was done there was no way to undo a trick. She had meant it to include him, to bring him over to the table, and yet she had mocked him. Magic was always mocking in a way. It was the process of fooling people, making them think they saw something they couldn't have seen. Every now and then fooling people made them fools.

"You fixed it?" Howard said.

"It's a trick," Bertie said. "A card trick. Remember? Kitty asked Sabine to do a card trick."

"Did you think I couldn't do it, is that why you fixed it?"

"Couldn't do what?" Sabine asked.

"That I couldn't do ESP, that I didn't have any?"

"Nobody could do it." Sabine tried to make her voice kind. "There is no such thing." She was not entirely convinced of this fact, but she felt it was important to say so.

"Well, you wouldn't know. You're a cheat." He tilted back his head so that she could see his eyes beneath the bill of his cap, so that she could see the damage done to his face by the train track. "You wouldn't even give a person the chance to try."

"Leave it alone," Kitty said.

"Don't you tell me what I can't do." And with that Howard Plate's hand swept down through the air like a bat.

Every single person at the table flinched backwards in their seat, as if the hand were coming down especially for them, but it didn't hit coming down. His hand struck as it came back up, catching the underneath edge of the table. It was the table that was struck rather than the people, and the table, which was pine stained to look like oak and lighter than it appeared, flipped up on its side, towards Guy and How and Bertie, away from Dot and Kitty and Sabine. The cards, which had brought about all the bad feelings, were the first to shoot up in a particularly spectacular twist on shuffling, followed by the coffee cups and varying amounts of coffee, both milky and black, followed by the table itself. Probably no one would have been hurt if they had just sat there and taken what was coming on. The coffee was no longer hot and the cups tumbled to the floor and slivered into pieces. How caught the table on his knees, but it wasn't very heavy and the blow was more surprising than painful. Bertie, however, saw it all coming. She watched Howard more carefully then the rest of them did, and when she saw his fist she tried to stand. In the second the table came towards her, she fell backwards in her chair, hitting her head with a dull crack against the wall. In all the confusion, the flowered pieces of coffee cups still spinning on the floor, the coffee still dripping from the edges of their chairs, they each distinctly heard the sound of Bertie hitting the wall.

How righted the table from his knees, looking first to see that he wasn't in turn pinning someone else, and then slipped down on the floor beside his aunt. The edges of her white sweater were turning brown from where the coffee was soaking through. He picked up her hand, the one with the ring, and held it.

"Bertie?" Dot crouched down beside her daughter and touched her forehead. Guy helped Kitty and Sabine pull the table into the center of the room, though any one of them could have managed it alone. "That was a hell of a spill."

Bertie was still in her chair, but on her back, like a drawing that needed to be rehung in another direction. She squeezed her eyes shut and then blinked them open. "Tell Howard to go," she said quietly.

"How's your head feel?" Dot said.

"Tell Howard to go."

"I didn't do a damn thing to her," Howard Plate said, his voice raising. "She fell out of her chair and now you're going to say I pushed her out." He rapped his finger on the table. "I was all the way over here."

"Howard, go on," Kitty said.

"I did not push her."

Dot tried to slip her hand under the back of Bertie's head and Bertie's eyes squeezed shut again. Dot's fingers came back a bright and oily red. Suddenly Sabine remembered having cleaned the light fixtures that morning, although it seemed like weeks ago. That was the reason everything was so bright now.

"Ah, Christ," Howard said. "Well, you've all got it fixed

now. There's your proof. There's your proof that I'm the bad man."

How was the biggest person in the room, the tallest, the heaviest, the strongest, though none of them would have thought of him that way. He would not have thought of himself that way. "Bertie, do you want to try and sit up?" he asked his aunt.

"Sure," she said, "but if your dad could go."

"Fine," Howard Plate said. "You don't have to ask me twice." He was across the room in four large steps. He opened the door with one hand and took his coat off the hook with the other. He was gone at the very moment How was lifting up Bertie's chair. Howard Plate did not close the door, did not remember or did not bother to. The cold air cut into the room and made Bertie smile. Dot kept her hand under her daughter's neck to help steady it. Kitty ran to close the door.

It was the barrette, the flat gold oval from Wal-Mart that held back Bertie's hair, that had bitten into the back of her scalp and scraped up as it met the chair rail on the wall going down.

"I can't quite tell." Kitty removed the barrette and tried to see what was beneath the fast-soaking curls. "You've got so damn much hair. But I'm pretty sure you need stitches."

"Maybe she has a concussion." Dot tried to peer into Bertie's pupils to see if they were evenly dilated.

"I don't have a concussion," Bertie said, her voice tired. "You should call Haas. He can drive me over."

"He can meet you there," Dot said. "We'll drive you over."

How was standing with Guy now. The sight of the blood had driven them back, away from the table. Their faces were pale, very young, suddenly identical. They looked as much alike as Kitty and Parsifal. "She going to be okay?" Guy asked.

"I'm going to be fine," Bertie said. "Nobody ever died

from falling out of a kitchen chair." She looked at her pair of nephews. "You call Haas. Tell him I'm okay, that I just need a few stitches, but he should come over to the hospital."

"Sure," Guy said. "He should come now?"

Bertie nodded slightly. "That would be best."

The boys turned and went together down the hall, opting for the phone that was farthest away from the kitchen.

"I've got to get a towel," Dot said, and headed down the hall as if she were following after the boys.

"Get a dark one," Bertie called to her.

Sabine leaned over and began picking up pieces of coffee cups, but they seemed to be everywhere. The floor had taken on the jagged topography of a bar fight.

"Bertie, I'm awfully sorry," Kitty said. She touched the back of her hand to her sister's pale cheek and held it there as if checking for fever.

"You didn't do anything."

"I didn't do anything is right." Kitty tried to wipe away the line of blood that was running down the back of Bertie's neck, but she only succeeded in smearing it. "Your sweater's going to be ruined," she said sadly.

Dot came back with a towel and an armful of coats. "Okay, chop-chop, we're getting out of here."

"One of you needs to stay here with the boys," Bertie said, taking the folded towel and pressing it gently against the back of her head. She winced. "Shit."

"They'll be fine," Dot said. The heater was set to seventy-two degrees, the cupboards and refrigerator-freezer were full of food. There was television.

"They won't be fine. They feel bad. We don't all need to go."

"I can stay," Sabine said. She wanted to be of help. She was the one who started everything, picking Howard from the

263

audience. That was why Parsifal was the magician. He knew who to pick, how to control the crowd.

"No," Bertie said. "Not you." She twisted her fingers through Sabine's to hold her there. Sabine squeezed. At least she understood how to comfort.

"My boys, I'll stay," Kitty said. "But for God's sake, get going or we'll all have to come in and give you a transfusion."

Sabine held the towel while Dot and Kitty helped Bertie on with her coat. The boys came back in time to tell them Haas was on his way. After that Bertie was in a hurry to go.

"Call me from the hospital," Kitty said. She followed them onto the porch and stood in the circle cast down from the light over the back door. The snow was so brilliant it seemed fake. "I want to know how many stitches." She waved, as if they were going on an adventure and she understood that she had to be left behind. Sabine was sorry to leave her. Kitty would feel guilty about this somehow. There was snow in her dark hair and she shivered, standing in the cold night without so much as a sweater.

"Goddamn Howard," Dot said, her eyes on Kitty as they backed down the driveway. "You can't go swinging your temper around without somebody getting hurt."

"At least it wasn't one of the boys," Bertie said.

"Well, it shouldn't have been them, but it shouldn't have been you, either. I just feel sick about this," Dot said. "You were the only one of my children who never had stitches. I always thought of that as a real personal success."

"I had stitches when they took my wisdom teeth out," Bertie said.

"Those kind of stitches don't count. I'm talking about emergency stitches, this kind of thing, everybody piled up in the car going to the emergency room, praying you don't have a wreck on the way over. Bertie was always so much more careful than Kitty and Guy," Dot said over her shoulder to Sabine, in the backseat. "I always said it was God's reward to me. He knew I didn't have the energy for another daredevil. She was always a lady. Never jumped off of tables, never wanted to play pirates using real knives. I always thought that would be such a high-class thing, having a kid that wasn't sewn up fifteen different ways."

"Well, I'm almost thirty," Bertie said, yawning. "This can't be held against my good childhood record."

"Your children are always your children," Dot said with authority.

It was early in the evening and completely dark as they headed towards town. Inside the houses that were so much like Dot's, the warm yellow lights clicked on, and Sabine could see the shapes of people passing in front of their windows, and she wondered if there were other strangers in town, a whole contingency of hidden people who had not meant to come there at all, people who meant to leave but couldn't find exactly the moment to go. She wondered if they were from all over the world, from every place she had ever been to with Parsifal, sleeping in their borrowed beds, drying their hands on guest towels. She wondered how it was they'd come to be here. Had their cars broken down? Had they spoken to a stranger in a restaurant and stayed to find out more? Had they come here to visit someone, some relative so distant that the blood ties were all but untraceable, and then somehow just fell into a habit? They had grown used to being there even as they longed to leave. They missed the beautiful places they were from. They missed the indigenous flowers, the good local supermarkets, their families, and still they did not know how to go. It was impossible that what was happening to Sabine could be happening to her alone.

Haas was standing outside the front entrance of Box Butte

General Hospital. Even from a distance they were sure it was him.

"He's going to freeze to death," Bertie said, leaning forward as they pulled up the front drive.

"I'm sure he'd rather freeze to death than wait inside," Dot said.

Haas had recognized the car and was there with his hand out, opening the door before they had come to any semblance of a stop. "Are you all right?" He reached down and unfastened Bertie's seat belt. His face was flushed with cold and worry.

"I'm fine," Bertie said.

"I told them inside you were coming." Haas wasn't wearing any gloves. He was trying to help her out of the car or trying to embrace her, it was difficult to tell. In his worry his hands went everywhere, as if he were checking for other injuries.

"You two go inside," Dot said. "Sabine and I'll park." But even as she was saying it, they were walking away, pressing themselves together into one person against the terrible cold. Dot watched them until they were safe inside the bright waiting room. She shook her head. "I like Haas plenty," she told Sabine. "He's a good man. But there's something about those two, the way they're so stuck on each other. It makes me nervous. I always want to leave the room when they're together."

"It's like watching something that's too private," Sabine said, thinking of the letters that Phan had written to Parsifal, how she had to put them back in the envelopes. *Most Beloved.*

"Maybe it's just that nobody ever loved me that way. Al sure didn't, not even in the beginning, and I didn't grow up around that sort of thing. I'm from another generation. Maybe I don't understand it or maybe I'm jealous, though God knows I'm too old to want somebody hanging all over me now." She smiled at Sabine, picked up a handful of her straight black hair, and then let it fall back into place. "What about you? Were you and Guy ever that way?"

Sabine smiled. The very thought of it. "Not us," she said, watching Bertie and Haas huddle together at the information counter, his arm around her waist. "It wasn't that kind of love." When Phan was in the hospital, when he was sick at home, Parsifal would hold him in a way she could not describe. It was the way Bertie was holding Haas now, holding on to him. They seemed to absorb one another through the skin.

Parking the car only consisted of driving about twenty feet to the left and turning it off. The lot was well plowed and lightly scattered with cars. Every car stood far apart from the next. No one took the risk of sliding into someone else's fender. When Dot and Sabine pushed through the door of the hospital, the nurse looked up from her paperwork and gave a smile that established her as both helpful and concerned.

"It's not us," Dot said. "My daughter, Bertie Fetters." Dot pointed to the double doors, knowing full well that was the direction they would have gone in. "Albertine Fetters."

"Of course," the nurse said. She had the healthy, big-boned look of a woman who should have been on a ranch, collecting eggs and putting out hay for the horses. Sitting at her desk in such a white uniform, she had the carefully studied attitude of someone who was pretending to be something she was not. "She went back with her husband. Do you want to go with them?"

"Naw," Dot said, walking away. "I've been. Let them be alone." She took up a spot on a battered two-seater sofa as far away from the nurse as possible and then patted the cushion next to her for Sabine to come and join her. "No big-city emergency room, hey?"

Sabine sat down. In their hurry to leave she had not put

on socks and now her feet were aching from the cold. "It is a hospital, isn't it?" Sabine hated hospitals, but this one brought up no unpleasant memories. It was just a large, well-lit room with a linoleum floor and mismatched furniture. If it weren't for the nurse, who was deeply involved in a magazine article, they would have been alone.

"I should know. There isn't one part of this place I haven't been. I had all three of my kids here. Kitty crushed a glass with her hand. Al pulled Guy's arm out of the socket—Lord, that was a gruesome sight. They stitched up my lip and my eye, taped up my ribs. So many things you couldn't count. We were the regular customers. There was a time I couldn't imagine coming in this place and not knowing the name of the girl at the front desk. The nurses all said hello to me when I saw them in the grocery store. Cops brought Al here the night he died. Tried to resuscitate him all the way over in the ambulance and then again when they got here. What a thought that was, bringing him back from the dead." She shook her head. "Kitty got married on the second floor. Of course, it was just a tiny little place then. They added all this on ten years ago, our last stab at prosperity. If you want to be somewhere that Guy spent a lot of time, then this is the place."

Sabine reached out to touch a rubber plant at the end of the love seat. For a minute she'd thought it might have been real. "Maybe I should drive out to Lowell," she said. "Take a look at the reformatory."

Dot turned to her, her mouth open. "Jesus, what a horrible thought. You wouldn't do that."

"Just to see it, see where he was."

"You forget about that," Dot said. Sabine knew the look on her face. She had seen it on Parsifal's face the day she suggested they ride out to Connecticut to see his parents' graves. "He isn't there. You wouldn't see anything but a bunch of crazy, terrified boys. Or maybe it's gotten better by now. It couldn't have gotten worse."

"You went to see him at Lowell?"

"Sure I went," Dot said quietly. "Two weeks before I had Bertie. I took the bus clear to the other side of the state, almost to Iowa and up north of Omaha. Worst sort of hellhole, like nothing I'd seen before or since. But Guy came in the visiting room so nice, his hair all combed. All he wanted to know about was how Kitty was and how I was, and when I asked about how he was doing, he shook his head and said he was fine. I was so embarrassed, being that pregnant, but I knew the trip would be even harder once I had the baby with me. When our time was up, he gave me a hug, just like he was only going off to bed, and he told me not to come back." Dot nodded. "I knew what he meant. He didn't want me to have to come so far, but more than that, he didn't want me to see him there. For me, that day was the worst of it. Worse than the day Al died and worse than the day Guy was sentenced. Guy would never want anyone going back to Lowell."

Sabine took Dot's hand. She felt vaguely relieved. Touring the monuments of Parsifal's youth wasn't the only thing that mattered. "So I won't go. You know I hate to drive in the snow, anyway."

"I appreciate that," Dot said.

Sabine never looked up when someone came into the waiting room at Cedars Sinai. It was part of the code of manners, that you let people have their privacy, that you let them read bad magazines or have a cry or go to the bathroom twenty times in a half hour and grant them the courtesy of not noticing. But Box Butte General was too small, and when they heard the door Dot and Sabine and the nurse all looked up in unison at the tall, thin man who came through it.

Howard Plate left a watery trail of snow on his way to the information desk. "I wanted to check on Bertie Fetters."

"Hey," Dot called out. She waved her hand so that he would have no problem identifying her.

Howard sighed and drummed the nurse's desk slowly with his fingers before turning and walking over. The nurse, always interested in the possibility of family drama on a slow night, watched until he was safely on the other side of the room, and then she went back to her magazine.

"What are you doing over here?" Dot said.

"I was getting ready to go on. I thought I'd just come by and check, make sure she's okay." He didn't look at Sabine. He kept his eyes on Dot. His hands stayed deep inside his pockets. "There's nothing wrong with her, did they say?"

"No one's told me anything. I imagine she'll take some stitches in the back of her head."

"Well, it's too bad."

"You shouldn't be throwing tables around," Dot said. Her tone was instructive: look both ways before you cross the street, never leave a knife point up in the dishwasher.

"Don't get started on me," Howard said mildly. "If I want to hear it I'll go see my wife."

"I'm not starting on you, Howard. I think it was decent of you to come by. I think you're a real son of a bitch for a million other things, but you're good to check on her."

He nodded his head slightly, accepting both the criticism and the smaller compliment. He looked tired. The map of scars on his cheek was red from the cold. "You don't need to say I was here."

Across the room, Haas slipped through the double doors and was almost in their party before any of them noticed. They were all startled to see him; the terribly pained expression on his pale face rendered him tragic. For a second they each imagined some improbable version of bad news. "Why are you here?" he asked Howard.

"How's Bertie?" Dot said.

"Twelve stitches. She's fine. She only minded because they had to cut out some of her hair."

"Twelve," Dot said.

"Why are you here?"

Howard Plate seemed completely unable to say. The bill of his cap tipped down, as if a strong wind had come up that might take it from him.

"He came to see if Bertie was okay," Dot said.

"You need to stay away from Bertie," Haas said. There was nothing threatening in his voice or the way he stood. His face lifted up and his glasses reflected the overhead lights and hid his eyes. He was a smaller man than Howard Plate by two inches, and he lacked Howard Plate's toughness in every way, the toughness honed in his hoodlum days, and yet there was no doubt that had they fought, Haas would have won easily. He would have been fighting for Bertie. "I know you're around," he said. "I know you're family, but when she comes into the house, you need to go."

"I was on the other side of the room," Howard Plate said. "I got nowhere near her."

"Doesn't matter. You say you got nowhere near her, and she got hurt. What that says to me is that you need to stay farther away."

"Don't tell me what to do." He shifted his feet so that they were a few inches farther apart. Howard Plate was ready. If something was to happen, at least it would happen in a hospital. Dot wouldn't have to drive anyone over this time.

"I am," Haas said, so quietly the nurse did not lift up her eyes. So quietly that Sabine almost didn't hear. "I am telling you." Then he went back across the waiting room and through the doors. Howard Plate watched him go. He stayed for a minute afterwards, watching, thinking about it. He seemed to have forgotten about his mother-in-law and Sabine. He had forgotten about the nurse. He stood by himself in the waiting room as if he were trying to decide whether or not he should go through the doors, pull Haas to the ground, and kill him. When he finally made up his mind and left, no one said good-night.

"My God," Sabine said. "And I thought we got a lot of drama in L.A."

"The things that go on in these little towns, you wouldn't believe them." Dot watched all the doors carefully to make sure that no one changed his mind.

When Bertie came out with Haas, her hair was knotted up on the top of her head. There was a large piece of white adhesive tape stuck to the base of her skull, with skin shaved freshly pink around the edges. She looked slightly dazed, as if her stoic good sense were finding its limits. Haas carried an ice pack in one hand, Bertie's hand in the other.

"Oh, Bertie," Sabine said.

"Twelve stitches," Dot said. "I can't brag on you now."

Bertie stood and stared at them with such complete blankness that Sabine wondered if they had checked her for a concussion. "I'm going home with Haas," she said finally, her voice a bare squeak. "I'm going to stay with him for a while."

"I think that's good," Dot said. "I think that's exactly right."

"You have Sabine," Bertie said. "You'll be fine at home."

"Absolutely fine. You two go on. Stay together. Absolutely right."

"I don't want you to worry." Her spiky eyelashes were collecting the first stages of what appeared to be tears.

They all stood frozen in their spots, waiting to see whether or not Bertie was going to cry. Finally Sabine picked Dot's purse up from the couch. "We're leaving," she said. "You two go home, get some rest."

Dot was only too happy to follow, and together they went quickly into the night. For the first time the cold felt like a relief. The night sky that the storm had left behind was black and clean, full of the milky stars that one could never imagine seeing in Los Angeles, even when there wasn't a trace of smog in the valley. The moon, which was nothing more than a white hole punched out of the Hollywood night, had its own landscape in Nebraska, as accessible as flour in a bowl. It lit their way to the car.

"I am giddy," Dot said. "Not that I'd want her hurt, not for anything, but I've got to tell you I was starting to think Bertie was never going to go."

"She's never spent the night with Haas?"

"I told her to. I said we're all adults here, but she'd just walk out of the room. She wants to protect me—from what, I have no idea." Dot started the car and shifted into Drive. When they slipped a bit to the left on some hidden ice beneath the rear tires, she didn't even notice. "Bertie was a big surprise. People don't wait fifteen years between having their children on purpose. To start on diapers again, the alphabet. I didn't think I could do it. Of course they had that *Sesame Street* by the time she came along, that was a big help. Guy was gone. Kitty had run off and married that nut. Bertie just stayed so close. She wanted to hold my hand everywhere, she wanted to sleep in my bed. I was tired, you know. I'd raised my two kids. I'd been through all that with Al."

"She loves you."

"And I love her, too. I couldn't love her any more than I do. God help me, she was a great kid, but she never left. She's going to be thirty years old in a couple of weeks. I've been telling her to marry Haas since the first week she started going out with him, and that was six years ago. Nothing comes in balance, Sabine. Your kids either vanish or they won't go away. You pray that one daughter will get married and the other one will get divorced, and there's not a damn thing you can do about either one of them."

Sabine knew that if she stayed long enough, she would hate Howard Plate like the rest of them did. She knew there were stories and reasons, and even without them he made a particularly bad impression. Yet there was a strange way in which she felt almost sorry for him now. The way he couldn't sit comfortably in any room. The way he was outside of his own family. "Do you think Kitty would ever leave him?"

Dot took her eyes off the road to look at Sabine. There was no traffic, only soft snow stacked into banks on either side. "She leaves him all the time. She leaves him, he leaves her. The boys move in, they move out. Kitty can go, she just can't stay away."

Sabine saw Kitty going to the car in the middle of the night, a few items carelessly thrown into a bag, the boys, bleary-eyed from having been woken up, trailing behind her. "I wonder why not."

"You can't really leave somebody in a town like this. There are only ten thousand people here. No matter where you go, you keep seeing them. You can't ever start over again. I understand that. I wanted to leave Al, but where was I going to go? I'd never lived anyplace but Alliance. I didn't have any money, I had kids. Howard and Kitty may well hate each other, but it's their habit to be together, so they keep going back. You want to stop doing something, you have to get away from it. You have to put it behind you."

"And you think that's what Kitty wants?"

"Sure it's what she wants, but she doesn't have any

confidence now. She's used up all her confidence on leaving. Kitty doesn't feel young anymore. She doesn't think, Well, I could still start over and do something else. It makes me sad. We've been talking about it for more than twenty years now, how she's going to leave Howard. It makes me tired to think about it still going on."

Dot stopped the car, but they weren't at the house and they weren't in town. They were up on a knoll, a swell of land no more than ten feet high with nothing on it. "This is where all the kids come to neck," Dot said. "Not in the winter, though, only the really hardy kids come here in the winter. There are all sorts of stories about people leaving their engines going to keep the heater on and then running out of gas and freezing to death. But in the summer you have to take a number and wait in line. In the summer this is all corn as far as you can see in any direction. My father had been to the ocean once when he was a young man and he said that the ocean looked exactly like this corn, only blue. He probably said it just to make me feel better about being here."

Even without the corn it was like the ocean. The ocean on some impossibly calm night when the water looked white in the moonlight. The ocean in every direction, as far as anyone could see; which made the knoll an island, which made them shipwrecked. "I did some necking here myself in my day," Dot said dreamily. "I love it here. I come by myself now and people think I'm crazy. I come up here to think things out. When I can see everything like this it gives me perspective."

"So what's the perspective?"

"That everything is pretty much the same no matter where you are. That everyone has their problems, everyone has a couple of things that make them happy, and that if I went someplace else or knew other people it wouldn't really change.

Of course now I don't want it to change, now I like where I am, but when I was younger, that used to give me real comfort."

There was never any point in taking someone else's comfort away, even if it was comfort from another time, but Sabine did not agree with Dot's assessment of the view. Things were better in other places. People had different lives. Many suffered less. Many were happier. Sabine knew without question that Parsifal must have come to this spot. What he saw was not a life that was the same in all directions. He saw New York when he faced east, Montreal when he faced north and when the sun came down over the never-ending yellow ears of corn, he faced south and west and looked towards Los Angeles. This was the very spot Nebraska youth would come to re-imagine their lives. Even if his father had dodged the bat and the Nebraska Boys Reformatory had remained nothing but an idle threat, he would have found Los Angeles. And yet surely Kitty came here with him, looked out at the flatness and dreamed about the west, so why didn't she get to go along? Why did she have to stay behind and marry some fool who slipped off a train? Kitty could have been the magician's assistant. She had all of her brother's potential, his humor and beautiful bones. Looking out at the flatness until it folded down against the earth's natural curve, Sabine thought it was the one thing Parsifal had done wrong. He should have taken his sister with him.

"It's getting late," Sabine said. "We should be getting home." We should be getting home before Kitty leaves.

"I'm just sorry that there was no one here to see us. Old Dot Fetters finally got somebody to ride out to Park Place with her. Imagine what the talk would have been."

The windows were dark and the driveway was empty when they returned. Without someone inside, the house could not possibly distinguish itself and Sabine looked down the street, trying to remember which one was home. Sabine had been so sure they would still be there. Howard was at work, there was no reason for them to leave. Wouldn't Kitty have waited to hear about her sister? Wouldn't she have waited?

"Looks like we have the place to ourselves," Dot said cheerfully.

But Sabine didn't want the place. She was tired, the hospital had done that. She was used to spending her days at home now. Sabine took the nightcap Dot poured, their secret ritual, formerly saved until Bertie was safe in bed; but even without the ice the bourbon failed to warm her. She took the rest down in a clean sweep, some tedious dosage of medicine, told Dot good-night, and went to her room. Sabine stood at the door and looked at the twin beds for a long time before choosing the one by the window. It was hard for her to imagine now, such a little bed holding two people.

"Mother?" It had been well over a week since Sabine called home.

"What a relief to hear someone call me that. Your father has been trying to teach the rabbit to say it, just to make me feel better, but the poor thing just isn't getting it."

"How is the rabbit?"

"Fat. Fatter-than-usual fat. You know, your father peels him grapes. It takes him half the morning. You can't buy peeled grapes anywhere."

"So give them to him with the peels on, that's what I do."

"He says the peels upset the rabbit's digestion."

"I never noticed."

"Then maybe your father is right, maybe it is happier with us. Tell me something, does this poor creature have a name?"

"His name is Rabbit. Parsifal named him. He thought it was minimalist."

"Minimalist," her mother said. "That's good. We thought maybe he had some sort of racy name you didn't want to tell us."

A dirty name for the rabbit. What a thought. "Nothing so interesting."

"So, Sabine, we love the bunny, we do. He's a lot of company for your father, but we'd be much happier if you came home and took him back."

"Is he bothering you?"

"Not the point. We want you to come home now. We miss you. We worry about you. Everyone at Canter's asks, 'Where is Sabine, when is she coming home?' What do we tell them? What in god's name is keeping you so long out there in cowland?"

Sabine took a sip of her coffee and stared at the empty kitchen where one man had been murdered and poor Bertie had had the back of her head split open. "That's the sixty-four-thousand-dollar question."

"Well, give us a hint. Are you finding out everything about Parsifal you ever wanted to know?"

"I am, really. He had a bad time of it. A whole lot worse than anything he could have made up. He and his sister, Kitty, were very close. She's told me stories. At least I can understand now why he wanted to change everything about the past, give himself a new background and start over again. I don't feel like he was lying to me anymore. It didn't have anything to do with me."

"So what is so bad about these people that he had to completely reinvent himself?" Her mother's voice had the tense edge Sabine knew. It came over her just before she started making demands.

"It's not these people. It's not anything that's going on now. There were a lot of problems with his father, and his father is dead."

"Come home, Sabine."

"I will."

"When?"

"Bertie's getting married next week. I addressed the invitations. I feel like I need to stay for the wedding. After that I'll come home. I promise."

Her mother kept the line silent for a minute to let her daughter know it was not the answer she was looking for.

"Mother?"

"Hum?"

"There was something else I wanted to ask you. I don't know why I've been thinking about it. I've had a lot of time on my hands. The days out here have been incredibly long." Sabine couldn't seem to get any further in her line of questioning.

"What is it you want to know?"

"Where did you and Daddy meet?"

"You already know that. We met in Israel."

"You didn't know him before that? You never knew him in Poland?"

"Why are you asking me this long-distance? We live five miles away from each other. You can ask me when you get home."

Sabine twisted the phone cord. Because Parsifal had never told her anything all the years when he was right there, either. "I've got no problem paying the bill. You were both from Poland."

"It's a country, Sabine. It would be like saying, You were both from California."

"Did you meet him in Poland?"

"Yes."

"Did you know him when you were young?"

"I didn't know him. I met him. I met him in a train station. That was all."

"That was all? You didn't know him, but you remember meeting him in a train station. Did you speak to him?"

Her mother coughed, maybe to let Sabine know that such conversations were detrimental to her health. She would be in her own kitchen. Sabine's mother always answered the phone in the kitchen. She would lean against the counter, stare out the window, and wait for the hummingbirds that dipped into the red syrup in her hummingbird feeder all year round. "It was the first time we were moved, not later. I had dropped the sack with my lunch in it. There was a large crowd and I hadn't held on to the bag tightly. Your father saw me sitting in the waiting area and he gave me half his sandwich. Then we were put on separate trains. That was all."

"That was all? You met him that once and then you didn't see him again until you were in Israel?"

"Correct."

"And then what? You recognized him, all those years later?"

The line was quiet again and then she heard her father's voice in the background. "Ruth?" he said.

"I'm fine," she said. She must have put her hand over the receiver. When she came back her voice was clear again. "That sandwich meant a great deal to me," she told Sabine. "It was the last truly nice thing anyone did for me for a while. That, and your father had a very nice face, so I thought about him some. It was like your Nebraska in that way, there was plenty of time."

He did have a nice face. It was her own face. She knew what he would have looked like then. She knew how kind he would have been, how he could offer something without it seeming at all like charity. He would have convinced her that he had never eaten a whole sandwich in his life. That she would be helping him, truly, by taking half.

"So where did you see him again?"

"In Jaffa. You know this story. He was working on a road crew and I was at a strawberry farm."

"And he saw you walking down the street and he asked if you were from Poland, and you said, 'No, I'm from Israel.'"

"We each knew who the other one was, but we never said anything about it. Things were different back then. People weren't so big on talking everything out. We had dinner together that night."

"You must have been so happy to see him."

"I was very glad your father was alive."

Glad that her father was alive, that he had given the sandwich, that she had accepted, that they were somehow reunited, that because of that Sabine was in Nebraska now. "Do you ever talk about it with him, that time?"

"Not now. Not anymore at all."

"Do you think about it?"

Her mother considered this for a moment. "Only enough not to forget it completely. The trick is to almost forget it, but not completely. So now I've told you that." She cleared her throat. "The fascinating story of my life. Do you want to tell me why you asked?"

"I want to know everything." Suddenly Sabine longed for her mother, longed to be with her, to hold her and be held by her. "I don't want to be outside anymore."

"You have never been outside," her mother said kindly. "You were born in the center of the world. No one has ever left you out for a minute. Now do you want to say hello to your father?"

"Yes." Sabine told her mother good-bye. She wished she could tell her other things, but she had embarrassed her enough for one day.

There was a pause, the handing off of the receiver.

"Sabine-Love," her father said. "You've made your mother cry. Did you tell her you were staying out there with the cowboys?"

"I was asking her questions about you."

"Then I should assume these are tears of joy?"

"Exactly," Sabine said.

Bertie wore her hair down and did not mention the twelve neat stitches in the back of her head. If anyone inquired about them she would say only that they itched occasionally. She didn't bring up Howard Plate's name or complain that any wrong had been done to her. She sat at her same chair at the kitchen table and made a specific point of reminding Sabine that she said she would come to her classroom and show off her shuffling skills, as if to make clear Bertie harbored no ill feelings towards certain chairs or shuffling. If anything, Bertie appeared happier after Howard pushed over the table that sent her head cracking into the wall. She spoke of nothing but the wedding now, hemming her dress or checking back in with the soloist. She was thrilled by the envelopes Sabine had addressed for the invitations. In this new life in Nebraska, where time had not only stopped but occasionally seemed to creep backwards, Sabine was happy to pour herself into the job and made every letter in every word a tiny piece of art. Bertie said she wanted to ask everyone to give the envelopes back to her so that she could put them in her wedding album.

But no one thought that the impending wedding or the sharp blow to her head were the cause of Bertie's sudden happiness. Since the accident she had not spent another night at home. She was there every day, picking up her clothes, sometimes staying for dinner, but by the end of the evening she had made her furtive departure, never exactly saying that she was leaving, so that Dot inevitably spent five minutes looking for her before realizing that she was gone.

"Did you see where Bertie went to?" Dot would ask Sabine.

Within a matter of days Bertie's room had metamorphosed into a guest room, neat and anonymous. The bedspread was folded over the pillows with the smooth regularity of a Holiday Inn. The closets were empty except for some summer dresses pushed down hard to the far end of the bar; a few pairs of sandals, stacked one on top of another, sat beneath them as if they knew to stay close to the dresses they belonged with. Her bottle of perfume and three tubes of lipstick were no longer on the dresser top next to the picture of Haas, which was not there itself the day after. Items began disappearing from the bathroom: shampoos and conditioners, dental floss, Nivea, hairbrushes, a vast assortment of headbands, hair clips, and ponytail holders, until the tile countertops appeared nearly bare. Bertie went quickly, considering it had taken her almost thirty years to go.

Howard Plate was also noticeably absent in the Fetters house, no longer dropping by for sandwiches and beers when he had a few minutes. He was not sitting in Dot's recliner, watching television with the volume up high, when they came home from trips to the market. Whatever message Haas had tried to get across to him had clearly arrived. What was surprising was that the lack of Howard meant considerably less of Kitty, who had been scarce since they had driven off to the hospital that night. She was around, picking up the boys, dropping them off, but she seemed to hang by the back door and excuse herself quickly. She was quieter then, distracted, as if she were late for someplace and could not exactly remember where it was she needed to go. Sabine was worried about her, but Kitty begged off conversation. Sabine, for one, missed her terribly.

"Kitty comes and goes," Dot said. "You can't get too worked up about it. You have to remember, she's got children, even if they're big children. It takes a lot of effort. And she's got Howard. Sometimes he decides she shouldn't be spending so much time over here. He nags at her so much, it's just easier for her to back off. I figure she doesn't need me nagging at her, too. He's just got his feelings hurt about Haas. He'll forget about it. Everybody will forget about it."

With the house getting quieter, without Kitty around to talk to, Sabine wondered how she would last until Bertie's wedding. Every day Dot checked out books for her from the high school library, Dickens and Thomas Hardy, Jane Austen. Anything that was not about a girl's love for her horse. Sabine was lonely and in her loneliness wondered if her gardener in Los Angeles was remembering to pinch back the pansies around the back patio. For the first time since Parsifal's death, she worried about the pool skimmer, the rug stores, and the unfinished architectural models that cluttered her drafting table like a bombed-out village. In her loneliness she felt herself drifting towards home.

Dot did not go back on her word. She did not worry about the whereabouts of Kitty or lament the absence of Bertie. Dot, like Bertie, seemed better off, though Dot was afraid to show too much pleasure in gaining an extra room for fear of hurting Bertie's feelings, and was certainly afraid to show that she missed her for fear of driving her home again. She didn't tell anyone how she really felt about things, except for Sabine, to whom she revealed her true plan.

"I'm thinking about making it into a sewing room," Dot said.

"Really?" Sabine was poaching eggs, trying to keep the water swirling at exactly the right speed. Just yesterday she had found a lone package of Canadian bacon at the grocery store, tucked away between the liverwurst and olive loaf, its date a full week before expiration. She'd decided to make eggs

Benedict for breakfast. Dot claimed to never have eaten eggs Benedict before, but she had seen it often in old movies.

"Take the bed out completely, the dresser, everything. I'd leave my sewing machine out all the time, leave the ironing board up, get a love seat and a little television. I've even thought of getting one of those exercise bikes. I've just never had the room for it before. Never had the money, either, and now I've got both, I figure, why not?"

"Perfect," Sabine said, speaking as much to the eggs as to Dot's plan.

"I can sew. I should make you something. I make clothes for Bertie and Kitty all the time, clothes for the boys. I think if I had a sewing room I might even be able to do some things professionally, alterations, something. I could get one of those dressmaker dummies. I've always wanted one of those. My eyes should hold out for a few more years."

"Phan sewed beautifully." Everything was right on time. The English muffins had popped, the Canadian bacon was patted dry, and the hollandaise was smooth, lemony-tart, and not too thick. Phan had taught her how to make hollandaise.

"I thought he did something in computers."

"He made his living sewing when he was in school." Was that right? She couldn't exactly remember. Had he sewn in Paris, or was it later? "He used to sew my costumes for the show. He was brilliant in that way."

"Maybe Guy was looking for a boy like his mother," Dot said.

"Not impossible." Sabine brought their breakfast to the table. A sliced orange, the little bit of parsley from the bunch she'd bought for the occasion, knowing full well the rest of it would go to waste. She had remembered to warm the plates.

"This is how people eat in Los Angeles," Dot said, as

pleased as she would have been if Elizabeth Taylor herself had brought the meal.

"Every morning of their lives."

"I feel like I'm in a movie."

They cut into their eggs, spilling the sweet yellow yolks across their knives. It tasted better than the best dinner Sabine ever had at the Rex, because this morning she was hungry, she had made it herself, and she knew that no one else in Alliance was having eggs Benedict on a Tuesday morning. "I have boxes and boxes of patterns that were Phan's, beautiful things, a lot of wedding gowns. I'll send them to you if you'd like."

"Wouldn't that be great," Dot said. "That will be the first thing I make in my new sewing room. Something that Phan liked."

That was the last time that either of them mentioned the idea of the sewing room.

Maybe if they had gone to work on it as soon as the breakfast dishes were in the drainboard, called the church thrift store and asked them to come and haul the furniture down the snowy back stairs as soon as possible, Dot might have made it. But as nature abhors a vacuum, families are unable to leave empty bedrooms sitting idle.

Breakfast was only two hours behind them. Sabine sat at the kitchen table reading *The Return of the Native,* feeling sleepy from the combination of a large breakfast and a slow plot. She planned to take a nap as soon as Dot left to go and dish up hot cafeteria food (How could she look at the food all day?). Dot was down the hall in her bedroom getting ready to go, putting on ChapStick and combing her hair. The room that had been Bertie's stood between them. It was free, no longer hers and not yet something else.

Kitty tapped on the window of the back door and then let herself in.

"Good," Sabine said, slipping the Alliance high school library bookmark into place. One came inside each book that was borrowed, to discourage the dog-earing of pages. "This gives me a chance to stop." Sabine was hoping this visit meant that Kitty was free for the day, that she wasn't working, and that her husband was. The odd combinations of their schedules were impossible to predict.

Kitty hung her coat on the rack by the door. Her clothes were ridiculously large, as if she had mistakenly reached into the boys' closet instead of her own. Inside the pine green sweater and black jeans there was only the faintest outline of Kitty's bones, like a child beneath a pile of blankets. "Dot's still home?" Kitty asked quietly, as if her mother might be both home and asleep. Kitty looked like Parsifal did before he died, too thin, brittle, and exhausted. Her blue eyes were red rimmed and damp. Her cheekbones threw shadows. It occurred to Sabine with a certain numbing horror that Kitty might be sick. There was a large yellowish patch on her neck.

"Dot's getting ready for work." Sabine leaned forward and pushed out a chair. Kitty sat down beside her. "You don't look like you feel very well."

Kitty checked to see if anyone was coming down the hall, in preparation for telling secrets. Sabine knew the look in those eyes. She had seen it when there was bad news about Phan. Kitty was getting ready to tell her things she didn't want to know. "I think I'm going to come home with the boys for a while."

"Are you sick?"

Kitty looked as if she didn't understand the question exactly. "No one's sick."

"I just thought—" Sabine shook her head. "Nothing."

"It's rotten timing," Kitty said sadly. "Bertie just about to get married. And you're here. Come to Nebraska to get a little rest. You must already think we're all crazy people."

Kitty and the boys here? Around the clock? Full, long days of company, days of Kitty. "Bertie's moved out," Sabine said, selling the sewing room down the river. "She hasn't been here a single night since..." She stopped. She thought of nothing to fill up the space in the sentence and so she left it empty. "Her room is free. And as far as you being crazy, I don't think you're any more crazy than the rest of us."

"I must be," Kitty said.

"What happened?"

Kitty shrugged, her bony shoulders shifting up like a coat hanger inside her sweater. "Nothing new, really."

"There she is," Dot said brightly, her purse held tight in one hand. Her curls had been carefully reformed with water and a little Dep from the tub on the bathroom sink. "You should have been here for breakfast. Sabine made eggs Benedict. It was brilliant, really brilliant." Bertie was gone, Sabine was here, there was the promise of a sewing room. Breakfast had been the crowning glory.

"I'm sorry I missed it," Kitty said.

Dot put her hand under her daughter's chin and tilted her face up to the light. "You look like hell."

"Yes, I do."

"Do you have a reason?"

"Same old, same old."

A cloud had passed into Dot's good mood. She studied Kitty carefully, as if she were trying to place her. "You haven't been around here much lately."

"Well," Kitty said, reaching into her purse for a pack of cigarettes. "That's about to change."

Dot let go of her chin and sat down at the table. "Let me have one of those, will you?" Dot didn't smoke, but pushed far enough, most anyone will have a cigarette.

"It won't be forever."

"If it's forever, it's forever," Dot said, because it was always best to consider what might happen. "You and I have lived together before. We did okay. You'll bring the boys?"

"Sure."

"Do they know it yet?"

Kitty passed out cigarettes to Dot and Sabine and then lit all three. "I'll tell them after school. I haven't gotten their things together yet. I need to go back over to the house."

"Does Howard know?"

Kitty took one slow inhale and then got up to find an ashtray. "I told him. I'm not so sure that means he knows. There hasn't been a lot of listening. I think he said a couple of times he was planning on leaving me, too."

In her white cafeteria uniform, her cigarette balanced neatly between two fingers, Dot looked like the old Zen master of failed departures. "Well, everybody can say they're going, but once you really go it's a different story altogether. Still," she patted her daughter's wrist, "you've left him before, Kitten. He got along."

"I was thinking that maybe this time would be it," Kitty said quietly.

"If that's what you want," her mother told her, "then I hope it is."

"I have to think about what's best for the boys."

"You do," Dot said, but no one made it clear if "best" entailed leaving or staying. She looked at her watch. "I can take off work. Call in sick, no problem."

Kitty shook her head. "If you took off work every time we thought it was over with me and Howard, you'd be unemployable."

Dot laughed and reached up to brush her oldest daughter's hair. "Oh, look at that," she said, stopping at her neck. "He got you there."

Kitty reached up and touched two fingers lightly to her neck. "I got off a couple of my own."

"That's the difference between me and Kitty. Howard socks her one, she socks him back. I never hit Al. Christ, it never even occurred to me. He would have put me through the floor."

"Dad was a lot bigger than you," Kitty said.

Dot shook her head. Size was not really the heart of the matter. "You've got more nerve than me. I never even left Al. Not really."

Sabine volunteered to go back to the house with Kitty to pick up some things, which meant Dot could go to work and only be a few minutes late, not that anyone would even mention it to her. This time of year everyone was late anyway, cars didn't start or they slid off driveways and lodged in snowbanks. Winter was nothing but a long excuse for tardiness.

Kitty and Sabine drove together to Kitty's house. Even with the heater turned to High they were cold. The cold air seemed to come at them directly through the windshield.

"So," Sabine said, "do you want to tell me?"

"Howard," Kitty said.

How handsome he must have been at twenty-one, before the fall from the train, lean and long legged, tan in the summer; his hair truly red then, a dark, new-penny color, edged in gold from working outdoors. Howard, standing by the side of the road, a wheat field spreading out behind him in every direction, his skin freckled and burned brown. Howard from a distance. Howard in a white T-shirt. Howard not saying anything. He was strong and brave and full of dangerous fun.

"What happened with Howard?"

"Ever since Bertie fell, we've been going at it pretty hard. We just fight. After a while we're not even fighting about anything." Kitty thought about it as the snowy little ranch houses shot past their windows. "I could tell you something he said or one thing he did, but it's not really like that. You just get tired. He keeps crossing the line, and I kept moving it back for him to try again."

Although she would never mention it, Sabine was unclear as to how momentous this trip to pick up clothes and move Kitty and the boys into Dot's house actually was. It sounded like departure was part of the cycle, the yearly autumn in their relationship, after which she settled back in for the winter. Kitty looked neither convincing nor convinced when she spoke of staying away this time. There was only a note of wanting in her voice, a tired desire. Staying away was a wish, like wanting a new winter coat or an extra fifteen-minute break at work or a sewing room. To Sabine it was a perfectly honorable wish: Kitty on her own, free to do better for herself; Kitty, who was in possession of all of her brother's potential, having the opportunity to put it to use. Not that there was any sense in trying to understand another person's marriage or to say, after two weeks of careful observation, that it seemed like the jig was up. The things that went into keeping people together and tearing them apart remained largely unknown to the parties immediately involved. Recently discovered sisters-in-law visiting from Los Angeles were more useful packing sweaters into suitcases than offering opinions.

"I hate to have you see my house," Kitty said when they were standing on her back porch. She fumbled with her keys, her wool-covered fingers unable to chose one from the many available on the ring.

Sabine waited behind her and shivered. She had not previously been invited over to Kitty's, although the house was pointed out to her from a distance as they drove by. The siding was a dull Dijon yellow where Dot's was white. The yard was deeper and there were fewer box hedges beneath the front windows, but the basic fact remained that Kitty had wound up almost exactly where she started.

"I haven't cleaned anything." Kitty's hand stayed on the back-door knob, waiting.

"I'm not coming over for the tour," Sabine said. The day was bright and blue, but there was a terrible wind pressing down on them from what felt like every direction. There was no real stand of trees to speak of between where they stood and Wyoming to slow down its roaring advance east. Sabine felt the metal hook on the back of her bra freezing into her skin, the finest knifepoint against her spine. She wanted to get inside the house, no matter what the house looked like.

But Kitty just closed her eyes and in the next moment covered her face with her hands and started to cry.

"Hey," Sabine said. She put her arm around Kitty and felt slightly warmer. "Stop that."

"I'm sorry," Kitty said.

"Why in the world are you telling me that you're sorry?" As close as she was, Sabine had to raise her voice slightly, as the wind seemed to carry the words directly from her throat and down the block.

"Sometimes I feel like you're Guy," Kitty said from deep inside her gloves. "All these years all I've wanted is for him to come back, to talk to me, and now that you're here everything is going to hell. You're going to go and that's going to be it. You're going to think, Thank God I got out of there. I won't see you anymore." The tears on Kitty's face froze onto her gloves and left glittering paths on her cheeks. A thin sheet of ice formed in the dip of her upper lip.

Every time Kitty had come into the room, Sabine had thought of Parsifal, the way he walked, his lovely face. "Of course you'll see me," Sabine said. "You have to forget about that. There are too many other things to worry about here."

"Don't worry about Howard," Kitty said, and sniffed. "I know he went to work."

The thought that Howard Plate might be inside had never even occurred to Sabine. She was talking about worry in a larger sense, worry down the line as opposed to the more immediate worry of an angry husband hiding in a closet. "Then open the door before we freeze to death."

Kitty looked up as if to notice the weather, tilted the broad planes of her face into the wind so that her hair wrapped around her neck and slapped into her eyes. She turned the key in the lock.

There was nothing so terrible inside the house. It was a private life left lying around, because no one had thought that Sabine was coming by to see it. Breakfast dishes from exactly one breakfast sat unwashed in the sink, a handful of plates were broken onto an otherwise very clean linoleum floor. In the living room there was one pillow, one peach-colored blanket, and one very faded comforter with the shadowy image of Superman making an upward departure, crumpled onto the sofa. The cushions from the back of the sofa were scattered on the floor. Everywhere they went there were clear signs of boys, tennis shoes, hockey sticks, assorted textbooks that one could easily imagine should have been taken to school.

Sabine pressed her hands against her ears, hoping that the blood would return. "It looks like a house," she said. "Like anybody's house. I promise I won't break off all contact because of it."

Kitty rubbed her cheeks, knocking the ice away. "What I mean is, I don't want you to think of me like this. I'm not always like this." Kitty collected two startlingly large tennis shoes from opposite sides of the kitchen and set them next to one another by the back door. She crouched down beside them and for no reason evened up the laces. "Or I am always like this and I don't want to be. Or I'd like you to think I'm not always like this. Hell."

"You have it all wrong," Sabine said. "I'm the one who worries. 'Who is this crazy women who married my gay brother before he died? How did she wind up in Nebraska when we'd never even heard of her?' If anybody's suspect here it has to be me. I'm not always like this, either, you know. I used to be a lot happier than this." She started to pick up the pieces of plate on the floor.

"Leave those," Kitty said. "Howard threw those."

Sabine looked in her cupped hands, heavy everyday china broken into chunks, the chunks covered with flowers and rasp-berries. She set them back down on the floor in a neat pile.

"So what were you like when you were happier?" Kitty said.

Sabine thought about the days before Phan was sick or before they even knew Phan. "I don't know how to say it. It had something to do with being younger."

Kitty apologized at the doorway of every room they went into—unmade beds, socks and underwear thrown on top of the clothes hamper, towels rolled into damp balls next to pillows. "Dear God," Kitty said, picking up handfuls of clothes off the floor of Guy's room. "Couldn't you just wait in the kitchen for an hour or so?"

"I've seen it now. I've been initiated."

Kitty shook her head, left the room, and returned with a box of lawn-and-leaf bags. "I'm just going to make a pile and you shovel it in. We can wash it when we get back to my mother's house." Kitty started throwing things in the direction of the single bed. Above the bed was a large black poster of the word PHISH, whose green letters formed into the shape of a fish. Sabine thought it must be some kind of inside joke she could not possibly understand.

Kitty bent over and started digging around on the floor. "When you're young and you want to have a baby because babies are so cute and everybody else has one, nobody ever takes you aside and explains to you what happens when they grow up. Maybe they all think it's obvious. I mean, if you know enough about biology to know where babies come from, then you should know that sooner or later they turn into teenagers, but somehow you just don't ever think about it, then one day, bang, you've got these total strangers living with you, these children in adult bodies, and you don't know who they are. It's like they somehow ate up those children you had and you loved, and you keep loving these people because you know they've got your child locked up in there somewhere." She stopped with two pairs of jeans in one hand and a windbreaker in the other and looked at the wreckage that she couldn't seem to make a dent in. "You love them so much and yet you keep wondering when they're going to leave."

Poor Dot, Sabine thought. She'd had five whole days to herself after forty-six years and even then she had a house guest. Sabine nosed the butt-end of a joint safely under Guy's bed with the toe of her boot. "I like your boys. But I'm glad they're your boys, if you know what I mean."

"Of course I know what you mean. I like them, too, but I wish they were yours."

Sabine looked into the tumble of clothes in dark green plastic. "There are no socks in this bag."

"Socks," Kitty said. "Right."

The point was never to take everything, just a cross section of the essentials, just enough to keep them from coming back to the house for a few days until everyone calmed down. This trip was for clothes, shoes, toothbrushes, things to meet immediate needs. Photographs, letters, the pretty blue glass vase shaped like an ostrich egg that had been her grandmother's, stayed exactly where they were. Kitty and Sabine each tugged a lawn-and-leaf bag out to the car and slung it into the backseat. As soon as the weight was out of their hands, they felt better, freer. For a moment it was as if they were loading up the car to go on a vacation. They would find a map in the glove compartment and head due south, not stopping until they got to Mexico. In Mexico there was no family. Sons, husbands, mothers, sisters, fathers, and brothers were the sole property of the United States. In Mexico there was only warm weather, only beaches, tequila, Kitty and Sabine.

When they got back to Dot's house, Sabine made lunch out of what was left of last night's chicken while Kitty sorted the laundry by color and type of fabric into huge piles on the kitchen floor.

"Every time I stick my hand in a pocket I hold my breath," Kitty said, and slid her hand into a pair of jeans. She pulled out a folded paper napkin covered in phone numbers, held it for a moment up to the light, and then tossed it onto the counter. "Piece of cake."

"Are the boys going to be very upset about this?"

"It's a break for them, too, a couple days of peace. They don't like to move around, have their routine upset, but the fighting wears them out. They'll worry about their dad, Guy especially. He's afraid of him, but he thinks Howard is basically misunderstood. Maybe he's right."

"You don't understand him," Sabine said, laying out four slices of bread. She had convinced Dot to switch over from white to whole wheat.

"I always thought if Guy had been around, my Guy, your Guy, it would have been easier for them. They could have had another man to watch, somebody else to try and be like. My father was dead, and thank God for that, and Howard's parents have both been dead for years. I thought at first maybe Haas could fit the bill. They like Haas fine, but he's so shy.

It's almost like he's too small for them. But Guy could have taught them things, how to have a sense of humor for one."

"You can teach them that."

"It's different when you're a boy. It has to come from a man, preferably a father."

"Well, it sounds like nothing came from Parsifal's father, and he turned out fine."

"Guy was different," she said, her hands sorting in an automatic rhythm. "He had so much to him. Hell, he went off to California and rewrote his whole life history. He could be his own father. My boys aren't like that. At heart they're followers, and there's nothing wrong with that, but they'll stay exactly where they are for the rest of their lives unless somebody shows them what to do." Kitty scooped up a bundle of white clothes with both arms. "I'm going to get started on this," she said, and headed down to the basement.

Of course the father Sabine would pick as a general role model to all boys would be her own. How happy she had been on the days he picked her up from school as a surprise and took her with him to CBS to prepare for the nightly news. Sabine sat quietly in the darkened editing room, watching him slice away at world events and tape them back together. President and Mrs. Kennedy stepping off the plane in Paris, waving to the dark and boiling crowd below them. Her father ran that piece back and forth, back and forth, again and again because Sabine could not get enough of them, his handsome smile, her delicate wrist disappearing into a buttoned glove. Once Walter Cronkite was in Los Angeles on special assignment and while Sabine sat on her stool he peered around the door. "Oh, thank goodness you're here!" he said to her. "We need you to read the news tonight." He managed a look of such sincere desperation that Sabine wanted to say yes. His famous face was thrilling in person.

"I can't read the news," Sabine whispered.

"Are you sure? Plenty of good stories tonight."

Sabine shook her head. Walter Cronkite wore the loveliest suit.

"What do you say?" her father asked her.

"No, thank you, Mr. Cronkite."

"Well," he said, his mustache spreading into a smile, "if you change your mind..." And then he waved good-bye and closed the door quietly behind him.

"That's the boss man," Sabine's father said. "Maybe you should think it over."

After the work was finished, Sabine's father said good-evening to everyone, secretaries, newsmen, copyboys, janitors. She loved the giant cameras that watched them pass with their lone eyes. She loved the clicking of typewriters down every hallway. She held his hand all through the building and down onto Fairfax Street, where they walked the four blocks home. "Here, you can walk," her father would say. "Here, the weather is always like paradise."

It was years before Sabine realized that her father only picked her up on the days when the news was especially good, when the film he had to edit was beautiful, so that Sabine grew up believing that the evening news was a daily reflection on the world's wonders. Her father did not speak of unhappiness. He did not brood late at night, alone in the living room. "What fortune," he said to Sabine when she finished her dance re-citals, showed her report card, walked into a room. "What fortune," he said when her mother brought the Sunday brisket to the table on a wide oval platter. "What fortune," he said on the day Parsifal married Sabine. Her father took Parsifal in his arms, kissed his cheeks. "Now I have a son." They all laughed, but he stuck with it. "Let me speak to my son," he would say to Sabine on the telephone.

"Forty-five years old and I have a father again," Parsifal would say.

Now Howard Plate's sons were moving two miles across town to live in their grandmother's house.

Kitty and Sabine did the laundry and did more laundry. They stripped the beds, folded underwear. Kitty ironed a few shirts and hung them in the closet in Parsifal's room while Sabine carried her clothes in neat stacks across the hall and laid them in Bertie's dresser.

"I hate to kick you out," Kitty said. "But you couldn't put those boys in a double bed."

"Of course not," Sabine said. "Don't even think about it." She did not look back over her shoulder as she left, but she felt the loss. She would miss the terrible plaid carpet, the baseball trophies with his name etched into the small metal placards, the nights of lying in the little bed and thinking about Parsifal. She found the bag of building supplies she had bought at Wal-Mart and moved them out with everything else. "I should make the boys a house," she said to Kitty. "I could make them a model, the White House or Monticello. I could even show them how to do it."

"Make them your house," Kitty said, dumping rolls of socks into a drawer. "That's what they'd like to see."

"Phan's house?"

"Your house, Phan's house. They'd be thrilled with that."

Dot brought the boys home at three o'clock. The three of them crept through the back door silently, unlaced their boots, and slipped across the floor in their sock feet. She had told them in the car coming over. It was the only thing that could account for such quiet.

"Hey," Kitty said, coming from Parsifal's room where she had just finished making up the beds. "You're home."

"We're home," Guy said, his tone and manner completely devoid of a living pulse.

"So you know."

How nodded his head while Guy slid towards the refrigerator, opened the door to shoulder width, and buried the upper half of his torso inside, looking for nothing in particular.

"They're taking it real well," Dot said, pulling off her mittens and then her scarf. "We had a good talk coming home, didn't we, How?"

"Sure," How said, his lovely hair flattened to the sides of his head from the stocking cap his grandmother had made him put on.

Guy stayed inside the refrigerator, his hips swaying back and forth as if he were thinking so hard about loud music he was actually able to hear it.

Kitty went over and hugged How. He was half a head taller than his mother and he rested his cheek against her forehead. When she let him go, she went to Guy and put her arms around his waist, pulling him both towards her and back so that he was forced to come out. "Aren't you cold enough yet?"

"Not quite," he said.

"Don't be mad at me, Guy. I really couldn't stand that right now."

He stood up, red faced and sad. He had gotten taller in the last week. "All right," he said, and put an arm loosely around her shoulder. "See?"

Kitty kissed his cheek hard. "Okay," she said. "We'll figure something out. Until we do, I've got your room all made up."

"Where's Aunt Sabine going to sleep?" How said.

"In Bertie's room."

"Then where'll Bertie be?"

"Enough questions," Dot said, not wanting to get into the matter of exactly where Bertie was sleeping. "There are plenty of soft surfaces and plenty of pillows. It's my house and I promise you that every person in it will get a good night's sleep."

"Sounds like a campaign promise to me," Guy said.

Dot handed him a cookie and he took it like a child. "Then I want to know what I get if I win the election."

"Sabine's going to build us a house," Kitty said. "A model of any house we want. I thought it would be nice if she built her house in Los Angeles."

"I've seen the houses she builds," Dot said, happy to take the subject beyond failed marriages and who got what bed. "Just exactly like real houses, only miniature."

"You know how to do that?" How said.

"That's what I do for a living," Sabine said, "in California."

"I thought you were a magician's assistant," Guy said suspiciously.

"You can't exactly pay the rent being a magician's assistant. I've been making architectural models for years. I mostly do it for fun now, to have something to do."

"Magician's assistant!" Dot said, and put a hand over her heart in a gesture of mock myocardial infarction. "Do you realize that we haven't watched the tape since the night after Sabine got here?"

Sabine thought Dot was teasing her, but when all the people in the room held the same panicked look on their faces, she asked them, "So what?"

"We watch it almost every night," Kitty said, her voice strangely nervous.

"We've never gone this long without seeing it," How said. "Ever."

They were guilty, Dot Fetters and the three Plates. For more than two weeks they had forgotten to touch the talisman that was their only connection to their dead son, dead brother, dead uncle. They had not paid him homage, their icon. They had forgotten.

"For God's sake," Sabine said, pushing Dot lightly on the shoulder. "Snap out of it. So you didn't watch a video. It's a relief. No one should watch the same piece of tape every night. It isn't healthy."

"You must think we've forgotten about him," Dot said in a voice so small it was not her own.

"But you don't need to watch it all the time. I'm here. I'm on the tape. You see me every day." She put her face near Dot's. "It's the same thing."

"Let's watch it now," Guy said.

Everyone looked at him. Guy wasn't one for coming up with answers, especially not the kind that made people feel better. "I'm going to put the tape in," he said, and went into the living room with crisp authority. The rest of them fell into line behind him, with Sabine at the back, going slowly to take her seat.

"I don't understand this," she said. "I know I should, but I don't."

"Sh," Dot said.

Guy hit the button for Play and stretched out across the carpet.

And there was Johnny Carson, still in the same tan suit, still with the same short silver hair and knowing smile.

"When we come right back, we have a big treat," How whispered. "For the first time on the show, Parsifal the Magician."

"When we come right back, we have a big treat," Carson said, balancing his pencil. "For the first time on the show, Parsifal the Magician." The pencil flipped and he hit it two times, eraser end to desk.

"So don't go away," How said. No one stopped him or told him to be quiet. They understood. They wanted to say the words, too. It had been too long since they had seen

Johnny Carson last, and the comfort of his familiar voice washed over them like a warm, enveloping breeze smelling of saltwater and lime blossoms.

"So don't go away," Johnny Carson said. The music came up and then the picture, the television and floor lamp running in their everlasting dance of love.

When the bull's-eye came on counting down three, two, one, they counted along. Even Sabine formed her lips around the words, though she didn't make a sound. She felt a strange sort of anxiousness, the way she would feel picking Parsifal up at the airport after some rare trip when she had not gone along. She would stand at the end of the gateway with all of the other lonely and longing souls and think, I'm going to see him again. She had to force herself to stand still, not push to the front of the line.

The great colored curtain parted like Moses' sea and they were borne onto stage, onto television, Parsifal and Sabine.

When Dot began to cry quietly, Kitty followed her, and then Sabine. This time she did not think about the way the trick was done, she did not remember how it felt to be there. She cried because she saw the man she loved at the height of his life and she missed him terribly. She cried from the pleasure of having a chance to see him again, even like this, reduced to two dimensions, his whole body the size of her hand. It was right to see the tape again, because tonight it meant something else entirely. It was not a magic trick but a slow, deliberate tango. He took her hand and laid her down. He lifted her feet and ran his hands down her legs in a way that was both tender and obscene. She was still, but not sleeping. She was still because he was making some sort of love to her on the stage, because he wanted her to be still so that he could dance around her. She was lifted by him, balanced on the point of the chair. Magic can seem like love. She was so far above them, her toes nearly scraping the colored gel from the lights. And then, from the very height of it, he brought her back, let her down gently, sweetly, and when it was over, he kissed her there on national television, and while everyone who saw it could feel what had happened in their bones, no one knew how to call it by its name. No small wonder that Johnny Carson would ask her out to dinner after that.

Carson came to them. He took Parsifal's hand. "Great," he said. "Just great. That's one trick you wouldn't want to blow."

"I haven't dropped her yet," Parsifal said.

He turned to the woman wrapped in the smallest bit of red satin. "And I certainly hope you'll come back to see us."

All eyes were on Sabine now, wanting her. She parted her lips to speak, but nothing she said would matter. She owned them all. They would take anything. "Thank you, Mr. Carson."

"Here's the windup," Guy said over Carson's perfect smile.

"Right back," Johnny Carson said.

"Lord," Kitty sighed, happy for the first time that day. "I do love that show."

How crawled towards the VCR on all fours and hit Rewind. "Oh," Dot said, wiping her eyes against her sleeve. "Maybe Sabine was right. Maybe it was good to take a break. I felt like I was watching it for the first time again." She looked at her daughter-in-law, who was mopping her own eyes. "Was he really like that? Was he beautiful like that all the time?"

"Every minute I knew him," she said in all remembered honesty. "I swear to God."

"Someday you're going to have to tell us how you did that trick," Guy said, but this time his voice was dreamy, full of patience. He would wait as long as it took.

"You never know," Sabine said.

It was all easier now. The thing they hadn't realized was missing was back again. The boys went to their homework, the women went to the kitchen to smoke and make dinner. Sabine sat at the kitchen table and sketched out a floor plan of her house to work from. Nothing had to be exact, so she drew without measuring lines. No one mentioned Howard Plate or this recent departure. They spoke of magic tricks, where to buy costumes like the one Sabine wore on television, and how Johnny Carson seemed like a very decent person in real life. Bertie came in and was there for nearly a half an hour before anyone mentioned to her that her room was gone and Kitty had moved back in with the boys.

"I'm awfully sorry about this," Kitty said to her sister. "Everything falling apart right before you're getting married. I should have waited. This morning when I left I wasn't thinking, and then it just didn't seem like I could go back."

"I don't mean this unkindly," Bertie said, "but you and Howard are always falling apart." To show that there were no hard feelings intended, she moved a piece of Kitty's hair out of her eyes and hooked it back behind her ear. "What the two of you do isn't going to affect me and Haas. I mean, we care, we want you to be happy, but it isn't going to spoil our wedding."

"That's all I wanted to know," Kitty said.

"Where is everybody going to sleep?"

"I know you think that I haven't exactly noticed that you've moved out," Dot said. "But as far as I'm concerned your room is up for grabs."

Bertie took a moment to stare at her shoes.

"Sabine's in your room, the boys are in Guy's room, Kitty's on the couch."

Because there was so much shifting around and so few

beds, Sabine thought this would be as good a time as any to broach the topic she had so studiously avoided. "And I'm going home on Sunday, which will free up some space." At that moment the refrigerator kicked off and Dot stopped stacking dishes, and the room was filled with a quiet unmatched in any windless Nebraska night.

"What?" Kitty said.

Sabine put down her pencil and tried to divide her gaze equally among her three friends. "It had to happen sooner or later. When I came here, I never thought I'd stay so long. You must all have been wondering when I was finally going to go."

"Don't say that," Bertie said.

"The wedding is Saturday and then Sunday I'll leave. I have to. I have to go home. I have the rabbit and the rug stores and the house to take care of. I can't just move in here."

"No one's talking about moving in," Dot said. "But you only just got here. You can't leave when you only just came." She kept her voice light to let Sabine know she wasn't taking her talk of departure seriously at all.

"Listen to me," Sabine said. "I'm forty-one years old. Everything I know is in Los Angeles. That's where I live. You saved my life, letting me come up here. I was so depressed over Parsifal, but I think I'm ready to try things out at home."

"So you're over him now?" Kitty said.

The room turned and looked at Kitty. Sabine's mouth opened and then closed, silent as a fish. She squeezed a kneaded eraser between her fingers. Over Parsifal?

"Kitty, Jesus," Bertie said.

Kitty closed her eyes and shook her head. "I'm so sorry," she whispered. "I don't know what made me say that. I just don't want you to go, is all. I didn't mean that. We all want you to stay."

"We're not going to talk about this now," Dot said. She opened up a cupboard and began to sift randomly through cans. "There's still plenty of time to think this over."

"I just wanted you to know," Sabine said, her voice coming out hoarse.

Dot held up her hand. "We're talking about this later."

"Sabine," Kitty said.

Sabine shook her head. "I'm fine." She picked up her pencil and quickly began to draw her bedroom at home, where she would be sleeping in what was only a matter of days. She marked off the French doors that looked out at the pool. She put in the indentations for the fireplace. She made a walk-in closet. Parsifal's clothes to the right, Phan's to the left. She had left her clothes in her bedroom upstairs.

As the evening went on, everything went in reverse. After dinner it was Bertie who left and the Plates who stayed. Everyone thought that Howard might come by, though no one as much as mentioned his name. Every rustle in the backyard made them sit up straight and lean towards the window. They were not afraid of Howard Plate. They worried when they thought he was out there in the cold, freezing to death rather than knocking on the window to come inside.

After dinner Sabine began measuring pieces of board and cutting them out with razor blades. She would keep the house very small, a little jewel box. Small was no good for architects, but it was perfect if somebody was actually going to keep the thing around for a while. Small was also more difficult, and she was interested in time-consuming projects.

"You make it out of posterboard?" How asked. He sat beside her under the swag light, watching her careful fingers trace the lines.

"Posterboard, plywood, playing cards, anything I can find. You should see the box of scraps I have at home. Everything is separated by thickness. I save the pieces of cardboard out of stocking packages, pastry boxes."

He watched the blade slide past the side of her hand. "Have you ever cut yourself?"

She turned her wrist over. "Once." The scar was still red and there were the smallest dots on either side where the thread had gone in and come out again.

How extended one careful finger and ran it against her skin. "That's awfully neat."

"How can you remember exactly what your house looks like?" Guy said.

"Don't you know what your house looks like?"

"Sure I do, but I couldn't draw it. I wouldn't know where everything went."

"I have a good memory for buildings, I guess. The same way some people remember faces." Sabine glued two pieces of board together, recessing the second piece slightly to make windowsills. Tomorrow she could look around for something to use for the glass. Sabine had never made a model of a house she had lived in before. She had very rarely modeled real houses. Making things that were already made meant that you had to suffer the burden of comparison. Usually what people needed to see was the idea of a house, the possibility. Once the poured concrete and supporting beams existed, a tiny re-production of it was nothing more than precious.

There was nothing to watch on that first night, drawing up plans, cutting and layering walls to dry overnight, but they sat with her at the table and watched her like a television. Finally, when it was late enough, Kitty checked the boys' homework and then herded them towards Parsifal's room, though they were years beyond anyone being able to put them to bed. Then she brought blankets and a pillow from the hall closet and started to make up the couch.

"You don't have to do that," Sabine said. "You're welcome to sleep in Bertie's room."

"Well, she can't sleep with me," Dot said, stretching her arms over her head. "I'm willing to take this welcome-you-back-to-the-nest thing just so far."

"I've put many a night in on this couch. I'm going to be fine here."

Sabine got up to wash the glue off the razor blade and off her hands. "Well, if you change your mind, you know where I'll be." There was not a great deal of sincerity in the offer. She was hurt by what Kitty had said and felt that if Kitty wanted to sleep on the couch she could sleep on the couch. Sabine dried her hands on a dish towel that was covered with fat blue ducks. "I'm going to bed."

"Right behind you," Dot said. She didn't offer Sabine a drink. The drink was their all-clear sign that everyone else had finally gone.

Kitty, who looked like the victim of some natural disaster standing there alone with her arms full of blankets, told the two of them good-night.

Bertie's room had been Kitty's room. Dot and Al had been in the room beside hers, Parsifal across the hall. That was the map of the family before the great shift in sleeping arrangements came: Al down to the cemetery, Parsifal off to his bunk at Lowell, and Kitty crossing the hall to make a place for her soon-to-be-born baby sister. Or maybe she just wanted to be in her brother's bed. Maybe she thought she would stay there when Parsifal came home and they would sleep in their matching twins, side by side.

Sabine had had that thought herself, sleeping in one of the two narrow beds: that somehow she and Parsifal were there in that room together, united now against any danger that had previously been for him alone. Comparatively, Bertie's double bed felt like a giant expanse of mattress, and she tossed and rolled, trying to find a place for herself that was safe in so much open space. How had she slept in Phan and Parsifal's king-sized bed? A single bed was all that anyone needed if they were alone. She took the extra pillow and pressed it against her back, trying to make herself feel hemmed in. She wondered what was going on across the hall, if the boys were talking, fighting, sleeping, pretending to sleep. She wondered if they realized where they were.

She pushed her hands into her pillow and closed her eyes. She thought about what it would be like to be home again, to have the rabbit snuggled hard against her back. She thought of her parents standing together in the airport, how they would arrive at least an hour early to make sure that they didn't get caught in traffic.

"Sabine?" There was a crack of light coming in from the hall and the dark outline of someone at her door. For a split second she thought Bertie had come back. She imagined herself curled up in the hallway with her pillow and blanket. "Are you asleep?"

"No."

Kitty came in dressed in a dark T-shirt and a pair of shorts, or maybe they were short pajamas, it was hard to tell in the dark. She sat down on the edge of the bed, facing away from Sabine, her hands holding tightly to her kneecaps.

"Did you decide not to sleep on the couch?" Sabine whispered, not wanting to wake up whoever else might be asleep. The walls in this house afforded all the privacy of Japanese scrims.

"It was a terrible thing that I said." Kitty's voice trembled. "I'm lying out there in the living room and I can't stop thinking about it."

"You've had a hard day," Sabine said, and with a sudden,

benevolent clarity, she knew that she was right. Kitty was simply in fighting mode. She had been fighting with Howard all week. She had packed up her boys and slipped out this very morning. "You're tired. Just forget about it."

"It surprised me so much when you said you were leaving. I mean, I knew that sooner or later you'd go, but when you said it—I don't know."

"Forget it."

"I know you'd never forget about Guy."

"No."

That was all there was to say about it, but Kitty stayed, hands to knees, looking at the wall in the dark in the room that had been her room three lifetimes ago. Sabine waited to see if there were something else. You never knew with these people, there was always some revelation lurking around the corner of every meaningful silence. "Are you okay?" Sabine asked.

"Okay," Kitty said in a way that meant, Just okay.

"Are you thinking about Howard?"

"Nope."

Sabine stifled a small yawn by pushing her mouth against her pillow. "Do you want to sleep here? You really don't have to stay on the couch."

"I should go back," Kitty said, staying perfectly still.

"Well, all right." Sabine would have been happy to have her stay. The bed felt so cavernous.

"I should go back," Kitty said again, and then stood up and turned around to face the mattress. "Good night, then."

"Good night."

When she said it Kitty put a hand flat on the bed, leaned forward and kissed her. It was not a kiss on the cheek, or a kiss that was meant to be a kiss on the cheek but lost its way in the dark and landed gently on the lips as an accident. Kitty

kissed her lightly, stopped for one second, and then kissed her
again. Two soft mouths made softer by the close proximity of
sleep, that dozing, nearly dreaming warmth that made people
affectionate and unembarrassed. Sabine, who had not been
kissed in this way for a long time, remembered the feeling and
kissed back, some instinctual code patterned deeply in the
cells. She kissed before thinking or understanding, and before
she could think or understand, it was over. The beautiful face
receded in the dark. Kitty smoothed down Sabine's hair as if
she were a feverish child needing comfort and then she left
without repeating her good-nights, leaving Sabine to rattle in
the four corners of her bed alone with something she had not
started. The door clicked shut. There was no proof that anything had happened at all. Sabine's body was terribly awake,
every inch of it ready as it had not been two minutes before,
all of it confused with wanting. Kitty had kissed her. Sabine
rolled from her back to her stomach and then onto her left
side. What should she have said? Kitty was out there now,
alone on the sofa where the cold air came in from the windows
despite Dot's vigorous caulking. Maybe Sabine should go to
her now, sit beside her, possibly take her hand, tell her something she had not yet thought of. Sabine touched her fingers
to her lips. There was no evidence. She rolled back onto her
stomach and waited, her eyes straining against the dark, for
something else to happen.

No one slept well in their new beds.

In the morning only Dot seemed fresh, mixing up pancake
batter from Bisquick. She was humming quietly to herself
when Sabine came in, a snappy tune that Sabine did not
recognize. Dot had wanted her house to herself but was so
accustomed to disappointment that she took it all in graceful stride. Guy was in the shower, a steamy marathon meant

to deny his brother even a tablespoon of hot water. How pounded on the bathroom door. "I said *now*!" he shouted.

Dot rubbed her hands in one quick, downward wipe on the dish towel tucked into the front of her pants and hustled down the hall towards the noise. "That thing will come right off the hinges," she said to How. "This house isn't built for high-impact fights. That, and your mother is still asleep, so keep it down."

"Sorry, Gram," How said, and twisted his bare toes into the carpet.

Dot tapped politely on the door. "Come on out now, Guy, or I'll come in and get you. I have the key, you know. I've seen you naked before."

The water shut off. A breath of steam rose from beneath the door.

Sabine sat down at the table wearing Phan's pajamas and Parsifal's bathrobe. She was a little bit taller than Phan and her ankles showed bare under the cuffs of the short pants. Dot came down the hall just as Kitty turned in from the living room.

"You're not asleep," Dot said.

"I wish I was." Kitty poured herself a cup of coffee and turned to Sabine. "Coffee?"

"Sure," Sabine said. She was looking for some recognition and hoping in a way that was weak and halfhearted that there would be none. In memory, the kiss had become less certain. It could have been friendly, familial, a good-night wish for pleasant dreams. Kitty was, after all, her sister-in-law, a married woman, however unhappily married. And Kitty was a woman. That made the kiss a trick coin, heads on both sides. Kitty and Sabine were both women, and despite their mutual lack of luck with men, they were not women naturally inclined towards women. Not that one kiss mattered.

One kiss between two half-asleep women in their forties. It was best forgotten.

Kitty handed the cup to Sabine with no brush of the hand, no secret message to decode.

"I'm on today," Kitty said to Sabine, to her mother, to anyone who might be listening. "I've got to get moving if my children will ever vacate the shower."

"Don't hold your breath." Dot flipped a pancake, a true flip, where the cake lost contact with the spatula and did one solo rotation in the air.

The coffee was black and Sabine got up to get some milk out of the refrigerator. Even though she had not been looking for an egg, there they were. This was the bathrobe Parsifal wore on omelette Sundays. The pockets were deep and lined in fleecy flannel. The robe itself had so much fabric that one could easily hide a half dozen in the folds.

"Sleep okay?" Sabine asked, taking back her place at the table.

"Too much to think about," Kitty said, her tone again implying exactly nothing. "The first night out of the house always makes me crazy." As in, cannot be held accountable for actions?

"So tonight will be easier. Boys!" Dot called down the hall. "Are you planning on eating this morning or are you just going to bathe?"

"I'm going to have to drive them in." Kitty looked at her watch with tired resignation. "The school bus isn't coming here."

Soon enough the smell of pancakes pulled the boys towards the kitchen, the sweet perfume of maple syrup calling them by name. Guy was exhausted from water that was too hot, and How was agitated from water that was too cold. Their wet hair curled darkly and dripped down their necks and into the collars of their ironed shirts. Even now their eyes were longing for sleep, and if their mother had said the deal was off, there was no need for school today after all, they would have wandered back down the hall in their somnambulist fog and curled into their beds like bears in winter. Dot put down plates of pancakes all around.

Kitty pushed away from the table. "I'm not going to have time."

"Always time for breakfast," Dot said briskly, a recording from a thousand mornings spent giving instruction on eating habits.

"Have something," Sabine said.

"You've been spending too much time with my mother."

"Something small, then." Sabine leaned forward and let her fingers slip into Kitty's soft hair, which had not yet been tied back for the day. The rest of them looked up. All eyes were on her, on her hand touching Kitty's hair, and yet not one of them saw the egg until the moment it was pushed, whole and dully white, from her ear. Kitty shivered and touched the side of her head.

They stared at the egg in wonder, as if it were the one thing that might save them all. "That is so cool," Guy said appreciatively.

Sabine handed Kitty the egg, and Kitty took both the egg and the hand together, squeezed them without enough force to do damage.

"Oh, I love it when you do that," Dot said, and smiled.

"Just like you promised," Kitty said to Sabine. "When I wasn't expecting it." She put the egg in the pocket of her sweater. "I'm going to take a shower with whatever water is available to me."

"Wear your mittens," How said to his mother as she headed down the hall. He waited until she was safely out of earshot before he leaned in towards Sabine. "Can you teach us that one, at least?"

"Palming an egg is no place to start. There can be a lot of mess."

"So a neater trick. Something," How pleaded. "If we're all going to be staying here together, you have to teach us something. It doesn't have to be how to turn someone upside-down on a chair."

Sabine thought over the options. "All right," she said, and put her napkin on the table.

"You don't have to do it while you're trying to eat your breakfast," Dot said. She was now left with two untouched plates of pancakes.

"One minute, that's all." Sabine went down the hall to Parsifal's room, her room, the boys' room. She could scarcely recognize it for the clothes that covered the floor. She only caught the smallest glimpses of her plaid rug. She knelt on the floor and fished the Mr. Mysto set out from under the bed. The magician still gazed at the children with evil intent.

"That old thing?" Guy said, wracked with disappointment. "You think we haven't been through that a hundred times?"

"I'm sure you have," Sabine said, careful not to tear the masking tape off the lid. "But you've never been through it with me. All I need are these." She took out the cups and balls and set them out on the table.

Dot sighed and took away the two extra plates. "If this wasn't educational I'd never let it happen while we were eating," she said.

Sabine hid the balls on the tops of the cups and they watched her do it and did not see her. It was something that Parsifal figured out when he was halfway through his career as a magician: People don't pay attention. They don't know how. They can smell guilt or fear from the other side of the Dodgers' stadium, but if you simply go about your business with authority no one can tell. "Three cups," Sabine said, unstacking the cups with the balls hidden inside them. "One ball." She placed it under the middle cup. "All you have to do is keep your eyes on the cup." She slid them easily—left to right, circle back, part the two, slip the third in the center. "All I have to do is make sure you're wrong." She took away her hands.

"That one," Guy said, tapping the correct choice on the far left. How nodded, sorry that he hadn't beaten his brother to the punch.

"And if there was money here, would you bet money?"

"Sure," Guy said.

"Then you would lose." Sabine lifted the middle cup and the ball rolled obediently forward. "And if you learn to do it, other people will bet you money, and they will lose." She shifted the cups around again, quicker this time. "Now?"

Guy kept still and let his brother tap.

"Incorrect," Sabine said, lifting an empty cup. "And if I add another ball?" She slipped one under the empty cup, let Dot choose this time, and lifted up a cup to show two balls, then did it again, this time uncovering the egg. "I know this set is old hat to you, but I think we can find a way to drum up some interest."

"You can teach us to do that?" How looked longingly at the thin metal cups, the egg, the little rubber balls.

"Can and will," Sabine said.

"Now we're officially late," Kitty said, pulling on a coat as she walked into the kitchen. "Let's move it out."

"We can't go yet," Guy said. "Sabine is finally going to teach us a trick."

"Well, then, won't we be happy to see Sabine later on?" Kitty said.

They moaned together, the sound of a low, lingering belly

pain, and shuffled off in search of boots, hats, gloves, and scarves, the extraordinary preparation for a trip outdoors. "Get all your books," she called to them.

"I will see you tonight," Kitty said, and kissed her mother on the cheek. "Tonight," she said to Sabine, and kissed her hard and fast on her forehead. It was a complete surprise, that kiss, as startling and cool as an egg pushed from an ear canal. Kitty was out the door, in a hurry to start the car, while the boys fell into a ragged line behind her.

"Later," Guy said, and slapped Sabine's hand, as if they were happily colluding now.

Dot looked around at the kitchen. It was a wreck of mixing bowls and hot griddles, of bacon that had not yet finished cooking but spit grease on every surface. Vast quantities of uneaten pancakes weighted with syrup littered the plates. "You're going to tell me it's too early for a drink."

"Probably not," Sabine said, picking up a plate and taking a bite, not because she wanted to, but because she knew she should.

"Well, the boys are okay." Dot sighed, defeated by her own maternal instincts. "Kitty seemed happier today than I've seen her since I don't know when."

"You think?"

"It won't last. Howard will come around. The boys will want to go home, but hell, let her have a little rest. She needs one."

"So you think she'll go back?"

Dot cut a triangle of pancakes stacked three deep and delicately mopped up a small puddle of syrup on the side of her plate. "Only if history tells us anything."

"Sometimes things change, every now and then."

Dot nodded, chewing thoughtfully. "Things changed for me and Al. I don't mean that to sound crass, but we kept doing it the same way over and over again, and then Guy stepped in and changed that. Not that I think Howard is like Al. They've got a whole other set of circumstances over there."

"So what could change it for them? Assuming that How or Guy doesn't—"

Dot put up her hand. "Don't even say that."

"No, I don't mean—"

"I'll tell you the one time I had hope was when Howard had himself a girlfriend. He moved out of the house, moved in with her. That made a real difference. He wasn't interested in going back and Kitty wasn't interested in having him. I could see her starting to get on with her life. It lasted more than six months. That was promising."

"So what happened?"

"Well, the girl threw him out, of course. If she'd had a grain of sand in her head she would have figured him out sooner or later. God, I would have given her every cent I had to keep him. She threw him out and then there was no place to go but home. He's got his name on the deed to the house. There's not enough money to buy another house. Howard and Kitty are fighting and he's sleeping on the couch and then one day, bang, he's not sleeping on the couch anymore. What do you say?"

"I don't know," Sabine said, not sure whether the question was rhetorical.

"You say, 'Hello, Howard, haven't seen you around here lately.' "

"How long ago was that?"

"Three or four years now." Dot pushed up from the table and started picking up plates. "There are some little birds around here who'll be mighty happy with these pancakes."

Sabine stayed at the table, tracing lines through her syrup with her fork, her mind full of her sister-in-law.

"Listen to me, Sabine. I know you like Kitty a lot. I knew you would from the first time I met you. I'd like her even if she wasn't my daughter. But you can't let yourself become overly involved with how her life's going to turn out. Bertie and I go around about this all the time. She thinks I should make Kitty leave Howard and come home. She thinks I can do that. But I can't and you can't, either. Kitty's going to play her hand. There's just no saying how long it's going to take her."

Sabine nodded. She had spent the better part of her life in love with one basically unobtainable Fetters. The idea of somehow setting her sights on another one, one that she had no idea what to do with anyway, was ludicrous. "You're right."

" 'You're right,' " Dot said. "Now, why don't my own children ever say that to me?"

Together Dot and Sabine cleaned up the kitchen, washed and dried the dishes and wiped the bacon grease off the stove, wiped up every amber bead of syrup that had been dripped off plates. When the hot-water heater had warmed itself up again, Dot went to take her bath while Sabine brought her work back to the now clean kitchen table and began to cut out the supporting beams for Phan's house. She found the task immensely soothing, the order she had to follow, the lining up of glue and razor blades and straight edge. In the monotonous details of the task she was able for a moment not to think about anything. She did not think about missing Parsifal, nor did she wonder about Kitty. She did not think about what it would be like to leave or stay. She cut and measured. She wrote long lists of numbers on the back of an old envelope and worked the math out in her head. Nothing comforted Sabine like long division. That was how she had passed time waiting for Phan and then Parsifal to come back from their tests. She figured the square root of the date while other people knit and read. Sabine blamed much of the world's unhappiness on the advent of calculators.

"You look like you're set for the day," Dot said.

Sabine looked up from her work. "Are you leaving already?"

"I've got to pick up some things for Bertie. I feel like with all the other stuff that's been going on the wedding is getting short shrift. They should have gotten married six years ago. It feels a little antichmactic now. I keep forgetting it's on Saturday."

"It took me twenty-two years to get down the aisle, and Haas likes girls, so don't complain. By the way, why did Bertie wait all this time just to get married in the dead of winter?"

"She's turning thirty. They were going to get married next summer, and then all of a sudden she decided she wanted to get married before she turned thirty."

"Good a reason as any." Sabine arranged a line of toothpicks.

"Are you going to be sitting right there when I come home?"

"Probably."

"Well, at least put some slippers on." She waved to Sabine and blew her a kiss.

As soon as she had closed the door Sabine understood what Dot wanted, just to have the house be quiet for a while, to have a couple of hours alone. She understood because the quiet was wonderful.

Sabine did not get up. She did not take a shower. She stayed in Phan's pajamas, in Parsifal's robe, and worked through the morning and afternoon in a state of transcendent concentration. Her hands pursued their delicate, complicated mission. She went over every detail of the house in her mind: the shape of the planters on either side of the front door, the curve of the driveway, the size of the swimming pool in relation to the house (Sabine made beautiful swimming pools, cut them to their proper depth on a plywood base, painted the inside blue, and covered the top in a rippling cellophane. Maybe she would make a yellow raft.) Every time Kitty's face floated towards her she shook her head and refocused her attention on a task. She liked to skip around in the way they had told her never to do in architecture school. She would connect two outer walls, stop to sand the base, gesso some cardboard, work on the garden. She cut out pansies the size of baby aspirin from a sheet of white notebook paper, cut slits in two matching shapes, and then slid them together using tweezers. Then she ran a violet streak across their faces with a toothpick. She had made an entire saucer full of pansies when she heard the high whining brakes of the mail truck. She put down the tweezers and flexed her fingers open and closed. Getting the mail was one of the tasks that Sabine had come to think of as hers, like shoveling snow and washing dishes. She hurried to get dressed, suddenly anxious to be outside for the sixty-second round-trip that mail retrieval required. She stepped into a pair of boots by the door (there seemed to be no sense of ownership about boots when it came to short trips) and went out the back door rather than the front, just to make her walk a few feet longer. Sabine barely noticed the freezing cold, the blue sky, or the howling wind. She was getting used to them.

She was thinking about the placement of the windows in the front hallway of the house on Oriole, trying to remember the number of panes in each window. She had walked all the way down the driveway and reached into the mailbox before she noticed the man across the street leaning on the front bumper of a parked Chevy Cavalier. The sun directly above their heads made Sabine squint. No one simply stood outside in Nebraska in February.

"Howard?" Sabine shaded her eyes with her hand.

He gave a curt nod of agreement but didn't say anything, as if he were waiting for someone else and didn't want to be disturbed.

"Are you all right?" Sabine said from across the street.

"Oh, hell, I'm fine. My wife left me and took my kids. How are you?"

"Do you want to come inside, have some coffee?" Sabine said, turning slightly towards Dot's house to show which way she meant to go. "It's awfully cold out here."

"I don't mind the cold."

"Well, that makes one of us." Sabine stuck the mail under her arm to put her hands in her pockets. "What are you doing out here?"

"Waiting for you."

"Waiting for me?" Sabine said. "Why didn't you come to the door?"

"You all made it real clear about how you felt about me coming around. You don't want me anywhere near you."

"I never said—"

"I'll talk to you where I want to." He stayed on the other side of the street, his long, thin legs angled down like a loading ramp.

"Okay," Sabine said. "Talk to me."

But her asking only seemed to make him wait. He looked down the street, his eyes fixed so hard on something that Sabine looked in that direction to try and see what it was. There was nothing down there. It was only more of the same. "She sure does talk a lot about you," Howard Plate said, looking off. "Used to be she talked about that brother of hers all the time, but once you came into town she fixed on you."

Sabine shivered. She hadn't planned to spend this much time outside. She had only dressed to survive the cold for a minute. She had left her hat and gloves inside. She had left her coat. "It's a big surprise, finding family you didn't know you had. It's been a surprise for me."

"You think we're family?"

"Dot was my husband's mother. Kitty and Bertie were his sisters. I think that makes us family of a sort. I certainly care for them a great deal."

"That explains why you came to see them so often."

Sabine took her hands from her pockets and rubbed them quickly along the outsides of her arms. It didn't take long for your skin to turn brittle, to feel the hard bite of the wind. "Howard, I'm freezing. I'm going inside." Where were all the neighbors? Where were the cars driving by in the middle of the day? Why was everything so quiet?

"I still haven't told you why I came to see you."

"Okay." She shifted her weight from one foot to the other, trying not to hop. "Why?"

"I want you to stay away from my wife and I want you to stay away from my sons. Things were fine when you were out in California." He said the word with particular hatred. "I want things to be fine again."

"Listen, this is Alliance," she said quickly, hoping to wrap this encounter up. "I don't know where I'm supposed to go to avoid seeing Kitty and the boys, especially now that they're staying here. Besides, I hardly think you can blame this breakup on me. Things were going great before I came to town and now they've all gone to hell?" I kissed your wife, she wanted to say to him. The words came up in her throat with a powerful urgency, and it was all she could do to push them down. I kissed your wife.

"Things might not have been great, but we were all living in the same house."

"Sometimes," Sabine said.

"Most of the time. Don't you tell me what goes on in my family. That's exactly the kind of thing I'm talking about."

"For what it's worth, I'm not the problem."

"It's worth nothing," Howard Plate said. He detached himself from the car and stood up. The street seemed remarkably small. With all the snow banked along the edges it would have been difficult for two cars to pass one another.

She didn't tell him she was leaving, that he would get exactly what he wanted if he held on for a few more days I know your wife, she wanted to say. "I'm going inside." Sabine turned around and walked down the driveway. The boots were an old pair of Dot's and they were too small for her. She was half walking on her toes.

"Maybe I'll take you up on that cup of coffee now," Howard Plate shouted at her as she turned around the corner of the house.

"I kissed your wife," she said quietly as she let herself in the back door.

Distracted now from the formerly seamless flow of work, Sabine took a shower, changed her clothes, and nervously straightened up the house. Howard Plate was not outside, she looked. There was only a perfectly harmless Chevy parked across the street. She was not afraid of him. He was a bully, a deep annoyance. She would not see him as a dangerous man. She made the twin beds in Parsifal's room and hung up the clothes, knowing it was probably not her business to do so, but it calmed her. The room, since she had so recently vacated it, had become mysteriously average. The baseball trophies and Hardy Boys books that had held her undivided attention for the past two and a half weeks were now simple decorations on shelves. She fluffed up the pillows and picked up three glasses (three?) from the night table. Then she went into the living room and folded up Kitty's bedding from the couch and put it back in the hall closet. For a minute she dipped her face into the sheets and smelled Kitty, the soap and cigarettes and wintergreen, which brought back the kiss, which led Sabine to close the closet door tightly.

By the time Dot came home with the boys after school, Sabine was back at work on the house. She had cut all the exterior doors and walls and made her windows out of two layers of freezer bags melted lightly together on a cookie sheet. She did not mention Howard Plate's visit. She had very nearly made herself forget about him and was only reminded by seeing the boys and their long and lean resemblance to their father. There were so many different angles from which to look at boys. They would look like their uncle, then their mother and then their father, depending on how you turned them in the light.

"That's the place," Dot said. She pointed the boys' attention towards the obvious. "That's exactly what it looks like."

"It's bigger," Sabine said. "And there's a roof."

"I wish you'd been here when my science project was due," Guy said, running a tender finger over a windowsill.

How sniffed around with moderate interest. "Are you going to show us how to do the cups and balls?"

Sabine nodded and held two pieces of recently glued board together. At home she had a vise. "Do you want to do that now?"

"I've been thinking about it," How said, careful in the ways teenage boys can be about not seeming to really want anything you might be able to give them.

So Sabine showed them cups and balls. It was no great betrayal to the secret society of magicians. The directions were, after all, written out in completely impenetrable English on the top of the box. There were diagrams of the trick in every cheap book of magic. But pictures never explained anything. Sabine set up the cups and the balls. "Leave the egg out for now, that's the tricky part. Basics first." She showed them how to hide the balls on the tops of the stacked cups, how to turn the cups over so that the balls didn't fall out, how there was no magic, just planning and acting. How and Guy, fresh from school's obedience, sat and watched, desperate as they never were in American history to give a perfect mimicking of the facts. "Once you learn how to do it, you never look at your hands. If you look at your hands, they'll look at your hands. You control the attention of the audience. You direct it. That's how you hide things."

Dot came over and stood behind Sabine. "Maybe you boys could learn how to do this, start up a brothers act, make your way in the world."

"We start a brothers act, I can tell you who's going to be the assistant," Guy said, never taking his eyes off Sabine's hands, which never stopped moving.

"There will be no slighting of magicians' assistants in my presence," Sabine said.

"Sorry."

"I'm ready to try," How said with great seriousness, his face fixed with the set determination of a batter waiting for the first pitch.

"Good," Sabine said. "Have at it." She slid the props across the table. She was pulling for How. She thought he was exactly the kind of boy who could make a decent magician, basically too introverted to do much with other kids his own age and therefore more likely to practice the tireless hours that were required. A boy who would fashion the persona of a magician like another boy might carve a turtle from a bar of soap. As much as Guy wanted the skills, rabbits, hats, assistants, he didn't sufficiently need them. People would come to him for other reasons. He wouldn't have the patience for the tedium, the repetition and failure that might one day put him on late-night television.

How took the cups and carefully placed the balls on top, his large, chapped hands trying to appear nimble and birdlike. He set up the cups without any of the balls scooting across the table and onto the floor, then he looked to Sabine for approval and direction.

"And then you say . . . ," she said.

"We're going to put this ball"—he held up the ball that he had hidden in his hand. A good palm job, although it was not a ball that needed to be palmed—"under this cup."

She liked his use of the first-person plural, his eye contact. "Good," she said. "Good."

How and Sabine skipped the cups around until Guy got bored and wandered off to watch MTV in the living room. How was tireless, a record set to Replay, so that at the end of every run-through he simply went back and started over again, each time repeating his patter with a musical freshness. Dot claimed a sudden urgent need to go to the grocery store to get away from the never-ending question, "Where do you think the ball is now?" But Sabine could take it. The wild tedium of watching someone else practice, of practicing herself, was a skill she had developed over the years. She spotted him like a gymnastics coach, sticking an arm beneath his back at the most perilous moment of the flip. He did not tire, get frustrated, grow sloppy. He worked.

"Do you think I'll be able to do the egg sometime?"

Sabine nodded. "You were born for it."

How put his broad hands down flat on the table. His nails were red, their beds crushed to a fleshy pulp by the constant efforts of his teeth. All his cuticles were stripped beyond the possibility of regrowth. "If you thought you could stay a little longer, it would really help me—I mean, to learn some of this. I should have asked you sooner, I know. I just . . ." He looked at her pleadingly, his sentence over.

"I really do need to go home, How. I'm sorry. You're going to be great, though. You've got what it takes to do this thing yourself. Your uncle did it. Nobody taught him magic." Sabine said this without having any notion of whether or not it was true. For all she knew, Parsifal's math teacher was a Blackstone himself. He may have passed on every secret in the book after the chalkboards had been wiped down.

Over the unbearable strains of electric guitars coming from the television in the other room, Sabine could hear How's labored breathing. This time of year, everyone in Alliance was breathing with difficulty. "Um," he said, staring at his damaged hands, his knuckles scraped and scabbed as a fighter's. "Do you think my mom might go and see you in California?"

"She might," Sabine said, never really having thought about Kitty in Los Angeles. "I hope she does."

He waited for a long time, mulling over her reply, preparing his next sentence as if he were culling the words out of an English phrasebook. "I'd like to come." He said this very quietly, as if he were overwhelmed by the burden of his own request.

"Of course you can come," Sabine said, and she meant it. She could take How to Disneyland, to the beach. He could lie by the pool. Her parents would like How, his sweet disposition and healthy appetite. She could hear his big feet slapping down the hall, coming in at night to practice magic in front of the mirrors in the master bedroom. The rabbit would be so happy—something to do. "You can come even if your mother doesn't."

His eyes turned up, so hopeful and filled with wanting that Sabine could not exactly meet them. "Really?"

"Sure," she said, and pushed the cups back to him. "Just practice."

By the time Kitty came home at six o'clock, How had something to show her that was nearly formed. You never knew if a trick was any good until you found someone to pull it on. His mother watched with rapt attention, sitting right down in the chair beside him when he asked for her, not stopping to take off her boots or heavy coat. She picked the cup that she earnestly believed concealed the ball and seemed to be thrilled when she was wrong. He had fooled her and she was delighted.

"Sabine taught you that?" Kitty had both hands on How's shoulders.

"Every move."

"I wish Guy could see this," Kitty said to How, to Sabine, to Dot, who had returned from the grocery. She did not mean How's brother, who was at the moment stretched across the living room sofa mouthing the words to a Smashing Pumpkins song along with the television. "He would be so proud of you."

And Sabine confirmed that this was true.

When, after dinner, they watched the Johnny Carson video (now back on the track of their regular habits) it meant something else again. Tonight it was about the possibility of becoming that young magician, and for a moment they each considered How in Parsifal's role. Sabine could even be his assistant, though How deserved a younger girl, someone who was not an inheritance but completely his own.

"A person would have to work awfully hard to be that good," Dot said to the room in general, as if she were noticing for the first time that what had been done so many years before in the NBC Burbank studios was difficult.

"I know," How said, his eyes never for a second leaving the screen.

Many hours later, when everyone was asleep or waiting to fall asleep, and Kitty came quietly into Sabine's room and sat down on the edge of the bed like a college girl come to tell late-night secrets, the thing she wanted to talk about was How. The thing that Sabine wanted to talk about she didn't begin to have words for.

"I think he has some real promise," Kitty said, sitting cross-legged in the dark. "I remember what Guy looked like when he was first doing tricks. He was younger than How, but there were similarities."

It had only been one trick, one afternoon of cups and balls, which was the place every person who ever had the most fleeting interest in magic began. "It's not like we've just found out he's Mozart," Sabine said, speaking rationally. "But I do think he'd make a good magician. He has the right kind of temperament for it."

"I know he's not Guy, but I want things to work out for him that way. I want him to be successful, happy."

"If you're talking about money, Parsifal was a successful rug salesman, not a successful magician. By the time we paid for costumes and equipment, we wound up making about a thousand bucks a year on magic, and that's when things were good. If you're talking about happiness, I don't know. I don't know what makes people happy." Sabine remembered Howard Plate and thought how happy she could have made him simply by telling him that she would soon be returning to California, how profoundly unhappy he would have been to hear the thing she had wanted to tell him, about Kitty and the kiss she was thinking of now. "I saw Howard today."

"Howard?" Kitty sat up straight, as if Sabine had seen him under the bed. "Where?"

"He came by this afternoon to talk to me."

"To talk to you?"

Sabine put her hands behind her head. Her elbows stretched past the edges of the pillow. "He said he wanted me to leave town. He seems to think I'm the cause of your problems."

"Dear God."

"It's no big deal," Sabine said, entirely unsure of whether it was or not.

"I'm so sorry about that." Kitty laughed. "And to think I was coming in to try and talk you into staying."

If there was some important information in Kitty's eyes, it was too dark for Sabine to see it properly. "You know I'm not leaving because of that."

In the dark, Kitty could have been a girl. She could have been the Kitty of years ago, sitting on her own bed, her brother across the hall. "Still," she said, "I'll see if I can't call off the dogs."

"You have enough to worry about with Howard. He's not going to bother me. He didn't bother me. Like I said, we just talked."

They sat there quietly for a while, both meaning to say other things. All the things that had made them brave the night before, the dark and the quiet, made them terribly shy now. "I guess I should go on to sleep," Kitty said.

"Are you working tomorrow?"

Kitty shook her head. "I'm going to help Bertie with a few last-minute things for the wedding."

"If I can do anything..."

"Sure," Kitty said. "Thanks." She stood up and patted Sabine's foot where it made a small hill beneath the covers. There was between the two of them so much disappointment and relief that Sabine found herself taking shallow breaths. Kitty slipped into the hall and closed the door behind her without stopping or saying good-night, and though Sabine waited, sure that this time she would think of the right thing to say, Kitty did not come back.

There is a tremendous crush in the Magic Castle. The secret panel in the bookcase is open and there are people filling up the foyer and the main lobby. The banister strains to hold back the people packed onto the staircase and they spill onto the balcony and down every corridor. There is a man Sabine cannot see pressing against her back and he pushes her hard up against the man who is in front of her. She can smell the sweet verbena pomade in his hair. Every magician she has ever heard of is here, every magic-store owner, every cabinetmaker and previous audience member, and mixed in with them are a thousand people she does not recognize. The crowd has a steady percolation of movement, although Sabine has no idea where the people want to go. Maybe they are trying to get to the bar, or maybe they are trying to adjust themselves to the ones who continue to flood into the room. Maybe, like Sabine, they are looking for someone. She is fortunate. She is taller than most of the people there, taller still for wearing high heels. There is a large group of Vietnamese surrounding her and she can see over their heads without difficulty. The men are wearing white dinner jackets with black ties, and all of the women are in evening gowns. All of the women except Sabine, who is wearing the sea-foam green assistant's costume that Phan made for her. She lifts her hand to her chest and touches the satin trim and tiny blue glass beads. She was at the Castle the last time she wore it. She and Parsifal did one last show three months before Phan died. Phan came with them. He was blind by then, but he sat in the front row and held his face up to the sound of Parsifal's voice as if he were watching. Magic means nothing to the blind, but Phan said he was very proud. Later he touched the beads on Sabine's costume with the tips of his fingers. "They're so tiny," he marveled. "I can't believe I ever saw well enough to sew all of those on."

So she is back at the Castle, wearing this costume, which can mean only one thing. With great difficulty, Sabine begins to turn in a circle, looking, looking. What she sees, finally, is not Parsifal but a beautiful picture of him, a poster for tonight's performance. It is larger than he is. He is painted in front of a flaming California sunset, his feet surrounded by sand and sea grass. He glows from the brilliance of the yellow that is behind him. His face is handsome and very wise. In the picture he holds the rabbit tenderly in both hands. PARSIFAL IS MAGIC, the sign says.

Sabine begins to fight her way to the greenroom. "I'm the assistant," she says, pushing her hands against the shoulders of the people in front of her as if she is trying to peel them apart. "I'm the assistant. Let me through." Inch by inch, she works her way forward. Even the people who want to help her can't. There is no place for them to move to.

She is exhausted, her hips caught between two men who have their backs to her. She is still a good twenty feet away when the door to the greenroom opens and Phan comes out, looking worried. She waves and calls to him, but he cannot hear her for the noise of the crowd. He scans the room and just as he is about to give up he finds her. His face is lit with joy and relief and he waves, his arm going madly overhead. "Sabine!"

Phan in his white dinner jacket and black tie looks like no other man in the room. He glows like Parsifal in the painting. He holds out his hands to her and she stretches towards them. He steps into the crowd as if he is stepping into water. The people part for him and flow around him, and he comes to her easily and takes her hand and pulls her back with him towards the shore. "We've been frantic," he says in her ear.

"Parsifal said he thought maybe you were angry, maybe you weren't going to come."

"I've been stuck out there," she says. "I couldn't find you."

"It's all right now." He squeezes her hands. She thinks that both of her feet have left the floor, that she is being handed forward through the crowd.

"Is he here?" she calls.

Phan nods. They are delivered, pressed against the door. "He's nervous, though. This is a big night for him. He needs you."

"Are we going to do a show?"

"We're in a real hurry."

"There are so many people."

"My family is here."

"What?" Sabine calls. They are so close and yet it is impossible to hear anything.

"We can't talk out here," Phan says, and tilts his head towards the door. "Inside."

They step through the door and everything is different, everything is quiet. So many flowers. An entire spray of tiny white orchids. White calla lilies; three dozen yellow roses, each as big as a teacup; pink globes of peonies dropping petals on the dressing table. Gardenias float in a shallow glass bowl. There are as many flowers in this room as there are people in the other, and the smell of them all together is complicated but not overwhelming, as if the flowers have been instructed to keep themselves in check. Phan keeps a tight hold of Sabine's hand. She keeps a tight hold of his.

"Look who's here," Phan calls.

"Really?" Parsifal's voice comes from behind a dressing screen.

"I'm here," Sabine says. It all feels so easy now, not like

Paris. She is not overcome, not surprised. She is only happy now. She is back with her family.

Parsifal steps out tentatively. The top button of his white tuxedo shirt is undone and the black silk ribbon of his tie rests loosely against his shoulders. His studs are the set of opals he bought in Australia, rimmed in gold. He is not wearing a jacket. His dark hair is as thick and as shiny as How's. He is as beautiful and whole as any man has ever been. "Look at you," he says.

"Me?" she says, and laughs. She crosses the small room, flowers brushing her bare shoulders, and opens her arms to him. "Look at you."

They hold each other. This is exactly what it was like to be held by Parsifal. She presses her face against his neck. "I miss you so much," she says.

He runs his hands in circles across the top of her back and then leans away from her so that he can see her face again. "But everything's worked out, hasn't it? It's all turned out so beautifully. I thought it would, but I didn't know for sure. And even when I imagined it I never imagined it going this well."

"What are you talking about?"

"Things with my mother and Bertie and the boys." He smiles, his head tilted, his eyebrows slightly down. It is the smile he gives her when the two of them understand something secret together. "Kitty."

"What?"

"Parsifal," Phan says from the door.

Parsifal looks up at him. "Oh, come on. She knows. I know, you know, she knows. There isn't a whole lot of time."

"Why isn't there a lot of time?" Sabine says, feeling slightly nervous. "What about Kitty?"

Phan shakes his head as Parsifal hugs her again. "Kitty is

fabulous. Don't worry about Kitty. Besides, this isn't even the reason that you're here."

They never had flowers like this before a show. It's like being in some strange sort of garden where things grow out of tables rather than the ground. "So why am I here?" Sabine says. She doesn't think there needs to be a reason. They haven't seen each other in so long. That they are together now is reason enough to be anywhere.

Now it's Parsifal who looks nervous. He glances at Phan, who looks at his wristwatch.

"It is late," Phan says. "We have to get things going." Phan opens the door a crack and looks out down the hall. "It's a madhouse," he says, still watching the crowd. "They'll tear this place down if you don't go on soon." He lifts up on his toes, leans his head out into the crowd, and then spins around. "Oh, my God. Parsifal, Johnny Carson is here."

"No," Parsifal says, and rushes to the door.

"You can't go out there now," Phan says, blocking his way out. "They'll eat you up. You can see him after the show."

Parsifal puts his hands on Phan's shoulders. For a second Sabine isn't sure if he's going to embrace him or push him aside. Parsifal leans forward, kisses him. "I'm scared," he whispers.

"You've done it a hundred times in practice. It's brilliant. You'll be brilliant." Phan buttons the top button of Parsifal's shirt and begins to tie his tie.

"You're going to have to tell me what's going on here," Sabine says. "You're making me crazy."

Parsifal turns to her, Phan's hands still at his neck. "It's a new act, I guess you'd say. I'm going to show it here tonight. It's amazing, Sabine. It's beautiful. I want you to be the assistant."

"But I don't know it," Sabine says.

Phan looks at his watch.

"There's nothing to know," Parsifal says. "You look stunning. We're a team. You'll be absolutely fine. Just follow my lead." He hands her a black-and-gold lipstick case from the dressing table.

"I have to know what the act is," Sabine says, drawing on her mouth in red.

A young man wearing wire-rimmed glasses and a headset comes in the back door without knocking. His eyes are frantic. "Now," he says, pointing to the door. "I'm sorry, but right now."

"Go, go," Phan says, giving them both a quick kiss. "I need to get to my seat." He is out the door.

Parsifal puts on his jacket and takes a handkerchief out of his pocket to wipe the perspiration from his forehead. "We have to go." He does not say this to Sabine. He mouths the words. He takes her hand and pulls her down the back hall to the edge of the stage. They are standing there together in the dark, side by side, as they have been on any one of a thousand nights before. Sabine doesn't ask him anything now. It's too late. You can never talk this close to the stage, but Parsifal turns and takes her face in his hands. He kisses her and says, "Remember this, okay? You'll love this."

Sabine has never been onstage before without knowing the drill, without having practiced the trick backwards and forwards for months on end. Then she remembers that first night at the Magic Hat, when he called her up from the back of the room, the waitress holding the Manhattan. She went with him then. She followed his lead like they were dancing. Now, at the Magic Castle in the pitch-black dark, Parsifal takes her hand. Their arms are twisted together and they lean into one another hard, the way they always did before a show, their mutual wish for good luck. He leads her onto the stage.

The second their feet touch the polished wood, the light

floods down on them. They can see only each other. Sabine can tell the size of a crowd by its roar, and the roar tonight is huge, bigger than Vegas, though that's impossible since none of the theaters at the Castle is anywhere near as large as the Sands. They are screaming his name. They are stamping their feet against the floor. They are applauding and the noise it makes is like an airplane splitting apart in midair.

Parsifal raises his hands to soothe them. The light reflects from his palms. "Thank you," he says. His voice is humble, genuinely overwhelmed. "My name is Parsifal." And they begin to scream again. He waits, he shakes his head. "And this is my beautiful assistant, my wife, Sabine."

She looks at him as the crowd calls her name. He has never introduced her as his wife before. Until that moment she has completely forgotten she is his wife. Parsifal lifts her delicate hand high in the air and she bows to the audience, to him. The sea-foam green of the satin combines with the pink lights to make her skin luminous.

"Tonight—," he says, but they are still roaring. "Please," he says, "please." He waits until they are quiet, but even the quiet is volatile, living. There is a charge in the air, as if anything might set them going again. "Tonight I will attempt to perform a feat of magic that, to the best of my knowledge, has never been attempted on any stage, at any point in time, anyplace in the world." This notion, that they are about to be placed in history, makes them cheer again. The audience loves them so desperately that Sabine feels frightened of their love.

Parsifal raises his hands. "This is, in all ways, an extremely difficult performance, and if it is to be accomplished, I will have to request absolute silence." They are off like a light switch. There is barely the sound of their massive, collective breathing. He motions for Sabine to walk in front of him. "Sabine," he says.

Sabine doesn't know where she's supposed to go or what

is supposed to happen. She wonders if this trick will involve her body, if she is in some way supposed to pass through him or be cut into pieces or float in the air, and while she is apprehensive, she is not afraid. She knows her work. She knows work in the deepest part of herself, and she knows Parsifal. She walks ahead of him. She has not noticed the table before, but there it is, center stage. It is a regular table, not a trick prop. It is waist high, with slender legs and a thin, solid top the size of a record album. With its slight proportions the table reassures the audience that it is not designed to hide anything. All it has to do is hold one deck of cards, which it does.

A card trick?

"Please pick up the deck," he tells her.

Sabine picks up the pack. It is absolutely good in its shrink-wrapped cellophane and its glued-down seal.

"Is the deck unopened and unmarked?"

"Yes," Sabine says, and holds it out to the audience. Parsifal never used marked cards in his life.

"Please open the deck and remove the jokers."

Sabine finds the tab on the wrapper and pulls it open. She breaks the seal with her thumbnail and pulls the deck out of the box, dropping the cellophane and the two jokers onto the floor.

"Please shuffle the deck."

Parsifal steps aside and Sabine begins to shuffle. She's glad she's had some practice lately. She waits for his signs, his hand in his pocket, his right foot turning in, but none comes. There are no instructions on how to stack the deck and so she doesn't. She shuffles for the art of it, for the form. She makes the cards move only in ways that are beautiful. When she is finished, there is a small swell of applause, but Parsifal silences it with a look. Sabine places the deck neatly in the middle of the table.

There must be a joke in here somewhere. It all seems a little portentous for a card trick, but when she turns to smile at Parsifal he is once again the man going into the MRI machine. He is Parsifal on the night of Phan's death. He is pale and his face is shining with sweat. Sabine can see the veins rising in his temples, and she raises her hand to touch him but he shakes her off. "Silence," he says, although this time he can barely manage the word.

He raises his right hand, as if he is lifting up the light scaffolding. The hand trembles beneath some terrible unseen weight. Then he lowers it slowly to the deck and taps the top card, one time, two, three. He stops to take a breath and Sabine wants to say to him, Forget this, whatever it is, forget it, but she is the assistant and she has to wait for his sign. He taps the deck for the fourth and final time. He sighs and smiles, a small, tired smile. He takes out his handkerchief and wipes his face again, making a slight nod of acknowledgment to the black hole that is the audience, because somewhere out there are Phan and Johnny Carson. "Turn over the top card and show it to the audience, please," he tells Sabine.

Sabine does not know this trick, but she knows a show. She lets her hand hover in the air above the deck for just a moment as if she is afraid of what she might find. She is not afraid. She picks up the card and holds it in front of her, making a sweep from left to right, as if such a massive, faraway crowd can actually see this little piece of cardboard in the dark. "Ace of hearts," she says, and puts the card face-up on the table.

"Second card, please."

The deck is not stacked. She is the only one who could have stacked it and she didn't. She holds up the second card. "Ace of clubs."

There is a murmuring in the audience that even Parsifal's looks can't quell. His voice is weak. "Third card, please."

They are waiting and Sabine makes them wait. She has never turned a card so slowly before in her life. "Ace of diamonds." There is a gasp now, and Sabine makes part of it herself. The audience is on their feet. She can feel them trembling, straining towards the stage. Her own hand is shaking. She knows all the tricks and this is not one of them. It was not possible to stack the deck.

"Fourth card, please, Sabine."

And when she lifts it up she cannot believe it herself. The audience comes on them like a wave, leaping onto the stage and sweeping Parsifal high into the air. They already know the answer. They do not need to hear her say it but she does, over and over again. "Ace of spades, ace of spades." Someone tears the card from her hand. Parsifal is gone, riding out on the shoulders of the people. He turns, he tries to wave to her, and she waves to him, good-bye. The table has overturned. The cards are everywhere.

"Sabine," the voice said. There was a hand shaking her shoulder. "Sabine, wake up!"

"Kitty?"

"Dad's here." How reached over and switched on the light next to her bed. Sabine raised up on one elbow. He was wearing sweatpants and a T-shirt with Mr. Bubble on it. His hair was rumpled with sleep.

"Your dad is here?" She had been dreaming about Parsifal. Parsifal and she were in a magic show.

"In the kitchen with Mom. You have to go talk to them. You have to get up."

Sabine pushed herself up from her bed and opened the closet to find her bathrobe, but How took her hand and pulled her forward. Parsifal was with Phan and they were happy. There were flowers everywhere. "Come *on*," How said.

Sabine stumbled down the dark hallway in her pajamas. The house was cold without her robe. Dot turned the thermostat down at night to save money.

"I won't put up with this." Howard's voice, too loud for being so late at night. Sabine didn't know how she hadn't heard it before or how Dot was sleeping through it now. The people who listened for Howard's voice had been awakened by it. The ones who weren't used to it slept through.

"Go home," Kitty said, her voice tired.

Guy was standing just outside the kitchen door, wearing only a pair of white jockey shorts. The light from the kitchen fell over the front of him like the light from a movie screen. He was watching, shivering, all of his skin impossibly pale.

"Go in there," Guy said when he saw Sabine. She put a hand on his bare shoulder and he leaned against her. He still had the warm smell of sleep on his skin. "He'll kill her," he whispered in her ear like a secret.

They were watching Kitty and Howard, who seemed to think that they were the only two people in the house who were awake. "Nobody's going to kill anybody," Sabine said, feeling clearheaded and brave. Parsifal had told her, Kitty is fabulous. He said it with such assurance that there was no way to believe it wasn't true. Howard was easy, a middle-aged punk. If she had to go up against him, there was no way he could match her. She left the two brothers behind her, huddled together at the door frame.

Kitty was sitting in a chair at the table, her hands covering her face. Howard was standing beside her, rapping the blade of a ten-inch knife against the table. In her life, Sabine had seen as many trick knives as real ones. Blades that were rubber and bent away. Blades that slid up into the handle and gave the illusion of stabbing. That's how they did it in the movies, in magic shows.

"Hey, Howard," Sabine said, rubbing her eyes. "You're waking everyone up."

He turned to her, his face full of the rage she had seen only on the faces of the teenaged boys who roamed Los Angeles. He pointed the knife towards her. "Go back to bed."

Kitty raised her face. She was crying or she had been crying. There was the smallest cut along the top of her cheek that was bleeding. She was bleeding. A delicate cut with blood so impossibly red that for a moment Sabine thought that, like the knife, it might not be real. She would take Kitty and the boys back to Los Angeles with her. That was the answer. Looking at the cut on Kitty's face, Howard, this same kitchen, it became clear. All of this was over.

"Go back to bed," Kitty said. "Take the boys with you."

Sabine shook her head. "I'm not going anywhere." She came over and took the chair next to Kitty. "Let me see your face." She put a hand under Kitty's chin.

"I'm fine," Kitty said. "Really."

"Goddamn it, don't you hear?" Howard Plate said.

"Perfectly," Sabine said, not taking her eyes off Kitty for a minute. She pressed a paper napkin left from dinner against the cut.

Howard took hold of Sabine's shoulders, the shoulders of Phan's white cotton pajamas, and pulled her to her feet. The neck of the pajamas caught her neck and made her head snap back and then up straight. The knife, which he held at a careless angle so that it could as easily go through her skin as not, cut her sleeve. In the hallway she heard a sound from the boys, a deep inhale. There were as many trick knives as real ones. Knives so useless you couldn't use them to open an envelope. For all she knew she was still asleep, or she had been awake before and this was now the dream. Howard's knuckles pushed against her collarbone and the soft skin of her throat.

"Howard," Kitty said, standing up herself.

"Listen to me!" he screamed at Sabine. He flung her back against the refrigerator and then shook out his hand as if he regretted having touched her. Four refrigerator magnets shaped like fruit fell to the floor.

Sabine pulled down her pajama top to set it right again, trying to catch her breath. No one had ever pushed her, had ever pulled her anywhere. "You need to go home," she said, coughing.

"I'm going home," Howard said. "I'm taking my family home." He was like the audience, just barely contained. He shook slightly, as if he were making an enormous physical effort to keep himself from killing her in his fury.

"They won't go with you," Sabine said.

"They'll do what I tell them to do." Howard Plate looked at Sabine as if he were only just now able to see her. He was trying to catch his breath. "Why are you here? Didn't I tell you to stay away from us?"

Maybe he could kill them. Maybe Kitty's leaving had made him mad enough and the dream she remembered really was a dream rather than a promise. Kitty is fabulous. Sabine had thought she could bluff her way through this, but when she opened her mouth there was nothing she could think of to say. She was afraid of him. It had never occurred to her that this might be the outcome. She was in Nebraska in a kitchen where one man had already died. What did she know?

"They want to come home tonight. My boys want to come home. Jesus. I don't have to explain this to you." Perhaps he meant to pound his fist against the table and forgot the knife was still in his hand, or maybe he meant to drive the knife into the wood, which he did. It went in with a deep thud and stood up straight, a gesture from an old western—cowboys, Indians. Kitty flinched against the sound and then, for a while, they were all quiet.

While each waited to see what the other would do next, Guy stepped forward into the light, all of his skin showing, his arms wrapped around his narrow chest. The elastic on his underwear had seen a hundred washings and sat down loosely on his slim hips. The white was not a pure white anymore, but a very, very pale gray. He had none of his standard bravado, no sway; but with all of his body showing, his youth and beauty were startling and they all turned to watch him. Almost naked, he glowed with celebrity the way his uncle Parsifal had that night on the Johnny Carson show. He came into the kitchen so quietly, with such timidity, that he appeared to be coming in not to stop the fight, but to offer himself up to it. How followed his younger brother, stepped just inside the door, onto the linoleum, and stopped. Guy moved ahead silently, as if clothing were responsible for all sound. They couldn't even hear his feet against the floor.

"You boys go back to your room," Kitty said. "This is all going to be fine."

Guy looked at the knife. He reached out two fingers and lightly touched the handle to test how securely it was anchored in the wood.

"Go on," Sabine said. She did not like to see him so close to the knife.

"Dad, it's late," Guy said, as if this whole story were about sleep and how they were being kept from it.

"Then get your naked self to bed," Howard said.

Kitty walked towards Guy and put her arm around her son, ran her hand across the beautiful skin of his back. "I'll take the boys to bed." She held out an arm for How, who came to her. They were children, sleepy and undressed.

"They're big enough to get themselves to bed." Howard's tone was halfhearted, his anger failing him. He looked at his wife, who was walking away. "You come back here when you've got them settled," he said.

Kitty stopped, her beautiful face suddenly rested and self-assured. Whatever it was was over. Guy had defused it somehow, had made it all different. "I'm going to sleep," she told her husband. "We'll talk later." And then she walked her boys down the hall.

Howard Plate looked at Sabine. She was the only person left in the kitchen. He shook his head in disgust. "She never minds me."

"It's late," Sabine said.

Howard rubbed his hands through his hair, rubbed his face with his hands, as if trying to coax the blood from the pool around his brain. "I only wanted them to come home. That's where they're supposed to be. I was in bed and I wanted my wife and my boys to come home." He looked around the kitchen, trying to figure out where the conversation about sleeping at home had gone so wrong. "You can't make Kitty do anything. She won't do anything you tell her to."

Sabine nodded. It was no time to argue the point. The back door was so close he could be there in a second.

"All right," he said. "All right. You tell her to call me first thing in the morning."

"I will," Sabine said.

Howard Plate, without a coat or hat, stepped into a howling snowstorm of solid whiteness that Sabine had not noticed until he opened the door. She closed it behind him, snow blowing over her bare feet, and turned the lock. It would be impossible to see the road on a night like this. He could drive off the shoulder, and if the car were stuck, back tires spinning great plumes of dirt and ice, and he decided to walk, how far could he go without a coat? How long could Howard Plate wander the streets of Alliance in the snow before lying down to rest for a minute and freezing solid? Everyone would remember this night, how he was half out of his mind when he went out into the weather. People freeze to death all the time, but never on the night you expect them to, never on the night you hope for it.

Sabine went and pried the knife out of the table with a solid tug and then put it back in the drawer so it would not be the first thing everyone saw when coming in for breakfast in the morning. She rubbed the cut in the wood with her finger. Another reminder. *Do you remember that night Howard came over and stabbed the kitchen table with a knife?*

Sabine headed back to her room but went to the left instead of the right without meaning to; force of habit. The boys lifted up on their elbows from their twin beds and blinked in the darkness.

"Did he go?" How said.

"He went home," Sabine said. "Everything's fine." It was amazingly simple, lying to them. They wanted to believe that everything would be all right, she wanted them to believe it.

"We thought we heard the door," Guy said. "Was he okay?"

"I think he'd calmed down." Thanks to you, she wanted to say, but maybe Guy wouldn't want the credit for sending his father away.

"Gram didn't wake up?"

Sabine shook her head. "Now you need to go to sleep." She went to Guy's bed and then How's, kissing them both on the forehead even though they were too old. It was not an ordinary night.

"Good night," How said.

"Good night, Sabine," Guy said.

Sabine backed out of the room quietly and closed the door. She liked to believe they were already asleep, that they felt so safe with her reassurances that sleep came without question.

Across the hall, Kitty was lying on the bed, staring up at the ceiling.

"How's that cut?" Sabine said.

"I shouldn't have left you out there with him."

"It was fine. He left without any problem." Sabine leaned over and looked at Kitty's face. She ran her thumb beneath the tear on Kitty's cheek. It wasn't so bad. No more stitches, at least.

"He's always going to be around," Kitty said, as if she had decided to take the rest of the night to puzzle out her life.

"He's not," Sabine said. She sat down beside her sister-in-law and took her hand. "He won't be in California."

"Lucky for you," Kitty said, her voice thoughtful. "He doesn't seem to like you."

"I want you and the boys to come back to California with me." All she didn't understand was why she hadn't thought of it before.

Kitty looked at her. "Leave Alliance?"

"In a heartbeat."

Kitty sat up and pulled a pillow into her lap. She had meant to go with her brother. She had meant to be the magician's assistant, see the ocean. "Leave Mother and Bertie?"

"Lots of visits."

"Oh, Christ," Kitty said. "I don't know." She looked up at Sabine. "I'm not so young anymore. I don't know how it would be to uproot everybody, have everything be different." She reached up and put her hand on the side of Sabine's face. Kitty's hand was as cool as a leaf. "You wait and you wait and you wait for something to happen, and then when it finally does you don't know what to do about it."

Sabine closed her eyes and kissed Kitty. A kiss that she liked to think would have been much better if she hadn't been so tired.

"We don't have to decide this right now," Kitty whispered. "It doesn't have to be tonight."

Sabine shook her head. "This offer is good. Permanently good." She stood up and Kitty stood up beside her and together they folded back the blankets. Now the bed was the right size, and Sabine put her arms around Kitty and held her against her chest. This was the thing that everyone had told her about, the thing that she had given up for Parsifal before she really understood what it was. Kitty pressed her face against the side of Sabine's neck. "I'm going to fall asleep," she said.

And that was when Sabine remembered what she wanted to tell her. "Just one more thing," she whispered. "I had an incredible dream about Parsifal and Phan tonight. I never remember my dreams, but everything in this one is still so clear."

"Tell me," Kitty said from deep inside the well of Sabine's arms. "I dream about them all the time."

Very early on the morning of Bertie and Haas's wedding, two perfect inches of powdery snow fell on Alliance, Nebraska, making all of the snow that was beneath it appear fresh and bright. The plows were back in their sheds by seven A.M. and by eight the sun was out and the sky was clear from Wyoming to Iowa. While the tides of her family rose and fell around her, Bertie stayed focused on what was to be the happiest day of her life. She would be thirty in two weeks and was old enough to remember to put together the proper package for herself: old, new, borrowed, blue. All of the teachers and staff from Emerson Grade School were there, as were the teachers from the high school, where Haas taught chemistry; the middle school; and Saint Agnes Academy. Cousins and second cousins came from Hemingford and Scottsbluff. Two came from Sheridan, Wyoming. Al Fetters' brother, Ross, came with his wife all the way from Topeka, Kansas, though no one had heard from them in years. In fact, the only member of the family not in attendance was Howard Plate, and no one had expected him anyway.

Kitty and Dot helped Bertie with her dress, which she had bought on a trip to Lincoln when she had first become engaged, more than two years ago. Sabine fixed Bertie's hair. She had planned to wear her hair up for the wedding but was afraid that the spot that was shaved in the back of her head for the stitches might show. Anyway, she said Haas had always liked her hair better down.

"Look at my three beautiful girls," Dot said, speaking of her two daughters and Sabine, whom she had come to think of as a daughter. "All of you grown-up and going away."

"We're pretty far past grown," Bertie said, putting gloss on her lips. "And as far as gone, well, Haas and I are only going to San Francisco for five days."

"And I'm not going anywhere," Kitty said.

"You're going to California." Dot picked up the back of Bertie's dress, shook it out, and dropped it.

"I didn't say I was going to California. You're getting things confused. That's what happens when you get old, Mother. It's Sabine who's going to California." Kitty smiled.

"You're going with her."

"I said the boys and I were thinking about going to visit for a while."

"Maybe a long visit," Sabine said hopefully.

"I don't know what we'll do yet," Kitty said.

"The problem with Kitty is that it takes her forever to make up her mind. Let me have some of that powder, will you?" Dot held out her hand to Sabine.

"This is Bertie's day," Kitty said. "Let's leave Kitty and all her problems out of it for once, shall we?" She attached a white net veil on a crown of white satin roses to the top of her sister's head. "There," she said, stepping away. "Will you look at that?"

Sabine brought the bouquet of lilies of the valley from the refrigerator. Everyone agreed that Bertie was a lovely bride.

"I should be crying," Dot whispered to Sabine as she slipped into the pew after walking Bertie down the aisle. "Pinch me. Make me cry."

At the reception people ate sandwiches cut into small triangles and a white wedding cake covered in frosting roses. A three-piece band played "What a Wonderful World" while Bertie and Haas danced their first married dance together in the church basement. Haas didn't look so shy now. He looked happy. When everyone else joined in, Dot danced with her brother-in-law, Ross Fetters, of Topeka. Sabine danced with Guy, and How danced with his mother, though the boys had made their position clear to them on the drive over: Absolutely no more than one dance. The dancing was the entertainment: dancing, lunch, and a champagne toast, even though it was only one o'clock in the afternoon. There was plenty to keep everyone busy, and yet Bertie had asked Sabine a week before if she would do a magic trick at the wedding.

"I'm not sure it really goes," Sabine said.

"Just one trick," Bertie said, twisting her fingers together. "Everyone would love it."

"I'm not actually a magician, no matter how I try and pass myself off around here. The truth is I've never performed by myself before. I don't think I'd be very good."

"Of course you'd be good," Bertie said. "Besides, if Guy was alive he'd do it. I bet he'd want to do a trick."

He would. He never missed a chance to do a little magic. He pulled Rabbit out of the punch bowl at their wedding, which was a hell of a trick. He had to have a special bowl and table made up and the rabbit got soaked coming out and turned a sticky pink. Everyone loved it.

"Just one," Bertie said.

Sabine relented. All week she had planned to do cups and balls, a complicated version whose finale required a half a dozen eggs and three live baby chicks, which, as it turned out, were not difficult to come by in Nebraska. But as of yesterday morning she had changed her mind.

Haas went onto the dance floor by himself. One wall was lined with heavy boots and coats. Hats, gloves, and scarves spilled from the pockets. He cleared his throat. "Everybody?" he said. "Excuse me."

The crowd, dressed mostly in brown suits and in dresses ordered through catalogs, shifted towards him. Haas seemed startled by their sudden attention. "We're very fortunate to-day because my wife's"—he paused to nod his head towards Bertie, so newly his wife "sister-in-law, my sister-in-law, the famous magician Sabine Parsifal, is with us today and we've asked her if she would please do a trick for us. Sabine?" Haas put his hands together and began a polite round of applause.

Sabine came forward carrying the base of a wooden podium that seemed to be about the right height. The trick was impossible. She had gone over it again and again yesterday. She'd shuffled the cards until her hands ached. No matter how much or how little she did to arrange them, they came out the same every time. She hadn't shown it to anyone yet, not even to Kitty. She didn't think it was such a good idea to do it at a wedding reception in a church basement, except that it was Bertie's wedding and this was, by a long shot, the best trick that she knew.

Sabine put her hands flat on the table. "I just learned this one," she said. "So be patient with me. Is there a volunteer? I'm going to need some help."

People raised their hands. People lived to help. Throughout the semicircle around her hands were pointing up towards the fluorescent lights overhead as if it were school and the whole room knew the answer. She had been hoping to use Bertie or Haas, but, of course, they were too busy holding each other's hands to raise them. She wanted to call on Dot or Kitty or one of the boys, just to have someone she knew beside her, but then people would be even less likely to believe that what was going to happen had really happened. So she pointed to the fifteen-year-old girl with the purple knit dress and navy blue pumps she was not qualified to walk in, somebody's bony, awkward daughter who had not appeared to have had a moment's fun for the entire wedding. The girl came forward shyly, unable to believe her good luck at having been chosen.

"What's your name?" Sabine said.

"Laney Cole," the girl said, and twisted a shank of her dark blond hair between her fingers. The Coles, Sabine remembered from the invitations, were the Wyoming cousins.

"Do I know you?" Sabine asked.

"No," the girl said, shaking her head to reinforce her point.

"Have I set anything up with you beforehand, given you any money?"

Now Laney Cole blushed and looked down at her feet. "No."

"You promise?"

The girl nodded her head, her face so red that Sabine decided to drop the line of questions before the child had a stroke right in front of her. "Okay. Now I want you to take this pack of cards and look at it. You tell me if the seal is good, if anybody could have gotten into it, and if it looks good to you, I want you to open it."

Laney Cole studied the package with considerably more care than the task required and when she was certain it was in all ways an average, legitimate deck, she opened it up and handed the cards to Sabine, who thanked her, threw the jokers on the floor, and shuffled them until they felt warm and pliant in her hands. The audience burst into a raving, spontaneous applause. Sabine nodded her head. "Here," she said, giving them back to the girl. "Now you shuffle them. Cut them up and put the deck in the middle of the table."

Laney Cole did a very decent basic bridge shuffle and then cut the deck three times and put the pack on the table. She had a nice face. You could tell she was going to pass through this phase and grow up pretty.

"Perfect," Sabine said. "Now don't leave. This is the hard part. I'm going to have to ask everyone to remain completely silent." Sabine wasn't sure about the silence, or about the enormous strain that had come over Parsifal when he tapped the deck. All she could figure was that it was part of the act, because she found she could give the deck four extremely careless taps under any circumstance of noise with an utter lack of concentration and the aces still raced to the top of the deck like horses to the barn. That very morning she had leaned out of the shower and tapped the deck four times with a soapy hand. Bingo. She ground down her teeth and half closed her eyes and gave four light but ominous touches to the top card. When she was finished she opened her eyes as if returning from a long fever. She shook her head and stepped back. "Okay," she said to Laney. "Turn over the top card and then hold it out to face the audience."

Hearts, clubs, diamonds, spades. The aces moved to the gravity of her hand.

The audience turned out a good solid round of applause, but it was hardly the rollicking enthusiasm they'd managed when she had shuffled the deck. They did not swarm forward and carry her out into the snowy streets of Alliance. No one, in fact, seemed to realize that something other than a good, if simple, card trick had transpired except for young Laney Cole, who was holding on to the edge of the podium, the ace of spades still clutched in one hand.

"How?" Laney whispered while the crowd dispersed, many heading back to the buffet table for a second round of cake. Her eyes were bright with tears.

"I don't know," Sabine said, touching her wrist. "I swear to you."

"And she thinks she couldn't be a professional magician." Dot came up behind Sabine and gave her a hug. "That was super."

"I thought you were going to do the one with the chicks," How said, looking slightly disappointed.

"Hush," Dot said, and swatted at him. "The one she did was fine. I only wished it was longer."

"I think you should have made yourself float," Guy said.

Bertie was bringing Sabine a piece of cake, the plate balanced on her open hand. The crinoline beneath her skirt made a gentle rustling, as if she were moving through a pile of fall leaves, and Sabine thought how wonderful it was to have the bride bring you your cake, the bride who looked so much like a cake herself, shining white and in every way decorated.

"Wasn't she wonderful?" Bertie said to her sister, who was standing beside her.

"Wonderful," Kitty said.

Bertie handed Sabine her cake. She had been careful to cut a piece with a frosting rose on top. "And if Guy had been here, I know that's exactly the trick he would have done."

Kitty and Dot looked at her. Bertie didn't know Guy. She had only met him that one afternoon when he came home from Lowell, and she was barely three then. She was always frightened of strangers as a child and when he came inside the house, she cried. "I guess that's possible," Dot said.

"No," Sabine said. "She's right. He loved that trick."

The Mary Ingraham Bunting Institute at Radcliffe College, The Guggenheim Foundation, The MacDowell Colony, and Ucross supported me at different times during the writing of this novel, for which I am deeply grateful. Other kinds of equally necessary support were given by my agent, Lisa Bankoff, and Frank and Jerri Patchett. I have long-standing debts of gratitude to Allan Gurganus and Nancy Grimes.

Books by Ann Patchett

Run
A Novel

ISBN 978-0-06-134063-5 (hardcover)

Tip and Teddy have been raised by their loving and possessive father, Bernard, who wants to see his sons in politics—a dream the boys have never shared. But when an argument inadvertently causes an accident that involves a stranger and her child, all Bernard cares about is his ability to keep his children—all his children—safe.

Bel Canto
A Novel

ISBN 978-0-06-093441-5 (paperback)
ISBN 978-0-694-52533-1 (unabridged audio)

"*Bel Canto* is its own universe. A marvel of a book."
—Robb Forman Dew, *The Washington Post Book World*
New York Times Bestseller
Winner of the PEN/Faulkner Award and the Orange Prize
NBCC Award Finalist

The Patron Saint of Liars
A Novel

ISBN 978-0-06-054075-3 (paperback)

Trying to keep her pregnancy from her husband and mother, Rose checks into a home for unwed mothers. Rose plans to give the baby up, believing that she cannot be the mother it needs, but when her time draws near she cannot go through with it.

Taft
A Novel

ISBN 978-0-06-054076-0 (paperback)

John Nickel is a black musician who is left with nothing but the Memphis bar he manages. He hires Fay, a young white waitress, whose brother, Carl, is in tow. Nickel finds himself consumed with the idea of their dead father, Taft, and begins to reconstruct the life of a man he never met.

Truth & Beauty
A Friendship

ISBN 978-0-06-057215-0 (paperback)
ISBN 978-0-06-058680-5 (unabridged audio)
ISBN 978-0-06-075599-7 (unabridged audio CD)

"A loving testament to the work and reward of the best friendships."—*People*
New York Times Bestseller

Reading Group Guides to these works
are available at www.HarperPerennial.com.
www.AnnPatchett.com